COLD REALITY

Kneeling at the back gate of the snowcat, I slipped off my goggles and face mask to peer through the crack between the doors. I never got a peek.

With a bang, both doors flew open.

Behind each stood a parka-clad Russian trooper and in the hands of each was an automatic weapon pointed directly in my face. The guy to the left had an AK-47 submachine rifle with the action already back; the other held a 9mm Makarov with a muzzle so large I could have poked my thumb in it.

It was only two against one, and those weren't the worst odds I'd faced on this trip. I leaned slightly forward and prepared to spring. . . .

FALSE CROSS

False Cross

Stephen Forbes

A SIGNET BOOK

NEW AMERICAN LIBRARY

PUBLISHED BY
PENGUIN BOOKS CANADA LIMITED

FOR POLLY

NAL BOOKS ARE AVAILABLE AT QUANTITY DISCOUNTS WHEN USED TO PROMOTE PRODUCTS OR SERVICES. FOR INFORMATION PLEASE WRITE TO PREMIUM MARKETING DIVISION, NEW AMERICAN LIBRARY, 1633 BROADWAY, NEW YORK, NEW YORK 10019

First Printing, May, 1989

2 3   4   5   6   7   8   9

SIGNET TRADEMARK REG U.S. PAT OFF AND FOREIGN COUNTRIES
REGISTERED TRADEMARK   MARCA REGISTRADA
HECHO EN WINNIPEG, CANADA

SIGNET, SIGNET CLASSIC, MENTOR, ONYX, PLUME, MERIDIAN and NAL BOOKS are published in Canada by Penguin Books Canada Limited, 2801 John Street, Markham, Ontario, L3R 1B4

PRINTED IN CANADA
COVER PRINTED IN U.S.A.

Prologue

In Tyuratam, Kazakhstan—the Cape Canaveral of the Soviet Union—there are no cheering crowds to hail a successful launch.

Tyuratam, like the Cape, is its nation's major facility capable of accommodating large orbital boosters, but unlike its Western counterpart, few outside the military are allowed access to Tyuratam. Soviet failures are carefully guarded secrets.

Nevertheless, the July 26 launch was witnessed. Carp fishermen on the distant Ozero Balkhash, coal miners as far away as the Karaganda quarries, shoppers in the streets of Alma-Ata, all central Kazakhstanis who looked skyward could see the plumed contrail of the giant SS-9 booster as it sought an altitude of two thousand miles.

This forerunner of the smaller SS-18 ICBM had been reconditioned for orbiting a massive, though strictly conventional payload if only in the sense that it was non-nuclear. The Kazakhstanis could not know its real function: to blast enemy satellites from the sky.

American antisatellite (ASAT) technology involves intercepting satellites by direct ascent with an F-15 fighter. At maximum altitude, a small missile is fired that launches a miniature homing device beyond the earth's atmosphere. Guided by infrared telescopes, laser gyroscopes, and miniature jets that can alter its trajectory, the basketball-sized homing vehicle impacts with the satellite at high speed. Theoretically, direct ascent can be used against any orbiting body in practically any orbit as far out as geostationary.

The Soviet system is not so sophisticated.

It is capable of destroying satellites orbiting within a very narrow range of inclination and at lower altitudes only.

Into this low orbit the three-stage, liquid-fueled booster had delivered its ASAT interceptor payload, six thousand pounds of explosives and pellets. The interceptor raced across Siberia at an inclination of 63 degrees, passed over the Pacific to South America and then on across the lower Atlantic to Africa. In less than two hours, it was back over the Asian landmass.

Toward the end of the second orbit, the interceptor had begun closing on a military reconnaissance satellite taking extreme sensitivity photographs beyond the infrared range.

A timer started counting down.

Some newer American satellites are equipped with evasive maneuvering capabilities. This one was not. Over central India, the ASAT interceptor overtook the satellite, approaching as close as its companion orbit would ever permit.

Detonation occurred automatically. A ton of high explosives propelled a thousand pounds of steel pellets in the satellite's direction. A poor percentage struck their target.

The damaged satellite was blasted into a new, rapidly decaying orbit.

There would be no proud announcements; quietly, cleanly, the failure-plagued Soviet ASAT program would log the interception a qualified success—the satellite, after all, would come down. Neither the Balkhash fishermen, nor the Karaganda miners, nor the shoppers in Alma-Ata ever learned what happened next.

What follows is the story of one American who did.

1

The Scorpion Issue

At latitude 83° south, all the rules are changed.

The stars do not rise in the east and barrel across the sky only to disappear below the western horizon; instead, they circle about a point overhead like a twenty-four-hour clock that perpetually gains three minutes and fifty-six seconds a day. Now one of the billion hands on the black face, an arrow-shaped constellation named Crux, pointed toward the south pole; in these latter days of July that meant only one thing: it was high noon. A subtle diffusion of orange light low on the opposite horizon corroborated this fact.

Temperatures were hovering at 44 degrees below zero—warm for late winter, cold enough to solidify the mercury in a standard thermometer.

Despite that, all ten members of our project had ascended to the ice. Without speaking a word they outraged the silence of the barrier with their stomping feet, their banging hands, and their explosive exhalations as the moisture of their breath, confronting 76 degrees of frost, was carried away crackling like a dry wood fire. Social responsibilities had not brought them out. Courtesy here does not demand a reception committee by hosts, and the particular guests we were expecting would be the last to insist upon courtesy. But there had been no break in the endless boredom of winter night for the preceeding five months, would be none for days to come, and therefore any excuse to disrupt the routine was an occasion not to be missed.

Natural order and social custom, however, are not the only rules that come under revision in this white continent. We'd been living with those for nearly a year and had become accustomed to an alien existence; today we were facing Antarctica's concept of international law.

Australians, Chileans, New Zealanders, Argentineans, French, British, and Americans all occupy active year-round stations below the antarctic circle, though most were well north of ours. But none of them—ourselves included—was so foolish as to make a dangerous, unexpected, and unannounced winter trek across the barrier known as the Ross Ice Shelf.

These visitors were Soviets.

They had radioed an approximate arrival time, nothing more. Of their intentions they had given us no clue. It didn't matter. We were in no position to stop them even though our station was established under the aegis of the United States government and was doing research of a potentially sensitive nature. The Soviets could go where they pleased, stay as long as they wished, and leave when they were ready with whatever they had learned. Under the covenants of the Antarctic Treaty of 1967, there wasn't a damn thing we could do about it.

An overhead flood put the unimposing site of Mensa Station in a cone of light, but the project members had moved outside the circle of illumination in order to spare their night vision for scouting the barrier on all sides.

Predictably, Nils Hellstrom was the first to spot them.

"I think I see a headlight," his voice boomed.

They gathered quickly; someone asked him where, and with one hand guarding his face from the gentle yet numbing easterly, he stretched out the other toward a third-magnitude pinpoint of light where Scorpio was circumnavigating the horizon with a clockwise crawl.

Mary Ingram's voice crackled. "That's Antares."

A couple of us had glasses trained toward the constellation.

"Since when is Antares a binary star?" one asked rhetorically.

I sensed them all stirring.

"Antares is a binary," replied another, Jules Digne, the meteorologist undoubtedly. "Faint blue companion. Not discernible with less than a six-inch telescope. However, neither of the two is capable of maneuvering around a dune."

That started a round of excited chatter.

In the darkness, with the bulky parkas and leather masks covering what of their faces the hoods exposed, it was almost impossible to identify one from another, except for Nils, who towered above the others and whose parka was accordingly tailored. Even their voices as they began to ponder with delight the prospects of new people and new conversations seemed indistinguishable. The snapping and popping made their words sound like the static exchanges we had with McMurdo Station, distant and too often incomprehensible.

I did not share their enthusiasm.

Those headlights should not have been out of Scorpio.

"Now, why," I asked, "would they be coming in from the northeast?"

Something in my tone aroused Nils to regard me curiously, but it was David Saperstein, our station leader, who lowered his field glasses and snapped, "Why shouldn't they?"

"They have no stations to the northeast of us."

He shrugged it away. "They have no stations on the whole barrier, we all know that, but they do have a southern station on the opposite side. They probably just deviated around an area of disturbed ice or a crevasse field and are now back on course. Their crevasse-detection equipment isn't up to ours."

"If that's true, they're deviating to the south now."

"What are you talking about?"

"Well, look, David, where do you suppose they're going from here?"

"What I suppose is that they'll tell us . . . when they want us to know."

"But you said yourself they have no stations on the barrier. They're going to cross the Queen Mauds."

"So?" Saperstein raised his glasses again.

"So they can't do that west of here. Or south. A winter crossing of the mountains is impossible without snowcats or tractors which have to cross over one of the glaciers—the nearest navigable one is Beaumont Glacier a hundred fifty miles to the north."

"Nimrod Glacier is less than a hundred miles north."

"And strewn with crevasses at the lower limits."

"Is there a point to this?"

I faced away, shaking my head and hearing Saperstein say at my back, "Our suspicious Mr. Masterson."

As Saperstein moved off to join the others, I glanced up at Nils. We alone were without face masks. Mechanically I studied his features for signs of frostbite. He was doing the same with mine. Then he winked and rumbled, "You think Mensa is a bit out of their way, huh, Peter?"

"Not far enough out to suit me."

He laughed. "Should we not release the balloon?"

"Don't be silly—either that or we start walking for McMurdo. Do you want some help?"

Another silly question. The crate—including the twelve-foot-diameter signal balloon, five hundred feet of line, assorted electrical hardware, and the helium tanks—weighed only three hundred pounds. "You start on the ice," he recommended, adding, "If you finish first, you can help me; otherwise, I will help you."

A dense fog formed immediately as he opened the hatch, and he and the fog together descended into the warmth and light of the storeroom. Two minutes later, as I was making an inspection of what little of our station was exposed to weather, he appeared rising out of the fog, carrying the crate on one shoulder as another man might a small load of firewood. I did not renew my offer, being the only one at Mensa—other than the meteorologist Jules Digne—whose responsibilities brought him onto the ice at least twice a day. I wasn't about to spend my limited surface time idly—watching the Russians approach—or to waste it—helping someone who needed my help so little as Nils Hellstrom was ever likely to need mine.

The vents had to be checked for frost accumulation. Ice buildup on the aerials and weather instruments had to be removed. Snowdrifts needed to be dealt with daily. Despite the resistance wire wrapping, I had seen the nine-inch-diameter vent pipes choked solid with humidity that had frozen before it could be discharged. Ice would bring the anemometer cups clacking to a halt. The thermograph and barograph leads would be encased in a block of ice, and the rime buildup on the support wires and radio antennae would be so thick a man could not encircle them with his hand.

And the drifts. The notion of massive snowfall here is a misconception. In fact, it rarely snows on the barrier, for it is too cold. But snow that is here never melts. It becomes superchilled into a kind of ice crystal, pure white and as tough as a grain of sand. Dunelike drifts move eternally across the icescape, constantly changing the face of Antarctica and burying any human attempt to claim its surface. The city of New York, transported intact to the barrier, would within a year be covered in drift to the tops of the World Trade Center towers. Despite the fact that our six-thousand-square-foot structure protruded above the surface of the ice by a matter of inches, huge piles had already accumulated to leeward, fanning out like the wake of a boat north and south.

For now, it could be shoveled. If it weren't, it would harden over the skylights and vents so that striking it with a pick or shovel would present so misguided a fool with a resonant ringing and a pair of very badly sprained wrists. After that, nothing less than a saw would dislodge it.

I set to work.

Much of the rime on the guys and aerial could be removed by flexing the wire and fracturing the ice. But I did so carefully, mindful of the fact that such temperatures will also affect the molecular structure of metal, making it as brittle as the ice itself. At 60 below, a length of half-inch wire cable can be snapped like a dry stick.

Even before I'd cleared the drift blocking the entrance to the huskies' shelter and had begun shoveling off the upper surface of the station, the set of head-lights was identifiable as a snowtractor and so were the four identical light pairs coming behind it. By the spacing of the headlights I guessed that each tractor was trailing a number of supply sledges. The convoy was not five miles distant—in less than an hour they would be here.

Most of the reception committee, however, had already dispersed. In fact, seven of the team had gone below. It might be presumed that cold had driven them back down, but I knew better. Nils was busily loosening the signal balloon to several hundred feet while David Saperstein kept watch with his binoculars for an acknowledging signal from the convoy; therefore, it was the two women, the four-man engineering crew, and Jules Digne who had gone below.

Work in the drilling chamber was carried out in twelve-hour shifts on a round-the-clock basis. So the engineers who were on duty had simply returned to it, and the other two, feeling their sleep imposed upon, had headed for their private quarters. Meteorologist Digne could handle cold as well as most men; the women could, in my opinion, handle it better. Subzero temperatures, as well as close confinement and endless boredom, somehow troubled them less than any of the rest of us, with the possible exception of the big Swede. A veteran of several polar expeditions north and south, Nils Hellstrom was, from my observations, troubled by nothing at all. But none of them was going to spend an hour in 76 degrees of frost waiting for the Russians to find their way in. For the moment the excitement was over.

Forty-five minutes later I was taking a much-needed break when Nils approached and put a hand on the shovel. I gave it up without argument. No false pride and no physical contests of manhood for me. Not here. I had already begun to sweat from the exertion, a dubious luxury one cannot afford in this climate.

He started moving great shovelfuls of snow about with ease. It would take more than such casual labor to cause him perspiration, but as he straightened a moment, I was reminded that no one is immune to the effects of bitter cold. His lips were dry and cracked and, worse, his skin was yellowed with frostbite.

Before I could utter a caution, he nodded at me. "Peter, you've a blossom on your nose."

I hadn't even known it.

The sting of my fingers as I removed both sets of gloves was absolutely indescribable, but resolutely I kneaded my nose and cheeks, wincing as the dead flesh slowly began throbbing into an agony of life. Nils was doing the same.

"Did they acknowledge the signal?" I asked him.

"Yes. But I think the balloon should remain up until they are closer. Even in good weather they could pass this base by less than a thousand feet and never know it."

That didn't sound to me like a very unhappy proposition and I was commenting to that effect when Saperstein stepped between us. He must have just come from below, for he held a thermos cup of hot coffee and through the holes in his mask I could see that the frost was gone from his eyebrows and lashes.

"Please," he said, "keep those kinds of opinions to yourselves, at least until after they've gone. We have the opportunity here to promote a little understanding and cooperation between our two countries or we can screw up and turn this meeting into an embarrassing international incident in which everybody, the company included, is held up for public ridicule."

"That's the worst you can see happening," I challenged him, "that we might be embarrassed?"

Behind him the hatch leading to the weather lock opened and Mary Ingram and Paulette Gruber were starting out.

"What do you see happening, Masterson?"

"Almost anything."

"Dammit, these are scientists we're talking about; Soviet scientists, sure, but scientists just like ourselves."

"Like you maybe; not like me."

Saperstein spun, "Hellstrom, can you control this guy?"

The big Swede smiled and shook his head emphatically. "Not even," he declared, "on my best day."

Ten months of cabin fever were boiling inside of Saperstein as he whirled back to me. "Perhaps, Mr. Masterson," he said just as the two women joined us, "you'd better start worrying about me, then. I won't have you jeopardizing the continuation of this operation, and if necessary, I'll radio the company about having you recalled. As long as I'm in charge we're going to treat these Soviets like Charles and Princess Di come to tea."

Here it was again. This seemed to be my theme song. At least the tune and the words were the same I'd heard so many times before. My facility for finding employment was exceeded only by my proclivity for losing it. The only job I'd held for more than a year was military service, and even there my early release had come with a clear understanding that while I was not exactly being kicked out, it would be a waste of everyone's time for me to put in for reenlistment. My commanding officer had been a man much like David Saperstein.

"Do you understand that?" he demanded.

My final words to the CO under similar circumstances had given me much more pleasure. But then, the antarctic is no place to go job-hunting. "I do," I said, grinding it out through clenched teeth. "Now you understand this: I don't like those guys and I don't want anything to do with them."

As I turned and strode off toward the weather shack, Paulette's quiet words were carried to me on the wind popping like a bowl of puffed cereal: "Why should they be any exception?"

When the Soviet tractors rolled into camp, the subtle glow on the northern horizon was only a memory and Achernar, the ninth brightest star in the heavens, was descending toward the south pole.

Mensa had turned out in force again to greet them. There was something offensive about those snowtractors; like most Soviet designed machinery they seemed to possess a malevolence beyond their function. In performance they were undoubtedly inferior to our modern cats. They vaguely resembled modified Weasels, the hardy half-tracks that had served American and British expeditions so well on both poles, but with heavier plating. The front end sported a wheel-ski combination while the tank treads on the rear axle provided locomotion. A high box cab would be cramped with two people; a covered bed in the back did not look weather-tight. Yet their appearance was threatening.

Here was the real outrage to the quiet of the barrier. Compared to the banging diesel engines and the clatter of treads on the ice, our clapping, stomping, and crackling of breath was absolute silence. Rather than relief from months of remote duty, this arrival struck me as a vile intrusion.

The lead tractor crunched to a halt just outside the periphery of our floodlight, and in military fashion, the others braked beside it forming a single closely dressed rank. The lines of sledges behind each formed the files. As though on command, the drivers began descending from the one side of their still-idling vehicles while men I took to be navigators dismounted from the other. All the while we could see many other members of the expedition discharging from the tractor beds, making formation behind and then marching around the side of the last tractor. We counted thirty as they did a smart left flank and came to attention in a double rank behind the line of drivers.

They were nearly goose-stepping.

Certainly this looked like no polar expedition I had ever seen. Granted, none brandished automatic weapons, though their bulky military-style parkas could have concealed any variety of machine pistols in hidden holsters. The men were of uniformly large size and moved with a uniform power that suggested athletic conditioning. All wore masks that, unlike ours, incorporated goggles and breathing filters. The overall effect was intimidating. But whatever else we might conclude of their expedition based on outward appearances, one very disturbing fact was plain to me, its interests were clearly not scholarly.

The drivers stood before the ranks while the others, the ones I had taken for navigators, collected near the first vehicle. There, a tall, maskless specimen in a black shapka, who had descended from the passenger's side, spoke to them briefly before approaching our tiny contingent. It seemed to me that as Saperstein left our midst to meet his opposite number midway between the two lines, he did so with reluctance and I believe that for the first time since coming to Antarctica, he was indulging in the one forbidden luxury of this unforgiving land—he was sweating.

I leaned sideways to remark to Paulette, "Don't you agree their scientists can drill better than our scientists?"

"Shut up, Peter!"

That wasn't the cold talking, or the close confinement, or the boredom. Paulette Gruber, like Mary Ingram and Jules and Nils and all the rest of our team, was just a little bit scared. Well, perhaps Nils could be excluded, but include me by all means. I was more scared than any of them because I was more sure.

After a few minutes Saperstein turned and waved us over. At the same time, the Soviet commander signaled to his officers and drivers. We were prodded into a rough sort of row, and the ten Soviets formed a line that started past ours exchanging courtesies.

A receiving line, by God!

So maybe I was wrong about the Soviets and David Saperstein was right. Charles and Princess Di it was.

Because their troops had remained in formation, we had them matched man for man, assuming you count our two women. And counting our women seemed only fair for reasons that became clear after I had met Comrade Zhizn. He had removed his mask to give us the benefit of his smile—what little benefit or smile there was. I'd seen them like his before: smiles that, in place of reaching out from the inside, are on the surface alone, reaching neither out nor in. I've been told I rarely smile, and it is the risk of having a smile such as his that restrains me from doing so. As he stepped before me, mechanically I studied a face . . . not for signs of frostbite. His were cold eyes but from irises so light a gray that they were barely discernible, a cold thin mouth so straight it might have been an incision. The yellow, lifeless texture of his skin was not the result of sub-zero temperatures. This was the face he had brought to Antarctica.

Had it not been for that face, I would have seen her sooner. Suddenly, Zhizn had stepped aside and she was just there, sticking her cold little hand out to me and saying, "My name is Lieutenant Asia Krokov; I am pleased to make your acquaintance."

Her eyes were bright; her smile was sincere.

"Well, well," I said gruffly. "My name is Civilian Peter Masterson; what's a commie like you doing in a place like this?"

She smiled again. And then she was gone, sidling to Nils on my right and repeating her introduction word for word.

I met two other comrades of no account before the Soviet commander, a colonel, no less, named Fedorev, offered me his mitt. He looked even taller at close range, somewhere between me and Nils, with a handsome, genial face and an easy manner that took me by surprise. Apparently he'd noticed my sneaking glances at his female lieutenant as she moved along the reception line; just as I espied her in front of our chief engineer peeking unobtrusively back down the row at me, Fedorev's voice brought me around, "Give it up, Mr. Masterson."

I raised my brows.

"When victory is impossible one must forfeit a fight in advance; there are some challenges that can be survived only if one declines to accept them."

I shook my head.

"That sounds like good advice, Colonel, for someone who thinks there's a difference between default and defeat. I don't happen to think that there is. Besides, if we made it that easy for you, you guys would own the planet.''

He nodded and smiled genially. ''We will anyway.''

2

Project Centaur

In these latitudes a welcome is hastily proffered. Once the last Russian reached the end of the reception line, a quick set of orders was issued in two languages and fifty souls queued up before the hatch to enter the weather lock.

Nils Hellstrom took charge, organizing them into groups of twos and threes. I stood beside him until the final group had descended, then gestured for Nils to start down without me, suggesting that he was group enough by himself—which was true—and insisting I would be right behind him—which was not.

The closing of the hatch left me alone on the barrier, certainly the only human within four hundred miles in any direction.

That was just the way I wanted it.

I moved beyond the circle of illumination, guided, through a darkness that was all but complete, by the sound of the five idling diesels, snarling like hunger-brazened wolves outside a winter camp. Of course, we could not infer from this that the Soviets' layover would be a short one. Shutting the tractors down even an hour or two would mean a grueling half-day spent with blowtorches on the transmission, head, and crankcase before the oil, frozen to the consistency of fudge, would permit the engines to be turned over.

The nearest tractor was number five in the convoy.

I headed for it.

Though the last of the midday glow was indeed gone, enough light scattered from Mensa's flood to make possible a general inspection of the tractor at this

closer vantage. I recovered the flashlight from my
parka pocket, hesitating only an instant before switch-
ing it on, for I was after something more specific than
a general inspection. The beam lanced across the hood
of the armored cab. I played it along the left side as I
moved toward the covered bed.

For what happened next I take full credit.

True the flash robbed me of what little night vision
I had acquired; the rumble of the engines was deafening. So I couldn't see or hear—but I could still think.
I should have assumed they'd never leave the tractors
unguarded.

My light danced around the corner of the bed, then
suddenly froze when it materialized a hideous appari-
tion; the tall bulky figure, his face disguised by parka
ruff and mask was, in the disfiguring glare of the flashlight, an antarctic spirit, a disembodied demon pieced
together of the bits and parts of barrier victims. My
first reaction was to take several large steps back. My
second was to extinguish the flashlight aimed at the
Russian guard's goggles and disappear in the darkness
before his own night vision could recover. I checked
both reactions. Odds were he had a flashlight of his
own and trying to run would be a fruitless effort and
an admission of guilty intentions.

Even as I considered that, a powerful lantern flared
in my eyes.

"Chta vam nusna!"

I forced a smile. "Just browsing," I said. He barked
Russian again, something I couldn't translate on a bet.
Pointing to the near tractor, I shouted, "Mind if I
have a look?" His reply was more meaningless barking, and a glove against my chest. Then he punctuated
both with a shove—a little shove but one that lost nothing in translation.

From out of nowhere came another figure just like
him.

This one was armed, not with a flashlight but with
an automatic weapon, and he was no longer concerned
about the political repercussions of displaying it
openly.

The muzzle was trained blatantly at my midsection.

Shoulder to shoulder they spat gibberish, gesturing from the tractors—an inspection of which I was apparently being denied—to the station and the hatch—entry to which I was obviously being encouraged. Though it was impossible to read their expressions behind the sinister facades of mask and goggles, the militant nature of their refusal and the machinelike quality of their voices from the breathing masks emphasized the futility of further debate. These were trained sentries who could not be moved.

No sooner had that realization come to me than both men suddenly, mysteriously moved, taking two startled steps backward.

I turned.

Nils Hellstrom stepped beside me. The odds had shifted in my favor.

"You didn't come down," he thundered. "Do we have a problem?"

"What we have is a couple of cub scouts who seem to feel this corner of the barrier is staked out. Is there a merit badge for watchdog?"

For someone who abhorred violence in all its forms, Nils had been handed the wrong-size suit. It would have crushed him to know just how intimidating his appearance could be.

"Maybe so," he said, "let's not start any trouble."

I had to agree. Any trouble would find its way through channels to Colonel Fedorev and what got to Fedorev would doubtless make its way directly to Saperstein. Nevertheless, as we turned and headed back to the light without once glancing behind us, I felt their watchful eyes upon us and I was more determined than ever to have a look inside those tractors.

This time I preceded Nils down the ladder into the weather lock. He joined me in the corridor that connected all the wings of the underground shelter. This, too, gave the appearance of having been staked out. The corridor was eight feet wide, a hundred feet long, and just then wall-to-wall Russians stowing their gear, lying, sleeping, or preparing for sleep. A traffic lane

down the length of the corridor and the doorways leading to the individual wings had been kept clear.

Nils and I proceeded single-file to avoid blankets
and bodies and turned into the minibar at the same
time David Saperstein, followed by Colonel Fedorev,
Asia Krokov, and two other Russian officers, crossed
the corridor farther along. A tour was in progress of
the private rooms of the Mensa staff.

"Hope you made your bunk this morning," I said
to Nils as he scratched initials on the chit and I popped
the caps on two bottles. We headed for our table.

Fifty years ago there would have been a single plank
top table with long benches on each side right here in
the middle of the room. No longer. Five decades has
taught us something about the psychology of close
confinement. One of our two pleasures after ten months
together was separate—admittedly small—dining tables, the other being separate—equally small—sleeping
quarters. Despite the fact that this was cafeteria,
lounge, conference room, and club in one, space was
still at a premium. The company considered five two-
seat tables adequate for a party of ten.

Nils and I would share one if our schedules coin-
cided. Two other tables had been pushed together by
the three junior engineers and meteorologist Jules
Digne, whom I collectively referred to as "the whitewall corps." Not without cause. Their faces were always shaved, their short cropped hair, forever
trimmed. I'd never heard them swear. I'd never seen
them slouch. They were middle-aged, average weight
and medium height. Sometimes I couldn't even tell
them apart. You know, the type who hold down jobs.
With Saperstein and Dolan they were nothing less then
deferential, disgustingly so, and while they didn't start
and end each sentence with "sir," they didn't need
to. When you look like they did and stand like they
did, what's the difference? I don't say they had no
business acting that way, but if they're going to act
that way, they've no business being in Antarctica. At
another nearby table would sit Saperstein and Dolan,
who were nevertheless members in good standing of
the "corps." Saperstein as Mensa supervisor and Do-

lan as senior engineer, and therefore Centaur Project leader, just didn't think it fitting they should sup with the troops—another damn silly attitude for the south pole. I mean if it was just a question of not wanting to eat with those guys . . . hell, I didn't want to eat with them. Neither did Paulette. Mensa's medical expert had her own table and her own reasons.

That left Mary Ingram.

Mary alone would have preferred the plank top table and benches. Only in that way could she have avoided playing musical chairs. Mary Ingram, the station's geologist, was a gem. In form as well as in frame. Everyone agreed. When the food was bad—the food was always bad—she had a way of brightening up a table. No one but Mary could join Paulette without conflict. A seat was constantly reserved for her among the corps—they ate in shifts—and would have gotten more use if the two Top Mackeroos hadn't so often pulled rank. Their smartness failed to put her off. On the other hand, she and Nils could have the grandest time together and his blond mane had never seen a comb; a razor hadn't touched his cheeks in months. He was a bear in chronic hibernation and had perfected an appropriate posture sitting or standing.

For a while, Mary had even dared sitting with me.

But you can only expect so much hardness.

Even from a gem.

Our mugs were not yet drained when Saperstein escorted the party into the bar; by this time, Comrade Zhizn had joined them. Zhizn—he turned out to be a major—was French-kissing a cigarette about six inches long, a Papirosi, two inches of Russian tobacco, four inches of hollow filter, and a drag like sucking on the exhaust pipe of a fifty-four Olds.

"This wing," Saperstein was saying, "contains our cafeteria; here, the lounge, and at the far end, storage for perishables. Like all the wings it is sixteen feet wide and thirty feet long."

Zhizn was unconcerned with those details. "You mean to say," he puffed, "you give your men alcohol?"

"Good heavens, no," said Saperstein. "This is a

cash bar. We charge them for it.'' He pivoted as Paulette Gruber came up. ''What's that?''

''A radio message, David. McMurdo.''

''All right, will you . . . ?'' He made little swirls with his hand indicating the five tour guests.

''Sorry, David, I'm treating two cases of frostbite.''

''Then can you get Bob—''

''Bob Dolan just left for his duty post—an emergency. And Jules is helping Mary make dinner for fifty people.''

Wearily, Saperstein regarded Nils and me. ''Peter?''

I started to decline, having warned him already what attitude to expect, but something restrained me. True, Fedorev's lieutenant was poking her head around giving me a look similar to the one I'd caught in the line, indicating interest. But my reason for acquiescing was more concerned with my interest than hers: I'd never talked to a communist named Asia before and had not yet gotten an answer to my question why she was here.

''Why not?'' I said, standing.

Saperstein bade his guests look about the cafeteria while he took Nils and me to one side so he could warn me to watch myself and request Nils to do the same. Watch me, that is. When he left, I issued other instructions.

''I'll be okay, Nils. Keep an eye on the weather lock for relief going up to the sentries. I want to know what kind of shifts they're standing.''

''Why?''

''Let's just say I'm a concerned host. I don't want them to catch cold.''

I led the five of them across the corridor to the administration wing, offices for Saperstein and Dolan and for Paulette's medical facilities as well as the little office shared by Jules Digne and Mary Ingram for their meteorological and geological studies respectively. They asked their questions. My answers were suitably cryptic. It was when we moved down the corridor to the wing west of the bar that I realized my attitude about the tour had changed.

I had expected to feel defensive with these Russians.

Instead, I found myself feeling rather sheepish.

And for a good reason. In my mind were images of Robert Falcon Scott and his dwindling party trudging through the worst of Antarctica's weather—which at its best is the worst on earth—on the return journey of a losing race to the south pole. By the time they'd come just to the east of the future site of Mensa Station, their supplies were nearly gone. Some of his men were walking off into the storm to conserve rations for the weaker members of the party. The gesture was in vain: Scott and his few remaining men would fall within miles of the base camp.

Even twenty years later, in 1933, primitive conditions were the unbroken rule. I could see a picture of Admiral Richard Byrd, the first man to fly over either north or south pole, spending the antarctic winter alone in a small buried shack three degrees north of here. A malfunctioning gasoline generator nearly asphyxiated him. The interior of the shack froze. Had relief not arrived several weeks early, he would certainly have died.

And then there is Hell's Flow.

Hell's Flow deserves its own chapter on the subject of hardship in the antarctic. And it didn't take an imagination to see the damn thing from Mensa; during the summer months a decent pair of field glasses would do the trick.

Two years after Byrd's, an expedition led by Willem Sturdevant attempted a crossing of the Queen Maud Mountains, which stretch from the coast at McMurdo Sound a thousand miles toward the south pole. Their crossing site was supposed to be a glacier due west of the location we had selected for Mensa Station. Exactly how far they managed to get or what calamity befell them is not really known, for Sturdevant and his party were never heard from again. Other, safer crossings were found. Philippe Cheval, his tractors delayed by endless waist-high undulations in the continental ice surface above that same glacier, sent an advance party down to reconnoiter an emergency detour to the barrier and home. After waiting a fortnight for his party to return and not daring to risk his tractors on a blind descent, Cheval decided he had no choice but to maintain his original course; half his remaining men were lost on the long leg north. Two decades passed before, in 1956, an expedition was launched by an Italian named Riga to trace Sturdevant's route. He found it. Or one equally treacherous. It is believed the latter-day party of seven explorers with their snowtractors and all of their supplies tumbled into a hidden crevasse midway up Hell's Flow, as the glacier had by then come to be known. At any rate, no member of the expedition survived to relate the tale. By the end of the decade, Hell's Flow was placed under international off-limits.

The history of Antarctica is written in that kind of sacrifice. That kind of suffering.

So naturally I was sheepish.

"Now, in this wing," I informed them with a dispirited wave of my hand, "is the gymnasium, movie theater, library, and game room."

It was true, of course, that the antarctic winter night passed for us more gently than it had for those who pioneered the continent. It wouldn't work to go back; there are not enough Byrds—or Scotts or Sturdevants—in the world to do the work that needs doing here. Nils Hellstrom was one such man. But his kind are rare and the company was forced to make duty tolerable if it were going to induce qualified personnel to come. Still, I couldn't help but believe the Soviet stations were closer to Byrd's accommodations than they were to ours, and I felt like a damn pansy showing them through.

The rooms were all brightly painted. Attractive photographs and paintings lined the walls. Interior temperatures never dropped below fifty degrees and the work wings were well illuminated day and night. Every convenience was to be found here to make the duty tours more pleasant.

Of course, any convenience or pleasantry in Antarctica must be brought in, and at no inconsiderable expense.

For example, there were skylights in every room but not a window to be found in the place. Mensa Station is actually carved out of the two-hundred- to four-hundred-foot-thick glacier that makes up the Ross Ice Shelf. Its design is at the same time impractical and mandatory—shaped like two capital Hs side by side and connected by their horizontal strokes. Each wing is therefore surrounded by ice on three sides, as well as above and below, which makes for maximum inefficiency in maintaining internal temperatures. Yet this had been the unvarying design of polar shelters even before the time of abundant thermal power. Here, we fear heat much more than cold. Specifically, we fear fire. Once started, fires are nearly impossible to halt, for the stuff about which might put it out is too frozen to be of any use. Shelter designs are meant to isolate a blaze whenever possible. There were fifty-eight fire extinguishers scattered throughout the station and every member of the project was responsible for knowing the exact location of them all.

The corridor connecting the eight north-south wings is eight feet in width. Each of the wings extending from it is exactly twice that. The explanation for this is simple enough: the particular ice-dredging monster that was hauled to this latitude the preceding summer to build the station carves a ditch exactly eight feet wide and ten feet deep into the ice.

Floors, walls, and ceiling were all prefabricated in Groton, Massachusetts, and shipped to Antarctica, where they were reassembled according to instructions that listed the last nut. So much is common. Less common is our modern source of heat. There being no fuel on the entire five million square miles of continent, anything that burns must be brought in. Formerly, that was fuel oil, kerosene, and later, bottled gases specially mixed for such temperatures. Mensa received all of its heat, as well as its light, electrical power, and hot and cold running water, from two nuclear generator plants. Clean, neat, trouble-free energy with the danger of fire virtually eliminated—such was the advantage of nuclear power in the antarctic, and each plant was so compact that it could be loaded onto the back of a sledge and towed to the site behind the Badger snowcats.

The only thing I had a tough time getting used to was putting on the damn rem badges whenever I entered the storeroom or project chamber. The engineers had to wear them on all duty shifts, certainly a small price to pay for a year's worth of heat and energy. One had only to step outside for a moment to truly appreciate the blessing.

Until we approached the end of the scheduled tour and the Russians discovered the Centaur Project, I thought the nuclear miniplant was going to be their major interest.

That and the two Badger snowcats.

After leaving the gym and library we crossed the corridor to the storage wing for hardware supplies. There was nothing about it that deserved more than a glance, with the possible exception of the power plant. Barely the size of two refrigerator boxes laid end to end, it had been tucked in an ice alcove near the doorway. One of the engineers was making some minor adjustments to the generator.

While everyone else mingled about checking the supply of crates and tanks, Comrade Zhizn moved over to it and stared. After a while his fascination became obvious, and Tom Elliston, the engineer, stood to explain its operation. It rankled me how obliging the entire staff was being to these guests of ours, as though only by giving them everything they wanted could we avoid the risk they might take it. I crossed over to eavesdrop.

"Like any nuclear plant," he was saying, "it's basically a boiler—it heats water. And we use plenty of hot water at Mensa, for space heating as well as for . . ." He hesitated as he saw me standing nearby. "But it also drives a small turbine mounted back here that generates all the electrical power for the station."

"You have just the one plant?" Zhizn asked.

"Actually, we . . ." Elliston caught my eyes again. "Er, for the general operations, yes. Just the one."

"What heating system do you use at the Nimsky Station, comrade?"

Zhizn turned slowly to me. "Nimsky Station?"

"Your southern outpost. Isn't that where you've just come from?"

"What makes you say that?"

"Curiosity."

"Is there a point to your curiosity?"

This guy was starting to annoy me; everything he had to say ended in a question mark. "There sure is," I said. "I gather the Russian custom when stopping by an American or British station down here is to start bumming antifreeze and fuel oil first thing. If we're now going to be supplying you with plutonium, we need to have some advance notice."

"Peter!"

Saperstein had come up behind me. Beside him was Colonel Fedorev. "Major Zhizn, please forgive Mr. Masterson. He has a unique sense of humor. Please, gentlemen, if you'll follow me to the garage I will be happy to continue my role as tour conductor."

With a hand, he led Zhizn away.

That was my cue to leave. I had twice while escorting them been unsuccessful in getting Asia Krokov's attention, and now, as they headed off, I approached her a final time with thoughts of a personal tour. But suddenly Colonel Fedorev was cutting me off.

"How do you like your work here in Antarctica, Mr. Masterson?"

I watched Asia Krokov move away with the others. "Don't you people read your own propaganda? I'm a capitalist dog. We don't like anything except money and here we don't get paid enough to like even that."

"So what do you do?"

"There's nothing I can do about it. You can't press for a raise by satellite. Besides, what if they decided to give me my walking papers instead? It's a four-hundred-mile walk to McMurdo, and in case you hadn't noticed it's cold out there."

He started to grin but fought the impulse back.

"I mean your job. What do you do?"

When I didn't answer, Fedorev pursued it. "You apparently know something about polar survival, yet Mr. Hellstrom is the resident authority. You are neither a meteorologist nor an engineer; you are not the

doctor and you rarely do the cooking. Miss Ingram is
the station geologist—though personally I would think
a station built upon ice floating on the ocean would
have more need of a glaciologist than a geologist—and
Mr. Saperstein is the official chief of operations. Naturally one wonders what your job might be.''

"Don't concern yourself with me, Colonel. I just
keep the flies off the important people.''

Again Fedorev controlled himself. "There are no
flies in Antarctica. There are no insects here at all.''

I shrugged. "I didn't claim to be overworked—just
underpaid.''

A smile spread from cheek to cheek; unlike Zhizn's,
this was a real smile and, taking into account the fact
that he was a communist, a real face. For a moment
I thought Fedorev was going to add something and so
did he, but a distraction spared me. We had passed
through the doors of the station's westernmost vertical
section, seventy feet long, packed from one end to the
other with the two cats, a dozen sledges, half as many
snowmobiles, all our equipment and tools, and the
lower cage for the dogs. It was cooler in here, by thirty
degrees, and the line of vehicles looked rather dreary
in the plain surroundings of the garage compared to
the rest of the station. Both the north and south ends
were inclined to the roof where massive trap doors
could be raised—with some effort—to move the machines in and out. The only indication of life came
from the large chain-link cage for Nils' huskies that
had access to the hut above by means of a circular
ramp that went right through the roof.

But that wasn't what had captured Colonel Fedorev's attention.

He stood mesmerized before one of the Badgers.
Unlike the Russian tractors, which had treads and skis
like overgrown snowmobiles, these cats incorporated
only a single set of very long treads—about thirty feet.
They were a little longer, some lower, but a lot wider
than the Russian models, factors that more than made
up in stability and safety what they cost in maneuverability. Aside from that, they were faster and more
powerful. One of these cats could haul half again as

many sledges as the old Weasels. A Badger could span a four-meter gorge and scale a 30-degree grade of ice. Their software was every bit as impressive as the hardware. There were outriggers on each side, frameworks projecting outward that supported platter-sized, downward-facing dishes linked to cabin computers. This echo-sounding equipment and the associated programming allowed the operator to "see" the integrity of the ice ahead, below, or even to the sides. These crevasse detectors as well as other electronic devices were advancements the Soviets had not introduced in their machines.

"I would love to sit in the cab," said Fedorev, who, when I pretended not to hear him, went to Saperstein and repeated his desire.

But he didn't get to.

Directly opposite the insulated doors was a second set of double doors that led farther to the west. The only identification on them was a carefully painted insignia of a creature, half-man, half-horse, holding in his hands a drawn bow. It was a regulation centaur except for the projectile along the bow, which was actually a drill bit instead of an arrow.

"Where does this lead?" asked Zhizn.

"That's private," I snapped.

Fedorev sensed an issue and crossed to us, saying, "I wasn't aware of any secret operations in Antarctica."

"If you were aware of it," I replied, "it wouldn't be."

Saperstein pushed out his palms. "Let's not have any trouble. Mr. Masterson merely said that it was private, not that it was a secret."

"Does that mean we get in?" Zhizn demanded.

I moved so as to position myself between the door and the Soviets.

"I guess we'll have to do it by the numbers, David. They're communists; this is a new concept for them. Mensa Station," I said, pointing to the floor, "is private enterprise." I gestured about us. "Everything in it is private property. And what's behind these doors is our private affair. Does that make it any clearer?"

"Now, now," said Saperstein. "It's not exactly like that."

The door swung open at my back.

Dolan came flying out in a panic, rushed by me, and nearly ran Saperstein down before he became aware of our presence. "Oh, David! God! We've got an emergency. Carl Johnson has fallen down the hole."

I saw Saperstein's mouth open in surprise and then close again without a word. What happened in the garage after that, I don't know. I raced through the double doors.

After twenty feet the passageway widened into a forty-by-forty chamber, only the central feature of which was of any interest: a grillwork dome mounted on a circular bulwark of ice about three feet high. It was possible to stand—as I was standing—and look through the framework into the center area. For a better view one had to climb four metal steps and mount the narrow gantry that penetrated the grille and bridged the fifteen-foot diameter of the dome. Ordinarily there was nothing much to see. Just a small pool. If you sat on the edge of the gantry, pulled off your shoes and socks, stuck your legs under the railing, and swished your toes in the water, you'd discover it was as warm as any hot spring.

Just then I was discovering that what wasn't really a spring, wasn't even there anymore. The water was gone. The hole looked like a dry well that disappeared in darkness deep below in the barrier ice.

Overhead a winch-and-tackle assembly was positioned to raise or lower flexible tubing beside the gantry and into the water; now the tube was swaying like a vine from a tall tree.

"We'd lost hole water," said Dolan, who was still breathless from having chased me back inside. "The packer had malfunctioned. Carl was taking some quick readings from the bottom monitor and suddenly the railing gave way. He went right over the side. Just disappeared without a sound."

"How deep are you?" I snapped.

"About a hundred and eighty feet."

"What's the water level?"

"I tell you there is no water. We lost twenty thousand gallons in twenty seconds."

"That's impossible! Unless you've cut through."

He shook his head adamantly. "No. The ice shelf here is nearly three hundred feet thick."

I had stepped to the gantry and was examining the broken weld on one of the railing stiles when Saperstein appeared. His decision about whether or not to allow the Soviets entry had apparently been made: Colonel Fedorev and the other members of the tour party were right behind him.

I paid them no mind but leaned cautiously over the rail. Taking a gentle hold on the tubing, I moved it gingerly from side to side while staring directly into the black eye of the hole. For ice, it got damn dark damn quick. Shouting into its depths was pointless: if Johnson were still capable of projecting his voice up 180 feet of vertical tunnel, he would be doing so; if voices simply failed to carry that distance with any clarity, there was nothing to be gained by calling down. I tried it anyway without result.

"You're the engineer," Saperstein charged, coming up to Dolan and waiting for my shouts to subside. "What do we do?"

"There's really nothing we can do," he replied. "I suppose we could lower a rope, but there's no possibility he's conscious enough to know it, let alone in any condition to hang on. Logically, the only answer is to move the rig and burrow a second shaft beside the first; when we get to his depth, enlarge it and tunnel across to him. Because of the top hole width, the two centers would have to be at least thirty feet apart, requiring that the chamber be enlarged."

"How long would that take?"

"Just moving the rig the thirty feet would take five or six days. Enlarging the chamber would take a month."

I climbed off the gantry. "Johnson hasn't got five or six minutes. Not if he's in the water down there—he'll freeze to death. If Dolan is right and the hole is dry, he may be dead now. Ice doesn't break a fall."

"What do we do?" repeated Saperstein.

"I agree that it would be useless to lower a rope; if he were conscious, he would be signaling on the tubing. He's not."

Torn and frustrated, Saperstein alternately faced Dolan and myself. Finally he blurted, "We'll try it anyway."

Paulette Gruber came running up; the look in her eyes spoke clearly that she'd been informed of the emergency. When I signaled to her, she detoured from Saperstein to me.

"Get Nils in here, Paulette." I held up a hand when she started to interrupt. "Don't argue. We don't have a patient for you yet. Tell him to bring that coil of climbing rope. Fast!"

She left.

Dolan asked if he should begin rigging a portable transceiver that could be sent down on the rope in an attempt to communicate with Johnson.

"Yes," answered Saperstein.

"Don't bother," I countermanded. "We don't have time to waste on gestures. There's only one thing to be done: we'll have to lower a man."

It took about ten seconds for that to sink in.

In the meantime, I moved back to the gantry and checked the overhead assembly as a belay.

"Nils will never fit down that hole," said Dolan at last. "He's too wide. It's fifteen feet across up here but it narrows continuously. Halfway down it's only three feet in diameter and the base is less than two. There's only one way anybody is going to get down there and still be in a position to get a hold of Johnson."

Without turning I said, "Nils isn't going down. I need someone on the gantry capable of lowering one man and lifting two back up."

Colonel Fedorev stepped forward. "I can have three dozen top men in here to assist you."

I shook my head.

"There isn't room for three dozen men in this chamber. And the rope has to be handled from the gantry. There's only room for one."

Having broken free the obstructing, damage railing

and set it to one side, careful that no pieces fell into the hole, I looked up to see Nils Hellstrom lumbering in leading a distraught Paulette Gruber. I had forgotten to mention that we might also need some carabiners and slings, but predictably Nils was more together. He had over his shoulder the two-hundred-foot length of nine-millimeter kernmantle and, in his hand, a full satchel of assorted ice-climbing gear.

I dug out my flashlight from my parka pocket and then discarded the parka altogether. After that, I took off the heavy sweater, too, leaving me in just a light cotton shirt.

"Wait a minute," Saperstein interrupted suddenly. "You, Masterson? After Nils, you're the biggest among us. Let Dolan go down."

"Not me," said Dolan.

"I'm the doctor," Paulette volunteered. "I should be the one to go. He'll undoubtedly need medical attention."

No one took her seriously. She wasn't lacking in gumption but neither was she shy of girth. Calling her two hundred pounds would have been sheer flattery.

Dolan grabbed her arm. "I don't think you understand, Paulette. Masterson isn't going to climb down. He's going to be lowered by his heels. Once he gets into the narrow part of the hole, he'd never get turned around; he'll be lucky to worm down headfirst to where Johnson has become pinned. And then he'll have to hang on to Johnson while they get hauled out."

Paulette Gruber's face blanched.

She said nothing while I stepped up to the gantry, swung my legs over the rail, and climbed down a metal ladder that ended several yards below on a foot plate. Three days before, the base of the ladder had stood on ice. The hole had been hand-sawn to this depth. Several minutes before it would have been ten feet under water. At the moment it hung in open space, equidistant from the sides, hovering over a black void.

The voices of those above me faded to a hush. They were replaced by a strange resonance, a rush not unlike that produced by a conch shell held to the ear—

assuming, of course, that the conch had a chamber fifteen feet across.

There was a breeze too, a chill rising up from the bottom. It didn't make sense, that it should be coming up. Yet it was coming up.

Nils was already on the gantry above me securing a sling to the framework overhead; he used another to belay himself to the opposite railing. Then he looped the rope around his massive shoulders and lowered the free end to me.

Several figures were positioning themselves around the perimeter of the grillwork. Some already had flashlights ready. I finished tying a bowline about my ankles, cinched my own flashlight to a short length of cord, and lashed that to my left wrist before drawing a double-edged boot knife and testing it between my teeth. Wordlessly, I nodded to Nils and then sat on the edge of the foot plate until the big Swede had taken in the spare rope.

"Two tugs for slack, Nils," I advised him. "Three to take in. Four means I've got him, okay?"

He nodded and, without having uttered a single word, started hauling.

My feet went up in the air and then I came off the ladder base and hung upside down over the shaft. Almost at once, I started down. Instinctively I held on to the tubing to steady my descent and worked it hand over hand, but the tubing was oddly less than taut and did little to arrest my swinging.

Light from a dozen flashlight beams swirled downward, reflecting with scintillating confusion off the irregular glacial walls of the frozen well. I descended into a cold kaleidoscope with a dynamic show of light coruscating about me. But that analogy broke down on two points: I was moving not away but toward the black viewing eye at the distant end, and it was the eye—not the show—that held me entranced.

Nils didn't waste any time lowering me to the limits of their visibility. Then, almost at the same time the diameter began narrowing radically, the light slowly died, and my descent slowed.

This shaft was neither round nor of uniform dimensions as would have been the case had it been drilled. No drilling apparatus had been used for the simple reason that there was no way to fit a derrick into the confines of a polar shelter. The process, being pioneered here, involved the use of superheated water to bore through the glacial ice.

The plastic tubing I moved along pumped several hundred gallons of hot water from the nuclear boiler to the bottom every minute. A heavy control nozzle, packer, and monitoring device at the end of the tubing slowly settled as the ice melted below it; the tubing was paid out; water was recycled at the top of the hole and sent back to the reserve tank on line with the boiler. Just three days of actual operation had gotten us to the present depth, but it had taken four months to get the equipment in working order. The process was truly a complicated procedure. Numerous and impressive safeguards were built into the system, but about then I was impressed only by the fallibility of our puny efforts to penetrate the massive Ross Ice Shelf.

The dark eye of the hole swelled. The walls narrowed inexorably. Cold and night smothered me like a wet blanket.

My left shoulder struck ice and then my right, too. I was gripping the tubing in front of my chest when both shoulders scraped the walls simultaneously. Ice snatched my hands and yanked them to my waist so that the flashlight, which I had foolishly failed to turn on, banged about in front of my face, clattering the ice and knocking glacial shards into my mouth and eyes. By then I could neither lower the flashlight nor turn it on, for my hands were pinned at my sides by the restricted circumference.

Down I plunged into the darkness. I craned my head to stare ahead. It was no good. If something were there, I would never see it; were I to see it, I could never prevent myself from colliding into it headfirst.

Again and again and through clenched teeth I shouted to Nils until the blade had slashed my lips and tongue and blood ran down into my nostrils. But the question of how well voices carried through the hole was settled when my descent continued unabated.

I thrashed my body like a snared animal.

All I managed to accomplish was to crack my skull against first the ice and then the flashlight time after time.

In desperation I began forcing my arms outward like brakes while I bent my legs and wedged my knees and feet against the walls. That slowed me some before a convenient bottleneck wrenched my shoulders and, in the process of bringing me to an abrupt, excruciating halt, darn near fractured them both.

The rope began to collect at my feet.

I waited.

Almost at once, the slack was taken up. Enough tension remained to steady me against a sudden fall and to take the weight off my shoulders, yet the line was slack enough to allow for signals. There were certain advantages to having the more intelligent of us remain above, and I thanked my stars that, having based the decision on size alone, the smarter of us was also a few sizes larger.

I gave three tugs with my legs and almost immediately began inching upward. Nils was pulling slowly, waiting for other instructions.

When the widening came, I shifted my arms below me, retrieved the flashlight, aimed up in front of my legs, and flashed it twice in succession.

I stopped rising.

A second later, I was going down again.

The powerful beam was able to keep the eye at a distance, but it created no kaleidoscopic entertainment. So narrow had the shaft become that all reflections were bent toward the bottom, where they died in darkness.

With my arms hanging, my shoulders and chest extended, I slipped past the restriction more concerned about the subfreezing temperature of the ice in contact with my bare arms and trunk than its negligible coefficient of friction. But the restriction was not, as I had hoped, merely a bottleneck. The shaft was tapering down, becoming inescapably narrower. Several times

I slowed to the point of stopping. Nils would hold a gentle tension on the line until I was able to snake farther along, reforming my body to the varying geometry of the shaft.

It was impossible to imagine a man falling through this confined space, despite its frictional coefficient, were he trying to halt himself at all. True, Johnson was quite a bit thinner than I was, but he had surely attempted to arrest his fall—unless he had been unconscious before he'd struck bottom—and I was doing precisely the opposite with dammably little success.

So where the hell was he?

Finally it happened. I became pinned so firmly in place that no squirming on my part budged me at all. I felt as though the extra square inches represented by the tubing alone were enough to stop me. It crushed my chest with the same pressure that gripped my sides. I was stuck good. And there was nothing they above could do to help me. Slack collected again at my feet. Nils might haul me back up. What might get me down? With a strength born of panic, I pulled myself down an inch at a time by shinning along the tubing. By that time, my body was chilled so badly that it shook with a palsied frenzy; whether this worked for or against my movement I don't know, but it drove me half-mad. There was one irregularity in the wall I knew I would never get by, and I spent minutes that Johnson could not afford, as well as sanity I myself could not afford, having Nils move me back up so I could chip away with the knife. Then I wormed by.

After what seemed like an eternity of squeezing along, contorting my freezing body and squirming snakelike inch by inch through that immensely cold damnable hole, my flashlight illuminated an obstruction below me that, even in the glare of my beam along the ice, could only be another body.

At the same time, the hole widened.

The ice eased its grip and I was lowered gently on top of Carl Johnson.

The beam picked up his upper torso and head. He was lying upright on top of the packer with his legs twisted through a gash in the side of the shaft.

Suddenly the incredible loss of hole water no longer baffled me.

Because the melting of new water in the reserve tanks is such a time-consuming process, the system is designed to conserve fluids at all costs. Once a fissure or crack is encountered in the course of boring, the bottom line monitor immediately senses the difference in volume between water pumped in at the bottom and that pumped out at the top and shuts off the flow. A tough rubber bag called a packer, situated just above the monitor, swells like a balloon to the limits of the shaft diameter to seal the crack. To keep the water from freezing again, circulation continues through a secondary aperture just above the packer.

It hadn't worked here.

This gash was so large that the packer had failed to seal it off, and hot water rushing through the portion of the gash above the bag had enlarged it as well as the rest of the hole bottom even more. The packer hung loose in this bottom swell, but it would never be pulled up through the restricted shaft.

I reached for Johnson. Having fallen feetfirst with his arms trapped over his head had probably saved his skull a good banging. That and landing on the bag. Despite which, his face was bloodied and more blood had spattered the ice around him. I tried to shine the light in his eyes, but there simply wasn't enough room. His hands were as cold as a corpse's, but mine were no warmer. Feeling for a pulse at his wrist was equally pointless: my own hands hanging down for so long were pounding with such a ferocity that I could never be certain if what I was feeling was his heartbeat or mine.

There was no option but to assume he was alive.

I gave Nils four tugs on the line, got a good grip on Johnson's wrists, and then tugged three times more.

Together, we started moving. He was lighter than me but still quite a load, and again I congratulated myself on having Nils Hellstrom available for the heavy lifting. No one else I knew would have been capable of hauling three hundred fifty pounds up such a height.

Surprisingly, the return trip was much easier. Having Johnson's weight on my arms stretched my body out just enough to reduce my width and make it possible to slip by the narrower constrictions. Of course, the work was Nils' going up. We moved higher and higher until the walls fell away and a faint light from above began to illuminate the shaft once again.

There was no way I could have been ready for what happened.

Suddenly, as though the rope had snapped or Nils had simply released his hold, I was plummeting uncontrollably back down the shaft. The light disappeared in an instant and we plunged into darkness.

If I dropped Carl Johnson, my own size would slow me down. Yet he would not survive a second fall if he had, in fact, survived the first, and I couldn't bring myself to let him go.

With his slim weight below me, and our combined momentum, we raced headlong past the restrictions.

The cold tore by, ripping at my shirt and burning the skin of my arms and sides. Instinctively I tried to spread my legs and brake the fall, but my ankles were solidly bound. Again, I attempted to wedge my legs across the circumference, but with his weight pulling me down the maneuver hardly slowed us at all. We shot down, Johnson and I, to our doom.

The impact was a nightmare. Mercifully I was knocked senseless when my head glanced off Johnson and struck glacial ice, ice so hard it can crack a tanker's bow. I came to some time later, but I was still dazed and remember little of what must have taken place. I do know that I was completely numb throughout; my head pounded below the weight of my body, which felt as though it had been telescoped into a length of about three feet.

Inch by inch, ache by ache, I straightened myself up.

As I did so, the length of rope tied to my feet came snaking down in my face. I shone the weak glow of the flashlight onto its end and then onto the bottom line assembly.

My recollection after that is sketchy. Somehow my

mind became convinced that, inverted as I was, another rope could not be lowered to us. I used the knife to slash the packer, and amid a small explosion of escaping air Johnson and I settled even farther into the hole. Still upside down, I must have hammered with the haft on the assembly release, breaking it free from the tubing before attaching the severed length of rope to the tubing end.

Nils told me later that while he was waiting for additional rope to be fetched, he felt three tugs on the tubing. Perhaps. At any rate it seems to be a fact that I used some of the rope to bind Johnson's hands together and then to tie a loop around my wrists to his, for when the winch was activated and I was pulled upside down to the surface at the end of the tubing, that is how they found Johnson hanging from me at arm's length.

We were both very much unconscious.

3

A Goat in Sheep's Clothing

The first thing I saw was Mary Ingram's darling dimples and the stars in her sky-blue eyes. I am convinced she cultivated the dimples with many an hour before a looking glass. On her way to becoming Miss Peaches and Cream or whatever the title had been. The eyes, however, like her brains, were a product of quality breeding. According to Saperstein, she had top credentials as a geologist. And he ought to know, but since I personally couldn't tell an agate from a feldspar, I would vouch only that she was the best-looking member of our team. That may not have been saying much. She was also undoubtedly the best-looking female in Antarctica, but again, of the twenty-five hundred or so humans currently populating the white continent, there can't be more than a hundred or so of the gentler gender.

Taking a good look at me, her eyes lost their sparkle and the dimples disappeared. "His face looks terrible."

Paulette Gruber leaned over me to adjust some dressings but spoke across the bunk to Mary. "His nose is broken, he has multiple lacerations and contusions. On top of that his face is frostbitten. How should he look, dear?"

For a doctor, and a female doctor at that, Paulette had a bedside manner that lacked any sort of gentleness—which shows the danger of gender generalization. Of course, depending upon the time of day, Paulette could have a very good excuse. When the Russian colonel was grilling me about the suitability

of Miss Ingram's specialization, he might have mentioned—and doubtless would have, had he known—
that it was no less unusual having as the station's
resident physician one of America's lesser known but
nevertheless foremost authorities on radiation medi-
cine. To a greater extent, the U.S. Navy Reserves and
the California Radiology Center, which had granted
her leaves of absence to work here, would have been
shocked to learn about Paulette something of which I
alone at Mensa, apparently, was aware: our good doctor was a junkie.

Her dispensary was more crowded than I had ever
seen it. At the foot of my bunk stood David Saperstein
with arms folded, awaiting an explanation. Dolan and
another engineer, Jerry Davis, hovered solicitously
near Carl Johnson's bunk.

As I started to speak, there came strenuous dissen-
sion; my mouth, having been cut badly by the knife,
revolted at the very idea of talking, and the bandages
wrapping my jaw abetted the mutiny.

Mary asked, "Will he ever smile again, Paulette?"

"No, dear. He'll only be as good as he was before."

Very funny. Rather than acknowledge such crude
humor I turned toward Johnson. All I learned by doing
so was that my neck muscles had joined the rebellion.
As for Johnson, his eyes were open but he looked
gone.

Paulette answered my unspoken question. "He
hasn't regained consciousness," she said, "and it's
unlikely that he ever will."

"Okay, Peter," snapped Saperstein. "Talk."

I talked.

At first haltingly, my rhythm improved as I accustomed myself to the cuts and dressings, and somehow
made it through.

When I finished, Saperstein settled into a somber
silence, but Mary spoke up quickly, "Peter, that was
really something! That's not the Peter Masterson you
pretend to be."

"What do you mean?"

"Holding on to Carl like that when the rope broke. Anybody else would have let him fall."

Of course I had considered that—and judged myself more harshly. The decision to hang on to Johnson meant that it was on my head if he failed to recover.

"How do you know what was going through my head, Mary? If I'd dropped him, he would only have fallen again from half the height he'd already survived. But his weight dragged me past the restrictions; without him I might have become wedged halfway down and never freed myself. I needed to get to the bottom. And as far as that goes, his body broke my fall much better than the ice would have."

Mary's face fell as she turned away.

In fact, nobody looked at me for a bit. Johnson became the center of attention, though true to Paulette's diagnosis, he never did regain consciousness while I was there; he just stared vacantly out the door and across the hallway.

Finally I asked Saperstein about Nils Hellstrom.

"Nils is helping to distribute food to the Soviets in the corridor. Do you want me to send for him?"

So he was back on the job I'd given him.

"No, don't," I said. "I wanted to ask him something, but it can wait."

"Ask me."

"That's all right, David. I'll wait."

"Well, I've got something to ask you." That was Dolan, moving in after checking to be sure the others were out of earshot. "About this crack at the bottom of the shaft."

"It was no crack—not even a fissure. It was a gaping hole. And what little I could see back inside looked a lot bigger yet. It opened up into a mammoth chamber. My flashlight wasn't powerful enough to illuminate the bottom, but I could hear moving water. A lot of it."

Dolan exchanged glances with Saperstein. "Probably some sort of subglacial chasm. Polynya maybe."

"And the water?" I asked.

"Seawater most likely," Saperstein said. "The polynya must penetrate the eighty or ninety feet to the ocean." He and Dolan nodded at each other. Dolan said that was a good thought and then together they faced me. Actually I might have believed it myself if I'd thought for a moment that either one of them did.

After a while I nodded my head, just to make it unanimous. "Yeah," I agreed, "that's a good one, all right. Say look, maybe I have got a question for the two of you, after all. At the bottom of that shaft I also noticed an unusual sensor on the downhole monitor. What exactly is it monitoring?"

Dolan spoke carefully. "Water temperature, gallons per minute, ice density, salinity . . . that sort of thing. You know."

"I don't know anything. I don't know, for example, why the display panel on the gantry would have a galvanometer scaled in roentgen units."

"What's wrong with that?"

"For one thing there are no minerals under the barrier. Certainly nothing that should be radioactive. So why would we need a Geiger counter on the downhole monitor?"

Saperstein silenced Dolan with an outstretched hand and answered for him. "This has nothing to do with your responsibilities, Masterson, and it should not concern you. Nevertheless, you know what this equipment was designed for . . . what this project entails. We're explorers. If we knew exactly what we were going to find, we'd be no more than miners."

"I still don't like it."

"Dammit, Masterson! You don't like anything at all. First you don't like Russians and then you don't like your job. Now I hear you're complaining to Colonel Fedorev about your salary. And you the highest-paid employee at Mensa."

I started to interrupt—that had to be the sheerest nonsense.

Saperstein pushed a palm at me. "I'm not finished. Here's something else you won't like, but you're not going to be able to do anything about it. I'm giving your room to Major Zhizn and Lieutenant Shokin. Be quiet and lie back! I started to say that Colonel Fedorev asked about quarters for himself and his three officers, and I offered to let them share rooms with some of us. When he refused to have his people mixing with ours, I agreed to vacate three rooms. Mary is going to bunk in with Paulette tonight; Johnson won't need his, and if you're going to spend the night here, then you won't either. I'm giving Mary's room to Lieutenant Krokov and the colonel will take Johnson's, but I still need one room for Zhizn and Shokin and yours is it. I'm not asking, I'm just telling."

"Okay, you've told me. I'll bet you feel better."

"I do!"

"Perhaps if you reminded Johnson here that these Russians are just a bunch of scientists, he'd feel better too. Tell him again how there's nothing suspicious in their arriving just as our boring process is getting under way. And how nothing will happen if we let them come in and take over the station."

"You're not blaming them for the loss of hole water . . . or for what happened to Carl!"

"There's no connection," snapped Dolan. "The Soviets didn't have anything to do with either one. Carl Johnson was all by himself on the gantry when the bore hole lost water. Elliston was on duty, but he had gone off somewhere and Carl couldn't find him—"

I said, "He was in the storeroom. Working on the generator."

"Carl came and got me," Dolan continued. "The two of us were alone in the drilling chamber when he fell."

"The first time he fell, maybe. Not the second time."

Saperstein was shaking his head.

"Mister, you're not just suspicious, you're paranoid!"

With that, Saperstein and Dolan about-faced together and marched out of the dispensary. When I remarked earlier that the Russian scientists drill better than our scientists, I wasn't including the members of the whitewall corps.

In the next hour the dispensary visitors drifted away. I turned down a bottle after seeing Johnson get his in

the arm, and settled for sucking soup through a plastic
straw. Before I finished, Nils Hellstrom stopped by for
a laugh.

"Well?"

He stopped laughing.

"Well, what, Peter?"

"What happened to that rope?"

"It broke."

"You're sure it wasn't cut?"

Hellstrom shook his head slowly. "I hope you didn't
say anything like that to Saperstein; he's already convinced you see bogeymen under your bed."

"I don't want his opinion. What do you think?"

"As a matter of fact, it looked as though it had
been." Nils was kind enough to answer the question
about the rope rather than about me. "Probably by the
ragged weld on the broken stanchion brace," he said.
"The rope was hanging right in front of it . . . you,
swinging back and forth. For that matter there might
have been a cut I didn't notice as it played through my
fingers. A defect of some kind. What more can I say?"

"Nothing. What have you found out about the
shifts?"

He chuckled again. "Knowing you, I was sure that
would be your major interest. Two hours. The second
shift was just posted."

I digested that.

"What do you want to do, Peter?"

"The temperature is dropping outside and we want
to be good hosts, don't we? Set out one of the electric
heaters."

"Okay. I'll do it straightaway."

"Not too soon, Nils. They'll appreciate it more if
you wait awhile . . . say, about ninety minutes from
now." I checked my watch—a painful exercise, as
every muscle in my body seemed to have joined the
rebellion. "Hold off until seven-thirty. Then shove it
out the weather lock. If you use the fifty-foot extension, it ought to just about reach beyond the hatch."

"Why not use a portable heater and take it right
over to their tractors."

"Well . . . these are communists, Nils. There's such a thing as going too far in trying to be a good host."

"And fifty feet ought to be just about far enough?"

I nodded, as that was still less painful than talking. "Anything else?"

"Yes. Bring me some clothes. My windbreaker, mittens, and cap—but be careful. Two heroes of the proletariat have seized my room. If they catch you taking my stuff out, they'll be sure it's secret documents."

Nils Hellstrom acknowledged the instructions with a frown, backed out of the dispensary, and moved off down the hall. After he was gone I turned and found Johnson watching his departure, too, with eyes that remained vacant, unseeing.

Twenty minutes seemed about right for dressing. So a little more than an hour after Nils returned with clothes, I sat on the edge of my bunk and regarded the pile: two pairs of woolen socks, finespun cotton windproofs with drawstrings at the ankles and wrists, two wool shirts, double-thick denim pants, reindeer skin boots, cloth cap, and canvas windbreaker. My tailored caribou parka lay on top of the pile. It had inside- as well as outside-facing fur and a wolverine ruff hood.

As stiff as I was, twenty minutes wasn't enough time by half. Before I poked my head around the corner of the corridor, Nils Hellstrom was already coming out of the main weather lock from having set out the heater.

There were six ways into and out of Mensa Station. The weather lock, situated on that horizontal stretch of corridor between the two side-by-side capital Hs was the one most often used. It was the size of a walk-in closet—and sure enough, there were parkas hanging on hooks and boots against the walls—in the center of which a ladder rose to a wooden hatch at barrier level. In addition to the weather lock there was an emergency exit from the storeroom, the lower right-hand leg of the westernmost H. We used this to bring in supplies when the small hatch and ladder of the weather lock proved too cumbersome.

After waiting for Nils to enter the lounge, I crossed

half the length of the corridor, observed the extension
cord running under the weather-lock door, and then
passed up both this and the supply-room exit. I pushed
through the double doors of the garage. The huge hy-
draulic deckhead hatches on the elevated ends of the
garage, which allowed the Badgers and sledges to be
moved in and out, were exits three and four. But these
would take hours to clear of snow on top before they
could be operated. Besides, I was hoping to slip out
unseen, not alert everyone in the station. Through the
next set of double doors was the Project Centaur drilling chamber, which had its own exit. However, I
couldn't be sure the chamber would be unoccupied
even though the accident had surely halted all boring
activity. And I couldn't be sure which of the engineers
who might be working there I could trust.

I was going out door number six.

A barking rose immediately as I stepped out from
behind the Badgers. But when I approached the cage,
the huskies quieted right down. Although they were
Nils' animals, I had spent a lot of time with them;
they had tested my skills behind a dogsled, found me
competent, and thereafter acknowledged my right to
authority. I entered the cage, giving Thor a pat on the
head. Huskies, like most people I know, are tough to
warm up to and generally my attitude is, Why bother?
There are rare exceptions. Nils and his prize lead dog
were two such animals. Most of the team were whelped
from the old bitch Freya, who was Nils' favorite, but
Thor was the first born and he was the biggest and
strongest as well as the smartest of the pack. He leapt
at me as I entered the cage, and then tried to follow
me up the ramp that led to their doghouse on the ice
up above. I nudged him back with a foot, steeled myself for the impending assault, and eased my head
through the trapdoor.

There are many words to describe Antarctica.

Barren is one word.

Frigid, bleak are other, equally accurate adjectives.
I liked it that way.

The rolling snow-packed glacier lay like a white
wool blanket on every side of me. Above, the sky was

as black as any sky ever gets on this planet. And the
stars are that bright. So bright were they, in fact, and
the landscape, so white, that it was possible to distinguish features of the barrier for a considerable distance. This is one of the only places on earth where
one can navigate with the unaided eye by starlight.
Across the night sky streaked a meteor; a new but
regular feature of our heavens, it might have been a
thousand miles up or a hundred feet, but I had decided
it was too periodic to be a comet and, judging by its
speed, too low to be a satellite in stable orbit. Whatever the thing might be, it was a punctual devil, ap-
pearing from the north almost hourly for the past two
days and quickly disappearing below the southern horizon.

Winter visibility, when the sky is clear, can only be
described as uncanny. Nobody knows exactly why.
Maybe it has to do with the aurora australis, an occasionally visible ionization of the Van Allen radiation
belt, which is in turn triggered by sunspot activity.
This was Nils' pet theory. Jules Digne felt it was tied
in with the annual disappearance of ozone above the
south pole. Each fall a hole developed in the ozone
layer the diameter of the antarctic circle, and each
spring the hole closed in. One of the meteorologist's
responsibilities was monitoring the mysterious, increasingly late reappearance of the layer in the last
several years, a matter of concern to scientists around
the world.

If you ask me, it's the cold. I don't know about the
visibility on a desert, but I know the antarctic; temperatures this extreme can account for anything. And
from this there is never a respite. The southern lights
will wax and wane, the ozone comes and goes, but the
cold is always around.

It's true there isn't a lot here to love, but what there
is divides very generously among the several hundred
who can take it. Five million square miles and not a
cop, a politician, or a bureaucrat in the whole place.
No dogcatchers or lifeguards either.

But there were the two guards, one standing, one
kneeling, both warming their hands in front of the

portable heater at the weather-lock hatch, which was practically in the center of the circle of floodlight. The alternate exit—from the storeroom—was also within this circle. I watched them from beyond the lighted perimeter. It hadn't taken them long to realize they could protect the tractors perfectly well from right there. They'd probably located the project chamber's emergency exit—even farther away in darkness—and discovered it could be opened only from below. They might even have toyed with the idea of checking the dog enclosure, but huskies have a way of keeping strangers at a distance.

On my belly I crawled to the fence, slipped out through the gate without letting any of the huskies loose, and then four-footed my way to the tractors. Not once did the guards look around.

Because I was late getting out I actually had only a matter of twenty minutes or so before a change of shifts would have me trapped outside.

There wasn't time to inspect the half-dozen sledges that were being towed behind each tractor. I had to assume that if there was something they didn't want us to see, it would be in the tractors themselves.

The first vehicle loomed over me in the darkness.

This time I did not turn on the flashlight.

Though I had taped the glass to a pencil-sized beam of light, I did not chance even that before crawling into the back of the tractor bed whose twin doors were latched but not locked; in only seconds, I was inside. The first thing my flash did was confirm one suspicion and dash an assumption: I was right about the beds: they were not weather-tight. I had been wrong about the armor plating: the walls were actually plywood painted to look like armor.

Benches were mounted along both tread wells. There was a small unfired heater forward and some rations on crude shelves. Lashed to the walls and ceiling was a myriad of arctic supplies—blankets, tins of food, tools, and weapons—all of it neatly stowed.

After a minute or two I slipped out again and proceeded to the next vehicle in line. One by one I checked the supplies in each tractor, and in each it was

the same story. Regulation arctic stores. All in neat
order. All innocently stowed. Little of it showed sign
of use; most had not even been broken into.

On the last tractor in line, actually the first vehicle
and the one from which Colonel Fedorev had descended, I found a different story altogether.

First off, there was a padlock on the bed doors. Despite that, a glint of light shone through a chink just
above the hinges of the left side. Rags and cloth had
been stuffed in all the cracks of the plywood joints to
insulate the interior, but one little hole had been
missed. By placing my eye close to the crack I could
make out a limited portion of the interior. An inside
wall was bare of equipment but had pinned to it such
a montage of papers in apparently random fashion as
to be all but white.

A shadow fell across its surface.

Instinctively I dropped a few inches and then returned immediately to the crack. It was an elderly man
silhouetted by a desk lamp; he was working in desul-
tory fashion at a panel against the forward wall, adjusting knobs and taking notes of readouts hidden from
my view. Very soon, he flicked some switches, stood,
and moved out of my vision to the other side.

I found another glint on the opposite door through
which I could just make out his figure on a bench bun-
dling up in front of a small kerosene heater. There
also, I had an improved vantage for inspecting the
panel. It looked like a comparatively sophisticated
communication set. I knew the Russians still used a
lot of tube stuff, which made their equipment bulkier
than our integrated models, and yet there was something about this particular transceiver that interested
me.

I advanced to the cab, eased open the passenger's
door, (knowing the idling diesel would smother the
sound) and slid in low along the seat. Through the
windshield I could see the light of Mensa Station and
the two guards in the much smaller radius of the electric heater's glow.

Cautiously I switched on the pencil beam and
guarded its light downward with two fingers pinched

over the hole. Illuminated on the floorboard was a variety of goodies, including a short-handled sledge that I knew to be a gear assister for changing speeds on a Russian-model tractor transmission. There were also some fuses and flares and a locked map case.

Something drew my attention to the windshield as I reached for the case. The hatch had opened and a pair of relief sentries began climbing out. They joined their comrades in front of the heater. A discussion ensued— serious business, probably a debriefing. I saw them pointing to the entrances and exits one by one. In only seconds, the first two would descend to the station and their relief would undoubtedly begin making a round of the tractors.

That left me precious little time to pick the lock.

Hurriedly I stripped down to the silk gloves and attacked the lock with a pocketknife. Despite my enthusiasm, I was expecting no prize, and not just because of the simplicity of the mechanism—rather, it was the Soviet penchant for secrecy. Likely the case contained nothing more valuable than a topographical map of Antarctica, one very much inferior to those we kept at Mensa Station in quantity or to ones obtainable by the general public from the American geodetic survey office for only a few dollars. By contrast, maps are usually classified documents in the Soviet Union; Red Army regulations permit only officers and higher-ranking noncoms to have access to maps or any type of navigational training.

When the case came open my expectations were realized.

Inside was a detailed map of our quadrant of the barrier, the middle region of the Queen Maud Mountains, and the plateau beyond them. A pencil line had been drawn from a position several miles northeast of Mensa to the station; the line continued back northwest to the Beaumont Glacier, up the glacier to the high plateau, that region of which is known as the Deception Reach, and then south along the reach to a featureless point just a hundred miles or so west-southwest across the mountains from Mensa. The line ended in that expanse of nothingness.

I looked up to see the relief guards beginning a swing inspection.

Returning the map to its case, I slipped out of the cab, eased the door closed, and knelt beside the front fender. All I had to do was wait until the two guards had circled out of sight behind the vehicles and then sneak back to the weather lock before they completed their inspection. I swore to myself when I saw them splitting up. They were going to start from different ends. I ran to the rear of the tractor, leapt the hitch, ducked behind the fourth tractor, leapt that hitch too, and emerged from between three and four in a dead sprint toward the weather lock . . . and stopped cold.

Of all the damn luck! The first two sentries hadn't yet gone below. They had to be frozen stiff, but there they stood over the heater waiting for the others to return. I'd never get in the weather lock or the supply wing hatch as long as they remained there. My only chance was to go back through the dog enclosure. But as I dropped to hands and knees and started across the open stretch of semidarkness, I heard a rustle of feet and a bark. My heart sank. Thor had come up the ramp. He'd spotted me. His eagerness alerted the two sentries under the floodlight and one started over. The guy called something in Russian to his buddies circling the tractors behind me. I couldn't go back to the vehicles and I couldn't go forward. There was nothing left but to move away at right angles into the darkness. I'd have to hide behind a drift until the furor died down and then find a way to sneak in. Even as the shouts and floodlights and swirling flashlight beams dropped behind me, however, I knew the foolishness of this plan. All the Russians had to do was send a man below and take a head count of the Americans to know who was out playing games. Until then, a flashlight beam could hit me at any time. One of the guards would step out of the floodlight or turn off his flashlight and spot me by starlight, a dark figure against a background of purest white.

Any way you looked at it, I was in trouble.

They were organizing something now. Their shouts had brought several huskies to the surface, and the huskies, in turn, were going crazy, barking and snarling.

I decided to double back. Create a diversion. Tackle whichever of the guards remained at the weather lock and fight my way down. With any luck at all—I'd had no luck so far—they wouldn't see my face. I started around. Halfway between my position and the dog enclosure I saw the project chamber's emergency-exit hatch crack open. A head popped out. Long black hair buffeted in the breeze.

There was no time to consider all the possibilities.

I scrambled toward it, put a hand on the Peeping Tom's head, and shoved it back down. Then I threw my feet through the opening and slipped in, closing and locking the hatch firmly behind me.

"I should have known it was you."

"Hi, Mary."

"You're kind of rough, aren't you?"

"Yes."

We had come down the circular stairway. She wrapped her arms around herself and shivered at the cold that had entered with us. I took off my parka and placed it around her shoulders.

She smiled. She looked gorgeous when she smiled. And when she didn't.

"But there's a streak of human in you, Peter."

"Forget it, Mary. I'm a lost cause. What are you doing in here all by yourself? Surely we won't be drilling for a while."

"Just collecting some records." As though to establish this fact, she gathered up a sheath of official-looking papers from off the control counter at the gantry. Some of these I recognized as printout sheets from the monitor assembly. "What about you?" she asked. "What were you doing up there making all that noise? Or more to the point, what are you doing out of bed?"

"Just collecting," I said.

With an arm around her waist I edged her down the hall to the garage entrance. "Come on, it's cold in here. Let's get out of here before someone finds us . . ."

"You mean before someone comes looking."

A minute later we were avoiding Russian limbs down the main corridor. The 60 degrees of the station interior felt as oppressive to my face and hands as had the extreme cold. We passed the weather lock just as the door opened and one of the guards stepped out. He looked at me. He looked at Mary Ingram. He looked hard at her parka and at the papers under her arm. One of the papers dropped out and fluttered onto the floor, and he looked at that, too. I reached down, scooped it off the floor, folded it in half, and smiled.

He wheeled without a word—he probably didn't know any English words anyway—and stalked off, no doubt in search of his immediate superior.

"So!"

I cringed as I faced her.

She was taking the parka off her shoulders.

"That's why you gave me the coat. So they wouldn't know it was you who'd been out there." She threw it at me. "I swear I don't know why I believe in you, Peter."

Mary Ingram stormed into the lounge. Even a real gem needs a pick-me-up after a knockdown like that.

The paper was a three-color computer-generated picture of the Ross Ice Shelf as seen from the upper atmosphere. We were right in the middle of it. A bright-red spot appeared to the west over the Queen Maud Mountains; around the red was an orange band that widened on the barrier side to a sort of a point. This, in turn, was surrounded by yellow. I guessed the outer diameter of the yellow may have been two or three miles except to the east. A yellow smear ran across the paper passing the orange point and extending well out onto the barrier to the small black dot that was Mensa Station.

On the top was some satellite information, including

an altitude and date indicating that the infrared photograph had been generated just the previous summer.

I stuffed the paper into a pocket, continued down the corridor, turned right at the dispensary/engineering wing, and ran smack into Asia Krokov with her hand on the dispensary door.

"That door was left open intentionally," I announced.

She turned with a start. "Oh! Here you are."

"There's a comatose man inside. I wanted the doctor to hear him if he came to and needed assistance."

"I don't understand, Mr. Masterson. The door's closed."

"Is there something you want?"

"I have to talk to you." Asia leveled her dark eyes on me and with some effort managed a smile. It was not an awful effort and the result was an awful smile. Her English, however, was exceptional, without any trace of an accent.

"Go ahead."

"This hallway isn't such a good place."

"My room is occupied at the moment, Miss Krokov. Zhizn and whosiz, your comrade lieutenant."

"We can use my room . . . Miss Ingram's room, that is."

"Somehow I don't think that's such a good idea—our going to your quarters. Why don't we just step in here."

I pushed open the door and allowed her to precede me.

Carl Johnson was no longer staring at the doorway. He was turned slightly to one side, facing the wall. As I went to him she spoke to my back, "What I have to say is private."

That irked me. You butt your head against a wall trying to explain to these communists about private enterprise and private business and private property; they look at you like you're speaking a foreign language. Now she wants to have a private conversation.

"Do you want to talk in English or Russian?"

Something about Johnson struck me as wrong. I

pressed a hand to his wrist and opened an eyelid; as a result of that, I didn't see her surprise. It was in her voice.

"You speak Russian?"

Johnson had no pulse or dilation. He wasn't breathing.

"*Nyet.*"

"English, then. But I must talk with you alone."

I turned. "You may speak freely," I assured her. "We are alone."

Quite suddenly she was beside me, her hands gripping my forearm. We stood side by side over Johnson's body without uttering a sound.

"He was a friend of yours?" she said at last.

"No. Just a man who needed my help."

"You tried to help him. We all saw that."

"Yeah. Yeah, I was a big help."

I noticed her noticing me noticing her hand on my arm.

"Is it all right if I call you Peter?"

"Anything but comrade."

"Peter, you must help me."

It was my turn to show surprise. "Look, Lieutenant. There's been some mistake. I'll admit I had my eye on you, but I do that. Guys like me look at girls like you. Don't take it as a compliment. Anyway, I wasn't looking to help. I think you ought to talk to Bob Dolan or David Saperstein."

"No, no. It has to be you. They frighten me."

I laughed. "Who? Dolan . . . Saperstein?"

"No, not them. Major Zhizn. Colonel Fedorev."

The names sounded different when she pronounced them, but there was no question about who she meant. "Your own people? What did they do?"

"It's what they will do if they catch us talking together."

"If that's all you're worried about, my advice to you is simple: don't talk. Or don't let them catch you. If you insist on talking and what you have to say is that important, maybe you really had better talk to Saperstein, after all."

Her grip tightened. "No, it must be you or no one."

"Okay, I'll listen," I said, reaching across to lay the sheet over Johnson's head before turning and easing her back into a chair, "but make it good."

She made it good all right.

Asia buried her head in her hands. When she looked up, there was a pitiable little smile on her face. Less awful than her first effort. She had nice dark features. Not beautiful, but pretty. Of course, her original attraction, that she was strictly a hands-off item, had begun to fade. Now that was being replaced by another kind of appeal. Anytime a man isn't attracted to a good-looking woman who has just announced it must be him or no one . . . well, that guy's problems are a lot more complicated than mine. By the time I'd rationalized that much, Asia had started to talk, and since I was the only one she could tell her story to, I decided to listen. "For twenty-eight years," she said, "I've been a good Soviet. Like a sheep. I've played the role of the sheep, worn the clothes of the sheep, and bleated the party line while those bastards sheared us and bred us and butchered us. Today is the day for shedding my sheep's clothing, and just look at me!"

Because my problems are basically pretty simple, I was looking.

This sheep business turned out to be her special allegory. Everybody in the Soviet Union, according to Asia, were sheep. Except for top party leaders and the government officials—they were wolves. I gathered that much of it only after a lot of stop and go. I made the mistake of asking her about shepherds and had to spend five minutes listening to her explain. The gist of it was that the shepherds were the government too. Apparently in the Soviet Union the wolves don't don sheep's clothing. In the Soviet Union the wolf dons the clothing of the shepherd. They don't go after a lamb or two; they go for the whole damn flock.

"I agree your analysis sounds rather forlorn, Miss Krokov, but I'm not sure what you expect me to do about it. What do you want from me?"

Her face, strong on appeal, looked up. "Freedom."

"You don't mean it!"

She meant it. Why, Asia wondered, did I think she'd come to me? I told her I couldn't imagine. That started a tirade. I had to help her, according to her. This was not a decision she had made on the spur of the moment. She'd been planning it for seven years. Women from the lower Ukraine do not attend Moscow University's School of Geophysics. She was and did. Twenty-eight-year-olds do not become accredited polar scientists. She had. For seven years she wore the sheep's clothing and never strayed from the fold. Her record was such that she was selected for overseas assignment over a dozen older men and senior members of the party. That was her plan. She had chosen a profession that one day would require her to leave the country. To come here. The Soviet mission in Antarctica is a determined, ongoing one, and Asia knew that she would be sent to this continent if only she could wear the sheep's clothing long enough. Here, where international law prescribes that representatives of other governments might also work close by. She knew her chance would come. It had. And scared or not, she was taking it.

I wasn't as unmoved as I appeared. "It all sounds okay, Miss Krokov, up until the part about representatives of other governments. I've tried to tell you people this is a civilian operation. There's no one here who can give you asylum, if that's what you're after."

She shook her head in bewilderment.

"But, Peter, you are . . . That is, we all thought you . . ."

I told her I didn't know what she was talking about, but actually I had a pretty good idea. Looking at things from her standpoint, it was obvious. I was a second in command with no clear job function and more authority than my position seemed to warrant. She looked at me and saw a facsimile of Major Zhizn. I'll wager she believed—as did I—that Zhizn's authority came directly from Moscow and the KGB without crossing Fedorev's chain of command. So she merely decided that things worked the same with us.

"You thought that I what, Miss Krokov . . . am CIA?"

"I don't know . . ."

"Let me satisfy your curiosity: the Central Intelligence Agency has as much interest in Antarctica as the KGB has in . . . in the back side of Pluto. Now it's your turn to satisfy mine. Where did this expedition of yours begin? How long have you been on the trail?"

She frowned at me as though it were inconceivable she would be asked to submit to a debriefing. "What are you asking me?" she said.

"You started the expedition about ten miles to the northeast of here?"

"Yes."

"You must have flown equipment in from Leningradskaya. Some type of cargo aircraft. Probably three or four. You offloaded the tractors and other equipment in the middle of the barrier."

"How can you know this?"

"Never mind that. What is your destination?"

"Destination?"

"Don't pretend you never heard the word. Where are you going? To the plateau? Across the Queen Mauds?"

"Yes, Peter. You say you're not CIA but you sound like CIA."

"Why didn't you fly the entire route?"

"We couldn't. The cloud cover prohibited it."

"Okay, I'll buy that. Landing a squadron of cargo aircraft on the barrier at night without runway lights or instrument approach was risky enough; on the high plateau—particularly Deception Reach—it would have been suicidal. Without absolute assurance of cloudless skies no aircraft would be able to descend. But that still doesn't explain why your expedition came here . . . to Mensa Station."

"You're going too fast, Peter."

I repeated the question a bit louder.

Asia made some noises to the effect that Mensa Station was merely on their way.

"No, it's not, but we'll let that pass for the moment, since we may be short of time. Tell me the real purpose of the expedition. What will you do on the reach once you get there?''

She shook her head. ''You don't understand. I'm simply a polar adviser. Colonel Fedorev and Major Zhizn have not confided in any of us the details of the expedition.''

I started to ask her about the old man in the back of Fedorev's tractor but thought better of it. If she did know about him, she wasn't talking, and if she didn't, there was no reason to let her know that I did.

''And now?'' she wanted to know.

''Now you've stumped me. We're not really in a position to do anything. Mensa is four hundred miles from the nearest installation. Too far to expect help. Right here in this facility Fedorev has more than thirty men who are undoubtedly trained combat soldiers. We've got Nils and me. You can see what kind of condition I'm in. The colonel's five tractors are filled with high-caliber automatic weapons. Nils has a bolt-action seal rifle and I have a pistol that tends to jam. We have no hold on them . . . no lever, and there's no chance he'll let you go or leave without you. You can try talking to Saperstein, but the way he feels about cooperating with your countrymen and playing by the rules, he'd never agree to give you asylum and couldn't back it up if he did.''

''It sounds as though you're saying you can't help me.''

''How can I? For that matter, why should I?''

Her eyes looked hopelessly into mine. ''If you won't, who will? If you can't, who could?''

Mary Ingram came immediately to mind, she having just confessed to believing in lost causes. I said, ''No one.''

Asia Krokov placed her palms on my chest. She hadn't stood up, but she was standing. She hadn't moved in, but she was against me. Her head fell back and her dark eyes looked directly into mine.

''What can I say to you, Peter? What can I do?''

She wasn't very good at it. Rather, she was now too damn good . . . having been not quite good enough a few minutes before.

If the original approach had been a little smoother or the transition from troubled refugee to seductress had been a bit more practiced . . . if the whole proposition didn't scream of hands-off, and if I hadn't just kicked in the teeth one very nice woman . . . well, it never would have worked. My rigid, heavily bandaged face gave her no clue as to my state of mind, but that was primarily because she wasn't looking at it. She was staring at the sheet over Johnson's body.

"I don't believe," Asia said, "that the Peter Masterson who dived into that hole to try to save this man will not help me now. I don't believe that."

"He was an American and an associate; you're a Russian communist."

"Am I a Ukrainian? Yes. Am I a communist? No. Perhaps if I came to America, you and I could be associates, too." Her full mouth remained open, revealing even teeth as white as polar snow.

The only thing to do was kiss her. So I didn't.

My eyes swept the medical room while my mind scrambled for an idea.

"We better inform the doctor about Johnson. You stay here," I ordered her.

"Where can I go?"

"I mean, don't leave this room; if you're not here when I return, I can't help you, understand?"

As she nodded and sat back down, I left, crossed the corridor to the cafeteria, and found Nils Hellstrom wolfing what was most probably his fourth plate of corned-beef hash.

He looked up as I entered. "You going out now?"

"I've been and back. Now I need to talk to Paulette."

He gestured to the other side of the lounge.

"Do me a favor," I said. "Go to the dispensary. Asia Korkov is in there. The Russian woman. See that she doesn't leave."

"Oh, no, Peter—"

"It's okay. She wants to stay. It's somebody else taking her out that concerns me. They may go looking for her any minute. Get in there. See that she remains and that no one else—and I mean absolutely no one except me—gets in."

He rose to his mountainous height. "What are you up to now, Peter?"

"Me? Nothing. It's her—Princess Di wants to defect."

4

The Water Carriers

Paulette Gruber exhaled a cloud of noxious fumes that came surging toward me like a billowing thunderhead. As I waved smoke from my face, Paulette's eyes narrowed, suggesting that only then had the features any meaning for her.

She was riding high.

"Get your ass back in bed, Masterson," she snapped.

What few manners Paulette possessed were reserved for the bedside. She ate—her portly frame indicated she did so to excess—and drank—in a like quantity— alone. Whether or not her manners or her habits were responsible for either I cannot say, as my own association with the other team members was limited to duty assignments, a result of which was that such gossip rarely found its way to my ear.

"I need to ask you something in private, Doc."

She started at sight of my jacket and cap. "The answer is no, you can't go outside."

"I've already been. Come on."

As I pulled back her chair—I observed Zhizn and the lieutenant—Shokin, I think—at Nils' and my table giving us the eye. Two of their pals seated at Saperstein's table had forced Bob Dolan to join the other members of the whitewall corps. Mary Ingram was there, too, surrounded by Tom Elliston, Jerry Davis, and Jules Digne. All looking pretty dour. Considering how excited everyone had been about the prospect of socializing with our fellow Soviet scientists, the room was divided up neatly along party lines. Maybe Fe-

dorev didn't want his people mixing even here, maybe
the accident had sobered up the Mensa staff, or maybe
we were just learning something about how communists socialize. After socializing the hall, they had proceeded to socialize a third of the private quarters, and
now forty percent of the dining space had been socialized right out from under us.

Everyone had gone quiet watching the two of us
leave. Dolan started to say something to me, but I
turned my back and led Paulette away.

"You know about Johnson?" I asked her in an undertone.

"What about Johnson? Is he conscious?"

"No. I left the dispensary door open so you could
hear him if he came out of his coma. You didn't close
it?"

"I did not. I've been in here for nearly an hour,
eating and then . . . relaxing. Shouldn't have, I suppose, but Nils assured me that as long as you were in
there with Carl Johnson, nothing was going to happen
to him."

"I wasn't there; something happened. Now I have
news: you've lost one patient and gotten another one."

"You're not getting away that easily, Peter. You're
in my care until I say differently and I want you back
in that dispensary—"

"Not me. Actually you'll be losing me, too, but I
was referring to Johnson. He's dead. And now you've
got another patient. The Soviet woman, Asia Krokov
. . . she's come down with something."

"Dead! How?" Her pace quickened.

"That's the first thing I want you to do for me.
Check him over. I want to know how he died."

"What do you mean how he died?"

By this time we had passed through the cafeteria and
reached the corridor, and though all the Soviets seemed
to be sleeping soundly, we crossed to the administration wing in silence.

"I don't know," I said once we had reached the
other side. "That's what I want you to tell me. Can't
you check for drugs in his system? Check the pillow
under his head for traces of saliva."

"You're suggesting . . ."

"I'm just curious, that's all." I held her outside the dispensary. "Don't go in just yet. Your other patient is in there."

"What's wrong with her?"

"That's the second thing you need to find out. She's got a serious disease. We may have to quarantine the station if it turns out to be communicable."

"What disease?"

"How should I know? I'm no doctor. Plague, perhaps."

"Plague!"

I shrugged. "Or it could be the flu. In fact, maybe it's just an incurable thirst for freedom. Paulette, the truth is Asia Krokov wants to defect, but she's come to the wrong place and doesn't know it. She thinks I'm working for the CIA and this is a government installation. Since I'm not and this isn't, we can't legally give her asylum, and under the circumstances we'd be pretty stupid to try. We couldn't win a fight with Colonel Fedorev and his Bolsheviks and they'd never stand by and see her come over. The only thing for us to do is to convince the Soviets that they have no choice but to leave her."

Twice Paulette Gruber had slumped against the door, bewildered, and twice she had come bolt forward in shock; the word *plague* will do that to medical people, and so apparently will suggestions of defection by visiting Russians.

Of course, in her case it might have been the dope.

Behind anxious eyes, she pondered her position. "I'm not sure just what my ethics and my oath allow me here, Peter."

"Don't talk to me about ethics. Junkies don't have ethics." She stiffened. Her slightly blurred eyes revealed an addict's fear of exposure. "What is the current euphemism for heroin? *Horse* is passé. *Shit* is crude. What do you call it?"

"Diacetylmorphine."

"Oh, that's clever. Do you buy yours from Walgreen? I know you didn't come to Antarctica with a dime bag. There are no connections here. But with a name like that you could stash a few kilograms right in there with the pharmaceuticals. What do you bet a rudimentary search by Saperstein will turn it up?''

She grimaced, turned, jerked open the door, and then stopped upon confronting a barrier of muscle and bone nearly seven feet in height. "Let me in, Nils," she demanded.

"Sorry, Doctor, but I can't do that."

I stepped in front of the crack. "It's okay, Nils, I'm here."

As he moved aside, Paulette gave me a crushing glare, transferred it to Nils Hellstrom, and then passed by him into the dispensary.

I stepped inside myself, trading places with Nils and asking him to continue his sentry duties in the hall so that we wouldn't be disturbed.

I introduced Asia Krokov to Paulette, briefed both on what I had in mind, and then excused myself to step outside while the two women worked out the kinks. Success or failure was entirely up to the pair of them. Nils and I were still in the hallway ten minutes later when Paulette came out and squared off with us, her expression a very unsettled one.

"Well?" I demanded.

"It'll never work."

I turned. "Nils, get David in here."

"Wait! I didn't say I wouldn't give it a try. Damn!" She pursed her lips. "We can argue a case of yellow fever. Cholera, too, or even plague as you suggested. Pneumonic plague."

"You mean bubonic plague?"

"No, bubonic is transmitted by insects. Not possible in Antarctica. But it sometimes leads to pneumonic plague or even septicemic plague, both of which are quite virulent."

"Sounds good . . . or rather bad. Are they contagious?"

"Extremely. Spread by droplets sprayed from the lungs. Septicemic plague is transmitted by touch. While bubonic plague is fatal in about fifty percent of the cases usually within five or six days, victims of pneumonic and septicemic plague—all but about five percent—die within as little as twenty-four hours. This is the Black Death, Peter.''

Nodding, I said, ''Based on what you've told me, it sounds like plague.''

''It may not be that easy. If the colonel or any of his men have even a modicum of medical training . . .''

I waved it away. ''Then we're finished anyway, so let's not worry about it. What did you find out about Johnson?''

''Well, he's dead all right . . . now. If you'd come to me immediately—''

''Forget that, Paulette. I know a dead man when I see him. What I don't know is what killed him.''

''Neither do I. I'm no forensic pathologist and quite incapable, even given the proper facilities, which are not to be found here, of doing an autopsy.''

''Don't you even have an opinion?''

''There's no outward evidence of the type of activity you suggested.''

''Okay, Paulette, thanks. Don't talk this around, huh?''

''Peter, I wouldn't dare repeat half the things you suggest. However, we both know that David Saperstein has to be told about that girl in there. And right away. Protocol probably requires him to be the one to inform the Soviet officials.''

I agreed and added that protocol would probably also give her the job of telling Saperstein, but I didn't add that Saperstein wouldn't have bought a thing that came from me.

''Give me five minutes and then bring David in,'' she said, wheeling and disappearing back into the dispensary.

Nils rumbled, ''What was all that about? The part about Johnson, I mean?''

''It's not important, Nils.''

The rumble became an avalanche. I looked up.

''You have an unfriendly habit, Peter, of telling people only what you want them to know. It was bad enough I had to learn he was dead by finding a sheet over his head. I'm not complaining—that's you—but I thought you should know I resent it.''

I shrugged and gave Nils my suspicions. ''When I left him to go outside,'' I said, ''he was flat on his back with his head propped up on a pillow looking straight ahead. I left the door open so if he came around someone might hear him. But when I returned, his head was twisted to the side off the pillow and the door had been closed. I just don't see that he would have regained consciousness, changed his position, and then died. And I sure don't believe he shut the door himself, so how can you explain it being closed?''

''Why try?''

''What are you saying? That I'm just trying to find an excuse to believe I didn't kill him myself? That I'm not responsible?''

''Peter, you're no more responsible than I am. I was holding the rope. If it was defective and a cut that bad slipped through my fingers, or if I allowed the rope to swing against the gantry, then I'm the one who killed him.''

''Don't be ridiculous.''

Silence fell over the little hallway; after a moment or two I suggested he start for Saperstein's quarters. A few minutes later they appeared around the corner, jockeying for position over and around our Russian guests.

Saperstein, trying to look purposeful despite a slightly disheveled appearance, stopped when he saw me. His hair was tousled, his clothes disarranged, and his eyes had a reddish cast. I added two and two. Saperstein is purely a social drinker and Colonel Fedorev wasn't anywhere around; the two of them were probably knocking off a few in one of their quarters.

''Are you in on this, Masterson?''

''Only in an advisory capacity.''

''I'll bet.''

I started to follow them inside the dispensary but a rude palm from Saperstein held me back. ''You and Hellstrom just wait out here,'' he growled.

So we did, standing at the doorway listening to the murmur of voices from within in case we should be summoned. After a while Nils thought to ask what I had discovered on my outing, and I was giving him a brief synopsis when the door came open. Saperstein emerged, looked us over again, and then turned to Paulette, who had come out right behind him.

"You really can't be sure of anything, can you?"

"I'm sure it's serious, David. What it is, I hope to learn before it's too late."

Having left the decision to her, I didn't know until that moment whether she had given Saperstein the truth or only the colored version that Colonel Fedorev was going to get. Apparently she had decided—wisely, I believed—that Saperstein would require color. Otherwise, he would never have gone along.

"She doesn't look all that sick," he insisted.

"Look, David, anytime you want to put on this smock and let me take over administration of Mensa Station, I'll be glad to change positions with you. In the meantime, you'd best take my word for it."

I could have kissed her fat cheeks.

"Could her condition be in any way responsible for Johnson's death?"

Paulette looked at me. "I don't see how," I said. "She didn't go in there until after he was dead."

Some few seconds passed once I'd finished talking before Saperstein unnarrowed his eyes and turned back to the doctor. "I'm going to let Bob know about Carl before getting into this with Colonel Fedorev." He left with Paulette, leering at me a final time before passing on.

Bading Nils remain on the alert, I slipped back inside and found Asia in what was, apparently, no longer my bunk with a sheet up to her chin.

It occurred to me that we had just been socialized out of half the dispensary but fought the feeling back because Asia Krokov—with any luck—was now one of us. I moved in closer. Saperstein was right: she didn't look that ill.

In fact, she looked fine.

"All right?" I asked her.

"Oh, yes."

Just as I thought. I looked around and spotted Nils'
tray with the empty plate of hash and condiments.

"Did you have dinner?"

"Yes. It was very good."

It had not been good. Jules Digne knew something
of Antarctic weather, but nothing about hash, and
while Mary Ingram had much to recommend her,
cooking was not on the list. Hastily I put some warm
water in Nils' empty glass, dumped in the contents of
the salt canister, and added the remains of the mustard
jar for good measure. "Here," I commanded, putting
the glass in front of her. "Drink this."

She took one taste and nearly gagged. I forced the
rest of the glass down her throat, and then she did. I
collected most of it on the tray, cleaned the rest with
a napkin, and approved the almost instant reddening
of the eyes and the odor to the dispensary, which de-
fies imitation.

"It's even better the second time," I said, waved a
good night to her, and slipped into the hall with the
tray.

"How's she doing?" asked Nils.

"Wretched," I quipped.

If my telling Saperstein about Asia was a bad idea,
then for me to be anywhere in sight when Colonel
Fedorev got the news was even worse. I persuaded
Nils to stand watch alone and to command my presence if he needed me. Given his bulk, I couldn't believe I would be. That done, I repaired to the lounge
to treat myself to a well-deserved solvent, intending
to dissolve the problems of the day, most of which
could be enumerated by bruise and bandage on my
body. Let me go on record as saying I am not a social
drinker. It's people, not ice, that take up too much
space.

But if I expected an end to the day's problems, I
was overly and uncharacteristically optimistic.

First of all, the commotion that ensued at the dispensary was enough to rouse several of the sleeping
Russians. I had positioned myself so that I had a good
view of Fedorev when he made his appearance. Even
from such a distance it was possible to determine that

he was livid. Zizhn was with him, colder and whiter and occasionally allowing traces of his special smile to be exposed. After several of the Russian officers and soldiers awoke and collected at the entrance to the administration wing, my view was blocked, but I gathered, during one period of silence, that Colonel Fedorev had talked his way into the dispensary for a conference with Asia Krokov. The uproar didn't resume until he came back out again and started across the corridor to the lounge with Saperstein and Zhizn by his side. Milling soldiers returned to their claims and a few even stretched out once again, but the murmurs and whisperings continued for some time.

Saperstein stepped behind the bar and began mixing drinks.

"I do not like it at all," Fedorev declared.

"I don't blame you, sir," Saperstein mollified him. "Neither do I, and that's a fact. According to the Antarctic Treaty, I must quarantine her here but not the rest of your party until it becomes established that her condition is contagious. As it stands now, Colonel, you and your men are free to go."

"Something is wrong. I cannot believe she can become sick so quickly."

"You talked to her yourself. Alone. Didn't she confirm that she had been sick since leaving Kampala and that she has held down no food in two days?"

"Yes."

Saperstein spread his hands while he led the two men to a table.

"Well, then?"

"I don't care. She is my polar adviser. I will not leave without her."

"I would prefer you not, sir. Until we establish that the disease is not contagious, I would rather no one leave."

For the first time, Zhizn made his contribution. "We must leave tomorrow morning on schedule, Mr. Saperstein. We will leave."

"If you absolutely must have an adviser, I can let you have one of mine. Nils Hellstrom and Peter Masterson are both experienced—"

"No, thank you," said Zhizn. "Not that we don't credit their skills. Mr. Masterson, I'm sure, is a very capable man, but we would not inconvenience you."

"I was going to suggest that you take Mr. Hellstrom. Masterson has other duties that will keep him busy for the next several days. However, Nils actually has more polar experience than Peter, as I was telling your colonel earlier, and I'm sure he'd agree to . . ."

I stopped listening. Colonel Fedorev had to be talked into continuing his expedition, but oddly, it was Zhizn who did the talking. All the time he did so, he was periodically giving me his best smile, which is to say it was the worst by far I'd seen across his cold white face.

When I finished the drink and rose to tell Saperstein that I'd have to find some place to spend the night, Zhizn's eyes never left me. I stopped at their table just as Fedorev was winding up a speech.

"It is against Soviet policy, and it is against my policy, to abandon one of my people under such circumstances. I am going to have to consider this matter very carefully. As you know, we have no medical man with our party. If there is a contagious disease among us, then it is possible that we will have other problems once under way. We might even carry it to another station. Maybe a quarantine is the best—"

"If that means, Colonel," I interrupted him, "that you'll be using my room for some time, then I'm going to have to find other quarters myself. Perhaps you have some room in one of the tractors where a man could spend the night. I bet your own tractor is fixed up real nice."

Fedorev glared.

That ill-humored smile spread again across Zhizn's lips and he shook his head slowly.

"Yes," he said, "very capable."

Actually, my plans were to spend the night on the floor of Nils Hellstrom's quarters, and as I moved down the corridor, a feeling of such exhaustion overcame me that I knew going any farther was out of the question. As it turned out I didn't even get that far.

Passing by Nils I must have faltered, for he was suddenly beside me, helping me into his room and onto
his own bunk.

We agreed one of us should be on duty outside the
dispensary throughout the night, and Nils was determined to take the first shift. I didn't argue with him
then, nor when he insisted it was silly for me not to
use his bunk while he stood watch. That night I slept
the sleep of the dead. It was still dark when I finally
awoke—and would be so for another few days at
least—but my watch indicated the hour to be after
seven o'clock in the morning. I jerked upright, nearly
screamed when still sore muscles objected, and then
lay back down. I rolled over more carefully. Nils was
stretched out on the floor.

"Dammit," I muttered to myself. He hadn't wak-
ened me and I had slept the entire night. I sat up,
kicked on pants, and yanked open the door.

The hundred-foot length of corridor was bare.

I stepped to the first intersection and looked from
the cafeteria around into the administration hallway,
even pulling open the dispensary door. Asia Krokov
was sleeping soundly in her bunk, but every other place
was void of human occupation. The storage room and
recreation wing were empty.

At the weather lock, I turned, ascended the ladder,
and raising the hatch, poked my head into the shuddering cold of polar morning. The flood illuminated
the few gray grim protrusions of Mensa Station onto
the ice, but nothing else to every side save the quiet
undulations of nomadic dunes and the living surface
of the barrier, a sea of ever-drifting snow that bade
them on. Wind that could shriek like a thousand ban-
shees was then but a whispering zephyr. There was no
sign of the tractors, no sound of idling diesels.

Nils had apparently remained on duty throughout the
night and turned in only late this morning after he was
no longer needed.

The Russians had gone.

An emergency meeting was called of all Mensa personnel immediately after early breakfast. Since the

cafeteria also served as a meeting room, we merely turned about our folding chairs until they faced David Saperstein.

"Yesterday," he began, "an aircraft went down on the high plateau about a hundred and eighty miles to the west-southwest. We . . . McMurdo, that is, has reason to believe there are at least some survivors. First thing this morning I had Bob Dolan and his men" —Saperstein indicated the table where the engineers were, as always, sitting together—"begin preparing the Badgers for an extended operation. McMurdo has asked us to launch an expedition as quickly as possible, get to them, and bring them back here."

Expressions of astonishment were traded among the occupants of the cafeteria's three groups, during which time Saperstein concentrated on the outside table where Nils and I were sitting. As Asia Krokov was seated between us there, his attention was not very difficult to understand. "Because I'll be remaining at Mensa," he continued, "I'm going to name an expedition leader. Nils?"

"Yes, David?"

"You'll be in command."

"Sure. Is Peter staying here, then?"

"He is not." Saperstein looked a challenge at me.

Admittedly, I had raised my brows in mild surprise, but it was the formal assignment of authority that struck me as odd, not his selection. Generally, leadership is given little play in the polar regions, where small groups of equally important individuals necessarily work for months at a time in very close confinement. Cooperation, not command, is the rule. And for such an expedition as this, it didn't seem necessary that anyone be placed in command at all.

"Any problems with that, Masterson?" Saperstein demanded.

"With Nils being in charge? Absolutely not."

"Fine. Nils, see to the supplies, sledges, gear, and dogs. Plan on an expedition lasting at least ten days and possibly two weeks or more. You can make other assignments as you see fit."

"Who all is going?"

"You, Masterson, Bob, Tom, and Jules. I think those five individuals should remain here for additional briefing while the others resume their duties . . . unless there are any questions or suggestions that concern us all."

"You realize," I ventured, "that by sending out the only two men who have any previous polar experience you're leaving yourself wide open in case of unexpected trouble here. I suggest either Nils or I should remain."

"Do you expect trouble, Masterson?"

"I said unexpected trouble. Anything is possible."

"Is that so?"

"The events of yesterday make that obvious. Several things have happened that are still very mysterious; this is no place to have mysteries unresolved. It's dangerous. Someone should be here who knows how to handle emergencies at sixty degrees below zero."

It was clear to me, watching Saperstein form his response, that he was boiling. And I knew why. "Didn't we learn this morning, Mr. Masterson, that Miss Krokov's illness was a sham, a product of your irresponsible imagination, and that she is as healthy as any of us here." Since Asia was present, radiant with health, and Paulette Gruber had confessed her part in the conspiracy to Saperstein over breakfast only minutes before, it was difficult to deny. "I tell you frankly, mister, that little maneuver might have cost lives. It very certainly will mean a diplomatic nightmare in the weeks to come and a loss of cooperation between us and the Soviets here in Antarctica. The required explanations will be very embarrassing for me personally, worse for Mensa. The very future of the Centaur Project has been placed in jeopardy. Nevertheless, this woman is here and she is fit for duty. I understand she is a glaciologist. An expert on polar conditions."

"With no practical experience."

"I think we'll make it all right, Masterson. Your suggestion is noted and rejected on its merits or lack of same. Are there any other questions?"

As the others drifted away—the three women, in a body; Jerry Davis, with instructions to continue preparations for getting the Badgers under way—Jules moved up into Asia's place and Saperstein, stepping to the engineers' table, began unfolding a large-scale map.

"We don't know exactly where the aircraft will . . . where it went down, but you'll be taking a directional receiver tuned to the international emergency transponder frequency, which should help you locate the site once you approach to within fifty or sixty miles."

"How many were aboard?" I asked.

"We don't know."

"What nationality was the aircraft? Where had it taken off from, where was it heading, and why, for Christ's sake?"

Saperstein growled, "I don't have the answers to all these questions, Masterson. I only know what McMurdo Station gave me. An aircraft down—survivors aboard . . . and their approximate position, all based, I would presume, upon radio traffic with McMurdo just before or just after the crash. Apparently the survivors are no longer in communication with anyone. But that doesn't prevent the aircraft's transponder from sending out a signal for us."

"Whoever they are," added Nils, "they couldn't last for more than a few hours on the plateau. At ten thousand feet, the temperatures will be in the minus fifties at best. We should have left yesterday."

"I guess there was some effort to have another station make a fly in, but weather over both coast stations, McMurdo and Little America, as well as the Amundsen-Scott facility at the south pole is windy and overcast. No possibility of getting any planes or helicopters into the air for at least a fortnight. The weather on the plateau"—Saperstein pointed to the map where the 150-degree meridian east intersected 85 degrees south latitude—"here along Deception Reach is apparently no better. So help not only can't take off, they couldn't have landed. The only option is a quick dash overland, and Mensa is the nearest station. I can't see any alternative and I can't refuse to commit our resources."

"I can."

Heads turned like magnets of common polarity to me, the one in opposition.

"You can see an alternative?" asked Saperstein.

"I can refuse. To me the whole thing smacks of intrigue; even if it didn't, I don't want to run up against those Russians."

"What has this got to do with the Rus—the Soviets?"

"Their expedition is heading to that same location on Deception Reach and they're taking the identical route you've outlined on your map."

Saperstein went rigid. "How do you know that? A crystal ball?"

There was no divination involved, nor even any remarkable recollection. I had recognized the route on Fedorev's map and here it was. The mountain crossing and the southbound course was the one taken by Sir Vivian Ernest Fuchs in his 1957–58 ninety-nine-day Trans-Antarctic expedition. Not coincidentally, the United States' radar string of remote unmanned dish depots is situated along the same line and for much the same reasons. I didn't bother Saperstein with that.

"It's a fact," I said. "You can take my word for it."

"Well, that's that," said Digne. "The Soviets will pick up any survivors. I mean, they may be communists but they'll surely take good-enough care of them until they can be transported to the proper station. For that matter, the aircraft itself and the passengers may be Soviet—there's plenty of them down here."

Tom Elliston nodded while muttering agreement.

Robert Dolan was strangely silent.

But Nils, shaking his head consideringly, boomed, "They may not know about the crash, and if not, they won't have the transponder receiver to find it. Their expedition could pass right by without seeing any sign of a downed aircraft."

"They know about it, Nils," I interrupted, "and

they have a very efficient receiver set. But it's not that
simple. Intrigue, remember? Saperstein got that radio
call from McMurdo yesterday afternoon when the Soviets were still here, yet he didn't tell them. So there
must be more to it.''

"There is more to it,'' Saperstein began carefully.
''I didn't know they were going to the site and I still
have only Masterson's word for it. However, I do
know that we still have to go, only now speed is of
even greater importance.''

Nils raised an eyebrow; Tom Elliston looked quer-
ulous.

I laughed.

''What's so funny, Masterson?''

''You are. Have we got a race on our hands to rescue some idiotic pilot and his passengers and crew?''

''Yes. But it's more than just the people. There's
cargo that must not fall into Soviet hands. We must
find it first. If we can't find it, we must make sure it
will never be found.''

''Oh, your own crystal ball? You forgot to mention
that when you said you knew nothing more about the
aircraft or what it was carrying. This is what I meant
by intrigue.''

''You and your suspicions. You were suspicious of
the Soviets' coming here; they've left without incident. You were suspicious of their looking around the
station; well, they looked and nothing happened. Now
you're suspicious of a Soviet expedition westward.
Nils,'' he said, turning, ''can we beat them to the reach
given an eighteen- or twenty-hour lag?''

Typically, Nils considered the problem without
emotion and with no consideration for personalities.

''Well . . . our snowcats are a little faster, one,
maybe two miles per hour at best. If we get off tonight
on time, they'll have a lead of a hundred miles or so.
The route north to the Beaumont Glacier, across the
Queen Mauds, and then south again to that point is at
least four hundred fifty miles. About five days' travel
for them. For us, a little more than four—in both
cases, assuming no holdups en route, which, as you
know, is a hell of an assumption. Theoretically we

could overtake them, but the margin will be very narrow if we do so at all."

Saperstein was frowning at the map.

"So what's the answer?"

"Why not take a shortcut?" I said.

"What are you talking about?"

I pointed to the Nimrod Glacier just north of Mensa.
"We're all aware that there are three routes over the
Queen Mauds from here—two really, since Hell's Flow
is impassable as well as being off-limits, the Nimrod
Glacier is strewn with hidden crevasses at the lower
and upper levels, and Beaumont Glacier is relatively
safe. The Nimrod route would be a hazardous crossing
for anybody, but much more so for the Russians without crevasse detectors, which is the reason they're taking the Beaumont route. However, if we can make a
successful crossing at Nimrod we could cut at least a
hundred miles off the trip."

Saperstein raised his eyes from a study of the map
but regarded Nils Hellstrom instead of me. "Well,
Nils?"

The question deserved some consideration. Looking
at the map it was easy to see a glacier as just another
strip of frozen real estate; all of us—especially Nils—
knew better. It wasn't difficult to guess what he was
thinking.

The massive ice sheets that cover Antarctica and that
comprise 90 percent of the earth's frozen water, would
(what with the accumulation of snowfall that never
melts) contain all the world's water in a few million
aeons were it not for one thing: the ice is constantly
returning itself to the sea. Relentlessly the continent's
crust of ice pushes toward every shoreline, feeding the
thousands of glaciers that breach the coastal ranges.
These three glaciers on Saperstein's map, as well as
hundreds more cutting through the Queen Mauds and
many others yet on the east side of the Ross Ice Shelf,
force the shelf inexorably out into the sea. From this
floating slab, as large as the state of California, icebergs, some the size of Rhode Island, calve at the shelf
front five hundred miles from the farthest point of land.

But the most remarkable carriers of water here are the glaciers themselves.

Glaciers are the bottlenecks where, ironically, the speed of ice flow is greatest; predictability, nonexistent; navigation, dangerous to the nth degree.

A glacier might move down the mountain as slowly as a few inches every year. Then again, it might push several yards in a day. They can range in width from a hundred feet or less, to many miles across. And because it is the movement of ice that creates and collapses the crevasses, glaciers also vary in their capacity to be navigated.

On some stretches, the Beaumont Glacier is like a highway, smooth and straight and with a gentle incline to the plateau. I'd seen other glaciers from the air that looked like a jigsaw puzzle or a cracked and dried streambed with slabs the size of football fields and the cracks between them wide and deep enough to swallow a fleet of snowcats like ours. On some, the cracks or crevasses run in regular parallel patterns, making a traverse relatively simple and travel up or down the glacier absolutely impossible.

And then there are the hidden crevasses. Drifting snow occasionally caps an open chasm in such a way as to make it invisible; the cap might accept the weight of a dog, a man, or even a sled. It might. But a tractor will inevitably break through the snow and go tumbling a dozen or a hundred feet to the bottom, where further movement of the ice will crush its iron shell like a wad of aluminum foil.

These indescribably powerful water carriers and their constant changing characters are the most dangerous aspect of arctic travel. In spite of this, they are often the only route for ascending the nearly two miles of altitude to reach the plateau of ice on the other side.

No doubt Nils was thinking about that in the silence that punctuated Saperstein's request, and I didn't for a moment envy the big Swede his position of authority.

"It might work," Nils mused, almost as though he were talking to himself. "The Nimrod Glacier is much rougher, it would slow us down considerably on the climb, and it would be risky even with the Badgers and their crevasse-detection equipment. But Peter is right: we would save hours by not traveling the extra miles north and then south again.''

As he had made no comments earlier, Jules Digne's interruption assumed a special importance. ''I hesitate to intrude into an area that is beyond my expertise,'' he said. Saperstein urged him to speak freely and he did so. ''I surely know nothing of glacial navigation. Yet as a meteorologist I feel it is my duty to remind the party that daylight will not return here for several days. At McMurdo, there is quite a bit of sun now and at the Beaumont Glacier there will be midday twilight. I assume this would make for an easier ascent. Nimrod Glacier, being farther south, will be in relative night for the entire outbound trip. Won't that complicate the climb?''

''Yes,'' Nils replied unhesitatingly.

With a sigh Saperstein straightened and looked about. ''Okay. I'll leave it up to the five of you.''

The two engineers exchanged expressions of dread while Jules Digne shook his head in a bit of preballot anxiety that challenged my grand notions of expedition by committee.

I snapped, ''It's a little late for that, David. You've put Nils in charge and now this is his decision to make.''

Saperstein regarded Nils with an odd intensity.

Dolan, Elliston, and Digne looked at Nils, too.

So did I.

''Against my better judgment,'' he said, ''I think we'll try the shortcut.''

It's hard to appreciate a woman's form at 40 below. A parka worth wearing here is so bulky that the figure of a Mary and a Paulette is almost impossible to distinguish. Even a face is a rare-enough sight; the balaclava is a mask that rarely flatters. Asia Krokov wasn't wearing one. She was bundled in furs, and the ruff of her hood exposed only a small oval of spanking pink. Dark eyes and features. Wide cheeks and a full mouth neither too wide nor too narrow. She was no Mary Ingram, that's true, but there was something about her and it wasn't hands-off.

Asia followed me from sledge to sledge checking the hitching and the lashing of equipment. I knew good and well she was freezing. But she was keen to learn everything she could, for, despite her admission that polar science was an escape route to the West, I believed she really loved it here as much as I did.

"For an expedition in a hurry," she said when she saw all the sledges that each of the two Badgers would have to tow, "you're dragging a lot of weight."

"Don't forget, Asia. This is as hostile a country as exists on earth. No one lives off the land here. If you want anything, you take it with you. These snowcats require a great deal of fuel and support equipment. Two hundred miles of trail flags make a big pile. And since there's always the possibility that much of the equipment and even some of the vehicles will be lost, everything necessary to sustain the expedition must be carried in double or even triple quantities."

As I finished talking we had moved behind one of the snowcats; Mensa Station and the other people helping us to load were out of sight. I turned around. There was nothing mechanical about my inspection of Asia's face. True, I noted that the pink had left her cheeks and the tip of her nose was a little too white, but that was merely force of habit.

"We need to get you warmed up, Asia."

"I'm not cold."

"Your face is cold."

Asia planted her clumsy fur boots right on top of mine.

The extra height put her mouth just inches away, and her arms around my shoulders were making arrangements to close the distance fast.

"What do you suggest, Peter?"

The tip of her nose brushed against mine.

She was daring me to walk away again without kissing her. So I didn't.

Walk away, that is.

We were stowing the last of the supplies into the second cat, Bob Dolan and myself, when I sensed someone beside me and, turning, found our team doctor beckoning me with a covert movement of her head. In spite of the fact that she had been quick to confess her part in conspiracy to David Saperstein and thereby relieve herself of any further culpability, Paulette Gruber had also been quick to join my conspiracy and had performed as requested. So without hesitation I followed her to an isolated corner of the garage and stood there while she sent her eyes around.

"Peter, I wanted to tell you one thing before you go. About Carl Johnson. You asked me to check his pillowcase for signs of saliva, thinking that someone might have used his own pillow to suffocate him. Is that right?"

"I thought it possible. I was wrong."

"I'm not so sure," she whispered. "After we agreed on our story yesterday, I changed the linen on your bunk so Miss Krokov could use it and I found something on the underside of your pillowcase: blood."

"My mouth was pretty bloody."

"So was Johnson's nose. I found traces of mucus, too. So I typed the blood. It was his."

"You're sure?"

"I'm sure it's his type, not yours. That it came from him can only be established by DNA matching and I don't have the equipment to perform that test."

"Well, well. What are you going to do about it?"

"Me? Not a damn thing, dear. You asked, and I'm telling you. As far as I'm concerned—officially, that is—it proves nothing; the last thing we need are rumors about Johnson being murdered, but all the same, I wanted you to know."

I thanked her and started to join the others when her hand brought me back around. "Please, Peter. Be careful on this expedition and hurry back to us."

"You, Paulette—worried about me!"

"Maybe. Maybe I'm more worried about who's staying behind."

I accepted her honesty and returned to work, making no attempt to console her with my conviction that the murderer was accompanying our expedition.

Night of the Fisherman's Bend

Nils Hellstrom ground the lead snowcat to a halt, poked his head out the door, and observed before climbing down, "There's a blow coming."

It was our expedition's first stop in twelve hours.

That otherwise not extraordinary event occurred the following morning at precisely six o'clock Mensa time—whose position, by way of clarification, 7 degrees and a few odd minutes west of the international dateline, put the station in the same time zone as Fiji or, closer to home, the Alaskan islands, extremities of the Aleutian archipelago half a world to the north.

Forty-two miles of ice had slipped beneath our runners.

In addition to maintaining such a dizzying speed, we had planted a hundred and twenty-two trail flags; alternated drivers in both cats twenty-four times; detoured two broken ice fields and eleven yawning crevasses, their blue-green walls slick with newly fractured ice; as well as made innumerable position fixes based on our magnetic and precalibrated gyro compasses, all highly speculative since the easterly deviation factor in that area was close to 160 degrees.

So much for the expedition's progress. I personally had drunk two dozen cups of oppressively black coffee and slept, by my calculations, a little less than half an hour.

Not that I had played no role in the group's headway, a distance that, facetiousness aside, was quite remarkable for antarctic travel any time of year.

Nils and I had agreed before leaving Mensa that either he or I should pilot the lead Badger at all times. That left the passenger's seat for a navigator whose sole employment it was to sit with his eyes fixed to the needles on the crevasse-detection meter—affectionately referred to by crew members as the Fault-Finder—ready to issue an alarm should it indicate a blind crevasse or any area of questionable integrity beneath the crustal surface. The third man piloted the trailing cat alone while yet another caught up on sleep in a small space cleared among the packed clutter of the lead Badger's cargo.

None of these distractions was so arduous as to require shift changes on the half-hour; it was the fifth man's responsibilities that regulated rotation.

Working off the last sledge of the rear cat where the bundles of trail flags were stowed, his job—at the flash of a strobe on the lead snowcat and a slowing of the train of vehicles—was to hustle a single flag to the head of the train, bore a quick hole in the ice by means of a hand-held brace, plant the orange banner by the time the last sledge had reached him, and then catch a chilling ride for another third of a mile while awaiting the next signal. After nine or ten flags any one of us— Nils expected—was ready to be relieved.

My lack of sleep was due to a further stipulation of duty assignments I had made in my own counsel— namely, that I would not close my eyes so long as Robert Dolan was alone either as the rear snowcat pilot or as flag setter. On only one occasion had he navigated while Nils drove; that had been my thirty minutes of sleep. On my other rounds in the makeshift bunk I lay belly to the frozen floor shaking like a man with the DTs as I stared through the crack of the tailgate for an obstructed but adequate prospect of the rear train.

The second pair of headlights remained about sixty yards back, illuminating a wide sweep of the barrier in addition to the line of six sledges roped to the tail ring of Badger Number One. Six more sledges were tied to the second cat.

As we would begin slowing, I could see the flag setter trot up the left side of the train, disappear past

my position, and then reappear furiously punching his
hole in the ice. Our pace would remain at half-speed
until a signal from the last sledge indicated he was
aboard, whereupon we would accelerate once again.
This time-consuming effort promised dubious returns
and even then only in the event we became lost or
others needed to find us, yet it was the only trail we
would leave in a roadless environment where vehicle
tracks are covered within moments of their having been
laid. Tradition additionally decrees that food storage
caches be set up at twenty-five-mile intervals with a
single tall flag on the mound and two rows of orange
pennants extending from the trail at right angles; however, we elected to forgo that safety feature in favor
of speed. After all, we were following what I confi-
dently believed to be the general route the Soviets had
taken, and they, being apparently even more pressed
for speed, had left not so much as a single flag.

Nils Hellstrom brought the Badger crunching to a
halt.

It was just six A.M., the hour agreed upon for our
first radio check with Mensa. Nils and I alighted and
moved to the cargo bed: he, to warm up the transmitter; I, to unload the level sextant and set the tripod.

The sextant is designed to measure an angle between
specific stars and a true horizon that even on the relatively flat Ross Ice Shelf is nowhere to be found.
Though the same instrument can be land-functional by
viewing the sky above a false horizon as a reflection
on a plate of liquid mercury, this procedure is of little
use in a land where mercury freezes solid. But by using a very sensitive alcohol-level base, I could still
compute star altitudes to within a minute of arc, and
therefore our position to an accuracy of plus or minus
a mile.

Here, as much as on the ocean, we were never free
of the stellar menagerie above; nor did we care to be.
The warriors, gods, and sundry mythological creatures
who gazed down with Olympian detachment upon us,
adrift on a veritable sea of ice, were often our only
emotional link with any civilization at all. The all-
covering ice, the utter cold, and the endless darkness

were Antarctica's and ours alone, but the stars, though they be millions of light-years distant, we could share with other humans in other climates barely a few hundred miles away. Ironically, it was these other climates that were too far off to fathom while the stars were at arm's length.

After telling Jules Digne to mark time for the third and final sighting and then reading him the figures, I turned to find Elliston and Dolan restowing the empty diesel oil drums on the fuel sledge, having refueled both vehicles.

Nils was still vainly repeating his call-up signal. "KFQ calling KFM, KFQ calling KFM."

"Nothing, Nils?"

"Not a peep."

Considering the power and quality of the transmitter at Mensa, I could only guess the trouble was with our portable unit.

Nils scoffed at the suggestion. "This unit," he declared, "is operating perfectly. I checked it over myself before stowing it away."

Nils looked about him as though to verify his earlier forecast. Even then a mounting westerly had begun raising a dense current of knee-high drift that seemed to have us all wading about in white-water rapids.

Digne paddled over with his almanac, sight-reduction tables, and clipboard, having already calculated our position. He handed his chart across.

After a quick glance, I offered another suggestion. "Let's assume one of two things: either Mensa can receive us but can't transmit, or we can transmit but we don't receive their return signals. Give them these coordinates and advise them we're maintaining our course."

He didn't like it. He wasn't to like my next idea any better, but I waited to advance this latest notion until after he had passed our position on to Mensa, signed off in the blind, and got our small expedition on the move again without wasting any time. The gale would worsen before it subsided.

Luxuriating in the aura of the cab's efficient heater, we removed our parkas and Nils even pulled back his sweater sleeves before getting a two-handed grip on the wheel and starting off. His giant's arms steering, tight and knotted with muscle, were like lines of six-inch berthing hawser round a bollard. Already he was smiling, reflecting on the phenomena of sky wave radio transmissions and the likelihood of our being in Mensa's skip zone. What did I think?

Nils Hellstrom was a carefree fellow and a commander from the same mold. Nothing seemed to worry him long and rarely enough to let on except to those like me who knew the big Swede's way. Such unruffled calm in the face of major calamities often had the effect of steadying his subordinates' nerves. In some ways that made him an exceptional leader and in another way it bothered me.

So I told him what I thought.

"There's a south-flowing fork in the Nimrod Glacier," I said. "It connects with the main flow about halfway up but we could shave two or three hours off our schedule by turning west now."

"I know the fork. It's never been climbed."

"There's no reason why it should be, what with the main flow of the glacier only thirty miles beyond. But it's navigable; I flew over it last summer."

"That doesn't mean a thing. The real hazards are the ones you can't see—you know that. What it looked like six months ago or even six weeks ago has no relation to what it's like now."

"It's a shorter route."

"Then it must be steeper, since it connects to the same glacier. Once we started climbing we'd be slowed down. We would gain nothing."

"We'd gain one thing: nobody would know what route we were on."

Nils was jarred. "That's rarely an advantage down here, Peter."

"These are rare circumstances. Here we are in a race without knowing the prize; for the past forty miles we've been following the general trail the Soviets must have taken and yet we haven't seen so much as a single trail flag. Are they—unlike us—simply too pressed for speed to plant flags or are they not even in front of us? Maybe they're behind us. Maybe they let us pass them by and are now following our trail of flags until it's convenient to ambush us.''

"So that's why you held off making your suggestion about a change in heading until after we'd relayed our route to Mensa.'' His voice had dropped half an octave and held more than a note of disapproval. "I don't suppose you advise that we call them up and tell them about this new route?''

"Are you kidding? Me, I wouldn't even tell Bob Dolan and the others which way we were going.''

Nils stared silently ahead. The rush of driving drift had nearly reached the doors; hard-grained crystals were blasting the rocker panels with a ferocity that challenged all but the most thoroughly ionized body paint, ricocheting off the hood and striking the windshield, threatening even to score the surface of the glass and render it translucent. Nils watched through the two rhomboidal patterns that the wipers nevertheless managed to clear.

After a moment he spoke. "You know, Peter, I may sound a little like Saperstein, what I'm going to say now, but you do show an unhealthy distrust of your own co-workers. I've noticed the way you clam up every time Bob Dolan is around and I've seen the sideways glances you've given him. Are you sure which side you're on?''

"Oh, I'm sure which side I'm on. I'm just not sure about my co-workers.''

"Dolan included?''

"No. Not Dolan. I'm sure about Dolan.''

"What about Dolan?''

"He's a murderer. I believe he killed Carl Johnson.''

For the second time Nils looked shaken.

I continued. "I might have bought Johnson's death as an accident. At least I might have believed that about his falling into the shaft. On top of that a practically new climbing rope snaps as Johnson and I are being pulled out. That's a hell of a coincidence. And in the dispensary he finally succumbs in very suspicious circumstances. It's like the man said: once is happenstance, twice is coincidence, but three times is enemy action. Anybody might have suffocated him while he lay there and half a dozen people who were in the project chamber after his fall might have cut the rope, but only Dolan could have pushed him into the hole in the first place. The two of them were alone there.''

"But why would he?''

"I don't know, but I have an idea. Dolan was missing for a while just before the accident and Johnson went to find him to tell him about an emergency . . . the loss of hole water. At the same time I remember that Major Zhizn was nowhere around. Just suppose Johnson found them together in circumstances that Dolan couldn't satisfactorily explain.''

"That's pretty weak, Peter.''

"I don't really think so. I admit it's pretty much circumstantial, but what other explanation is there? Dolan was acting suspicious when I questioned him and Saperstein about a Geiger counter on the downhole assembly. It's even possible Saperstein is in on this with him. You have to admit that a lot of strange things have been happening to us. This radio failure is only the latest—maybe it's skip zone and maybe it's not. Actually, I feel like a jerk when I think of all the sleep I lost trying to keep an eye on Dolan while he drove and punched flags, only to have him alone while he was sleeping, or supposed to be sleeping, not three feet away from where the portable radio is stowed. So now I'm asking myself, is something going to happen to us if we hold this course and they prefer it that we can't radio for help, or has something already happened at Mensa that we're not supposed to know about? If we did pass the Russians by, they could just as easily have doubled back to Mensa and be responsible for Saperstein's failure to acknowledge our radio signals. Whatever the answer, I'm tired of playing along. We do the expected: leave flags every foot of the way and radio every step to Mensa. I say we stop acting like fools and do something they're not expecting.''

Nils agreed that no one would expect us to take a

more dangerous route up the glacier if it didn't save us any time. "But," he added, "if Mensa is in trouble, our responsibility is to help them however we can."

I'd caught him perk up when I let it slip about possible trouble at Mensa and knew immediately it had been a mistake. Nils wasn't the kind to ignore a responsibility like that. "And turning back," I said quickly, "is exactly what the Russians might want us to do if they have gone ahead. Don't forget, we're in a race."

We drove several moments in silence, an act of deliverance in which only his vocal chords, and mine, participated. Meanwhile, the vents blasted a high-pitched storm of hot air; crystallized ice crunching under the cat's treads spoke a veritable demolition; the creaking, grating, and rasping of every movable machine part on the Badger screamed for fresh lubrication; and the ten cylinders of the diesel engine just opposite the thin, uninsulated firewall sequentially fired their revolutionary barrage. Had we envisioned an affair with silence, we would have found it as illusory as the presence of the stellar figures above us.

Shortly it seemed to me the time had come to signal the flag setter, but Nils showed no inclination to retard his pace. After a while he pulled the clipboard over with a hand and studied it carefully.

"There's this to think about, too," I said at last. "If we continue our present course, we'll still be on the barrier by 6 P.M. tonight when we stop for the next radio check. But if we turn west, we'll begin climbing sooner and should have some altitude before check in. With elevation, if we still can't raise Mensa, we'll at least know the problem isn't a skip zone."

He was nodding slowly. Then suddenly, he eased off the throttle and activated the strobe on the roof. Within a few seconds, Jules Digne came trotting by us from the back carrying his flag and ice brace.

Nils signaled him from the open window and, when Digne came closer, said, "Forget it, Jules, you ride up with Dolan. We're going to make some speed."

I leaned back and smiled.

The surface of the barrier was a rolling plain beneath the drifting snow, generally featureless in this region and rarely treacherous. Once the expedition moved into the lee of the Queen Mauds and the drifting snow retreated to mere inches above the ice, the powerful headlights of both cats put the reflective surface in daylight for a hundred yards ahead of us and for half that on each side. It was cold. Astonishingly so. But even here the plummeting temperatures had signaled comparatively stable conditions and clear skies.

Neither had there been any hint of trouble below the surface. Not once had the detectors recorded any blind crevasses and at no time had events proved our equipment remiss.

Up to that point the trip had been excruciatingly dull. That was precisely the way we wanted it.

By noon we were far enough north that the orange cast to the midday sky was positively illuminating. For nearly three hours, we were able to extinguish our headlights and still see a quarter-mile in every direction.

An outline of the Queen Maud Mountains materialized to our left.

We stopped twice to take celestial readings with the level sextant, and both times—after personally conducting the sightings and calculations—I corrected our course onto the branch of the Nimrod Glacier.

Slowly, the icescape began to rise. Not long after the glow on the northern horizon was gone we were climbing a determined slope. Gentle hillocks in the ice became a series of low ice hills, and later the ground to each side of us steepened into miniature sierras that directed our train onto the frozen river that flowed between them. And as the north and south banks sought the perpendicular, dark splashes of boulder, crags and granite buttresses, at last projected through the frozen veil. It was the first time in nearly a year that any of us had seen a sample of the earth's apparel that wasn't ice or snow or some white and frosty combination of the two.

While still logging occasional time with the curiously inanimate crevasse-detection needles, I was idly performing some pilotage—essentially window navigation—by studying the range of mountains ahead of us. It was a ragged swath torn across the star-riddled sky, both as black as a devil's dream but distinct one from another due to the lack of stars along the lower edge. Stealing a quick glance at Nils, I could see he was paying as little attention to the glacier as I was to the Fault-Finder. However, Nils was not lost in the opaque splendor of the Antarctic mountains but in his own thoughts.

"I want to tell you something," he said suddenly in the manner of a man seeking sanctuary in a confessional.

"Go ahead."

"What you said about Dolan and Saperstein . . . Remember you questioned them about the Geiger counter on the hole assembly?" I acknowledged the remark and urged him to continue. He did so. "It was before that, when we pulled Johnson out of the hole— Dolan saw it too and noticed my reaction. Later, while you were unconscious, he and Saperstein approached me about keeping what I had seen to myself, and I agreed."

The surface gale had returned. Confronting the thousand-mile barricade mountains, off-shore winds swirl and eddy in search of the routes of least resistance to the sea, inevitably finding the same paths taken by the descending glaciers. Even on still days the cold air of the high plateau settles onto the barrier by spilling down the ravines with a speed and power uncommon to barrier winds. However, the character of these surface blows are unique to the glaciers. Being swept clean, for the most part, of loose snow and what remains being larger and more densely packed, the glacial drift rarely leaves the surface by more than a few inches. And all glaciers are different, just as they are different from the barrier. Nimrod undulated with dips and bumps at almost regular intervals like a troubled river frozen so swiftly that even the swells were captured in ice. The surface foam washed beneath our treads creating the illusion of speed. The river came

to life and made us feel like salmon heading for our
spawning grounds or perhaps—considering the unnatural nature of our task—like logs attempting to ride
the flume back to the high forests from which we were
felled.

As I waited in vain for Nils to continue, our snowcat
crossed onto a flat oval as smooth as a skating rink.

"But now you're going to tell me," I insisted.

"Yes," said Nils. Another pause. "Carl Johnson's
rem badge. You had rushed into the chamber without
putting on a badge but Carl's was clipped to his jacket
flap."

"So?"

"So . . ." He swirled his right hand in the air as
though encouraging me to state the obvious and relieve
him of the distasteful duty.

"You mean it was discolored?"

"Discolored, hell," he blurted, his patience clearly
overtaxed. "That badge was almost black."

Much later, after it happened and the calamity that
unexpectedly befell us had claimed its casualties, I returned again and again to my thoughts and my actions
in the moments following Nils Hellstrom's strange
revelation. Not for the purpose of self-recrimination in
the matter of my performance during and after the
crash, for there would have been no point in that. It
was just before that bothered me. Was I observing the
Fault-Finder? Was I seeing it? I believe so, and yet it
is also possible that my eyes were again at the mountains beyond the warm and so very temporarily safe
confines of our cab and my mind was considering the
various implications suggested by the facts Nils had
given me.

That aside, there's no doubting what happened next.
The bottom simply and suddenly and without the
slightest warning dropped out of the glacier.

The ice shuddered.

We felt the snowcat settle about a foot.

Too late I whirled to the Fault-Finder and saw the
needles jerking. But their movement, even were it a
reading, no longer meant a damn thing, for by that

time the entire cat was shaking as though Nimrod Glacier were the epicenter of a Richter 10 earthquake.

I swung open the cabin door and leaned into the weather, craning my head to see the ice below us. What I saw scared the hell out of me.

It looked like a jigsaw puzzle with about half the pieces gone.

Nils had to make the quickest decision of his life.

When the ground opens up, or starts to, a driver has two choices: he can get into reverse as quickly as possible—which, I admit, would have been my choice or almost anyone else's choice, given the fact we were climbing a 10-degree grade. The alternative is to accelerate, assume you've already passed the worst of it, and use what forward speed you've got to try to make it across. Of course, that takes guts.

Which Nils has in the abundance his anatomy suggests.

Before I could advise him that huge sections of the ice were collapsing right under our treads, I felt the diesel engine jump into high revolutions and the snowcat lurch ahead. But what the hell! It was probably even money. And the decision had been made. There was no turning back.

"Go! Go! Go," I shouted.

Go he did. The cat accelerated again. I saw Nils open his door and get ready to throw himself out just in case. A second later, I was gone myself. The two of us had never encountered any situation like this, but we had considered it often enough and had spent enough time together that my role did not require further discussion.

I launched myself headlong onto the tread well guard running the length of the snowcat. So slick was it with collected drift and ice that I nearly slipped right off the back into the crevasse. I grabbed the ladder rail as I went by, braked painfully with the one arm, and came flying in a half-circle to dangle from the lowermost rung, my legs hanging over open chasm.

All of the central pieces of the puzzle had fallen.

It had become a gigantic black tear across the glacier fifteen or twenty feet across and several times that in length. Great hunks of drifted snow that had covered the opening continued to collapse from both edges so that the crevasse progressively widened at almost the same rate we moved away. Worse, we were running out of rope. Already the first tow sledge was being pulled near the downhill edge. Strapped to its back were twenty-four drums of fuel for the cat. I scrambled up the ladder, swung open the tailgate, and shook the man in the bunk who, only seconds before, had been blissfully asleep. It was Bob Dolan.

In the box with him was a wealth of equipment I could not bear to lose, but at a glance there was only one thing that we didn't dare to lose.

"Grab the radio," I yelled, "and bail out."

The shaking of the snowcat bed had already waked him. My shouts did the rest.

He began scrambling to his feet as I turned away.

With one hand on the ladder I reached down to the quick-release knot that secured the tow rope to the tail ring.

My task should be as simple as it was vital.

I groped blindly at the knot, found the free end, and pulled. Nothing happened. I pulled again. Nothing. The cable was stiff with ice, and the weight of the sledges had drawn it taut. Even so, a minimum tension should have slipped it loose of the tail ring. Having tied the hitch myself, I knew that was true. Yet it wouldn't budge no matter how hard I tugged.

Across the crevasse, the first sledge had approached the edge and the others were right behind it.

I leaned over, grabbed the cable with both hands, and put all my weight into the effort. But it was just no use. The cable was not coming free. Somehow, my knot had become cinched tight.

I shouted for Nils. Amid the roar of the fully revved diesel, there was no chance he would hear me.

Dolan was swinging off the back of the snowcat with the radio under an arm. He landed on secure ice. I called for him to have Nils halt the Badger at once before the sledges were pulled into the crevasse. He ran forward while I bent down again to try untying the damn knot. By this time my bare hands were numb and useless; in this cold and with this wind chill human flesh will freeze solid in a matter of minutes. My fingers had already done so.

The ice stopped fracturing. Our Badger began climbing away from the opening. On the other side the sledges closed on it at the same speed and the cable was far too taut, the knot pulled too tight, for me to undo it.

I watched in horror as the fuel-drum sledge—a four-meter sled like the others—slowly poked over the edge. But the crevasse was now twice four meters in width. When the runners were halfway out, the sledge dipped its yoke into the abyss and plunged across.

Frantically I drew my boot knife and started slashing away at the thick cable. This was an act of desperation. With its inner rope core and braided metal sheath, the cable had incredible tensile strength, remained flexible at almost any temperature, but required something more than a blade to cut.

The fuel sledge remained stable only until its runners left the ice and then, supported by a single rope in front and another tying it to the after five sledges, rolled onto its side and began spilling drums. I prayed they would all fall, but by the hollow sound of them banging off the glacial walls it was only the empty ones that had. The full ones were still too well secured. I worked like a maniac with that knife, not even slowing to count the crashes of the drums as they struck bottom—the sled itself had slung too low in the blackness of the crevasse for me to see how many were left. But I never heard any hit bottom.

Very quickly the second sledge, containing tents and food supplies and—ironically—at least a couple of good ice axes, had dropped too. Then the third started over and the fourth took its place at the edge.

The snowcat halted.

So too did the awkward dangle of sledges.

But not for long.

Nils appeared to the side in time to witness the fourth sledge with all of our tools, heating fuel, and tractor spares teeter on the edge, overbalance itself, and dive into the black abyss. In the second it took Nils to perceive my problem, we had a whole new one. The additional weight sent a convulsive yank along the cable.

Two things happened in such quick succession that had I not known them to be cause and effect, it would have been impossible to separate them in time: the snowcat lurched . . . and Bob Dolan plummeted into the crevasse. Somehow, he was back in the box, though I hadn't seen him climb in. I felt the lurch; something flew by my head, something small and dark; I swung about at a high-pitched scream. Bob Dolan was clawing at air on the edge of the tailgate, a look of hysteria frozen on his face. Before I could rise, he flipped heels over head and disappeared into the darkness.

His scream died abruptly.

The Badger seemed to shudder and then, incredibly, began sliding back.

Almost at once, the treads engaged. When I looked around, Nils was gone. Back into the cab. But despite his swift action and the power of the Badger, poor traction, the grade, and the tremendous weight of the four sledges hanging across the crevasse were simply too much. Even though the drift sweeping below me made it appear that we were making good time up the glacier, the black slash inching closer and closer revealed the lie of this view.

The tailgate of the Badger edged out till I was perched over oblivion. Below me was the tail ring and the cable that defied my knife, and below that was nothing but darkness.

Nils was back. His failure confirmed by abandoning the Badger in gear. He had come for me.

We both knew I would never get the rope cut in time.

Once the midpoint of the treads came over the edge . . .

A crazy idea popped into my head but I didn't get a chance to consult Nils. A cry erupted from below. We traded glances for a moment and then, as one, looked down into the crevasse. Dolan was still alive down there. Hanging from the fuel sledge. Or maybe the sledge below that one.

I don't know whether I would have tried it if we hadn't heard that cry.

I stood up on the tailgate, my mind made up.

"Don't do it, Peter," shouted Nils.

I launched myself into a sort of swan dive without any pretense at good form. My body became swallowed up by the night. Something struck my chest a shuddering blow. I bounced, caught something in my hand, and then lost it in the same instant. I was falling again. This time the blow came to my back. As I rolled off the second sledge, I made a blind grab, caught a runner in both hands, and wound up dangling in darkness.

Above me the headlights of Badger Two had ignited the swirl of ice into a surreal display. None of this penetrated the crevasse. The radiance of heaven cannot shine into hell and nothing reached into that pit.

Bob Dolan was there, though. I could hear him groaning. With every slip, every slight movement of the sledge, another moan would come from just over my head. I got my feet on the runner, climbed up, found Dolan clinging to the bindings, and pushed him forward onto the yoke, which was tied to the cable.

"Start climbing," I ordered. I located one of the ice axes on the packing and moved up behind him. He hadn't budged.

I put my mouth inches from his ear and bellowed, "Dammit, I'm going to chop the cable above this sled whether you're up there or down here—now start climbing!"

He implored me not to do it. Disgustedly, I wrenched his head backward so he was looking straight up. Silhouetted against the shimmering storm was the entire back section of Badger One, its treads protruding a third of the distance across the crevasse . . . and still coming.

That it would be pulled in on top of us was only half my concern. Just as likely was the possibility that the partially slashed rope on the Badger's tail ring would give way and send the four sledges, Bob Dolan, and me to our doom.

The cable was hanging at something close to 45 de-

grees; climbing it would have presented no real challenge in light clothes and gloves. In parka and mittens
it was a joke. That was Dolan's problem—he couldn't
seem to hang on. My problem was altogether different.
The same metal sheath that made the cable strong
enough to tow massive loads and all but impossible to
cut, was so super chilled that I couldn't let go. Every
time I pulled a hand away, great patches of skin stuck
to the metal. My palms grew thick and gummy with
blood that congealed almost immediately upon exposure. I blessed every drop of blood. If it hadn't been
for this, I would never have been able to hold on; the
feeling and the strength had left my hands long ago.

Dolan continually slipped onto my head; halfway up
he started to panic and his feet kicked me so violently
that I was forced to scramble up under his legs and
virtually heft him up the rest of the way on my shoulders.

When he climbed off my back I knew we had
reached the fuel sledge.

I waited until he had found a secure hold on the fuel-
drum bindings before backing down out of his reach.
There was no more skin on my hands. The blood had
frozen solid. It was all I could do to grip the ax handle.
My first three blind swings missed the rope altogether
and each time I nearly lost the ax.

Then I felt and heard the sharp ping of metal cutting
metal. I had not only hit the rope but caught it on the
tow ring where it would be easiest to sever. I swung
three times more on that mark, hitting twice.

With the fourth blow, I felt something give. But the
feeling was wrong. Our sledge should have swung
against the uphill wall of the crevasse. The release of
all but the one sledge—I'd hoped—would save Badger
One. Instead, we were falling. I forced myself to look
up.

Something in me died.

It was no longer light above. The immense black
form of the snowcat eclipsed the stormlight. Completely over the side, it seemed to hover in space even
as it came hurtling toward us at a terrifying speed.

I reached up and with a single motion grabbed Dolan's parka and heaved him and myself out into space. He screamed. It was for both of us that he did so. For only a moment we fell and then landed heavily against the tent sledge just as it was swinging back toward the downhill wall. With my right hand I drove the ax deep into the tarpaulin and with the other slammed Dolan hard against it. The tarpaulin ripped. Dolan started to fall; mercifully, we both found purchases and well for us that we did, for I do not believe I could have held him another second.

An incredible rush of air swept beside us. We couldn't see the snowcat as it fell but we could sense it. Feel it. The thing could not have missed us by more than a few feet. Then it was gone.

In its wake, we hit the crevasse wall with such force that the runners and most of the remaining framework of our sledge were shattered. Some of the supplies must have broken loose, for as I struggled to hang on to the bits and pieces still tied together with webbing, I was pelted by a rain of largely unidentifiable objects. That sled was like a kid's kite after a violent confrontation with the pavement, a bag of sticks and twine and material.

There came a horrendous explosion of metal and ice, man and nature in collision. The snowcat and fuel sledge struck bottom. The fuel ignited. The crevasse became a volcano of sorts as a fireball erupted from the depths, billowed yellow and red fury, and rolled upward, filling the crevasse with an intense heat and light. In that one dazzling moment hell spewed a brilliance such as the heavens have never seen.

I unburied my face to watch the fireball rise out of the crevasse.

As it did so, I searched the wall of ice above us. The fifth supply sledge with the cable hanging from its yoke was protruding from the upper edge. While I watched, the cornice began breaking away. The sledge angled into the crevasse, lowering us into the oblivion of delicious incandescence.

I reached into the shreds of tarpaulin and pulled out one of the metal tent stakes. By stretching to arm's length I could just get a hand on the wall of ice. Although the fire was no longer a hellish blaze, it was enough to illuminate a narrow crack no wider than my little finger. I pushed in the stake as far as it would go, reversed the ax, and hammered it home to the eye.

By the time I had pulled loose a short length of nylon web the sledge had almost settled beyond my reach of the stake. I shook the ax free from my palm, slipped one end of the webbing through the stake's eye, and tied it off. Then I tied a double figure of eight on the other end, inserted my foot, carefully stepped across, and let the sling take my weight. It held.

The sixth and last sledge was poking over the side.

I called for Dolan. There had been no time to test the sling's strength with me, and there would be none with Dolan. It would have to do. Now. Dolan was already well below me. I told him just once that he could take a hold on me or he could die. He didn't argue. Whether it was the pit looming below, the inexorable descent of the sledge, or his recent narrow escape I don't know, but he wordlessly worked both arms around my legs and held on.

No sooner had he done that than the sledge dropped.

One after another, four more sledges plunged past us, disappearing into the infernal reaches, fuel for the dying flames.

As quickly as the blaze had flared it was gone.

Dolan and I hung there in a darkness that was, if anything, even more complete than before.

An incredible silence settled down from above.

This silence was broken by urgent voices calling back and forth from one side of the chasm to the other, panicked cries from the downhill side and from the other, a booming voice giving orders that to us, below, were unintelligible.

Two powerful flashlights ignited directly above us and dispatched beams into the depths of the crevasse. The twin beams arced about like aerial searchlamps exploring the nether void instead of the skies. This was our chance to call out. Or at least to look into the face of the devil below us. We were both silent. And we did not look down.

More orders in the same booming voice.

A flashlight was lofted across the crevasse. Moments later, a bright circle of illumination was skimming over the wall above us. To our right side. Then, as though guided by a sense beyond sight, it played across our backs.

I still had my foot in the one loop, which was very fortunate, since my hands had not the strength to hang on. Dolan had a firm grip on my other leg and his left arm entwined in the second loop. We swung gently back and forth.

A cry went up.

After what seemed like the better part of an hour but was probably no more than the few minutes it took Nils to circumnavigate the crevasse and locate a rope, one was lowered to us, its end properly noosed. Dolan went up first, then the rope came snaking back down for me.

"Pulling you out of a hole," Nils said quietly once I knelt on firm ice, "is getting to be a habit with us, Peter."

My breaths were coming slow and deep only with great effort—the air was far too cold to permit panting—and I was trying hard not to shiver within the blessed warmth of the blanket that had been thrown over my back.

Nevertheless, I was able to admit in a moderately normal tone that I hoped he did not break his habit until I was able to curb mine.

Jules Digne and Tom Elliston comforted Dolan, who lay a distance to one side, his eyes closed, his breathing labored, and his groans to my way of thinking largely histrionic. That and a bloody appearance must have given them to believe he was in much the worse condition, and I agreed until some time later when it occurred to me that the blood on him was mostly mine. Days would pass before my hands would be worth using; I had also suffered some serious abrasions and a couple of deep cuts along my left forearm where I'd hacked myself with the ax without even realizing it.

There were exchanges of consolation, of gratitude, and of nervous glee. I wasn't hearing any of them and I wasn't really seeing them either. I was seeing in my mind's eye a picture, one that had never left my mind since I'd begun trying to slip the towline.

The picture was of the cable that rove the tail ring. And the knot: two internally hitched rounds—not ice and not tension—make a fisherman's bend impossible to slip. More important, two skilled hands—but not mine—had tied it.

"What are you thinking about?" Nils wanted to know.

I told him, grinding the words out between my teeth. "The fisherman's bend," I added, "is a goddamned anchor knot. With weight on it, you can either untie the thing or you can use a nail file to cut through the anchor shank; the second would be only a little more impractical than the first." As I spoke, Jules Digne had come over in order to catch the last part of our exchange.

"I thought you used quick-release knots," he snapped.

"I do," I acknowledged.

"Well, who tied those?"

"I did. A double-slipped hitch. They've been re-tied. At least the one and probably all the others, though we'll never prove that now."

Digne nodded but refrained from letting any appreciable conviction find expression on his features. Neither did he sound convinced when he asked, "Who was monitoring the Fault-Finder?"

Elliston had approached after half-supporting, half-carrying Robert Dolan off into the lee of Badger Two. Now he matched Digne's accusatory glare. Even Nils was regarding me closely.

"I was," I admitted. Then after a silence, "To answer your real question, I don't believe it registered at all. The only thing I can think of is that it was sabotaged, too. Someone was very concerned that neither the snowcat nor we survive the first field of unstable ice that we came to."

Judging by the looks Elliston and Digne exchanged, I was not winning any converts that night.

"They were nearly successful," Nils said quickly. "We may not yet. An expedition dependent upon a

single snowcat is a bad risk. Should we lose it to another accident or to mechanical problems, no one
stands a chance. If we expect to complete the operation, we'll have to pick the safest possible route, and
that will inevitably mean one even longer than the one
the Soviets are taking."

"We should turn back to Mensa now," said Digne.
I whirled to him. "We're not turning back."

"Well, there's no point in going on," Elliston
snapped. "Anyway, you're not the one to say; you're
not in command." He went on to expound his position, his and Digne's, that the loss of so much equipment and supplies effectively mandated the expedition
be scrubbed.

Nils Hellstrom raised his brows at me.

While there was no doubt whose part Bob Dolan
was going to take, I nevertheless insisted that we talk
to him, for the time had come to bring my own suspicions into the open. The only way to prevent a
wholesale mutiny was to reduce their majority by at
least one, the one who was unquestionably a saboteur
and a traitor and very probably a murderer, too.

As we moved to the snowcat something drew my
eyes toward the speckled garland of stars that is the
Milky Way, banding the southern celestial hemisphere. My first thought was an Olympian sign. Perhaps an omen that the course I was about to take
augured well for our future. But it was only a solitary
pinprick of light making its hourly southbound way
across the heavens.

6

The Act of a Ram

That section of the Milky Way was particularly rich in high-magnitude stars, globular clusters, and gaseous nebulae. Such a field should have made the mysterious traveler difficult to resolve, even granting its most unusual speed; however, at the moment it caught my attention it had entered the black void just north of Crux known as the Coalsack—a dust cloud many thousand times the size of our solar system that obscures all illuminating matter beyond. Though I had assumed as much already and the knowledge advanced me very little, I now had evidence at least to believe the strange object moved within the confines of our galaxy. As it streaked into the center of the four-point constellation, more commonly referred to as the Southern Cross, I heard Jules Digne sneering, "Bob, there's three of us for turning back."

Nils Hellstrom flushed slightly. "I'd like to question Bob about that myself," he rumbled.

Before he could do so, I held out a hand and stepped in. "I have a few questions to ask Dolan first," I said. "Such as what the hell you were doing in the snowcat after I told you to bail out? And what did you lose over the side?"

Dolan's voice broke twice before he could answer. When the words came they were weak and tremulous. "The transponder locator."

That stunned me badly. I had forgotten all about the transponder locator. The loss of that device was bad. Worse than being without the radio as far as I was concerned, and only my carelessness was to blame for

our not having it now, since I should have told Dolan
to grab that and to hell with the radio.

"Sorry, Peter. I was trying to help. I had every reason
to believe the snowcat was lost. And I knew that locator
was the one thing we couldn't get along without."

"And now it's gone," said Elliston. "Without it
there's no possible way of finding that downed aircraft. We can't succeed."

Digne agreed and added that Dolan obviously needed
to get to the nearest doctor. "I think Bob may have
some cracked ribs. He's coughing up blood. And his
right leg is either twisted or sprained. Hell, it may
even be fractured for all I know."

One of them suggested we take a roll right then as
to who was for going and who was for staying, and
Nils, instead of asserting his authority over polls, reminded everyone that we still hadn't heard from Dolan
himself on the matter.

Propped on an elbow, Dolan struggled to survey us
before turning a wan face to me. "I agree with Peter,"
was all he said, though he hadn't even been within
hearing of our conversation.

"You mean to say," asked a startled Digne, "that
you want to go on!"

"No. I don't want to. But I know we have to. That's
the only reason I tried to recover the transponder locator. I knew we had to continue and could conceive
of no way to do so without that device. I can't think
of a way now. But it's up to all of us to go on. It's
for men like Masterson and Hellstrom here to come
up with the way."

Cold attends every gathering on the barrier, either
in person or by proxy of wind and weather; in any
moment that man yields the floor, its forces can move,
second, and carry an adjournment. So it was then.
Nevertheless, I yielded. I held off making charges
against Dolan pending an occasion that was more appropriate, after all. Our team leader took advantage of
the opening.

"Well, if this were a democracy," Nils observed
with a wry smile, "the decision would now be in my
hands. And it is in my hands, though this is no de-

mocracy. Here's what I say: it's now after five P.M.; in less than an hour we'll attempt another radio call to Mensa. Until then we've all got plenty to do. Jules, I want you to clear enough room in the back of Badger Two for three to ride comfortably; set up a portable heater and a lamp. What supplies in there we can't leave behind, divide among some of the sledges. Tom, check out the Badger. I want to know the condition of its Fault-Finder. Run some tests if you have to.'' He regarded me stone-faced. ''I know you'll want to check out the hitches on the other sledges, Peter. When you've finished, better get some of the maps and be prepared to inform Mensa of our position. I'm going to poke around a bit and see about getting out of here before I have to warm up the transmitter.'' Nils swept the faces of his dispirited command. ''Once I've consulted with Saperstein I'll let you know my decision.''

In Antarctica the expression ''chilled to the bone'' is in no way idiomatic. Even moderate exposures to this kind of cold can cause stabbing, unrelenting pain in the base of the spine as well as in the joints and extremities; it is a pain that reaches right down to the marrow.

I had not been exposed that long, though I was shivering violently.

So I wasted no time fighting into my parka. Nils insists that spare outfits be stowed in every snowcat; these would have been invaluable had he not shown equal foresight in pulling out both our parkas when he had abandoned the cab for the last time. My own, which I'd had for years, was of the finest quality and I had no desire to break in another. But my gloves were of no use to me in any case. I held my hands out board-stiff while Nils slipped his own mittens over them. Though only my fingertips were yellowed with frostbite, the blood caked on my palms, now frozen a cherry red, made them as useless as paddles.

I went immediately to the rear of the snowcat and inspected the tail-ring knot. There it was—the double slipped hitch that I'd put there myself the previous day. It wasn't what I had expected to find. Apparently it wasn't what I'd hoped to find either, for I was immediately conscious of my disappointment. When after walking the sixty yards to the end of the train it became clear that the other hitches were equally innocent of tampering, I found myself almost praying Elliston would discover the Fault-Finder smashed beyond repair, even though it was our only chance of getting through. On the walk back I nearly succeeded in justifying that to myself.

Elliston hailed me from the cab of Badger Two. "Thought you might like to know," he said. "I ran an inspection of the Fault-Finder equipment and I don't believe it's been tampered with." He added that if it were sabotaged it had been done so ingeniously that he couldn't detect it.

I broke the news to Nils on a high hummock of ice.

"In a way, that's bad, Peter. I'd almost rather they believed someone was out to sabotage the expedition than that they lose their confidence in you or me. As it stands, there seems to be precious little evidence to support your version of what happened."

"That's a fact," I agreed. I didn't add that it wasn't losing their confidence that rankled; the lack of supporting evidence had forced me to examine the possibility that Digne and Elliston were right . . . about me. Perhaps there had been no sabotage at all. Apparently Nils sensed this.

"Of course," he said quickly, "Badger One was the designated lead vehicle—everyone knew that. It was the only vehicle that would need to be disabled."

By marking our three previous celestial fixes onto the map and extrapolating for the last few hours of progress I was able to come up with an approximate position. Once Nils contributed the results of his scouting, we were able to fix our position to within a few miles at worst. By that time it was nearing six o'clock.

Nils took extra care warming up the transmitter and making the proper adjustments. Again he started his call-up routine.

"KFQ calling KFM; KFQ calling KFM. Come in, KFM."

When he released the transmitter button, static crackled in the speakers.

"Mensa, this is KFQ; KFQ calling Mensa Station. Do you read, over?"

Static.

Being more patient than I am, Nils kept up the routine much longer than I would have done or was willing to listen. Shortly I interrupted him by asking, "You're sure there's nothing wrong with your radio?"

"No," he said, "I'm not. At first I thought so. It checks out, but really, all I know how to do is monitor these LEDs. If there is something wrong it will take a person more knowledgeable in electronics than I am to fix it."

"Or break it?" I remarked cryptically.

Nils tried his call up a few more times before stepping away from the radio. As though lost in speculation, he faced the distant barrier laid out below us like a huge black bay. Actually the barrier is a bay; the major difference between this and any other—be it the Bay of Biscay, the Bay of Fundy, the Aegean Sea, or even the Gulf of California—is simply that the barrier is larger. It is larger, in fact, than those four combined. And it's perpetually frozen. Maybe he was thinking about how big and black and cold it really is.

I was pondering something even bigger, even blacker, and even colder. It seemed to me we could try the glacier banks as a possible route onto the high plateau of Deception Reach. On the other side of this range was a perpetually frozen continent the size of the United States and Mexico combined. Our job was to get there; nothing else mattered. That was the major difference between Nils Hellstrom and me. I was thinking that if we abandoned most of the equipment . . .

"Peter!"

"What is it?"

I joined him looking down and back, following the line of his outstretched hand, which indicated an area just below the far horizon. He called for Digne to bring his field glasses and then spoke in a lower tone to me.

"Maybe they can't reach us. But it looks as though they're trying to send us a signal."

Where the blackness of barrier and night sky became one, a tiny dot of light shone like a third-magnitude star. I would never have noticed it myself, but then I did not have Nils Hellstrom's eyes. It is true that at night on the barrier, where there is no reflected city light and no artificial illumination whatsoever, a lantern can be seen for ten miles—a bonfire, for five times that distance. Yet we were nearly a hundred miles from Mensa, and once one knew where to look, this shone quite clearly. By this time Digne had come over with Nils' binoculars, and after adjusting the diopters and scanning the region, the big Swede passed them over to me.

"It's too big to be a signal fire," I said.

"But it is in the direction of Mensa," he insisted, "and there's nothing between us on that line and nothing beyond for two thousand miles."

I was nodding in agreement. "It is Mensa, Nils; it has to be. But for a blaze that big the whole station would have to be on fire."

From that moment there was never any doubt about Nils Hellstrom's position with regard to going back. No one even called for an official roll. We filled up Badger Two from the diesel drums on its own fuel sledge and sped down the glacier with what was in any case and regardless of conditions a foolhardy pace. It was a wasted gesture. Even at our best speed we couldn't reach the station in less than twenty hours and by that time the fire would have long since burned itself out.

It was only our good luck that we didn't tumble into an open crevasse or wind up crippled at the side of the glacier with a piston rod through the head or a busted track spun into the rocks.

Our rash pace didn't end at the glacier base. Neither did our luck. Rather than take a heading that would pick up our flag trail where it had stopped, we adopted a course that intersected the trail several miles along at a shallow angle, giving us the best chance to run across one of the flags. We needn't have bothered. At five o'clock in the morning our headlights picked up a fluttering orange banner not a hundred yards directly across our path.

From that time on we rarely missed a flag.

Occasionally the mileage gauge would indicate that a third of a mile had passed without our seeing the next marker, and then Nils or I would turn the powerful flood atop the cab into a wide sweep of the terrain, find the flag, and continue on course.

Only twice did the floods fail to pick up the bright orange of the flags. Both times we followed established procedure: marked our position, made a tight circle, and then, once the gyro compasses indicated we'd come 360 degrees, increased the radius by a hundred yards. When the flag was located, we would use compasses again to start off in the right direction.

It was slower than just holding a speed but faster by far than missing the station by two miles and making another thirty before finding it out.

We had stopped only once, for refueling, soon after finding the trail. Everyone worked fast and efficiently but with a grim determination.

There had been no jubilation upon finding the first marker, though such an incident would normally have had us clapping one another's backs, congratulating each other more heartily for the blessings of chance than would we have for the skillful navigation required to give us the edge. Later, when we finished stowing empty drums and returned, shivering and stiff and with our white faces merely crusted caricatures of our former features, to the warmth of the Badger, there were no joyful ejaculations.

There was no joy in us.

Every man knew that finding the trail had saved us many hours on the barrier trying to locate the station by dead reckoning or, worse, by guess and by gosh. But we were just that sooner to the horror of a burned camp. In the same way the torrid atmosphere of the snowcat and the mugs of scalding coffee had the proper restorative effect on us physically but could not relieve us of the knowledge that for any Mensa survivors the punishment and the suffering continued.

Happily we were not burdened with the extent of the destruction, the full measure of our companions' ordeal. This only struck us as we moved within sight of the camp.

We had just missed a flag and slowed to survey a radius. The searchlight revealed a dark smudge off our left side and I descended to inspect it at closer quarters, unalarmed, for it is not unusual for a flag to be knocked over by the weather. I knew at once it was not a flag. And that was alarming, since the odds are astronomical, regardless of where one stands in Antarctica, against any living thing having stood there before. Not until I cleaned its surface of ice did I recognize the object as a partially burned piece of crate from Mensa's storage wing. I stood. Farther south was another smudge. Then another. As I walked, Nils kept pace in the snowcat.

We entered the nucleus of the destruction and the Badger's headlights bore the gruesome tale to us in an unexpected, ugly splash of black on white.

Blackened bits of insulation, wood, and metal littered the icescape. Mensa itself was traced in ashes like a charcoal sketch on purest bond. That picture had been drawn a day before when fire had claimed the station completely. Today the barrier had claimed the fire. While nothing remained unscorched, there were no longer any flames to be seen. No lights shone above nor from within, and we could see into every part of the gutted station from where we stood. Ever-driven skud was drifting behind each of the many embered bits and piles; it was sweeping over the edge of the open roofs and filling every room and hallway. In another day yet the scene would change to one of chalk on the blackest slate, for the final picture—when the barrier claimed the destruction—would be drawn in white.

Mensa was a dead station.

Nils was first out of the snowcat. He moved to the chain-link enclosure, lifted a section of fallen fence, and knelt beside one of several carcasses.

"Thor?" I asked. It was burned too badly to tell.

"No. I think it's Loki . . . Thor's brother."

Digne and Elliston climbed out of the back. They helped Bob Dolan down; the three of them stumbled in shock toward the ruins. Nils and I went to the garage and descended the ramp to the lower level.

Only a thin insulation had covered these walls. They must have gone up like flash paper. The roof deck had gotten the worst of it. Burning roofing material had fallen onto the spare sledges and dogsleds. Our snowmobiles were buried to the seats in soot and snow. By starlight we crossed the snowdrifts to the inner station, pushed through the skeletal remains of the double doors. Nils produced a flashlight and ignited it down the corridor's length.

I swallowed hard.

Charred beams crisscrossed the corridor bracing walls, consumed by fire and now merely cinder and soot-scarred ice. Little remained even of the floor; of the roof, nothing. Piles of priceless equipment lay as ashes to be buried in drift. The stench of wet ashes and cold smoke still hung in the darkness.

We called out. Our voices rang with an eerie empty sound down the length of the shelter. More frightening yet was the silence that answered our calls.

We searched all of the wings in turn. With each one we came to we found the same story: no object untouched by the fire; no sign of any survivors. By the time we left the cafeteria and started across to the administration wing we were joined by Digne and Elliston who informed us that Dolan thought better to remain with the snowcat.

"Check the quarters," I said to Nils.

Digne, offering to help, followed him out.

Armed with his own flash, Elliston trailed me through the dispensary, meteorology office, and finally into the radio room. I borrowed his light on a sudden notion and shone it onto the transceiver set. Its big panel face was black but only superficially burned. I turned it around, pulled off the loose backing, and illuminated the interior. Here it was. Someone had found a function for that sledgehammer other than changing gears in a Russian tractor. There wasn't a component or circuit board in one piece or any two wires still soldered together.

When Elliston poked his head around, I remarked, "I'd say it's been tampered with, not so ingeniously that we cannot detect it."

"But thoroughly," he agreed.

We met Nils in the corridor and exchanged reports of no success in locating casualties or survivors.

"The project chamber?" I suggested.

Nils nodded and the two of us left Digne and Elliston to continue in the main station while we crossed through the garage and into the Centaur Project.

As everywhere, drift was filling the chamber like sand in an hourglass. Here, where the roof was a complete loss, the level of drift should have been highest, and so it was. Nils and I were three feet off the floor; he could nearly have looked right over the ten-foot walls onto the barrier. This chamber should be the first to fill. But it would not. In fact, if Bob Dolan was right about his shaft penetrating all the way to the ocean, I doubted its time would ever run out. The four walls sloped inward like white talus and even the base ran down toward the gantry. But the height of the circular bulwark supporting the dome's iron grill determined the maximum level of fill, additional snow spilled into the shaft as fast as it drifted over the walls—this room was both ends of the hourglass, filling and emptying at the same time.

"There's nothing in here," said Nils.

"What's that you're standing on?"

Nils pointed the flashlight at his feet. A square cornered black surface protruded from the slope of one wall. "What the . . . ? It looks like the top of one of the cafeteria tables."

We scooped enough snow aside to find a burrow below the tabletop and looked inside. Judging by the amount of space underneath I guessed all five tables had been pushed together. And there, wrapped in coats and blankets, huddled in a common heap, was the most chilling collection of bodies I ever hope to see.

Nils, who was the wrong configuration for burrowing, held the flashlight while I crawled inside to count heads and check for survivors. I was not optimistic. They looked ghastly in the glare of the flashlight, almost cadaverous. And small wonder. I doubted if the temperature under there came close to zero. Though it was somewhat warmer than the rest of the station, the difference was hardly enough.

Even more moderate temperatures can seriously aggravate heart conditions and affect people with asthma or emphysema. But asthmatics and heart histories do not qualify for detail in Antarctica. These were all people in excellent physical condition who had been frozen to the point of death.

All three women and one man.

I grabbed Paulette Gruber's bare wrist. It was unbelievably cold. Yet even before I had gotten a pulse, she stirred slightly and groaned.

"Better get them into the snowcat," I announced.

"Should they be moved?"

For the first time in days I almost felt like smiling. "They're not wounded, Nils, they're hypothermic. They've got to be moved to some place warm. The sooner, the better." As serious as that situation was, finding any of them alive gave me a huge sense of relief.

One by one I handed them out the hole. While carrying Paulette Gruber to the snowcat, Nils must have encountered Elliston and Digne, for they showed up to take Mary Ingram. Nils returned for David Saperstein and then I carried Asia Krokov myself.

By the time I had her in the lighted warmth of the Badger, the others were already coming around. Doctor Gruber was the most energetic. She was not only conscious, she was giving orders, attempting to administer to Saperstein and Mary—both of whose heads were heavily bandaged—and diagnose Bob Dolan at the same time. She glared at me as I set Asia down and spoke in her best bedside manner, "You took your time getting back, didn't you, dear?"

"We made the best time we could, Paulette."

Saperstein raised his bloodied head.

"Nils tells me that if the expedition had not diverted to the glacier ahead of schedule on your suggestion

you would never have seen the flames. Is that correct?"

"Not quite. I didn't see the flames. He did."

Dolan interrupted by asking suddenly, "Where's
Jerry?"

It was the oddest thing. Everyone exchanged glances
but not randomly. The four exposure victims looked
only at one another, and the five of us only at them.
A silent vote was taken while we watched and it was
decided three-to-one that David Saperstein should be
the one to speak.

"We don't know for sure. Presumably he's dead."

"How? The fire?"

"Bob, I'm so sorry . . ." That was Mary.

At least it was Mary Ingram's blond hair, a comma
of which spilled out from the bandages around her
head. That was all. The once beautiful features of her
face were swathed in dressings that would have made
her otherwise unrecognizable. Holes had been left for
her nose and mouth and two more for her eyes. Doubtless they were her eyes, but they didn't look it. These
were dark and lackluster. The stars had gone.

"What happened?" Dolan demanded. "Was it the
fire?"

"No, he must have been blown up. Mary saw him
going into the storage room just before the explosion
came." Saperstein shook his head with a baffled frown.
"The reactor, we thought, but apparently not, because
it's on a safe shutdown. Must have been the fuel stores.
Whatever it was, it literally rocked the barrier and
scattered burning debris all over the station. The project chamber caught next, but soon the fire was everywhere. We were fighting our way through the garage
when Paulette reported another blaze in the radio
room."

"I'd taken Mary to the dispensary," Paulette Gruber
explained. "She'd gotten facial burns from the blast.
Smoke started coming from directly across the hallway, and I raced in with a fire extinguisher."

"Then it was in the quarters. Yours, Masterson,"
Saperstein continued. "We'd get it controlled in one
area and it'd break out somewhere else. I tried split-

ting us up and covering the whole station, but eventually there were too many fires in too many places for us to cover. Mensa was gone. A complete loss. We'd have been gone ourselves if it hadn't been for Mary. It was her idea to hole up there in the project chamber where the fire had already burned itself out.

"She saved all our lives," said Saperstein.

"In another day," I added, "you'd have all been dead. If the fire hadn't come during our call-up, we wouldn't have returned in time. An hour either way, we'd have been on the move and never seen a thing."

Saperstein glared at me. He had, he said, already acknowledged that single bit of luck in the misfortune of the event. When I pointed out that people who survive by luck in these climates don't live very long, he challenged me to tell him what more could have been done and I sensed Nils starting to contribute. I stopped him with a hand. Anything either of us could say would be a slap in the face to Asia Krokov. After all, she had been the polar adviser in Nils and my absence. Any steps that were not taken, or were taken improperly, were as much her responsibility as Saperstein's.

"Anyway," Saperstein concluded, "it was a . . . a horrible thing. A tragic, tragic thing and I'm just glad that it's over."

His eyes hadn't left mine. I knew what he expected. He was waiting for me to declare that the thing was no accident. That the fire had been arson. That Davis' death had been murder. And maybe, just maybe, he was expecting me to add that the horror was not yet over.

So I didn't say a word.

It was Paulette who spoke. "Was this thing just an act of God or is there a maniac among us? Which is it, Peter?"

She expected me to choose. So I didn't.

"Neither one, Doc. This was the act of a wolf."

Nearly ten hours passed before I had an opportunity to modify that conclusion. By then the situation had improved in two respects. Mensa Station, or at least a small part of it, was again habitable, and so I spoke in the comparable spaciousness of the combination library and theater. The second improvement was my partner in conversation: it was to Mary Ingram I modified.

Nils and I had replaced the roof to that one wing. Laying some charred beams across the span on four-foot centers and thwarting those with shorter lengths of burnt lumber, we created a skeletal structure capable of supporting the scraps of tarp that went over the top. It was not very strong yet, but then it didn't have to be. We brought the flexible boring tube onto the ice and sprayed the tarp with warm water from the holding tank. The water froze almost as soon as it was exposed to the air. Only three coatings were necessary to bring the thickness of ice to an inch; in less than two hours it was almost a foot thick and we could have walked across it. The roof would be continually augmented and strengthened by drift as the days passed.

Meanwhile, the others were busily engaged with bringing supplies into that wing, canned food and other nonperishables rescued from the cafeteria storeroom as well as crates of foodstuffs from the expedition's supply sledge.

Robert Dolan had fashioned a stove heater using a blackened fuel drum and some ventilation pipe. A surplus of firewood lay about for the picking. Despite appearances, a great deal of the structure was only superficially burned. Nils gathered at least two cords worth, stacked it along one wall to dry. Elliston rigged a lighting system by stringing the sixty yards of sledge signal cord from that wing to the backup portable generator cannibalized from the Badger.

After Mary and Asia Krokov had finished tidying up and the heater had raised the temperature above the freezing mark, the two rooms began to take on a quite livable quality even if it was the kind of stark livability that only an Admiral Byrd, a Robert Scott, or a Willem Sturdevant could fancy.

I was in the back area wiring the last of the light sockets when Mary wandered in, apparently examining the underside of our roof with keen interest.

"Just be sure you don't let the temperatures in here

rise much above freezing,'' I told her, "or you'll start to melt the darn thing. But freezing is adequate so long as you stay bundled up, move around, and get enough to eat.''

She turned, smiled nervously from beneath the dressings, and came nearer. "Yes. It's a wonderful idea. I'm just sorry that . . . you know, Peter, about moving into the project chamber—''

"That was your idea?''

"Well, I'd always heard that was the rule. Burrow in and conserve heat. Wait for help to arrive.''

"You didn't hear that down here. Why didn't you listen to Asia?''

"As a matter of fact, I did . . . on both counts.''

"Look, Mary. There's two kinds of rules. Those that apply to the rest of the world and those for this one. In Antarctica all the rules are changed. If you're lost on the ocean, in a desert, woods, even in a snow-storm, that may be just dandy. Hole up and wait to be saved. Not here. In the first place, there's little chance anyone can get to you in time even if they knew about your problem, could find you, or were prepared to try. When you lie down in this continent you get buried— it's that simple. Give up and you're dead. You should have known that. But so should Saperstein and Paulette.''

"A man like you can't appreciate how frightened we were. I was scared out of my mind and so were all the others. I still am. I don't know what's happening and I can't believe we're going to get out of this alive.''

"You'll make it.''

"I just keep wondering . . . If you had been here, maybe this wouldn't have happened. We might not have been burned out; Jerry Davis might not have died.''

"Saperstein was a damn fool. There's no question of that. Not just taking your advice but in letting the fire beat him. He should have realized it was arson, but he just couldn't believe anyone could want to burn down his station. I think he's right; no one did. I believe it was intended as a signal for us. One that would make us abandon the race against Fedorev's expedition. That's why it came precisely at the time we'd arranged as a call-up. That's why it continued to burn in one area after another. The arsonist couldn't take a chance Saperstein would bring it under control before it was spotted.''

"You said it was the act of a wolf?''

"A wolf in sheep's clothing. A ewe or a ram, I can't say. Probably a ram, and I thought I knew which one but now I'm not so sure.''

"One of the four of us?''

"Not necessarily. Time-delay incendiaries could have been planted before our expedition had left. It could have been anyone. Anyway, it was no act of God. Saperstein realizes that now. Too late. Since he knew about the damage to the radio twelve hours before, he should have recognized the fire as arson immediately. Had he, Saperstein might have saved more than he did.''

"How?''

"By recognizing that there was no way to save it all. If, instead of scattering his people and having them fight all the fires at the same time, Saperstein had concentrated you and his fire-fighting equipment on one or two key wings, and let the design of the station do the rest, he might have saved a little. The cafeteria with its stores of food would have been one good place to make a stand. The project chamber would have been even better. Its natural isolation would have allowed a fire break at the garage. You could have moved supplies in before they were burned and ensured yourselves of the power and heat.''

"Is that what you would have done?''

I shrugged. "Who can say? Our expedition had problems of its own. We lost a snowcat and half our supplies. Dolan was nearly killed. If I'd been here there's every possibility that accident would have been avoided.''

"Nils told me all about it.''

"Talk to Jules or Tom; they have a different story. I can give you the highlights if you're really interested.''

"I'm not."

"You should be. It's the story of another damn fool who mistied the sledge hitches and was stargazing instead of monitoring the crevasse-detection equipment. That bit of foolishness nearly killed three people and could have doomed everyone if the expedition had continued, as of course the fool advocated that it do."

"That's rather severe, isn't it?"

"On the contrary, I thought they were quite generous. In their place I would have suspected a carelessness approaching criminal negligence. Jules and Tom might have charged that I suspected the actual danger we faced—which I did—and simply failed to take necessary precautions to protect the expedition. To such a charge I could only have pleaded no contest."

She pursed her lips and shook her head in disgust. "Peter Masterson, do you know what's wrong with you?"

"I have a pretty good idea, yes."

"I know you do. That's what's wrong, dammit!"

This was an extraordinary display. In all the months I had known Mary I had never heard her voice raised in anger. She was the single even-tempered soul at Mensa Station, never succumbing to the effects of close confinement with nine other psyches less stable in nature. Even I could not incense David Saperstein to the point her calm appeals failed to soothe him. And more than once she had brought my outrage under control before I rendered injury to one of our co-workers. Now it was my turn. I wondered coldly if she was working on my problems as a diversion from her own.

"Look," I said, "don't let it vex you."

"Vex me! Why, you egotistical . . ." She paused to laugh.

"Egotistical, am I?"

She shook her head. "No. No, I'm sorry to say, you're not. Egotists aren't like most people. Most people rate themselves by the judgments of others. If they're told again and again that they have worth, they believe it. If they're always told that they don't measure up, eventually they believe that, too. After a while they cede the right to judge themselves at all. Egotists are different; they don't seek anybody else's opinion. They rate themselves high regardless of what others think.''

I was watching Mary Ingram closely. But what I saw was a face swathed in bandages. Dressings are not necessary for first-degree burns, particularly here at the south pole, where infections are rare. Even second-degree burns, which rarely cause permanent scarring, don't require dressings as long as she'd been sporting these. So either the burns were more serious than Paulette had led us to believe or the dressings were required by Mary's morale.

Or both.

''But you, Peter. You're no egotist. It's true you're too conceited to take anybody else's opinion for anything. Let alone on the subject of which you're such an expert. You have to judge yourself, don't you? Your problem is you're too damn mean to give Peter Masterson a break. Even the benefit of the doubt. You set impossible standards for yourself, and when you fail to meet them or when you can construe your actions as failing to meet them, you condemn yourself.''

I was getting tired of this. If there was one thing I didn't need, it was a beauty-queen analysis. There had never been a shortage of adulation flowing her direction. At least until a day ago.

''When you look around,'' she continued without a stop, ''you see that no one else is meeting your standards either. You've never stopped to consider that your standards are unattainable and that you're the only one who's even coming close. You're suspicious of every decent impulse you've ever had, so you suspect everybody else's motives, too. You distrust your actions and so you distrust everyone. Your standards have made it impossible for you to like yourself, impossible for you to like anyone else, and as a result, impossible for anyone else to like you.''

I growled, ''Your Freudian slip is showing.''

''What are you talking about?''

''What was it, Mary? Kumquat Queen? Look at you. You went from child beauty to honor student to polar explorer. Who was doing the judging when you were

parading around in that bikini with the ribbon down
the front? Did they satisfy you that you were pretty?
Did they convince you that you were courageous when
you came to Antarctica with your new PhD? The same
PhD that was of no use to you here other than having
somebody else's signature on your IQ. I never heard
you complaining about it until now, when you figure
you're no longer pretty, you've lost your courage,
and your brainy ideas might have cost the lives of four
people. So now's a good time to decide the only opinion worth a damn is your own and plead for merciful
judgments.''

She had gone stiff. "That was very cruel of you,
Peter.''

"You can prove me wrong, Mary. Take off the bandages.''

Her head moved slowly back and forth. "Everyone
has his cross.''

"Fine.'' I said. "You bear yours and I'll bear
mine.''

I turned away.

She came to me in the garage while I was removing
ice, ash, and debris from the three snowmobiles. Not
Mary, Asia Krokov.

The others had paraded by to the library, some hobbling with support, some stumbling on their own. All
hurrying for the newer, warmer quarters.

Asia was the last.

She was standing over me when I looked up. As I
rose, she wrapped both arms around me and buried her
head in my chest. It was a damn silly operation, bundled up the way we were. When at length her head
fell back, I leaned over and we kissed for a long moment. That was even sillier. Our lips were too numb
to feel and the frosting on my mustache and four-day
growth must have been a godawful unpleasantness.

After a while, she stepped back, smiled in a sad
way, and left without having uttered a word.

Nobody had given it any thought except Nils Hellstrom and me, and nobody had really concerned him-

self with it except Nils, but there was still the problem of the missing huskies.

They were his dogs and Nils wanted to find them.

It lacked a few hours of noon but already the northeastern horizon was sending a hint of effulgence racing across the icy reaches and high into the winter sky. That day could give us our first glimpse of the sun in nearly five months. It was too light for the flashlights to be of much use. Yet a heavy hoarfrost settling onto the barrier obscured objects more than a few yards off.

Any individual sorties were out of the question; despite the fact that I was as ready for some warmth as the others, I agreed to accompany him once the shelter was prepared for occupation.

We made a search pattern of concentric circles. I remained just in sight of the station while Nils, holding to a like position at twice the distance out, shouted and whistled. If he hadn't been so adamant that the dogs would answer only to his voice, which would be drowned out by the snowcat's diesel engine, we might have searched in comfort. But he was. So Nils circled while I kept between him and the station, calling out if he seemed to be straying too far.

On the upwind side we were able to extend our circle, but as we swung downwind of Mensa it was a different story. Blowing frost hit my eyes like frazil, needlelike spicules of ice so light even a light breeze can drive them horizontally, so sharp they can pierce the skin. More often than not the station was lost in a rush of white. Downwind of me, Nils' calls died for minutes at a time.

The last time had me worried. I had shouted twice for him to close in and was about to take out after him when three big huskies ran past me. The others came in with Nils.

He had found them huddled together behind a distant mound with the drift burying all but their nostrils. He might have passed them by had not Thor bounded out. Even at 40 below, the dogs were warm enough, but they were ravenous with hunger and desolate for companionship.

While we were installing them in the garage, Asia

approached us with word that a meeting of all station personnel awaited only our presence. The library was crowded with all nine of us inside, but in this country the lie of more-the-merrier generally takes a backseat to the truth of more-the-warmer.

When Saperstein was informed of the success of our search, his first reaction was to comment that the dogs might come in very handy in the event our food supplies ran short. Nils, who is no sissy as concerns the harsh realities of arctic survival and has eaten his share of dog meat over the years, nevertheless launched a glare across the room that left little doubt as to what Saperstein's main obstacle would be in performing that bit of butchery.

Meanwhile, Saperstein, engulfed in a mound of blankets like a Middle Eastern mullah, head wrapped in his red-stained turban bandages, spoke with the mufti's matter-of-factness. "As a matter of fact," he continued, "our expectations are precisely that dire." He looked at Robert Dolan and from him received a ready nod of his black face in grim endorsement. "We do not have enough food supplies to last the two months until our relief arrives. Two weeks at best—no more.

"Now all that is bad enough," he resumed after a pause. "Naturally you wonder about the possibilities for summoning assistance. I'm afraid the news there is no more reassuring. Our radio is destroyed. We have the portable set, but its range is insufficient by half to reach the nearest post, McMurdo Station. As for outfitting another expedition, all of Mensa's spare diesel fuel went up in the fire and what came back with the first expedition is not enough to make the five hundred miles. Two hundred fifty perhaps. Three hundred at best. Bob?"

"Yes, sir. That is the situation."

Saperstein held out his hands. "We are here to explore some options."

Nils' voice boomed behind me. "Won't the company order a fly-in when we miss our radio schedule?"

"They might or they might not. They won't if they

can't and Jules assures me that the cloud cover now over the reach will be coming down off the mountains any day. Others will follow. It might be weeks before the company becomes alarmed. More weeks could pass before clear skies return. No. We've got to do something. We've got to take action.''

Then, by God, he turned and looked straight at me.

Everyone was seated except for Nils and myself, the two of us having never really settled in. Mary, like Saperstein still heavily bandaged, sat with Paulette and Asia to my left. They weren't crying. But they were gearing up. On my right, Dolan had gone into a whispered conference with Digne and Elliston. Their expressions were distastefully forlorn, no doubt pondering the palatability of poorly stewed husky.

I stepped forward. ''David, get these people out of here!''

''What! What do you mean?''

''We need to discuss some matters in private.''

''Can't it wait?''

''It's not waiting. We need to discuss this.''

Saperstein stirred. ''This concerns us all, Mr. Masterson. All our lives. Frankly I would prefer not to discuss it with you privately. That is not to say that I have nothing to say to you on the matter; on the contrary, I owe you an admission as well as an apology, but I feel these are things that everyone should hear. It now appears you were right when you warned that the Soviet stopover here would mean trouble. You were also correct when you suggested that either you or Nils should remain at Mensa while the expedition was gone.'' He swept a hand to indicate the remodeled room. ''It is obvious to us at this point what experience can accomplish. In view of that, I offer you my apologies.''

''Keep 'em. What about recovery of the material from the crash site?''

''That matter is finished.'' Saperstein turned to Nils. ''Is there any way now that you could overtake the Soviets?''

The big Swede shook his head. ''They've now got better than a three-day lead. If we started out on the same route as before and had nothing but good luck, we'd make up one of those days. But it would be fool-hardy to risk Beaumont Glacier with just the one trac-tor. In fact, I would refuse to lead such an expedition. We'd have to follow the Soviets' route up the some-what safer Nimrod Glacier. That, of course, would have us relying upon our tractor's superior speed to gain ground and we'd never recover more than a few hours on that score alone.''

"Well," Saperstein said, head bowed, "as far as leading that expedition, this may be an opportune mo-ment to make a further admission." He looked up. "Peter, it was my intention to place you in charge of the expedition. Those were my instructions from McMurdo. But your reckless handling of the Krokov matter convinced me that you were too irresponsible. However, I assume that in this case you concur with Mr. Hellstrom."

"He's talking facts. You can't argue with facts."

Saperstein nodded. "That seems to settle the matter. If you have any suggestions as concerns our current situation, I'm sure we'd be only too happy to hear them, Peter. Everyone here can attest that your pre-dilection for trouble is surpassed only by your uncanny talent for surmounting it. Have you any ideas?''

I thought about it for a moment and then nodded slowly. "There is one way."

"We're listening."

"If we sent a small team north with the portable radio and all the fuel, they just might get close enough to McMurdo to raise somebody. Of course, they would have to limit their outbound range to half the fuel; since they can't reach McMurdo, they'll need the other half to get back here. Particularly if they can't make contact. It's a slim chance, but it just might work."

"Indeed it just might," commented Saperstein.

"Unless anyone has a better idea," I added.

No one did. At least none they cared to advance.

"Peter," he said, "I hope you are prepared to lead such an expedition."

I might have smiled right then. It would have been appropriate. Having considered the alternatives carefully before the meeting commenced, Saperstein knew what the job entailed as well as I did but he had preferred that I make the suggestion. If half the snowcat's fuel didn't get the expedition within the portable radio's range of McMurdo, then the expedition leader would be under the gun to drive farther and farther north until one of two things occurred: either they did move within range, were able to raise McMurdo, and convinced them to launch an immediate rescue expedition of its own and hope it located the snowcat on its way south; or the Badger ran out of fuel and the team, lost, without power or heat, was forced onto the barrier afoot and a hundred miles from the nearest human habitation. Damn right he hoped I was prepared to lead it!

So I nearly smiled.

"David," I said, "I wouldn't have it any other way."

7

Second Sign

"You don't have to do this," said Mary.

"If I had to," I replied sharply, "I wouldn't."

David Saperstein interrupted in order to change the course of the discussion. "Of course he doesn't, but he knows someone does. How many more do you want on the team, Peter?"

"Two, not counting Nils."

He flashed a look of mild surprise behind me before wondering, "Don't you have to ask him if he's willing?"

A sound like that of thunder rolling beyond the distant Queen Mauds came from the direction Saperstein had faced. Nils Hellstrom was laughing.

Without turning I remarked, "If I had to ask him, I wouldn't want him."

"You're suggesting you both go? I don't get it. Your reproval of me for that error in judgment has been more than vindicated."

I waved it away. "The damage has been done. We were on the defensive then and had to be prepared for whatever they threw at us. Well, they threw it. Now we're reacting."

"All right, who else do you want?"

I indicated Saperstein himself with a nod. "We don't want anyone who hasn't recovered." I looked right to Elliston, Digne, and Dolan. "We don't want anyone who isn't willing to stick it out. There'll be no more referendums on turning back." I looked left. "We don't want—"

"Any women?" snapped Mary.

"Don't be silly, dear," replied Paulette. "Peter doesn't discriminate. He hates everyone."

"I started to say that we don't want the only doctor."

"I think," said Saperstein, "you've about eliminated every one of us here." He looked slowly around his command. "Who does that leave?"

"It leaves me," said Dolan. "I'm volunteering."

There was a period of silence after which Saperstein spread his hands. "Can you try it just the three of you?"

"I'll go alone if I have to; four would be better."

"I'm going."

Every head in that dark little room turned as one to Asia Krokov.

"Have you thought about what you're doing, dear?" Paulette Gruber asked her.

"If I had to think about it," she declared, "I wouldn't do it."

The expressions that faced that poor girl ran the gamut from bewilderment to simple confusion. Me, I didn't understand it myself, but she was obviously a woman after my own heart. I extended a hand to welcome her to the team.

Saperstein began a rundown on what information he wanted communicated to McMurdo, but I wasn't really paying attention. In the first place I saw Nils making notes; in the second, I was sure Dolan had already been given every bit of this before the meeting had even been called. What's more, I had absolutely no intention of getting close enough to McMurdo to communicate anything at all.

But I perked up when he offered to have everyone pitch in to get us ready to go. I declined—with an explanation: I told him that one case of sabotage was enough for me. "If anyone arranges to strand this final expedition in the middle of the barrier," I said, "starve us by a loss of supplies, or stick us at the bottom of another crevasse, I want the saboteur to be stranded, starved, or stuck right beside us."

"What are you talking about?" Saperstein whirled to Dolan. "Bob, what is he talking about?"

"This fire could have been started by the Russians," I explained, underscoring the "could have been." "They could have set time-delay incendiaries to ignite long enough after their departure that they couldn't be held accountable and still soon enough after that our own expedition would be delayed or—as it turned out—recalled. We all know the reasons for that. The same might be said for the destruction of the radio. Your radio, David. We didn't test it before leaving; all we really know is that it worked when you took your call from McMurdo four days ago. The Russians could have sabotaged it anytime after that. Even the Fault-Finder equipment on the lead Badger could have been tampered with while they were still here. But not the towlines. Those lines were not secured until the sledges were loaded; once the expedition was underway, we never halted. Those knots were retied here, at Mensa, by one of us, before we left."

Saperstein's expression was one of astonishment. "I'm hearing about this for the first time," he stammered. "I was told the snowcat's loss was an accident."

"Well, we don't really know it wasn't—" Digne began but was brought short by an elbow in the side from Bob Dolan. What Jules meant, Dolan interpreted, was that we had evidence of sabotage but no real proof. After that it became so quiet that that cold, dark room took on all the gaiety of a mausoleum. Dolan rose and then Asia, too, and together they followed Nils and me into the garage.

We began moving the snowmobiles up onto the ice. "Where do we put them?" Nils wanted to know.

I told him to kick the bundles of flags off the last sledge and strap both snowmobiles on it.

He looked at the flags and raised a disapproving brow.

"Again you don't intend to leave a trail?"

"Nils, if I could help it, this time we wouldn't even leave tracks."

After that we hitched three dogsleds on behind and onto them transferred some of the spare blankets, pemmican, prebundled emergency supply kits, as well as dried meat for the huskies, which I had agreed to take along as a favor to Nils. He would hardly have been a tolerable traveling companion knowing the only thing that stood between his dogs and the stewpot was a hungry David Saperstein.

I had two encounters before our departure that require inclusion. Both women and both with surprise announcements. The first came just as our packing was winding down and was with an individual who was making a habit of seeing me off. But then, I knew Paulette Gruber as a woman of habits.

"Peter!"

Her hiss was very nearly a shout and I left my duties to follow her once again behind some blackened piles well out of sight and earshot of the others.

"Peter, I need you to do something for me."

She didn't need to say it. I could tell by the look of blind panic in her eyes exactly what she was going to ask.

"How much do you have left?"

"Only what I'd kept in my medical kit for emergencies. Enough for a few days. A little longer if I stretch it. But the trip back to McMurdo could take several weeks. Even if the weather clears and they fly us back, it may be impossible for me to . . . to make any arrangements."

"What do you want from me? I said there were no connections in Antarctica, and that goes for McMurdo."

She clenched my parka with unnatural strength. "Please, Peter. When you reach them on the radio you could tell them that we have some injured and need—"

"Forget it, Paulette."

"You must help me!"

I shook my head emphatically and pushed her hands away. "Like the man said: you shit in your own Post Toasties."

The second encounter was with Mary Ingram. With her bandages removed I almost didn't recognize her. The scars across her face weren't as bad as they might have been, but they were more than bad enough.

Whether or not this damage was only the result of burns or if the burned tissue had been further destroyed by subfreezing temperatures I couldn't say. But I knew it would be a long time before men fought for her presence at their table without an element of pity; that she would ever look as good as she had before was doubtful.

I made a nasty remark about everybody coming one at a time to see us off. I owed her that much.

"Peter, please don't be mean. I . . . I came to tell you I was sorry. For everything I shouldn't have said. For everything I should have said and didn't."

"Forget it, Mary. They average out."

"I think I know what you're doing."

"Do you?"

"Why you're taking certain people with you. Trying to be sure that whoever is responsible for this doesn't remain here with us. Isn't that it?"

"I don't know what you're talking about."

"You don't have any idea who . . . ?"

"I have plenty of ideas."

"Then you'll be careful."

"Yes. I'm being careful right now."

Her eyes fell and she turned. I watched her go. I saw her turn around before she started down into the garage and stare at me sadly. From that distance and in that light she looked as good as ever.

"Peter, you're the hardest man to like I've ever known. It takes an almost superhuman effort just to stay near you. You demand the best from people. You don't tolerate anything less. And anytime a person decides it isn't worth the effort, he's no good at all. She isn't. Any woman who could do more than tolerate you would be an extraordinary woman indeed."

"Thanks. I think."

"I've never been an egotist. But I've always believed in myself because so many others always believed in me first. I don't care about any of their opinions anymore. What they think. I'm good. Perhaps I'm even a great woman. Because, you see, I love you. I always have."

By the time I'd recovered enough to think of a suitable reply, Mary Ingram had disappeared below.

Twenty minutes later we were gone too.

I had been wrong about the sun: it would not make an appearance that day. The faint blush of light had started at about 90 degrees true; waxed to a genuine glow on the north that, as Dolan might have observed, gave us evidence, but no real proof, of the sun's existence; and then waned as it worked its way west. When the four of us trooped back inside to make our farewells, there was only a suggestion of illumination. No doubt the tiniest segment of solar radiance would appear the following day. Yet I doubted, judging by the manner in which the five solemn faces acknowledged and returned our well wishes, that any of them would see it. They were burrowing in again. Larger quarters, yes. A little more heat and food this time. But burrowing in nevertheless. And I wasn't sure which of our fates—theirs by remaining at Mensa or ours on what was perceived to be our mission—they regarded with the more dread.

I was driving as we used the fading sunlight for a compass heading.

Dolan and Asia were in the back bundled up in front of the portable heater and lamp. Nils was beside me chastizing by glances instead of by words my abandoning the northerly trail of orange banners.

The dogs ran to the side on loose traces.

Owing to the Queen Maud Mountains, it wasn't long before the sunlight had completely disappeared and darkness claimed the barrier once again. And again, the western horizon was bordered by the ragged swath of black torn from the lower edge of the starlit heavens. But this swath had climbed much higher than the Queen Maud Range itself. This was the line of overcast, now over Deception Reach but which, according to Digne, was moving down onto the Ross Ice Shelf.

In another twelve hours, we would have lost even the minimum solace the celestial dome provided. It is a strange fact that the clear nights are colder in the main than those when the sky is covered. But it is also true that overcast here has a sinister character all its own. Partly cloudy skies are rare. When the clouds come to Antarctica it is an invasion of impenetrable gray gloom; an ominous blanket rolls over the land like a mirror image of the pack, crushing any hint of spirit in the fainthearted, in the lost, snuffing any glimmer of hope. It seems even colder, though somehow it is not. It appears much darker, and somehow it is. A kind of frigid desolation sets in as the whiteness of rolling pack and the whiteness of rolling clouds darken moods and defeat men who are sandwiched between frozen fear and dark despair.

After only one of those hours, I halted the Badger.

"Stay here," I told Nils. "I'll be back in a minute."

I moved to the box and opened the door on a haven of light and warmth. Asia and Dolan looked at me in surprise.

"Bob? Do you mind stepping down?"

Dolan worked his way out and stood beside me. The leg didn't appear to be bothering him tremendously, but then I didn't know how high was his threshold of pain.

I was about to find out.

"You wait here, Asia," I commanded, closing the door and stalking off into the darkness with Dolan at my heels. I moved about thirty paces away before turning, waiting for Dolan to come up.

He stopped in front of me. "What's up?"

I hauled off and drove a fist into his face with all of my two hundred pounds behind it.

Dolan fell backward off his feet and landed hard on the ice. I know he hit hard, for I saw his second grimace of pain after he was down and I can testify that this particular ice has the same blow-absorbing qualities as reinforced concrete.

He was several seconds coming around. "Are you fucking crazy," he groaned, rubbing his jaw.

"That was just to get your attention. And to make you realize I'm serious. I have a few questions to ask and I want answers, or else."

"Or else what? You're gonna beat me to death?"

"I could, but I won't have to. Look around you,
Dolan. Which way is Mensa from here? How far is it?
And what are your chances for finding it alone if you
start walking now? You ride with us by my sufferance—
piss me off and you hike."

"What's wrong with you? Have you gone mad?"

"I want to know what's going on. Saperstein is keeping something back and you know what it is. If I don't
find out about it, I'm leaving you behind."

"I know nothing that will help you reach Mc-
Murdo."

"That makes two of us. But I sure know this much:
David Saperstein would never have sent us racing over
those mountains without giving someone precise instructions. Nils didn't have them and neither did I. I
think you did. I was there when you were first told
about our expedition up onto the reach. You wanted no
part of it. Then you were alone with Saperstein and
something changed your mind. You voted to continue
at all costs. Now, what do you suppose could be the
reason for that?"

His sudden laughter was a nervous bark. "Ha! You
tell me, Masterson. 'We can't refuse to help,' was David's appeal to us. Do you remember what you said? 'I
can,' you said because it smacked of intrigue. What
changed your mind? You suggested the route up Nimrod Glacier. You scotched the vote. You convinced Nils
to take a dangerous shortcut and then favored pushing
ahead even after half of our equipment and supplies
were lost."

The truth of Dolan's argument hit me more solidly
than any punch he could have thrown. But there was
no time to analyze its significance, for I had not come
out here to learn something about me. I growled back,
"We're way beyond that, Dolan. Spill your guts or pick
a direction and start walking."

Letting him ramble had been a mistake. Time, and
hearing his own argument, had allowed a measure of
Dolan's confidence to return. He eyed me almost arrogantly and announced he may have a better notion of a
direction to head than I realized. "I guess I know Peter
Masterson a little better than you think. What do you

bet," he demanded, "I reach Mensa by taking a compass heading due east?"

I reached out, got a grip on his parka collar, and yanked him close. "Mister! You ain't got no compass!"

He nearly stumbled and fell when I shoved him away.

His eyes had registered a mild alarm, as though doubting if only for a moment just how well he knew Peter Masterson after all.

"I'm going back to the snowcat," he snapped. With that he whirled and started off.

I caught his shoulder, spun him back around, and clipped his cheek with a roundhouse right. This time he landed facedown, his body splayed in a twisted pile. He took longer struggling to his feet. About him now there was a look of real uncertainty. And concern.

In his eyes, concern gave way to sudden desperation. He started to shout, "Ni—"

I swung again, knocking him to hands and knees.

For long seconds he knelt there, his breathing half alien whimper, half stertor, no doubt caused by a bloodied—possibly broken—nose. Without even trying to rise, his head came up and confirmed both. The blood was Dolan's but the face belonged to someone else. His real uncertainty had been replaced by conviction, his concern by real fear. He knew now I would do what I threatened, and he could easily figure how that affected his immediate chances for survival.

"Well, Dolan, we're going. You can follow us if you choose, but you'll only take yourself farther and farther from Mensa. You can't be sure which way we're bound. And your chances for getting back will become increasingly remote. But since it's already impossible, that may not worry you." I turned and strode toward the snowcat.

"Wait!"

I stopped.

Dolan was fighting to his feet with a gloved hand covering his face. He was not kneading his nose but, rather, checking it for damage.

"What information do you want, dammit?"

"I want everything."

He brought the glove in front of his eyes. There may have been some evidence of damage but no real proof—skin tissue yielding to frostbite bleeds little to start with and what blood there is congeals rather rapidly at 40 below.

"All right," he nasaled. "But for Christ's sake can we get back in the snowcat? This is going to take a while."

It wouldn't have taken so long at all if Dolan had just spilled it. But once he was back in the relative warmth of the Badger and enough time had elapsed for me to bring Nils in to join us, Dolan had lost his prime. We had to pump every bit of it out of him one damning admission at a time.

"What happened to you?" asked Nils at sight of Dolan's roseate bill.

"He fell on the ice," I replied. "How clumsy of him."

"Peter hit him," said Asia, leering at me suspiciously. "Three times." Apparently some things had flowed fairly freely while I was gone.

"How clumsy of me." I looked expectantly at Dolan. Asia and Nils looked expectantly at me. "Bob here," I said at last, "has things to tell us."

And even then, I twice had to threaten him with a short stroll onto the ice. If Dolan had counted on the big Swede to take his part he was disappointed. Nils doesn't approve of violence—which is just as well considering his size—but neither does he approve of deception, or those who practice it.

"I want to state right at the start," Dolan stated, fingering his nose for sympathetic effect, "that neither David Saperstein nor I had any notion that any of this was in the works until he got the call from McMurdo Station. Even then he only knew what they told him. And he was only acting as they ordered."

"How does McMurdo presume to give orders to us?"

"Well, it's the nature of the polar environment. And our mission here."

"What does testing an ice-boring process have to do

with taking orders from the United States government?''

Dolan shook his head. ''If you weren't so damned
independent you'd understand. You know what this
project entails. Subcrustal mining requires too much risk
and expense to be undertaken by any business without
official blessing and support. We have no reason to believe that minerals exist in enough quantity underneath
the ice crust to justify the costs. Except for one particular element.'' He regarded Asia dubiously.

Something clicked. I said, ''You're looking for
uranium?''

''That is the underlying aim of the Centaur Project.''

''I thought the U.S. had adequate resources within
its own borders.''

''Of low-grade uranium, yes. Most of the high-grade
deposits of uranium ore in uraninite or pitchblende in
the U.S. have been seriously depleted. A couple hundred thousand tons of uranium ore in carnotite deposits
are our estimated reserves at the present. That stuff
averages twenty percent uranium oxide, recoverable
for upward of thirty dollars a pound. When that's gone,
and it probably will be in another five years, we start
looking for even lower-grade deposits recoverable at
even higher costs. As the price of uranium ore rises,
the necessity of searching remote locations grows and,
with it, the feasibility of profitably recovering ore once
thought not worth the cost. Satellite analysis of Antarctica has suggested the possibility of pitchblende deposits on a scale with those in Czechoslovakia and
Zaire. The problem is that much of the deposits here
are buried in upward of two miles of ice. Our barrier
project is designed to establish that the hot-water boring system can prove a financially sound method of
reaching the uranium deposits.''

''Well, this is not my area,'' I said, ''but I understood the new fast-breeder reactors were supposed to
make more efficient use of the uranium fuel.''

''Oh, they do. They actually 'breed' more plutonium than they use. And unlike the water reactors, they
don't require enrichment of the uranium fuel, which

further wastes energy. But America has found itself in
a nuclear-energy quandary. Our fear of all things
nuclear—particularly nuclear waste and nuclear-waste
sites anywhere within the continental borders—has made
it practically impossible for the power establishments to
construct new plants, the fast breeders. So we continue
to fuel the older, less efficient models that deplete our
uranium reserves at an accelerated rate and pile up the
nuclear waste. And where do we put it? The populated
East Coast pressures Congress to explore the West for
a dumping ground. The folks in Texas don't want it
under the fields of Deaf Smith County. Nevada screams
at the possibility of Yucca Mountain being selected.
Washington citizens pass a statewide referendum against
Hanford becoming the nation's nuclear-trash site. The
states with basalt mines turn a thumbs-down to geologic
disposal within their borders. So what was the government to do? Military defense waste is at least as great
a problem—by volume if not by level of radioactivity—
as the nation's power plants combined. Something had
to be done."

Dolan was going on, but I held up a hand to stop
him. It had been my mistake for asking the question,
but it sounded to me as though he were trying to justify
something the U.S. government had already done instead of something it was just looking into.

In spite of that, I knew what he was saying was true.
The government had funded studies to explore every
disposal possibility from rocketing the hazardous material into space, to sending it to the bottom of the
ocean. I'd even heard of a study made a couple decades back that had suggested burying it under the
antarctic icecap. There was always somebody with
arguments against any proposal. Some pressure group
or political organization to stop any plan from becoming implemented. Eventually I knew the government
would have to take the responsibility for the problem
and adopt a scheme regardless of who didn't like it.
But this was no place to solve that dilemma.

"Whoa," I said. "This is all terribly interesting but
too far afield for me. Have you found uranium at
Mensa?"

"What! How could there be?"

"You've found nothing under the ice?"

"There's nothing under Mensa but ice—ice and sea-water. Mensa is only a test site for the hot-water boring process. So we can experiment under conditions less severe than those on the reach."

"In that case how do you explain Johnson's dosimeter?"

That stumped him.

Instantly Dolan turned a sharp glare onto Nils. "I don't," he said after facing me again. His hand came up. "The fact is, I can't. If I knew . . . But I don't. Saperstein and I have discussed it but we don't have any answers."

"All right, I don't buy that, but let it go for a minute. You're looking for uranium. Why all the secrecy?"

"I shouldn't have to describe the situation to you and, frankly, I'd rather not—not in front of her." Dolan was giving Asia a sidelong glance. Anyway, he was correct. The situation was pretty obvious, probably even to her. A dozen nations including France, Britain, Australia, New Zealand, Chile, and Argentina all claim territory here. In fact, all the land north of the eightieth parallel is claimed by at least one country. Only the United States and the Soviet Union make no claims of territory at all. And only the U.S. and the U.S.S.R. refuse to recognize any of the other territorial claims. My personal opinion has always been that both countries are poised to claim it all. The Antarctic Treaty requires all nations involved to set aside their challenges and work in concert to develop the continent; I wonder how long that treaty would last if any of those countries learned there was uranium here. Their reserves of uranium, after all, couldn't be any greater than ours. And those without the nuclear-power facilities either possess the nuclear bomb or are making efforts to do so.

"Okay, okay, are we now to understand that these survivors up on Deception Reach are a couple of uranium prospectors out looking for the mother lode?"

"There are no survivors."

I raised my brows at that. "But surely the aircraft

had a pilot. And if no one's been up there, how do you know there are no survivors?''

"Because there is no aircraft."

Nils and I exchanged grimaces of betrayal.

"What crashed?" I demanded.

"A satellite. One of our reconnaisance satellites."

"One of yours? How many do you have?"

"United States, I mean. It was a military satellite."

"When did it go down? And where?"

"Where? The location you observed on that Russian map is the calculated site. They're after it too, the Russians. After all, they're the ones that shot it down."

I turned to Asia Krokov. "What do you know about this, Asia?"

She was shaking her head in earnest. "Nothing."

"This was four days ago, Bob? Five?"

"More like a week. That's all I know. Why they shot it down or what they hoped to gain by it David wasn't told, but obviously they're out to salvage whatever's left. The satellite stopped transmitting infrared photographs when it was hit. Washington doesn't know what it may have photographed since being thrown over the antarctic but we were ordered to recover an impact-proof film canister."

The infrared rang a bell. "Is this the same satellite that took those photographs of Mensa and the mountains just to the west? The ones from the project chamber?"

"Dammit! How do you know about those?"

"Does it matter?"

"Of course it matters; that's classified information."

"It's also a year old."

A squall came up to one side of us: Nils clearing his throat. "A year, a month, or a week," he said. "It makes no difference. That film canister may be impact-proof but it's not antarctic-proof. Even with the transponder locator we would never have been able to find it. After a few days on Deception Reach there is no possibility that anybody's going to recover any part of it. You were talking about the severe conditions up there. Brother, you have to see the reach to believe it. By now it will be buried under thirty feet of ice.''

"It's not buried,'' said Dolan.

"How do you know?''

"Because it hasn't been up there a week.''

"You said—'' Nils started.

"I said it was shot down a week ago. But it didn't come down. The satellite was in a highly inclined orbit and the explosion merely placed it into an elliptical polar orbit. A very unstable polar orbit.''

"So when did it crash?'' I demanded.

Dolan pulled back his parka sleeve and ostentatiously examined his watch. "According to McMurdo,'' he said, "about this time tomorrow.''

I had a feeling that Dolan was still holding back. But what he knew that he wasn't telling I couldn't fathom. Yet it was easy to figure the rest. The string of remote radar dishes set at unmanned depots along the perimeter of Deception Reach was probably capable of picking up a low satellite in such a highly inclined orbit making its perigean passage over the southern continent. Armed with that data, I had no doubts the military could calculate within a few square miles where the satellite would come down. Those radar depots were as much a part of Dolan's story as the mininuclear plants at Mensa or the commercial reactors in the United States, for no batteries could withstand the months of isolation or the draining cold of the plateau. The depots were powered by strontium 90 capsules, a radioactive element generated from chemical processing of spent reactor fuel during which uranium and plutonium are also recovered.

"All right, Masterson,'' said Dolan, "now it's your turn. Let's have it. Did Saperstein have you figured correctly?''

Nils and Asia turned simultaneously. A short silence was ended by Nils, who could contain himself no longer, asking, "What did Saperstein figure?''

Dolan smiled, knowingly. "Ask Peter.''

"If you're asking are we still in the race," I said, "the answer is yes."

"That's only the first half of it, Masterson. The rest has to do with winning. Answer this: are we, or are we not, making for Hell's Flow?"

In the year I had known Nils Hellstrom that was the first time I ever saw his face devoid of color. It wasn't to be the last. However, on the subsequent occasion cold had drained the life from his face; just now, it was fear. He pivoted to me again, slowly, mechanically, and as he did so, his complexion regained its normal ruddy shade, and then more until he was almost livid. For a second I felt I may have to remind him of his attitude on physical violence. Then, just as suddenly, he climbed out the back and disappeared.

Antarctica respects no one's secrets but her own.

What this land herself has buried she guards with the tenacity of a Cerberus. About my secret, her three heads were positively garrulous and would have made a gift of our destination to anyone with the senses to understand.

She had sent wind howling down from the mountains with a kind of fury I had never seen. This was the shriek of a devilish creature, and the nearer we approached Hell's Flow, the louder its cries sounded. They came out of the distant white beyond our headlights' glare raising a storm of hard-grained snow and propelling it straight into our windshield. I could have navigated by that alone. When the wind slacked or the snow began to blow across our nose, invariably, I would need to correct our course into its line of fire.

Temperatures plummeted. By the hour cold drove the alcohol level on the outside thermometer scurrying into the reservoir. There was no place for us to hide. When the insulated walls of the Badger proved insufficient for 80 degrees of frost, we could do nothing but retreat into our parkas and push onward.

Mile by mile the flat, unending plain transformed into a broken field of crisscrossed ridges, open chasms, raised platforms of ice, and rafted slabs that protruded from the shelf like huge white submarines frozen fast in mid 45-degree vaults to the surface.

Those were the three heads of Antarctica.

Wind and cold and ice we could sense. But Antarctica has a fourth head and this too we could sense. It was in our mouths—a foul taste that no amount of swallowing and no quantity of coffee, regardless how black or oppressively acrid, could wash. We could smell it in the air as well. A stench like that of sweat and decaying flesh.

Antarctica's fourth head is death.

Our senses told us it dwelt in Hell's Flow.

From there death had traced its icy finger in a semicircle at the glacier's mouth connecting prominent granite obelisks on each side and defied any human to cross the line. A custom in Antarctica obliges explorers to name any curious or distinctive feature of this featureless land; accordingly, the mouth was known as Satan's Gate. But for more than twenty years, no one had accepted the challenge.

The charts had no symbols for wind or cold or even for ice of the variety beneath our treads, constantly changing formations that rose, fell, opened and collapsed, and generally underwent a myriad distortions at the hand of the relentless glacier and the unimaginable pressure behind it. However, there was a most glaring dashed red line on the chart that described the glacial snout of Satan's Gate. And a similar arc in red ink at the upper limit of the glacier defined the high boundary. Between the two no trespass was to be condoned.

By nine that night we had approached within a matter of miles from the lower boundary.

Nils had relieved me at the wheel three hours before when I had asked him, but with the exception of the few words necessary to make that request, I had said little and he had said practically nothing at all—at least not to me.

To be fair, we'd seen little of each other in that time.

Once the icescape began to deteriorate I stopped the snowcat again with the intention of having Dolan and

Asia begin keeping a watch on the sledges. Should one
of the tow ropes break or some supplies spill, we would
not discover what was missing until it was too late.
Though I wasn't about to order Asia, or even Dolan,
onto the trailing sledge in the middle of a winter night
with temperatures falling into the minus fifties, they
could drop the tailgate and use the after-facing spotlight to keep an eye on things.

But when I got back there I changed my mind.

I ordered Dolan up front to monitor the Fault-Finder,
explaining that we had begun to encounter unstable
ice. "Tell Nils to maintain our heading," I told his
back.

Closing the doors above the tailgate allowed the box
to hold much of the heater's output, and by lying on
my stomach, peering under the doors, I could still observe the trailing sledges.

Almost as soon as I had positioned myself, the
snowcat lurched ahead. Then, very soon after that, the
lamp was extinguished behind me and I felt Asia moving out at my side. I turned to find her pink little oval
face studying mine.

"Did you and Mr. Hellstrom kiss and make up?"
she asked.

"There's hardly enough makeup in the world to fool
me into kissing his big mug," I said. "He's pissed,
all right, but he'll get over it."

"Pissed?"

"Pardon me. Disturbed."

"I too am deeply pissed, Peter."

"Is that so?" I was watching the line of sledges, or
pretending to. The huskies were tied individually to
each side of each sledge to prevent them from fighting
as they ran. The traces were too short for any husky
to reach the one behind or ahead of it, and sledges
separated them on each side. I was thinking that perhaps there should be something keeping Asia a little
farther from me, but then it had been the prospect of
being close to her that had lured me into changing
positions with Dolan in the first place.

"Do you think there's a chance we will see . . . the
Soviet expedition?"

"A very small chance, yes."

"If they see me, they'll know I'm a traitor."

"You're no traitor, Asia. You've committed no treason against the Soviet Union. You've simply defected. It's not the same thing."

Whereupon I got a speech. The gist of it was this: to me, or any American, she might not be a traitor. But in the Soviet Union that's just what she was. Russian, she told me, has no word for defector. There are emigrants and there are traitors, and any person who leaves the country is one or the other. An emigrant would have papers. She had none. Therefore she was a traitor. If Asia were seen with me, she would be returned to Moscow and sent to prison. Or killed.

"Of course I knew that when I allowed you to volunteer," I told her. "But you're the only one of us who speaks Russian. You alone might have a clue as to what their intentions are or what they might do in any given situation. I need your help."

She drew back in astonishment.

"You want to find them!"

"I wish there were another way, Asia. But we have no choice. There's fuel back there for less than two hundred miles and a radio here with an effective range of about half that in the most ideal of conditions, conditions that rarely prevail anywhere in Antarctica and do not now prevail at McMurdo, five hundred miles away. It's a portable radio for minor sorties from the station, not major expeditions. There was never any thought we could reach McMurdo by radio no matter how far we managed to get. Saperstein and Dolan never figured we'd try. I don't blame you for being mad at me. I don't blame Nils either, for that matter, but he, at least, brought it on himself. He stood there and announced he would refuse to take an expedition with only one snowcat up the Nimrod Glacier—compared to Hell's Flow, the Nimrod is an interstate highway."

"He said he would refuse to lead it. He would not have refused to go if you were leading. It's your deception that made him mad. Nils Hellstrom would follow you into hell, and you know it."

"Well, I won't try to deceive you. This expedition will make every possible effort to locate those Russian friends of yours."

"What are you going to do?"

"Exactly what Saperstein did figure. The only source of fuel within five hundred miles is that Russian expedition. With them is also the only radio capable of transmitting as far as McMurdo. And, most important, we know pretty much where they're going to be tomorrow or very soon thereafter. Once Nils realizes that, I don't think he'll stay angry."

"And me?"

She was close—too close for me to focus well—staring into my eyes.

"I'll do the best I can to protect you."

"Do it now, Peter. Hold me."

I reached over and extinguished the spotlight.

Someday I would try to find a warmer place to kiss her. Minutes after we separated, we were kneading each other's nose and cheeks, laughing like schoolchildren at the pain.

Then she was on her back looking up and smiling. "Never have I seen such stars."

Or so many. "It's an extraordinary country," I agreed.

"Look there," she said suddenly. "A falling star!"

I looked up.

"In that sign. It falls so long. Like an airplane."

"A sign? You mean a constellation?" I asked her.

"Yes, a constellation. You call it the Southern Cross?"

"Yeah, that's what we call it."

She asked if it could tell us which way we were going.

"It can if you know the time of day and which day of the year it is. And if you have the right sign. In the case of the Southern Cross, Asia, you have to be careful. That's a second sign. Another constellation altogether."

"That isn't the Southern Cross?"

"It is and it isn't. Two of the stars are part of one

constellation and two are part of another. The four stars together so closely resemble the Southern Cross that they are often mistaken for it by other than experienced navigators. It's called False Cross. But it's really not a constellation at all. If you navigate by it you'll wind up ninety degrees off course.''

''Where is the other one?''

I stuck my head farther out and indicated the western third of the night sky. ''Already lost behind that overcast.''

As I switched the light back on, Asia's falling star, my hourly visitor and Dolan's satellite, was skirting the line of clouds, racing for the southern horizon before the same fate overtook it. The satellite would have made three more passes above the cloud ceiling while Asia and I cuddled under the blanket with only a crack for guarding the trailing sledges. When the snowcat stopped again, clouds covered the better part of the sky. I climbed down and went forward, passing Dolan on the way back.

''Like to drive?'' asked Nils.

''Delighted.''

The barrier here looked like a demilitarized zone. Huge craters lay to every side of us. The beautiful symmetry of the Ross Ice Shelf had been blasted into every imaginable configuration. If a squadron of B-52s had made a flyover dropping one salvo after another of the highest megaton bombs and the resulting destruction allowed to refreeze instantly in place, the outcome could not have been any more a scene of confusion than that which was revealed in the glare of our headlights.

''Time to call in the first string?'' I kidded Nils.

He shook his head. ''No. But I figure us to be within a few miles of the boundary and I wanted you up here. You inspire confidence. Also I'll need you handy when the ice opens up so I can remind you that I was against coming.''

''Nils, the last thing you'd ever say is I told you so.''

He nodded. ''That, my friend, was the point.''

I noticed Nils kept a weather eye on the Fault-Finder

and quickly learned the reason. No sooner had we started off than the needle began doing a tarantella. Swinging slow one moment, swishing to a quick three-four time the next, it indicated ice below us varying in strength and integrity so quickly that by the time we could decipher the reading and react to it, the danger was past.

At a shout from Nils I brought our speed to a crawl.

"We hit a small pocket back there," he said.

He didn't need to add that it had been simply a matter of luck we had not fallen through.

There was no way to reverse the train without stopping and turning each of the sledges around individually. To avoid that we crept along, choosing our paths carefully. Several times the Fault-Finder prevented us from taking seemingly innocent routes that were in reality impassable, carefully covered traps that would have collapsed under our treads.

Luck remained with us. That, and Nils' years of experience over every manner of frozen terrain, got us through the demilitarized zone and into the war.

When our headlights struck a mammoth granite monolith that shot from the ice like a rocket and disappeared above the glare into the darkness, we halted. It was so distinctive a piece of natural architecture that it seemed unlikely more than one could exist on the continent. But, in fact, another nearly identical monolith stood not a mile away.

These are the twin towers of Satan's Gate, which mark the boundaries of the flow. One stands to the north, the other to the south, separated by a mile of glacier mouth. Only it isn't called a mouth. Glaciologists refer to the leading edge of a glacier as a "snout." It's normal for a small stream to issue from the snout, the source of this water being the thin layer of slush upon which glaciers "slide." No such stream had ever been witnessed spewing from Hell's Flow. But that hadn't stopped someone from giving it a name: the Styx. A glacier such as this? It must be there. According to myth, the River Styx encircles Hades like a moat; across it the souls of the dead are ferried; none of them ever return. It proved too fitting a title to ignore.

We descended from the cab and set to work.

Never have I known such fierce cold. It was impossible to face the glacier and that horrendous gale. Hell's Flow itself is so steep and cut into the mountains so deeply that the cold mass of air on the reach spills down in volumes and speeds that approach hurricane force.

Not surprisingly, no one was anxious to stand idle.

In those bitter conditions, hunched into our parkas and wrapped in every available protection for face and hand, we began offloading the snowmobiles.

Nils busied himself with a blowtorch on the first snowmobile that came off. Dolan helped me bring down the second machine; the two of us then refueled the Badger. As we finished, Nils had his snowmobile started and departed on a quick reconnoiter to verify our position and locate the least unlikely route of ascent. Meanwhile, Dolan suggested an inspection of the granite obelisk with the idea that a grotto he'd spotted on the south face of it would make an excellent location to stash emergency supplies. I, greatly impressed that he been able to spot anything at all in the up-wind direction, approved the suggestion and sent him along with a few precious tins of foodstuffs and blankets.

Asia and I got one dogsled hitched to the second snowmobile; we were strapping on additional supplies when Nils returned.

After moving his machine into position in front of the other dogsled, he made his report. "This is the north side," he shouted. "But I don't believe we'll ever get the snowcat across to the south. The snout is high and long. We'd have to move well out into the broken field to get around it. I couldn't even make it in the snowmobile. Couldn't even see the other pillar."

"Can we ascend on this side?"

"Do we have any choice?" cried Nils.

Dolan appeared beside us. Listening to the roar of that wind was unavoidable; confronting it was a hardship we shunned whenever possible, and so I hadn't seen him approach. I literally shuddered even considering facing the wind and drift up the twelve-mile length of Hell's Flow.

He opened his mouth and worked his lungs. "What!" He repeated his message still louder. After the third time he threw up his hands and gestured for us to follow him to the rock tower.

The four of us crossed to the south face and ducked into a low opening. Instantly the wind quieted; our voices became audible at conversational volumes. Dolan pointed to an extension of the cave that began descending at the same time it worked back into the mountain. "It's too dark to see down there," he said, "but the place is cavernous."

Nils disappeared and returned in a moment with a flashlight, which he shone down a rough ice-hewn staircase. Ice still covered the lower rocks but the walls and ceiling were cold granite. Dolan was already half-way down.

We caught up with him at the bottom, where the cave widened. The meager illumination from the snowcat's assortment of spotlights that had found its way into the upper level was nowhere in evidence here. We could see nothing except for a narrow blade of light that Nils swung this way and that to keep the darkness at bay. As he did so, a chamber of immodest dimensions was revealed.

"This is as far as I got," Dolan admitted.

We straggled into the chamber.

The only wall that eluded Nils' flash was the western one. He advanced in that direction. The rest of us followed him in Pied Piper fashion, mesmerized by the circle of light on the weird waxworks walls and the retreating darkness. The cave continued an unobstructed descent.

We worked deep into the mountain, lower even than the glacier itself, before the beam identified a recess to one side, which Nils explored with his light. Other recesses appeared. It occurred to me that rather than a cave, we were descending a catacomb with each vault larger, more imposing than the last.

We never did find the end of it.

Nils' beam was playing along a rocky slab when it

froze like a spotlight on a stage performer. I stopped beside Nils; Dolan came up short opposite me.

We stood stock-still and silent.

It was Asia who reacted first. She had slipped between Nils and me, beheld the figure before us, and instantly suppressed a sharp inhalation by clapping both hands to her mouth.

"My God," Dolan stammered. "What is it?"

I didn't say a word. It would have been melodramatic to tell him that this was the fourth head of Antarctica—that we were looking at death. And since I had no other way to describe it, I said nothing at all.

8

Beyond the Twin Towers

I've never been accused of prescience but my feeling that the ice-coated ceiling and walls amounted to a waxwork backdrop was right on the mark. The wraith-like figure before us stood as stiff as a wax mannequin, his arms held outward in eternal warning. Two glassy eyes stared at us from out of a gaunt face as white and slick as paraffin. A thin coating of ice was responsible for the sheen; an incredible case of dilatory decomposition had seen to the rest. Even I didn't realize how accurate my feeling had been until Nils shifted his flashlight to the left. There was another—this one, prone, eyes locked on the ceiling. Like the first, his regulation arctic clothes were threadbare but remarkably intact, considering they were several decades out of date. Eventually we found a third corpse in a similar condition, death mask and all, in the next vault down. The three looked precisely like wax figures in a gallery of horror.

Madame Tussaud would have been green with envy.

Finding the first two had dampened the group's enthusiasm, but not Nils'; he moved off down the catacomb slashing his light to and fro. I struck a match to inspect the one corpse more closely, wondering how many years had passed since he'd first been propped against that wall of ice. If there were any injuries on the body other than some facial lacerations, I couldn't see them. Dolan remained beside Asia, murmuring, "They must be members of the Riga expedition."

She asked how they could come to look like they did, but he didn't have an answer.

Nils called my name from farther down the catacomb. The rest of us stumbled toward his voice until we located him kneeling over the third body and shining the flash on its ghoulish face, saying, "Doesn't he look familiar?"

He did not! No one else thought so either.

"I can't be sure," said Nils, "but this looks like some photographs I've seen of Willem Sturdevant."

"Nonsense," snapped Dolan, "that was more than fifty years ago."

Asia was incredulous. "Why aren't they"—she waved both arms in search of an English word—"gone?"

"Antarctica is an icebox," I told her. "Toss an orange peel on the ground and it'll take a hundred years to decay. We're not in a cave. It's a crypt. And another fifty years from now, or even a hundred and fifty years from now, it still will be."

"Who they are," said Dolan, "is of minor importance. What I want to know is how they happened to get in here?"

"Perhaps they sought shelter from the cold," said Nils.

"And just sat down and waited to die?" Dolan didn't believe it. "Where are the other members of the expedition? What happened to them? Surely they got farther than the glacier base. If they'd had trouble up on the flow and these three made it back here, why didn't they strike out onto the barrier? They had supplies. And they would have made more ground than this before giving up."

There were no supplies in that cavern. I pointed that out. Then I reminded him that fifty years was a long time for him but not necessarily for the glacier. "If they'd become trapped in one of the slower-moving parts of the glacier, it might have taken them years to get this far."

"Did the glacier carry them in here?"

"You tell me. And when you've finished, explain this." I grabbed Sturdevant's parka, which was—like that of the first man we'd found—rigid as rusted mail. Their clothes could have stood by themselves and had probably been responsible for holding the one man against the wall until the body itself had frozen solid. "Parkas, pants—all of their clothes—have been soaked."

"Are you saying that they drowned?" asked Nils.

"That's easily explained," Dolan interrupted hastily. "Most likely there was a thaw some years back and the ice above them here dripped down."

I doubted that. However, not having lived in Antarctica the last fifty years, I was really in no position to argue. Anyway, the argument was running down. None of us really felt like staying, and very little encouragement was required to herd everyone out of the chamber and back up onto the ice.

No one spoke another word except Asia, who walked close beside me on the climb and once near the entrance turned and asked me if I thought the four of us would end up like that.

"Asia, honey," I said, "everybody ends up like that."

The eerie ululation of the west wind was a hellish welcome to the present. Once back to work lashing supplies on the two sets of sleds, we found it difficult to think of any other time or any other set of problems. In spite of that, the sight of those bodies never left us. I was to see their faces in my mind all that night, but just then, it served as an introduction to Hell's Flow that filled us with a sense of foreboding.

Sturdevant had been one of the best. While his equipment may have been inferior to ours, his polar experience, his polar skills, and his polar sense were second to none. The world had always taken it for granted he had died scaling Hell's Flow. But we were here now, trying in darkness what he had tried in daylight, and we knew damn well he had.

Nils descended into an uncharacteristic ill humor. Unlike Dolan, Asia, and even me, he was too accomplished a polar explorer not to know the impossibility of our task. For him, this ascent was the beginning and the end. To me, Hell's Flow was just a shortcut.

"I don't want the woman monitoring the Fault-

Finder," Nils declared when I tried to assign positions.

"You'd rather she drive?" I asked, somewhat surprised.

"No."

When I reminded him that Dolan and I would be on the two snowmobiles and there was no other position for her but monitor, Nils argued that Asia had no experience. "She is," he snapped, "the least qualified of the four of us."

"She won't be," I replied, "after tonight."

Begrudgingly, Nils allowed her to sit beside him and moved the Badger into the lead position.

While our snowmobiles, capable of speeds up to sixty miles an hour, were vastly more maneuverable, their low-set lights served only to reflect a dazzling display off the surface blow doing more to blind us than illuminate our path.

Despite its lumbering pace and comparatively poor maneuverability, the Badger had the powerful roof-mounted headlights to illuminate the glacier for several hundred feet ahead, and the Fault-Finder to look below the ice ahead of us for as much as a dozen yards.

Nils even rigged up a code system on his flag-setter signal light so that Dolan, fanning off his left quarter, or I, off the right, could be warned of unsafe ice.

However, the first and most conspicuous warning was ignored. We began the ascent by passing between and beyond the twin towers of rock.

From there the glacier abruptly began angling up at nearly 10 degrees—steeper than the steepest sections of other antarctic glaciers—and quickly began assuming even more precipitous grades. It rises two miles in just over twelve miles of length. And Hell's Flow doesn't wind like most glaciers; in fact, it doesn't even dogleg. The flow shoots straight down a wide ravine with hardly the slightest deviation.

In short, there is nothing to impede the advance of ice.

Advance, the ice of Hell's Flow does. It is nowhere near the largest of glaciers. In fact, it is relatively small. But more ice travels down Hell's Flow in a day than down any other three glaciers on the continent, combined, over the course of a week. For decades, Black Rapids Glacier in Alaska had established the record for glacier flow—during the particularly heavy snowfall winter of 1936–37—by traveling almost a hundred feet per day. That was before photographic overflights of Hell's Flow, from outside the already established off-limits zone that extended to air traffic as well as ground, confirmed consistent daily travel in even the driest of winters of more than a hundred yards.

We could actually hear it moving.

When the wind would momentarily abate and at points where the stress was greatest, the most horrendous wail would rise from the ground. It was close to the grating of twisted metal but much worse—more like the sound a framed structure makes before being ripped apart by tornadic forces, the sound of thousands of boards simultaneously breaking and tens of thousands of nails simultaneously wrenched from place. It is a terribly unnerving, terrifying wail.

Even the dogs were affected by it.

I'd never seen the wind bother them, or the cold, but as they followed the last sledge, staying between Dolan and myself, they whined continually. Their fearful eyes searched in all directions. Thor never faltered, but some of the other huskies, Freya included, would stop for no apparent reason, glance all around, sit, howl once or twice, and then suddenly leap forward to catch up with the others. That was unheard of.

We kept to a walking pace.

From my position I could see Nils' tack. He was holding to the flatter strips of ice, avoiding the obvious deformations as well as the more subtle patches that were windswept smooth; these to him signaled weaknesses below. He steered clear of major hummocks, gave wide berths to unusual pressure ridges and upthrust slabs.

Whether it was the Fault-Finder or Asia Krokov's interpretation of its readings that he didn't trust, I don't know, but even from fifty yards behind him I could tell we were not navigating by that instrument alone.

When he signaled weak ice for no apparent reason and hooked left, I smiled inwardly. Less than a mile up, the glacier had begun to outmatch his innate senses and the sum of his polar experiences. Dolan and I held to the left. Almost immediately, he signaled more bad ice and again turned away from the grade. He tried three times to cross a region of the glacier and turned back each time. His traverse continued until the Badger's headlights reflected off a high wall of ice running straight down Hell's Flow.

Nils halted the snowcat there.

"There's no way around it," he shouted when I came up.

"What's the trouble?"

He gestured above our position all the way across the glacier. "An area of weak ice that runs laterally. From the north side to this wall."

I studied the wall. We'd seen it farther down and the lights showed it extending well up ahead too, splitting the glacier into two different levels. What had caused it I couldn't begin to say. It was the kind of ridge formed by sea ice that confronts landfast ice. Tides and ocean currents will cause ice pack to fissure and pull away from ice attached to the shore; when they come together again, the difference in elevations will often be many feet. Yet this was not pack ice and I could think of no rational explanation for the wall's presence.

Other deformations had disturbed me the same way.

Glaciers come in every description, but Hell's Flow was the only glacier I'd ever seen that looked like a moonscape. This faulting was one such feature. But there were others: craterlike depressions pockmarked the surface. Lunar clefts or rills were matched here by open fissures that cut deep scars into the ice. Pressure ridges zigzagged down the hill. And massive slabs of ice thrust up from the glacier like the volcanic cones formed by uncalculable turmoil beneath the surface of the moon. But this was not the moon. No meteors bombarded Hell's Flow; no tides or tectonic forces were at work here.

The effect was sobering, and completely mystifying.

"We will have to descend half a mile to get to the other side," declared Nils, gesturing to the wall.

Two steps forward and one step back. No.

"Wait a minute," I said. "Let me try something first."

I fed gas and roared off with my snowmobile, not even slowing until I neared the opposite side of the zone Nils had indicated. It was noticeably grainier, like a composition ice that had been sanded smooth, where even the flat sections of glacier could use some heavy planing.

At the other side I dismounted and walked back. Once in the middle of the weak area, I stopped and pounded the ice with my foot. That was not really too foolish and not really very bright. What was strong enough to support my machine would most assuredly support me, but what would support my machine and me together might not begin to support the Badger.

I came and opened Asia's door. "Step down, honey."

When she was out, I jumped on her running board and shouted through the open window to Nils. "Shall we try it with a little more weight?"

He didn't start out right away. He double-checked the Fault-Finder, played with the throttle, and then eased the cat ahead. Inch by inch he moved the tracks onto the band of smooth ice. Once there, the engine dropped to idle and the cat held its position. Nothing.

Based on his earlier performance, I fully expected Nils to argue against going across. Instead, he merely raised his brows and looked the question to me, his expression totally impassive, as though it were really of little concern to him if we advanced or not. Once I had believed that nothing ever troubled this man. When something finally did I should have known it would be Peter Masterson; I had managed to crack his phlegmatic character. Now it was back. He had come to grips with me and with Hell's Flow.

I signaled him to proceed.

Again we started slow. I myself would have taken the Badger across at top speed, but not Nils. It had to be this way. The ice below us growled and groaned as each link of the track lay down; sweat poured off my forehead and down the back of my neck. On Nils' face there was nothing.

I could feel my heart pounding in my fist that gripped the mirror frame. Two, three beats per second. The seconds and the beats came and went as the snowcat crawled ahead. Then we were across.

I stepped down and took my first breath in a long time.

The sledges awaited their turn.

"Okay," I shouted, "bring 'em over."

One by one the sledges crossed without incident.

Dolan came over with Asia on the back of his machine.

"What's it read now?" I asked Nils as I caught him checking the Fault-Finder meter. He nodded, saying that it seemed much better up ahead. "It looks," I told him while helping Asia back into the cab, "that we can push the readout just a bit."

"I don't know, Peter . . ."

The glacier didn't wait for him to punctuate his skepticism. There came from behind us a thunderous explosion, and I turned, wide-eyed, in time to see the destruction. If the snowcat were a submarine hunter that had just laid its barrage of depth charges, the results could not have been more devastating. The whole rough-grained region just collapsed in an eruption of broken ice that left a zone of utter blackness across our wake.

The ground shook unmercifully.

I had stepped to the ice in astonishment but I had not released my hold on the Badger—knees that feel like my knees felt are not to be trusted completely—and even so nearly fell to the ground as the reverberations caught me.

When it ended, I just stood there.

Nils should have said something; someone should have.

They never had the chance.

A second explosion sounded ahead of us. I whipped around and saw an area the size of a baseball diamond fracture into countless pieces and settle. The result was a massive depression that would be impossible to navigate.

Only two things emerged clear. It was a safe bet that this was the source of the craters that pitted the glacier. That was the first. Second, "pushing the Fault-Finder," would not warrant further consideration.

The Badger's lights revealed a portion of the crater that had cracked the ice all the way back to the crevasse behind us. We were trapped by those two pits and the high ridge wall with only the narrowest trail left between the wall and the crater.

As each sledge passed, ice continually broke away. By the time it was my turn, the path had narrowed to a few feet.

Such obstacles became more and more commonplace.

One danger after another took us into the night.

We stopped often for Dolan and me to warm up in the Badger, and each time we did so—after shorter and shorter periods of time on the machines—it took longer and longer for us to regain our strength.

The wind-chill factor was off the scale. We were wearing full facial masks and goggles and still the wind found its way into every smallest crack or tear, freezing our flesh in a matter of seconds. The cold worked through our gloves and pants despite the insulation. My legs lost all feeling below the thighs. Ice picks stabbed into my lower spine. I was in agony just working erect once the snowmobile stopped. Then I would have to pull my hands sideways off the ends of the handlebars and it would be many minutes later, in front of the heater, before my fingers would uncurl and I could remove the gloves.

Worst of all, though, were the times we spent on the move. The myriad lights weaved and arced over the icescape, finding, more often than not, nothing but shimmering, blinding bits of blizzard on which to reflect. The result was a dazzling circus spectacular that did little to illuminate our way and succeeded only in making a mind-boggling nightmare of navigation.

Crevasses collapsed in the darkness to each side of us. Some of them we saw and others we only heard, or felt by the vibrations along the ice. More than once the vehicles became disabled in the tumultuous deformations.

Nothing but luck spared Dolan a broken neck when his snowmobile careened into a depression that took all four of us to extricate. As it was, the accident seemed to aggravate the injury to his right leg. He limped back to the Badger, declining our offers to examine the wound. The offers were not made gratuitously—even minor injuries are potentially dangerous here and I feared that Dolan's was worse than we'd believed. Nils broke a track link on a slab of ice that he swore was not in his field of light before he had driven through. Only a good assortment of spares and tools, not to mention several precious hours, kept the snowcat in commission. Later, I swerved to avoid a crevasse and struck one of the sledges locking my ski in its runner. Before Nils stopped the snowcat, the two had become hopelessly entangled. When we finally got them separated, the snowmobile required replacement and repairs that wasted more valuable time. It was no consolation that subsequent inspection by flashlight could not reveal the presence of any crevasses in the area.

These were the four heads of Antarctica as I had never encountered them before. Furious wind never calmed. The death throe cries of ice never died. And cold intensified as we ascended. The taste and the smell of death were gone, but we didn't need either to know it was waiting in every opening of the ice.

Hell's Flow allowed us no relief.

Halfway up the glacier we had miraculously survived every peril—except one. We had approached Hell's Flow with a wary respect. Now we knew it better, well enough to regard the second half of the climb with horror. We had succumbed to fear, and I knew this to be the greatest peril of all.

It was apparent, studying Dolan across the little

stove on one of our latter breaks, that his nerves were shot. I doubted if mine were in much better condition. For several hours I had been conscious that my hands gripped the bars of the snowmobile with unnatural strength. My arms ached as much from unending strain as from the cold. I could not relax. My mental state was comparable to an amphetamine high; I was days without sleep, yet my eyes were wide and I shook with nervous energy. This mental intensity was every bit as draining as the physical activity involved in piloting the snowmobile.

I tried to play it down in front of the others, but my cool veneer was as transparent as the thinnest sheet of ice and, like it, as liable to shatter in the storm or melt here before the stove.

The last straw came once we were on the move again and I was in my position off the snowcat train's right quarter. There had been no warning on the signal light, so neither Nils nor Asia had any forewarning of weak ice. Likewise, the glacier itself had presented us no intimation of trouble.

What I saw was the third and fourth sledges drop bang out of sight. Then the fifth followed the others into a dark hole that had appeared out of nowhere and swallowed them up as though they had only existed in my mind.

I raced ahead to disconnect the tow rope, tying it to the fuel and tent-supply sledges. Nils, alerted to the disaster, had stopped the cat immediately. It was too late.

The last three sledges were gone. They lay in a smashed heap twenty feet below the surface between two sheer walls of blue-green glacier ice. Among the broken chunks of ice in semidarkness it was impossible to say how much of the supplies, if any, might be salvageable. Most of the rations surely would be. I slung a rope over the side and ordered Dolan below with his flashlight. After lowering him down, I rappelled into the crevasse behind him and used my knife to slash the bindings and wrappings and make a rough haversack for Nils to haul to the surface.

Food and medical supplies I placed in the first load,

about a hundred pounds' worth, and signaled him to
begin taking in.

The sack was at the top being unloaded when I heard
Dolan cry out and saw his flashlight beam arc into the
sky. Then one of the sledges came hard against my
legs and I went down too.

Asia screamed.

The flashlight had fallen into a crack at our feet. It
shone on the uphill wall. So startling was what it revealed that I was slow to act. When I made a grab for
the flashlight, the case imploded and the light winked
out. What had shocked Asia now startled me the same
way, to the same degree.

The ice was bearing down upon us.

All glacier ice moves, but never before had I heard
of ice that advances so rapidly that it can be detected
with the unaided eye. This wall had moved several
feet in the few minutes I'd been down there; and as
its speed would be unretarded by mere trifles of min-
eral and flesh such as we, it would close to the downhill side in a matter of seconds.

I shouted for Nils to lower the rope.

Dolan grabbed for the free end and started climbing.

Left in darkness, I listened to the glacial vise sliding
closed. The grating, rasping wail drove right through
my brain. Then came the sound of wood and metal
being crushed into kindling and scrap—all the supplies, into so much garbage. With my back to the
downhill wall I felt the other at arm's length. Then my
arms were forced to bend by a billion tons of unstop-
pable pressure.

I sensed ice just inches from my face.

The rope came flying down.

I could never have climbed out in time. Thank
heaven for Nils' incredible strength. No sooner had I
found the knot than he virtually yanked me from the
mouth of the crevasse, which crunched shut at my feet.

What had been a gaping wound was now a ragged
scar.

I lay there gasping for breath. In fifty years, our
supplies would reach the barrier. In a thousand, they
would reach the ocean where, eventually, they would

be calved with the other bergs and drift north into the Atlantic Ocean to be deposited onto the ocean floor. I had come that close to making the trip.

Dolan was sitting on the second and now last tow sledge and held his head in his gloved hands. "I'm not going on," he said.

I stood. "We're over halfway up. It doesn't make sense to turn back now."

"I can't go on. I've had all I can take."

When his head came up, I saw he was telling the truth.

I suppose I looked just as bad. My hands were shaking. I was breathing for two people and my heart was doing things that were, to aerobics, what a four-minute mile is to running in place.

"I suggest we locate a stable stretch and pitch a tent for the night," said Nils. "In the morning we can decide what to do."

It was bad advice, but that's what we did.

We made a rough circle of the equipment, tying a few of the huskies to each machine to keep them from fighting or running away, and then we erected the fiberglass hut in the center. A four-piece shell that technically sleeps only three, it was the only thing we carried suitable for the kind of winds that blew day and night, winter and summer, down that glacier. I needed food badly and we had enough left to eat well. I needed rest even more, and while I got very little of that, I wasn't alone.

Rest meant relief.

Hell's Flow would never allow it.

Nils was again the exception. He occupied a third of the space, reclining against one wall with his head propped on pillows, peacefully smoking a pipe that he had produced from a handy pouch once the lamp was going. When the lamp was turned down, Nils went right off to sleep.

Throughout the night, Dolan, who lay beside him, fought the worst case of the heebie-jeebies I'd ever witnessed. His quiet trembling ceased for but brief intervals and only then in favor of fits of palsied frenzy.

It didn't make me think any less of him.

In fact, if I'd lain still, I might have done the same.

The glacier suffered its own case of the shakes. Frozen pellets the size of marbles pelted the exterior without pause. It raised such a clatter that we could have slept more easily with our heads thrust under the hood of the diesel engine. Through this backdrop of violence the fracturing of ice would rise to a crescendo, climax in a thunderous explosion, then set the shelter shaking so powerfully it threatened to dismember. Each such explosion would seize Dolan in another fit of shivers and moans.

I was just as bad, each time breaking from Asia's embrace, leaving the shelter and making a round of the equipment to verify that nothing had been lost.

After one collapse that sounded too close, I returned to find Nils lecturing Dolan on his technique for facing the dangers of the glacier.

"We all died," Nils said, "the moment we started up. That's the whole thing. At least, we're as good as dead. We can no longer choose when or where or even how we die. We die here. If not on this spot, then on the next, somewhere on this glacier. We die tonight. Now. If we survive this minute, then we die in the one that follows it or the one just after that. We die the same way Sturdevant and Riga and all the other explorers died here—cold and alone. Hell's Flow has our names written down and marked for death."

"You're saying there's no hope?"

"That's right. There is none. But whether there is or there isn't, you've got to assume that you're dead now. That way there's no point in being afraid. Fear is an instinctive reaction to danger, the possibility of death. But for us death is a certainty. We committed suicide. Why look back? You, me, Asia, even the dogs . . . we're all dead. Once you accept that, Bob, you'll be able to face whatever Hell's Flow can throw at us and you'll decide to face it in the only dignified way. For that is the only decision left us now, that of choosing the way we go."

It was a good speech.

And I admired anyone capable of resolving such a conflict within himself. I know I never could. But for

Dolan's part, he hadn't been in any position that afternoon to consider philosophy. Nils and Asia had been
in the Badger throughout the climb, where it was 50
degrees warmer, 20 decibels quieter, and immeasur-
ably more favorable an environment for such rational
deliberations.

Dolan watched me crawl back under the blankets
between himself and Asia before saying, "What about
Peter? You don't think he's dead, too?"

"I don't really know," Nils replied. "I'm torn between feeling nothing can defeat Peter Masterson and
believing no one can survive Hell's Flow."

At some point during the night I was defeated by
exhaustion. I'd made a dozen trips outside. The others
were becoming more and more irritated at my crawling
over their legs and opening the door for the weather,
and I began to wonder if I would survive my companions. When I did sleep it was fitfully. I neither tossed
nor turned, for there was no room for either, but I
awoke often to horrendous disturbances. The last time,
I lifted my head at the distinct aroma of hot coffee and
pemmican. The kerosene lamp was up again. And Nils
was busily preparing breakfast on the top of it.

"Have you been out?"

"No, Peter. But I've looked out. It's still early."

My watch confirmed it. I noted that Dolan was
awake and Asia was not, slipped on my boots and
parka, collected the flashlight, and crawled outside to
check the equipment. It was black as Hades but midmorning light could not be three hours off. We would
be well advised to wait it out if the one hundred eighty
minutes didn't put too much of a strain on Nils' count-
down.

The huskies perked up immediately from the shel-
tered lees they had selected behind the equipment.

Directly in front of the entrance, my snowmobile
and sled were drifted so badly they might pass for a
hummock. It would take hours to dig out, so we would
be unable to depart before first light at any rate. The
Badger and both sledges we had drawn across the glacier uphill and windward of the shelter. Snow piled
four feet high against them, even over the hood.

Owing to our shortage of fuel, the diesel engine had been shut down. Another two hours with blowtorches.

When the light passed along the two sledges, I stopped. No drift piled in front of the second for the simple reason that it did not present a front to the weather. Long tethers had spared the animals, but the sledge itself had been crushed flat along with all the supplies strapped to its back. I moved close to examine the wreckage. It looked precisely as the last three sledges must have looked after being ground to pieces by the closing crevasse.

Yet there was nothing here that could have been responsible.

I had moved to the downhill side of camp, shining the light in a wide arc, when it occurred to me something was missing. There were several hummocks a fair distance away but no snowmobile. Dolan had left it within a few feet on this side of the shelter—now there was nothing.

Numb with certainty, I directed the light at my feet. There, drawn on the glacier floor, was a ragged edge that, as I traced its outline with the flashlight, described a flattened oval. A crevasse—at least it had once been one. It was filled to the top with drifted ice so that only a settling along the sides revealed where the broken crust had fallen through. Somewhere below, buried under God knew how many tons, was a snowmobile and dogsled with half of our remaining rations and gear.

I went back inside to give Nils the bad news.

The marking off of names had begun.

Also buried there was Freya, the grand dam of his team, and two other valuable huskies, dragged to their doom by collar leads while their desperate yelps for assistance had been drowned in the clatter and thunder of Hell's Flow.

Half a mile and half an hour after heading out, our expedition finally encountered a familiar feature. It was gratifying to recognize something but disconcerting that what we recognized the feature to be was six hundred miles from where it had any business being.

By all appearances, it was an icefall.

Across the width of the glacier a jumbled mass of ice boulders littered the surface in the same way it does the ocean at the edge of the barrier. The smaller among them were the size of a standard refrigerator, the larger ones, as big as a cold-storage warehouse. Here was a berg-choked sea, except the sea remained frozen; the icebergs, locked in place; and the space between them, often too narrow for even a rowboat to negotiate with safety.

Our Badger could not proceed.

The others held at the lower limit of the icefall while I took the snowmobile on ahead to find a trail.

If I had had misgivings about bringing the snow-mobiles, what with Dolan and me being driven half-mad the first part of the climb, I had them no longer. This was precisely where they paid off. And that was not all. It could just as easily have been the Badger that sank under the ice during the night, and without this machine, the four of us would now be afoot. There weren't enough decimal places on a pocket calculator to compute our chances of surviving a march to the nearest outpost. Unless that outpost was no more than a few miles distant and lit with a pyrotechnic display that would have put a July Fourth celebration to shame.

A band of light marked the eastern horizon between the distant barrier and the low overcast, the latter of which now seemed to extend to the limits of the sky. It was sufficient for me to navigate among the boulders; I had no need for the Badger's powerful floods. Nor for the Fault-Finder. Any surface that could support the kiloton pressures of these towering boulders could support my snowmobile with ease.

Once inside, I felt like a tourist at a polar pantheon. Bulbous columns soared over me. Some leaned together. Some had toppled onto others. I passed under arches that I couldn't have reached with a snowball and others that made me duck my head. A few might have been here since Sturdevant's time, but many looked as though they would be dislodged by a brief warming spell or a good swift kick.

I meandered for the better part of an hour. Most of

that time I spent weaving in and out of snow-white canyons that dwarfed my machine and me, like a rat in a white maze. Occasionally I was forced to turn back when the path became pinched off. I would pass between boulders so close at times both handlebars scraped ice. Again and again I stumbled upon a path wide enough to accommodate the Badger only to have it narrow before it joined another or wound its way through. Twice during the search I'd reached the up-hill side. There, the icefall ended in the same abrupt way it had begun. And the glacier beyond looked much as it had before, generally smooth and devoid of the kind of obstructions these boulders represented.

I cranked the skis around and fed gas.

To get the rest of the expedition through—that was the problem. But what nagged me was how this pre-posterous phenomenon came to be here.

They might have fallen off the mountains to either side. But I doubted it. Not in just this single band. Certainly there was no other glacier above this one from which they might have calved, for at the top of Hell's Flow begin the high plains of Deception Reach.

Nils was pacing restlessly when I finally returned. "You've found a path?"

"Maybe. It'll require a couple of modifications."

I gestured to the Badger's reinforced bumper.

Another time Nils would have frowned on such treatment of his equipment. But now he was dead, or as good as dead, and I guess he didn't feel the argument would be dignified. He slammed his door and engaged the engine.

For Dolan, the loss of his snowmobile was a god-send. He had moved onto the snowcat—more accu-rately, he moved onto the nearly empty fuel sledge, for there was no room for him in the cab and the box was no place to ride over hostile ice.

I could sense an optimism in the expedition for the first time. A relief from the ever-present perils. It was morning. We had a limited visibility. The glacier here was on record as being reliable. And yet as we headed back into the icefall, something inside of me could not believe it. Hell's Flow would allow us no relief. I shrugged off the feeling; one case of prescience was enough for an expedition.

Dolan's cry came just as his sledge was about to follow us in. I spun the snowmobile in a half-circle and raced to the rear.

Even before he stretched out a hand to point to a boulder midway along the edge of the icefall, I could feel the glacier tremble. It was another quake, like those that we had felt throughout the night.

The boulders began to shudder.

The one Dolan indicated, a roughly spherical ball of ice about the size of the Badger and at least as heavy, dislodged from the front line and started rolling down the glacier. It took flight over a hummock, hit the ice twenty yards downhill with a resounding explosion, and went bouncing its way down, picking up speed after every rebound.

It was so astounding a phenomenon that some little time passed before it occurred to me the mystery of our smashed supply sledge was solved. I shook myself free of the trance.

The tremors had strengthened. Nils and Asia had come running back; all around us, boulders were shaken free of their frozen foundations. One after another on the front edge broke loose, fell forward with a crash, and then rolled from one flat surface to the next, continually gathering speed down the glacier. Their acceleration was carried back to us in a series of sonic booms. Still others moved down to take their places.

There was nowhere to hide. At any moment the icefall could become an avalanche of astounding proportions. I didn't care to be downhill of that.

I popped the clutch and leapt up beside Nils. By that time it was impossible to make myself heard. I waved toward the icefall, hooked my skis in the direction of the path, and watched Nils jump into action. I raced off. When I cranked my head around to check, the Badger was hot on my tail. We roared down my path with every revolution we could coax from our engines.

Ice under us shook so violently as to make guiding the vehicles a sick joke; my belt track whipped me from side to side, and steering control—skis operate poorly when off the ground, which, in this case, was more often than not—became virtually nonexistent.

To each side mammoth sections of ice upended and crashed. The path I had staked out was no longer a path at all. Debris had buried it completely. We ended up at high speed down an alternate route that had not even existed when I'd passed through before.

A column that looked as big as the Washington Monument came crashing across my way. Without thinking, I accelerated under it, and only when it shattered behind me did it occur to me that the snowcat was now trapped back there. I hadn't reckoned on Nils Hellstrom. For a corpse he showed amazing resiliency. No sooner had I turned out on a side route in search of a detour for him than a massive shelf shifted its weight and Nils came whipping through like a madman. Regardless of the performance characteristics for which the Badger was warranted, I have no doubt that had its designers been here to witness this trial they would have been aghast that the snowcat was still in a single piece and running. Nils was somehow able to get more out of that machine than had been put in.

When we came against a barrier that completely blocked the path, we actually waited for several minutes for some of the obstacles to be jostled enough that we might slip through. The Badger could not turn around. Any one of those minutes, we might have been checked off the glacier's list; a dozen times we should have been pulverized. It was no credit to our skills that we were not.

Two columns collided. In the aftermath of frozen shrapnel and through a cloud of snow, I saw the snowcat climbing a 45-degree mound of debris that was left. It was only rated for 30. I followed in its track.

Moments later, a large mass tumbled out of our way, revealing the naked glacier. I almost laughed as we left the last of the boulders behind us.

We regrouped just up from the icefall.

About us the huskies began to gather; Thor was bringing up the rear nipping at the heels of those in his command who showed faint heart.

I had stepped to the driver's window to congratulate Nils when I turned at the sound of approaching thunder. Another boulder shot off the hillside above like a twenty-ton cannonball and came bouncing down past us to strike the back of the icefall.

We were not out yet.

"There must be another one up ahead," I shouted.

Nils turned a sick face to me and I suppose he was set to tell me what I knew already, that we could not survive another. But then he lost expression. Instead, he nodded and jerked his thumb to the back. "My turn again," he said.

I assumed my position off his left quarter. I had to admit that the very thought was overwhelming. In a way this was even worse, for here we had no choice in our tack. We had to go slow while the Fault-Finder showed us the safe route, and we had to remain there while the boulders came careening down the glacier at their hellish speeds.

If you figure, as we did, that we had exhausted a year's quota of luck, then in the thirty minutes that followed we used up a lifetime's supply. The quaking eventually subsided. Before it had, a dozen boulders had passed to the side of us. Some were too close to believe. Nils did his best to maneuver the snowcat away, but considering our relative speeds, doing so was a bit like a battleship dodging kamikazes. Of course, in our case, the relative sizes of the combatants would have to be reversed.

There was only one occasion when by rights we should have lost it. A boulder had struck the side of the mountain just uphill and glanced suddenly, directly toward the snowcat. There weren't two seconds for getting out of the way. There wasn't a prayer. The boulder took one bounce not ten yards in front of us, and just dropped through the ice. It all but disappeared from sight. Only the very top protruded from the circle of a massive crater around it.

Nils told me later that his Fault-Finder had indicated the glacier ahead to be completely firm.

By early afternoon we found the source of the boulders.

In a way it was another glacier, after all. The upper third of Hell's Flow was, for some reason, attempting to override the lower level much as pack ice will raft itself on the ocean. An overhanging wall—called an icefront—had formed the width of the glacier, and from it, particularly during quakes, icebergs were calving. Rather than falling into the ocean, they struck the lower level of ice where the rounder among them went hurtling down the mountain.

We traveled one end to the other in search of a route. The resulting icefall had created several piles that reached nearly to the top, but none was wide enough to accept the Badger.

"We can't abandon the vehicles," said Dolan. "We can't make it without them."

Nils growled at him, "That's only half the story; the other half is we can't make it with 'em."

I climbed up the top of one of the higher piles and surveyed the situation. On the upper level I looked around some more. "It'll take some muscle," I reported to the others, "but we can make a narrow track the snowmobile can scale."

"You're suggesting we abandon the snowcat?" Nils asked.

"No. That should be avoided at all costs. But there are some major cracks up on top. If we plant some explosives we can blow a good portion of this section of the icefront down. There should be enough of a hill left for the snowcat to climb."

"What explosives?"

I pointed to the three barrels of fuel still strapped to the sledge.

Dolan objected. "Gasoline doesn't explode: it burns."

"Gasoline vapors explode. A five-percent fuel-to-air ratio. Pound for pound it's more powerful than dynamite. We don't even need the barrels; we can just pour some gas down into the fissure and wait for the fumes to build up. Top off the Badger first—we can't pull the sledge up that grade—and then we'll use what's left to blow the face of the icefront down."

That didn't convince Dolan. He argued that without

all the fuel we would never get back to Mensa. We couldn't spare a gallon, let alone two or three barrels. I didn't even hear him out. Rationally I was still limping along; emotionally I was no better than a maniac. I didn't give a good damn about getting back to Mensa. The only thing I cared about was reaching that Russian expedition. If we didn't, we'd never get back anyway, and if we did, there was plenty of fuel for the taking. Explaining that might have helped, but maniacs don't make explanations.

After two hours of backbreaking work we had engineered a ramp of sufficient width to accommodate the snowmobile and its single dogsled. We loaded one drum onto the sled, roped it down; then, while I drove the snowmobile, Nils and Dolan struggled alongside to prevent the drum from toppling. After two more such trips, the drums were in position and Asia was working a hand pump to spray the fuel down into the fissure. Tarps were placed across the opening to prevent the fumes from escaping. The Badger was moved out of the lower fall line. My fellow expeditionists knelt upglacier from the fissure. I stepped just close enough to lob in a flare.

The explosion was everything I could have hoped for.

A billowing cloud of frozen particles rose from the destruction, out of which massive chunks of ice were sent rolling down the glacier and smaller bits and boulders avalanched the lower level. As the cloud settled, a rough grade of white scree leading right to the top was revealed. We set to work at once making it passable.

When at last the snowcat poked its nose over the edge with Nils at the wheel, Asia, Dolan, and I stood, mutely willing him on.

We were all numb with fatigue and fear—dumb with cold. Hell's Flow had drained us of every emotion. I don't know how the others regarded me at that point, but they looked and moved and even sounded like automatons, machines half-frozen into immobility but still, mechanically obeying instructions, autonomically carrying on against hopeless odds and in spite of any and all rational considerations.

We went back to dodging hidden crevasses and weak ice with machinelike indifference.

The slope was noticeably flattening. The summit should have been within sight had we the vision to see it, but we lacked that kind of vision. To us, the summit was a goal we approached with logarithmic deceleration, nearing but never quite reaching the point.

The snowcat's Fault-Finder had twice saved us from deceptive crevasses before the snowcat established again a worth of itself in a region of all but impassably twisted crevasses.

Hell's Flow had become a kind of maze again, and again we were rats searching for a way through. Only this time, the walls were not around us and above us but below us, cut into the glacier. Deep, often wide clefts that ran first one way and then turned suddenly and incxplicably at oblique angles, had formed a curious pattern of viaducts—tortuous elevated passages weaving circuitously in routes that more often than not dead-ended before they had gone far. We never found an actual path that traversed the maze. Fortunately, with the snowcat, we didn't need to. Its long tracks were able to bridge some of the narrower crevasses and eventually take us through the region.

When the last of the crevasses was behind us, Nils stopped and bade us gather for a final break.

"How far?" asked Dolan, his face deathly white and his teeth tapping out a rapid tattoo.

"Two miles, three," I said.

We had paused outside the box and were staring upglacier to where the white of the ice and the white of the drift blended with the whiteness of the overcast.

"What can we expect up ahead?"

I shook my head. "I haven't expected a damn thing we've already run into. I can't even imagine what lies up ahead, let alone expect it. Maybe it's a cakewalk beyond here; maybe there's something much worse than anything we've yet—" I turned. "What is it, Nils?"

"I don't know. A sound."

Just then I heard it too. It was coming from up the glacier, distant yet closing rapidly. It was a sound like nothing I had ever heard before. Far more raucous than that of icebergs calving from a glacier. This was the clamor of ice being literally torn apart and crushed at the same time. On a colossal scale. It drowned the rumble of the snowcat. Then it drowned out the roar of the wind.

The glacier began an ungodly quaking.

This was such a shocking movement that we tumbled to the ice and, working on hands and feet, found the Badger literally bouncing and moving off down the slope.

Then we looked up Hell's Flow.

It came at us like lightning—a ragged black line the width of a four-lane highway tearing its way down the glacier, first this way then that but always in our direction. I had never seen anything like it. Nor had I ever heard of anything like it.

Such things are not supposed to be.

Zigzagging toward us was the glacial equivalent of an earthquake fault. The glacier was simply tearing apart, and the resulting chasm was approaching us at a breakneck speed.

It zigged and headed right between the Badger and the snowmobile. Directly at the four of us.

Nils and I hesitated until the final second; Dolan and Asia raced for the imaginary safety of the snowcat. On impulse I jumped, grabbed Asia by the collar, and threw her back directly in the icequake's path. Nils followed my lead and tossed Dolan, screaming, in the same direction.

My instincts had been right.

At the last moment the fault zagged and shot directly under the Badger. Nils and I leapt to the side just as the glacier split, creating a chasm more than forty feet across. One second the snowcat was there; the next it was gone.

I rolled to my hands and looked around frantically, trying to assess our situation.

The quaking had not let up. Incredibly, it was intensifying. The chasm was constantly widening. And the opposite side appeared to be sinking as it moved away. I didn't realize how criminally stupid that assessment was until a heartbeat later, when it was too late. What became immediately evident even to me was that our side of the chasm was undergoing a rapid destruction. The unceasing vibrations were causing large sections on our edge to break off. Some bergs—for that's what they were—simply toppled down the side of the chasm while others slid out of sight in a kind of slow motion, almost like living things clinging to the safety of the wall.

I tried to stand and wound up back on my face.

My stomach felt like it was riding in an express elevator. That's when I knew. The opposite side of the chasm wasn't sinking; our side was rising! A massive upheaval was pushing us higher and higher, and the result was the fracturing of all the weaker ice along our edge.

Before I could shout for everyone to crawl farther back, a telltale crack raced between us and the snowmobile. It outlined a quarter-acre shelf of ice. Almost as soon as the crack surrounded us, the shelf lurched free of the edge and settled about eight feet into the chasm.

Then it crunched to a violent halt.

With a frenzy born of panic I got to hands and knees, pushed myself into a crouch, and dashed for the edge behind us.

Nils, between me and the edge and just then getting clumsily to one knee, looked up and saw me coming. He turned as our shelf began sliding downward again, and could see there was no hope for me to make it . . . none even for him with his extra reach.

Somehow he intercepted me.

I had launched myself into an upward dive. But the edge was rising faster even than was I, and the shelf had pulled away from the side enough to expose a minor chasm of its own into which I would fall when my hands failed to find a purchase on the sheer ice of the wall.

A hand came under my chest; another found my leg. And suddenly I was flying. Nils had tossed my two hundred pounds into the air as though I were a child, and he'd thrown me precisely toward the edge with the additional force I had needed.

My gloved hands found a grip. My chest struck ice wall with such force that I just hung there for a moment, stunned, burying my face against the glacier.

As I looked down I could see the shelf with Nils, Dolan, and Asia clinging to the top, continuing to settle in fits of stops and starts. Its base was pinched between the chasm walls, moving down as the walls moved apart. Steadily, the shelf slid out from below me.

What yawned beneath my wildly swinging feet was a thing that my mind could not accept. I was hanging above the Snake River Gorge, whose granite walls had suddenly frozen. Not so the Snake River, a hundred yards below where the sides of blue-green all but met. Only it wasn't the Snake; it was the Styx. And it wasn't a river. It was a raging floodwater, a torrent of froth and fury that rushed down the mountain with ungovernable speed.

Such things are not possible.

My feet only slipped when I tried to climb up. My gloved hands fought clumsily, madly at the slick lip of ice. Somehow I worked my way over the side and lay there on my elbows staring down in disbelief.

The shelf with my three companions was still settling. And it was tipping too. They were scrambling for the high side to keep from sliding off the edge and plunging the two hundred feet into the water. There was no hope for their survival. The chasm walls had stopped coming apart . . . now they were coming back together. The fault was closing. For what it was worth I now knew what had caused the strange vertical embankment running down the glacier at the lower limits. When the opposite wall came against mine, there would be such a formation. That much didn't occur to me until later. The only thing I knew then was that the closing chasm was crushing the shelf. The resulting fragments would plunge into the Styx. Nils, Dolan, and Asia. They would drown in the frigid water long before the walls came together. And their bodies would wash into . . . where? Perhaps into an underground burial vault like that in which Sturdevant and his men were eternally entombed.

I raced to the snowmobile and grabbed the rope we had used for binding the fuel drums. It was barely thirty feet. My hopes were sinking as I lowered it over the edge. Nils balanced himself at the top of the rapidly steepening shelf, plucked Asia off the ice, and held her over his head as high as he could reach. She was a good twenty feet short.

I guess I went a little bit crazy.

Things had come too fast. There had been no time to recuperate from any trauma before another was upon us. The satisfaction of surviving one catastrophe had always been crushed beneath the next. And it had been that way for two days of climbing.

Something inside of me snapped.

I found myself back at the snowmobile, jumping on the kick starter with more energy than I would have supposed was in me. I unhitched the sled, wound my rope into a coil on the seat behind me, and straddled the machine. A criminal psychiatrist might have a word for what the insides of my brain were going through. If I had then brutally murdered a dozen people, my insanity defense would have been ironclad. But it wasn't homicide on my mind: this was suicide. And I knew it was a charge for which I would never stand trial.

The opposite wall was fifty feet beyond. It was also lower by at least the twenty feet this rope was short. All that registered later. At the time I recall only the high-pitched whine of the two-cycle engine at full revolutions. With a psychotic calm I made a single pass to gain speed and then, standing against the handlebars, accelerated toward the precipice.

Ice raced under my feet at thirty, then forty, and finally sixty miles per hour and more.

The edge raced toward me at that same speed.

Then it was gone.

I sailed off into nothingness.

The snowmobile—red-lined—screamed across the chasm. I caught a fleeting glimpse of boiling rapids far below, of Nils and the others clinging to the uphill side as the shelf tipped even more acutely. Their faces turned upward to me.

The opposite edge came leaping toward me with the same astonishing speed. But not fast enough.

I was going to be short by a matter of inches.

Instinctively, I stood on the machine and leapt away. The crash of the snowmobile against the wall was lost in my own jarring fall upon the ice. My body landed shockingly hard, then slid a good thirty feet before I came to rest beneath a hummock. As I shook myself into consciousness and looked around, I spotted the rope, still neatly coiled at arm's reach.

Scooping it up, I scrambled to the chasm and threw the knotted end over the side.

The snowmobile had struck the wall below me, shattered, fell in wreckage to the shelf, and slid down the incline into the water. Nils and the other two were crossing the shelf to this side.

This time the rope snaked to the bottom just inches above Nils' grasp. He again pulled Asia off the ice and hefted her over his head. Once she had a hold on the rope I pulled her up. Dolan was next, and he was at least half again as heavy. I thought I would never get him to the top. He was smart enough to try to help by bracing his feet against the glacier wall, but from where I lay it appeared to me only one of his legs was worth a damn and my arms had to make up the difference. At last he came to the edge and Asia helped him over.

The look Dolan gave me wouldn't have been a great deal different if I really had murdered twelve people. "God damn," he said. "Just when do you stop, Masterson?"

"Can it wait until after we get Nils?"

Together we might have pulled the big Swede to the top, but as it was necessary to dangle the rope by leaning over the side, there was no way for two men to get a hand on the end.

I ordered Asia to take a good hold on one of my legs, Dolan the other. Only then did I lean over the side with a two-handed grip on the knotted end.

Below me the shelf was breaking up.

Nils, balancing precariously, stared into the rapids. He was precisely the type to walk off into the storm if he thought by so doing he could help out the team. Here he wouldn't have to take a step. He could just let go or lean over or do nothing at all and save us the trouble of trying to save him.

I called for him to take the rope. He looked up doubtfully. "If you fall," I shouted down, "I'm jumping in after you." The shelf fractured a final time and dropped out from under his feet; Nils made a leap, got a grip on the end of the rope, and hung there while the gorge opened up below him and the broken bits of the iceberg shelf tumbled into the water only to be carried downriver at a mad velocity.

I could no more have brought him up than I could, at that point, have climbed the rope myself. But this was Nils Hellstrom. Hand over hand and then using his legs, he shinned up as though rope climbing were an Olympic event, his participation in which permitted real competition for only the silver and bronze. In only seconds he was clawing his way over the side.

We lay on our backs for the longest time, taking air in dangerous quantities considering its temperature and the consequent effects on our lungs.

Then we got to our feet and inspected the remains of our little expedition. "The Badger is gone," I said between pants. "And the snowmobile. The dogs and the sled are back up there." I pointed to the opposite side of the gorge.

My ribs felt as though they were stove in and my left arm hurt like hell, but I was in no mood to mention it. When Dolan finally tried to stand up, I could tell his leg was more serious than he'd led us to believe. And where I'd thought both Dolan and I were in bad shape emotionally, Asia was apparently much worse. She was showing the unmistakable and dangerous symptoms of imminent shock.

But we were all four of us alive.

A quarter of a mile farther on we found where the fault had begun and, from there, were able to cross over. We descended the same quarter-mile to recover the sled and the dogs. By then the fault had all but closed, yet the sheer twenty-foot wall was hardly climbable. The sled was where I had left it and so were Thor and two of the dogs. Nils rounded up another four by doing some calling and sending Thor out after stragglers. The rest were simply gone, most assuredly dead, though we were never to find out how. Using the lines and traces, we hitched them to the sled and started back toward the summit.

The upper reaches of the glacier were strewn with crevasses and cracks. We were like ants on an elephant's back. Several times the sled alone allowed our progress. We would push its three meters of length across minor crevasses and cross it like a bridge, dogs first, and then us. The top half a mile we hand-pushed the sled along in front of us, sometimes taking thirty minutes or more to portage icefalls and cliffs. When we came to some massive crevasses through which we were forced to lower the sled, use it as a ladder for us, and then lift it up the opposite side, Dolan became adamant that we leave it behind. Nils and I were way past arguing the point. This was our last piece of equipment. And we were hanging on to it.

Not until the slope had leveled off and the surface had become more accommodating did we rehitch the dogs to their traces and push on with some speed.

Half an hour after that, we made the summit.

The high antarctic was laid out before us like a sweeping white plain. The only visible features were the nearby nunataks, mountains sufficiently lofty—in this case eleven and twelve thousand feet—that their uppermost peaks protruded through the two miles and more of crustal ice, exposing tiny hillocks of rock like minor islands in the deepest of seas.

Only the last of the midday glow remained up ahead, almost directly in our path. I used it for a heading and moved off ahead of the dogs.

Nils called me to halt. He was standing at the very apex, ignoring the sweeping majesty of Deception Reach in favor of looking down the wide ribbon of white that acted as a highway for the rushing flow of drift washing down through the mountains to the barrier. From this perspective Hell's Flow looked beautiful and almost serene. But it had been no highway for us.

He turned to me with a look of perplexity.

"We're the first humans to ever do this," he said. "One of us should say something. We should do something."

I remained stock-still.

The others too kept an awful silence.

Nils shook his head and at length lumbered to the sled and mushed the dogs off in the direction I had taken.

In the Body of the Enemy

We only got about a hundred yards.

I wanted Hell's Flow behind us. I wanted to cross that imaginary dashed red line that had outlined the head of the glacier the same way it had the base at Satan's Gate. There was no logical reason for doing so. The bergschrund, or semicircular crevasse commonly found at the head of glaciers, was absent here, a clear indication of firm footing. But the Peter Masterson who knew such things and whose actions were accordingly guided had been an early casualty of the climb. Myself, I was past logic and taking no chances.

Unbelievable things had happened to our surroundings in those hundred yards. Hell's Flow was indeed behind us. Once upon the reach we found ourselves asea in an ocean of white. The few scattered peaks that breached the frozen foam were a rocky reef on which no ship would ever be lost. Beyond was the bewildering expanse on which no ship would ever founder. No sooner had we turned our backs to the glacier and mountain crests and begun walking than they vanished as though they had ever only existed at all in our darkest dreams.

At the base of a last rocky outcrop that bordered the reach I called a halt and suggested that it was time for an inventory of our remaining supplies.

The emergency pack on the dogsled revealed a not immodest supply of equipment including a good compass, flashlights and fresh batteries, maps, field glasses, flares, tarpaulin, pemmican in good quantity, a four-man nylon tent, and blankets, as well as a few

other items that could easily come in handy. There
was even an odometer drag wheel, which we could
attach behind the sled. Then Nils opened a padded
case and exposed an object the size of a coffee can. It
was a portable burner for melting drinking water and
maintaining a good hut near the freezing mark but very
little more. The four of us closed in around it with
faces too frozen and minds too numb to express the
emotion that was in us.

We anchored one side of the tarp to the sled and
staked down the other two corners as best we could
before convening inside. For more than an hour we
hovered around the glow of the burner like Stygian
witches with our hands outstretched, our faces unflat-
teringly reflected in the pathetic little flame, spell-
bound by the stubborn defiance of the chunks of ice in
the toylike thaw pot. As each tiny pool of warm water
formed in the base, a tin was sent around the coven
circle to be tossed off with the eagerness of a magic
potion or an elixir of life. Between drafts we munched
pemmican in unmannerly large mouthfuls, our hands
being otherwise engaged against the Bunsen burner–
sized flame.

"I've heard of subglacial rivers," said Nils at last.
Dolan looked up and regarded him warily.

"Me too," I said. "But never anything like that."

"There must be a huge underground feeder . . .
from deep under the rock; the continental ice shelf
doesn't melt but well below ground the temperatures
are a little warmer. If a source exists and a feeder takes
it to the crest, then its course below the glacier could
be responsible for much of the movement and defor-
mation of Hell's Flow."

Asia, able to gather we were talking about the Styx,
asked if we thought this is what had happened to the
other expeditions.

Nils nodded in thoughtful assent. "Probably. Assuming the volume of water in 1945 was a fraction of
what it is today. Had Sturdevant's party broken
through a crevasse like that one and plunged into the
water, they would have been swept down a network
of tunnels. The cave we found them in was undoubt-

edly formed by erosion over millions of years, so it's not fanciful to suppose they were washed into it.'' He looked pointedly at me. ''But not by that river . . . not the way it is now. That torrent would have smashed their bodies into pulp against the granite walls of the cave, not laid them neatly down in their respective tombs. And that's not all: it's now moving with too much speed and volume for such a twisted route. You saw it. Blasting straight down the mountain as though a dam had burst. And the effects on the glacier were catastrophic. So much so that I'm tempted to speculate the source of the water is something other than a simple underground river.''

''There's no point in speculating,'' said Dolan.

I told Nils to go ahead and speculate.

''Geyser. A huge one.''

I nodded slowly. ''That would explain a lot. Only heat and plenty of it could deform a glacier so completely . . . cause it to undergo such devastating disruptions. Subjected to constant thawing and refreezing on a huge scale, ice would naturally be prone to cataclysmic disruptions.''

''That's not all,'' added Nils. ''Most glaciers have a foundation of clear high-density ice, flowable, yet still viscous. Extreme heat from an underground geyser can have melted the base to slush. No wonder it moves so damn fast!''

I appreciated what Nils was saying: in effect, Hell's Flow might be little more than a massive ice-choked waterfall of Niagaran width and depth.

''Of course,'' he added, ''all that is speculation. But one thing is clear to me: whatever Hell's Flow was when Sturdevant attempted his climb in 1945, it's much worse now.''

After checking his watch Dolan made to speak and I thought for a moment we might get an opinion based on his engineering expertise. But all he said was, ''Crest Four should be coming down anytime now.''

''Crest Four?'' I demanded.

''The satellite.''

It struck me that he had just changed the subject, and not very cleverly. As absurd as it seemed, I was left with the immediate impression that Dolan knew things about Hell's Flow that Nils and I did not. My impression was apparently shared, for even Asia was giving him a queer sidelong glance.

I slipped outside. The overcast was quite total. Any hopes of seeing the satellite come down were less than remote. If it were to fall within a mile or so, there was a small chance we would spot it. Or if it were to explode on impact, we might see that from a distance of even ten miles. But I doubted we would find ourselves within a hundred miles of the crash site, let alone ten. And I couldn't believe it would explode. There'd been plenty of press and counterpress in the last few years about the possibilities of nuclear weapons being put into orbit—there is no rationale in orbiting conventional weapons—but I didn't think we'd done it yet. And even a downed nuclear device doesn't explode; radioactivity might fry the crash-site locals or anyone else who's stupid enough to approach without protective equipment. The whole area might even be uninhabitable for an aeon or two. But it doesn't explode.

With that cheery thought in mind I crawled back inside.

"You can forget it, Masterson," Dolan was saying.

"What do you mean?"

"Any object plummeting into the atmosphere will glow enough to be visible for miles but only in the upper atmosphere. This cloud cover is a few hundred feet off the ground, and by the time the satellite hits, there will be so little left, traveling at such a velocity, that you won't have a prayer of seeing it."

When next we emerged from the tent all traces of midday light were gone.

The expedition continued in darkness with the batteries in our flashlights reserved for emergencies and for making compass readings on regular schedules.

Asia rode in the sled, wrapped in blankets so that not even her face was exposed. Her condition seemed to warrant it, even more so than Dolan's, whose lame pace held us to a crawl.

It was unbelievably cold here, much colder even than the barrier. I suspected the temperatures were in the minus 70s but without an alcohol thermometer—not included in our emergency supplies—there was no way to corroborate this. Fortunately, the wind had abated to a gentle movement almost directly against our backs that, though it stung our faces bitterly when we chanced to face around, did more to urge us onward than to slow us down.

Eventually Dolan traded places with Asia. His limp had grown progressively more severe, retarding our pace by the hour. While I had to order him onto the sled and Nils practically had to force him to comply, our speed improved measurably even with Asia walking beside me, letting my arms take much of her weight.

Her condition too had deteriorated steadily. She had become increasingly listless and by late evening she was completely remote. Somehow, Asia had divorced herself from our situation. Beside me, her legs accepted my cadence but it was a dumb performance, involuntary, much as her lungs drew breath, exhaled their crackling clouds, and her heart tapped out its shallow if syncopated beat. I didn't know whether this was from the effects of the shock or if it was just her way of resigning herself to the interminable cold and endless misery with only one possible relief in sight. It worried me terribly, for I had begun to care.

Nils was just Nils. The old Nils. Like Asia, he was apart from the reality of our trial but above it, not beyond. His spirits rejuvenated me until I felt that the Peter Masterson who had died on Hell's Flow was undergoing a sort of reincarnation.

But Dolan's was the true conversion. Some men are lost in crisis; Dolan found himself. He became a different man entirely, and for the first time in the year we had been together, I liked him.

He positioned himself at the rear so that neither Nils, who was manning the sled, nor I, in the lead, could observe his pain. Whenever I would turn around, his pace would turn suddenly strong and several times I caught him running to catch up, his face drawn in agony. He dismissed suggestions we break by saying he had just caught his stride, and as for the leg, he "didn't dare to baby the damn thing." When we did break

Dolan would be right there helping to upturn the sled and set up the tent. He was the last inside, the last to drink or eat, and the first to volunteer for watch duty outside. After barely a mile of riding, he rolled out of the sled and insisted he was fortified enough to walk.

By late evening we had left the rocky outcrops behind us at least five miles. We were on the perimeter of the high plateau, but judging our position by topographical features alone, we could have been anywhere within a thousand miles. For there are no features here. Any sheet of white bond can serve as a relief map of Deception Reach.

We navigated in the darkness by dead reckoning, using compasses, watches, and the odometer.

My flashlight had given out after numerous heading checks and I had borrowed one from Asia's pocket while she slept. As far as I knew, hers had never been used and yet the cold had sapped every microwatt of its stored power. I didn't know what kind of batteries the Russians were using, but they weren't the match of ours.

Unfortunately none is the match of antarctic weather.

Beside me Nils raised his own flash and turned it on the compass face. Though he had used it much less than I had mine, the pathetic orange glow that barely illuminated the needle and bezel was heartbreaking. Our NiCd batteries were the best available and rechargeable too, but in this climate they were good for only a fraction of their rated amp-hours. Of course, there was nowhere within a week's travel to recharge them.

"When do we turn?" he asked me. "David said the crash was more to the south, though you've been holding due west since we left Hell's Flow." He was right, in spite of the fact that the compass was showing our heading as almost precisely due east.

"We don't," I replied.

"You don't want to beat the Russians to the crash?"

"Don't be silly, Nils. What hope would we have of finding that satellite unless we could see it fall and at least give ourselves a heading? For that matter, what hope would we have for finding it even if we did see it fall?''

"What hope did we have for scaling Hell's Flow? After that, Peter, I'm not concerning myself with odds anymore. I don't say we're coming out of this with our toes or even our skins. After all, we still have to get back to Mensa and that means giving Hell's Flow another chance at us. But you have done more than I would have believed possible; I know you must have some plan for recovering the canister.'' I admitted it. "All right, then, you just tell us what we're going to do and we'll say 'yes sir' and do it.''

So I told him what we were going to do.

For a moment he just faced me, looking drawn and grim in the orange reflection. Then he swallowed, once, and dipped his head. "Okay,'' he said.

Despite a flagging pace and considerable justification for holding our position until morning, we continued westward through the night. I was determined that we must make at least twenty miles from Hell's Flow before stopping.

The breaks came more and more frequently. We needed every one. I saw my face mirrored in theirs and I looked pretty bad. Our exposed skin had been rather red after the first break leaving Hell's Flow. By nightfall, the burner flame revealed a gray-yellow cast to our noses, cheeks, chins, and brows. Blisters had begun to form. Chilblain had set in. Our hands and feet were badly inflamed. The emergency medical pack contained syringe and heparin, but I had held off dispensing any of the drug until our conditions would have proved irreversible. Frostbite is a condition of restricted blood vessels under the most exposed areas of flesh in which the bodily fluids literally begin to freeze. It is not painful. Neither is it fatal, though loss of the body parts is inevitable. If the condition is not treated and circulation is not restored, the onset of gangrene follows. Gangrene is equally painless, but it is very definitely fatal. Heparin, an anticoagulant, is produced naturally by the liver, but studies in Japan, where examination of atomic-blast victims revealed that radiation induces an excess of heparin in the body, further established that an overdose of the drug can lead to massive bodily hemorrhage. This proved every bit as fatal as gangrene. I was no doctor and no one of the others knew more about such matters than did I.

Eventually, however, there was no alternative.

The injections, thankfully, had an almost immediate effect, and the effects lasted for several hours. But after a series of injections that had taken us into the following day, our heparin supplies were exhausted and our symptoms had returned.

By midmorning when the odometer confirmed that the twenty miles had been reached, our chalk-white faces once again sported patches of lifeless tissue. We established our most secure camp of the trip on a shallow swell of ice in the midst of nowhere and prepared to sit for hours or possibly even days in the subfreezing temperatures of the tarpaulin tent. To a man, the prospect held an almost intoxicating fascination.

Twenty miles out from the headwall overlooking Hell's Flow was approximately the intersection of the Fuchs Expedition's Trans Antarctic route, a small leg of which I had seen traced along the map in Colonel Fedorev's tractor. It was the general north-south course of polar explorers traveling to or from the south pole from the Ross Ice Shelf, and for good reason. The same reason had led the U.S. Navy to install along here its nuclear-powered radar string. This route parallels the mountain range closely enough that the peaks—particularly farther north—were often in sight as landmarks and always within a day's travel by snowcat. At the same time it held away sufficient distance from the mountains to avoid the unstable weather conditions they fostered. And along this swath of reach from one end of the continent to the other, compass headings are easily made and suffer at once the least and the most deviation, as Fuchs was first to discover.

No sooner was the tent erected than Nils began tending to his dogs while the rest of us scurried inside. Dolan got the burner going, Asia sat between us transfixed at his operation, and I prepared to brief them on strategy. "The Soviets," I announced, once the flame was burning and Nils had joined us, "will come from due north." I indicated the proper bearing by pointing to a tent wall inasmuch as directions with an utter absence of reference points mean nothing. "Of course, if they're on schedule, they may have already passed this point. We can hope that they've been delayed en route. There's a good chance they have."

Bob Dolan furrowed his brows in dismay. "You talk as though you want to run into them?"

"Everything depends on it."

"All right, we find them. What next?"

"First of all, we make sure they don't see us. We lay to one side until they pass by and then slip in behind them. We'll try to follow them to the crash site."

"Then?"

"Then we'll move in and relieve them of the canister."

"Just like that?" He wasn't arguing. Dolan wanted it more than I did, but he was bright enough to see the plan still had a few kinks. "There are forty of them and they're extremely well armed," he added, mentioning only the most obvious one. It had surely occurred to him as well that it would be impossible for us, on foot, to match the speed the Soviet tractor train would be making for more than a matter of yards.

"I like to ad-lib my way through the details, Bob. In any case I have a few ideas."

Dolan tried to smile but found his face yet too frozen. "That's what we're counting on," he said. His eyes moved from Nils to Asia and then back to me. "And I don't resent your implication that the particulars are best left with you." By his glance I suspected that he knew Nils and I had already discussed some ideas. Yet when he spoke again it was only to volunteer the first watch.

Nils pushed him down gently and worked his way through the flap. As Dolan settled gratefully back, I started to ask him about his leg but almost immediately he was asleep and was still sleeping thirty minutes later when I went out to relieve Nils.

The absence of references was indeed complete.

Like the ocean, the African Sahara, or the Argentinian pampas one direction was now the same as another. But here, that bewildering description extended up and down as well as to all sides. There was no texture to the overcast. It was an opaque white of gentle undulations. And it reached to every horizon. If it were moving, I couldn't tell it. In fact, for all I was able to tell, we might have been standing on our heads with our feet in the clouds. Somehow the light of late morning cleaved the halves of our white universe, but it wasn't even possible to determine from which direction the light shone. Our altitude might have given us our first glimpse of the sun in nearly six months, but it was not to be. And it wasn't the cloud cover that was responsible. While the altitude was higher, so too was our southerly latitude. This section of the reach in these days would be graced with six to eight hours of twilight and nothing more. I only wished it were less. Headlights would be visible for five to ten miles at night, but in this dayless gloom that proceeds directly from dawn to dusk it would be too bright to see their headlights from more than a fraction of a mile and too dark for us to see the machines themselves from a fraction of that.

There was really nothing else to do but wait and see. And sit. Some men—Nils, for example—can just sit for hours at a time in almost any conditions, but I cannot. I started pacing. My legs took me around the camp while my eyes wandered far beyond that perimeter. After a very short time I had made a discovery: holding twenty feet away from the tent, I could make the circuit in precisely forty-five paces. After thirty laps I learned it was possible to work a barely noticeable path into the glass-hard surface of the icesheet. One step to the second, forty-five steps to the lap, forty laps, looking all around but concentrating on the north. As tired as I was, it sure beat sitting.

Nils can do it. Nils Hellstrom's conscience is clear.

Taking the expedition to this point had been surprisingly easy. But then, taking for me had always been easy. I was able to take chances with other people's lives and take responsibility for their deaths. It's

easy enough when you don't care. The one thing I
could never do was give. I couldn't give up and I
couldn't give in. I'd always felt that was good. Now,
I was not so sure. If the Soviets held to the route, they
would intersect our course here. But the operative word
was 'if,' and the question nagged at me: would the
Soviets hold to the route? It was the alternative that
really galled: had I brought three people out here
merely to die? Three people. One I admired. One I
had begun to like. A third I had begun to love.

The opportunity to ask Dolan about his leg came
when he relieved me in another half an hour, but he
waved my concern aside before the words were out.
The hour's rest, he assured me, had done him wonders.

Back inside, my shivering had only started to come
under control when Nils looked a question to me. I
glanced at my watch and nodded.

"I must take a turn, too," said Asia.

"No."

I lifted my brows at Nils. His attitude toward her
had obviously undergone a revision since we'd begun
the climb up Hell's Flow. Then I'd gotten the impression he hadn't cared if she froze or not.

"I'm okay," she said, turning to me. "I can do
it."

She wasn't all right, but she had improved. Despite
the obvious evidence of frostbite, her face had more
color, she was smiling, and her eyes were bright. In
spirit alone Asia was hardly recognizable as the woman
who had lain near death in the sled or sat staring dully
each time we made camp.

Nils' voice rumbled, "I just don't think it's a good
idea."

"She's all right," I said. "But if it'll make you feel
better, I'll go out with her."

Of course that was silly, but it was a way of keeping
peace in the ranks, and if I were going to pull double
duty, I wanted to enjoy it. We huddled together under
a blanket with only my head protruding to scan the
sallow junction of ice and sky.

"Why is it called Deception Reach?" Asia asked, her voice muffled from within the blanket folds.

"Because it is," I said, "what it is and where it is. A wide expanse of territory. A plain or, as here, a frozen terrain." I felt her arms around me and bare hands exploring the fastenings of my parka. "This plateau changes little in appearance or elevation for hundreds of miles to the west. Your nearest station, Vostok Two, is out there in that direction." I indicated the west but she couldn't have seen me because, having unbuttoned my parka front, she was burrowing headfirst inside. "Five, six hundred miles. And the scenery changes remarkably little between here and there. No formations. No landmarks. No nothing but ice. The same to the north and south for a thousand miles. Due south of us is the geographic south pole. Of course the pole is due south of everywhere in Antarctica, but as you know, the magnetic south pole is not south of us at all; it's right off the coast of Antarctica in the direction of Australia, just north of you." Something warm and wet was dancing circles on my chest. Her fingers found the tie string of my pant silks and immediately she began gently, slowly nibbling her way lower down. "Er . . . I should say just north of your coastal station at Leningradskaya. Obviously the deviation factor for compasses is high all over the continent but nowhere higher than along this strip from the coast to the south pole. A hundred and eighty degrees. Compasses here indicate that north is due south and south due north."

She kissed my stomach.

When I paused, she murmured seductively, "What about the pole south of me?"

If you think it's hard wooing a girl in front of two other men you should try it in 100 degrees of frost for thirty-minute snatches during which time you're both bundled to the crown. Particularly when one of the parties is two days without going to bed and two years without the best reason. That was the story. On my own watches I paced. I would grab a half-hour break and then go out with Asia to stand hers. Or sit. Or . . .

I don't recall how many rotations had passed before I poked out of the blanket to find Nils towering over us. Darkness had settled over the reach, but I could make out his huge frame facing off to the southwest.

I sat up hurriedly and scanned the northern horizon. Nothing. I looked up. "What is it, Nils?"

"There. Off to the south."

I turned and saw them. They were coming toward us, all right, but not from the north. Sometime before we had reached the intersection, or perhaps during the twilight hours, the Soviet expedition had passed us by. They had recovered the canister and were now heading back the way they had come.

We were flat on our stomachs behind a gentle dune of drift when they passed us a hundred yards to the west. Not until another hundred yards had been put between us and the last sledge of the last tractor would we dare to move.

It was quite a procession.

Seen from the side, moving by at parade speed, the thirty vehicles with their glaring floodlights were more intimidating than anything that could have rolled through Red Square.

As might be expected of a fully regimented expedition, each sledge was uniformly packed and the order of sledges behind each tractor was the same. The first two of each were tents, rations, and various supplies. Behind those trailed the flag sledges, fuel sledges, and finally the snowmobiles. But despite the electric pageantry involved with the night passage of so many vehicles over mysterious terrain, not a single human being was visible.

Their headlight display did illuminate a fluttering orange banner well up ahead on their course.

I nudged Nils. "They set trail flags."

He nodded. "And are now recovering them."

"What does that mean?" whispered Dolan, though with the roar of five diesel engines they couldn't have heard us had we shouted at the top of our lungs.

I turned and searched the darkness for his voice.

He was lying flat beside Asia on the sled. Nils, who

had somehow coaxed even the six huskies into a crouch, knelt behind the stowed equipment. No one moved. Nothing we wore or exposed would reveal our position by reflecting light with the exception of our faces, which stared at the spectacle with the intensity of children at a Macy's parade; the dune and the ruff of our parka hoods conspired even to obscure these in deep shadows.

"It could mean they don't want anyone to know which route they took," I said. "It might mean they don't want anyone to know they were even here. But the Russians always pick up their stuff when they go, so it probably just has to do with being stingy or short of trail flags. I don't care. For us it means we can not only predict their route but the distances between stops."

Dolan started another question but I told him to just keep his eyes on the tractor train. They had barely traveled across our path when the lead vehicle slowed perceptibly and a figure rolled out of the box behind. He trotted back to the flag I had seen, bent to the ice, and worked the shaft out while the train proceeded by him at its persistent pace. By the time he had it free and had stacked the flag on a sledge, the fourth tractor was passing him by; he scrambled behind it; hands reached out from the box to help him inside.

"They had thirty personnel in the boxes," I said, almost to myself, but Nils was agreeing. "If they're all moved to the forward two boxes and assuming they staked the standard third of a mile, then they can make ten miles before stopping to transfer personnel again to the front."

The wooden gates of the box slammed shut. One by one the sledges of that last tractor passed us by.

As the drone of diesels began to fade, I turned again. The long shadows of my companions were running out to the southeast. "We've only got one shot at it," I warned them needlessly.

Three hoods bobbed in the half-light.

When I turned back, the caravan was disappearing—pushing aside the darkness only long enough for the trailing sledges to slip by before the night closed in behind them—like a worm digging a hole through earth that leaves no sign of its passage.

There would be no eyes to the rear.

"Now!"

I leapt over the dune and hit the downslope in my best sprint. From behind me came the sharp report of Nils' whip. It was hardly necessary. The dogs were well rested and eager to run; my flurry of movement had been all the impetus they needed, and I doubt if Nils could have held them back at that point, had he tried. Immediately the dogs were up and driving against their traces.

In my left hand was a coiled length of rope also tied to the sled. If the others fell behind, I would help pull. Just then, as Thor slowly passed me, the rope hung slack.

We were gaining on the sledge very slowly. It was barely fifty yards ahead but my initial burst of speed was finished. It had been months since I'd had an opportunity to run, years since I'd even cared to. And not a single item of my arctic wear, from the heavy fur boots on up, were designed with speed in mind.

Despite all that, I was beginning to outpace the dogs.

I'd gone a couple hundred yards when the sled had edged up beside me; now the dogs were falling back. Ahead the sledge was still a good thirty yards and seemed to be pulling away. I looked back and saw Nils behind the sled not only running flat out but pushing with all his might as he did so. He was like a machine, powerful, indefatigable, with an output that could only be calculated in horsepower. His legs pounded the ice like pistons and the condensation gushed from his mouth in a virtual contrail. Heaven knew what he was using for fuel. Nils was giving it everything he possessed, for he knew as well as I did that if it were necessary for me to begin pulling, we were all of us finished.

Another hundred yards fell behind us. And another.

My chest was heaving, taking in superchilled air in volumes that would soon prove suicidal. Faced with the task of raising the temperature of each inhalation in each second 150 degrees, my lungs—like any lungs—simply began frosting up.

Sweat poured freely off my head and chest.

The result was almost ludicrous. On the outside I was burning up at the same time my insides were frozen so badly they threatened to seize.

When I stopped running I was going to be in the worst kind of trouble. But I couldn't think about that— I couldn't think about stopping at all. I rallied my remaining strength and struck out with second wind. My legs drove against the ice. Twice I almost stumbled. The third time I went down and saw my lead on the huskies as well as the distance I'd closed on the sledge over the last hundred yards disappear.

Worse, I lacked the strength to rise again. A minute earlier my lungs had known exquisite pain with every inhalation; now they were numb. My throat and chest had become a single heavy block of ice. The effect was very much like a blow directly to the solar plexus. My breathing came in gulps and stammers but my chest had ceased to participate.

Somehow my feet moved under me and I came up running.

Again we were keeping pace with the tractors, but that was all. They were much faster than we suspected. The plywood siding made them lighter than the armor we'd believed they carried. I'd been a fool not to consider that.

We raced on and on.

Then the tractor train seemed to stall.

The engine drone subsided and far up ahead I caught the silhouette of a man rolling out of one of the boxes.

It had been a momentary pause only, but it was all we needed. In three desperate leaps I grabbed the frame of the sledge and threw myself aboard. In the same movement I rolled onto my stomach, rove the length of rope through the tail ring, and started taking in slack.

I risked a glance up the side.

The silhouette was bent over another flag and working it out of the ice not halfway up the caravan.

In a matter of seconds I had the sled pulled in so close I could hear Thor panting a rhythm on the Jew's harp; only then did I tie it off. Nils stepped on the runners and rode them until the subsequent slowdown when the flag puller was taken inside. At that point he raced up beside me.

With the drag taken up completely, the huskies had no difficulty maintaining the pace the tractors set. Asia and Dolan clung to the sled; Nils and I lay back between the snowmobiles.

Several flag stops came and went before I was able to move. Several more before I dared try.

At last I sat up.

My parka lining, all my inner layers of clothes, were damp and cold. So was I, inside and out. But the feeling was nothing like it would be once the moisture compromised the material's ability to insulate effectively. Better to walk or move around, but this time I would just sit. All of us would sit. And for quite a long time if our figuring about the Soviet procedures was correct. Still, that little inconvenience was the least of my concerns.

I felt like the kid who grabbed a lion by the tail.

"Okay, you got me," the lion might have said. "Now, what are you gonna do with me?"

At the time I thought the four hours we rode on that sledge were the longest, coldest I have ever lived. Of course, I could not then know of the four hellish days that were to follow.

One of those hours was far behind us before the caravan came to its first stop. We crouched, huddling and shivering in the darkness, while the crackle of voices and the stomping of feet carried back to us over the idling of diesel engines. Within minutes the sounds—all but the diesels—faded away.

A flashlight started toward us down the right side of the caravan swinging purposefully, sometimes playing along the ice, sometimes exploring the vehicles up ahead. Sledge by sledge it approached until the fuel drums just beyond us burst into illumination; immediately afterward the flash blazed in our direction. Nils and I held our breaths as the pool of light flitted among the snowmobiles lest the tiniest wisp of our condensed exhalations be reflected. Abruptly, the beam darted away.

While the flashlight beam swung its way back to the front we helped Asia and Dolan onto the sledge beside us.

Nils put the dogs on leads and allowed them to run behind instead of being tied to their traces. No sooner was he back aboard than the sledge lurched forward.

Those were the really dark hours. We knew it would be a long time before the next stop and feared it would be much longer yet before we could get off and hope for any relief. The four of us huddled against the machines and lay still. They, like me, may have kept unwilling count of the intervals of rising and falling engine speed. Two decelerations for each flag, three flags to the mile, and ten miles between stops. There was only that to affect progress, for no geography ever checked our speed. The caravan glided with unfaltering routine over endlessly level, unfailingly smooth terrain that slipped noiselessly beneath the sledge's runners. Sometime between ten and eleven o'clock that night I lost count of the decelerations and never tried to pick it up again.

We were miserably, bitterly cold. Regularly and more and more frequently I pulled off my gloves and massaged feeling back into my fingers, rubbed life into my face, which became layered with a shell of frozen condensation. For my feet and legs there was no assistance.

My body shook uncontrollably. Not from either fear or fatigue. I was just damn cold, and so were the others. In these climates wind and humidity play as much of a role in survival as the absolute temperatures. There was a little breeze at the time, but it came predominantly from our starboard quarter and acted merely to negate our head speed; the air, as was common, remained relatively dry. And while the minus 50s is certainly cold by traditional standards, for Deception Reach it's positively balmy.

The real problem was now with us. My parka and

those of all of us were designed to maintain body heat to temperatures at and even below those we endured. But only so long as they remained dry. Once damp, the weather seemed to reach right through. I could not steady myself. Nils suffered the same fate. Dolan and Asia, who had not exerted themselves, should have been better off, but I suspected their weakened conditions had lowered the thresholds to their limits of endurance and that they would not last much longer than would we.

So we shook. The tremors at last became so violent that the involuntary effort began to wear our systems down all the more and so to reduce their tolerance to the cold. It was a cycle that would end in only one way.

Eventually, it became too cold even for shivering.

Our bodies yielded to the futility of any method for maintaining internal temperatures, of which shivering is only the most desperate. As a result, when midnight came and the caravan stopped again, the frozen silence we held during the subsequent transfers of personnel and inspections of vehicles was no credit to our nerves.

It had become a matter of physiology. I ran against that again when I tried to slip off the back of the sledge. Fluids that collect in the joints are second to suffer after the extremities have succumbed to superchilling temperatures. The joints quite literally begin to freeze. Not without considerable suffering I coaxed my legs and arms to bear my weight to the edge, dismounted, and adopted an agonizing hobble to the sled in pursuit of the blankets. By fashioning a kind of lean-to against a pair of the snowmobiles there was sufficient room for all of us to crawl inside.

Moments later, we were on the move.

Dolan had waited only for the reassuring acceleration of the engines before asking—through numb and bleeding lips that reduced speech to a mumble—how much farther we would hang on. I replied that I certainly hoped not much farther, but once that had been said, there was really little left of which I could be certain. Pictured in my mind were the maps I had often perused, photographs and drawings I had studied. But the truth was we had placed a bet against long odds in a land where Lady Luck seldom smiles on man. She is eternally cold, the quintessential frigid woman, and in the final analysis, no lady at all.

One-thirty the following morning found us peering through the snowmobiles as crews thirty feet ahead of us moved fuel drums off the sledge with military precision. Empty drums were returned half an hour later. It was the longest stop of the night. And the coldest.

The entire tail of the caravan was lit like a circus during that operation. It was certain that one or more of the half-dozen flashlights there would eventually find suspiciously unauthorized stowage on the snowmobile sledge or—more likely still—behind it in the form of the sled and dogs another thirty feet back. But they did not.

It had been my intention to keep a watch to both sides of the caravan, but not long after we had resumed travel I must have fallen into a kind of sleep. As a result, it was Bob Dolan who shook me and brought me up.

"There," he said.

His outstretched arm indicated a blinking red beacon well to the east of our course.

I reached a hand under the blanket to wake Nils, whose arguments that space and blanket shares be made on the basis of proportion rather than portion had gone unchallenged.

"It's time, Nils."

Asia stirred too, eyes widened in fear. "What is it?"

"This is our stop, honey."

While Dolan prepared to release the dogsled and the huskies, Nils went to work on one of the snowmobiles, undoing the straps that bound it to the sledge. I collected half a dozen five-gallon cans of snowmobile fuel, leaned out over the right runner beam, and lowered them to the ice one at a time so that they did not topple but rather passed back in a line to one side of the sled.

"Ready, Nils?"

His growl confirmed it.

At my signal Dolan freed the sled and animals. Then the three of us pushed the snowmobile to the back and eased it over as noiselessly as we could. It banged once striking the ice, slid several feet under its own momentum, swerved, and came to a rest slightly askew but upright.

I turned to Dolan and issued rapid instructions. "There's no time for reviews and no need—you know what to do. With any luck at all, we'll see you in an hour. Two at the outside. Don't wait any longer than that, once you reach the depot. That's an order! Do your job and then try to make it back to Mensa on your own. Remember, no headlight as long as ours are in sight." He nodded and turned, steeling himself for the leap. "And, Bob . . ."

He faced me again. "Yes sir?"

"Good luck to you."

Dolan smiled. His lips split in half a dozen places as he did so and the blood froze immediately upon exposure. His face was pockmarked by patches of gray and yellow. If he survived, which seemed unlikely, his nose and cheeks would require surgery. He would probably lose toes if not his leg. I had no doubt he was in extreme agony with nothing to look forward to but the prospect of an extended and arduous trek, alone, across the earth's most hostile environment, with which he was substantially unfamiliar and for which he was totally unprepared. Yet he smiled. I could not fathom why.

He shook hands with us, nodded curtly to Asia, set his jaw, then dropped off the back with an ungainliness matched only by that of the snowmobile, and landed with a concussive force only slightly more severe. Trying to favor his right leg, he lost his feet altogether and tumbled onto his back; not until he had made two complete rolls did he wind up facedown on the ice. Before the fragile afterglow of the caravan lights had evaporated and allowed the darkness to fold about him, we saw Dolan fighting awkwardly to a stand and starting back in his by then familiar—if so recently exacerbated—game stride toward the snowmobile.

I had Asia keep an eye on the beacon. Then Nils and I moved forward until we were looking across the thirty feet of ice and towline that separated us from the sledge up ahead. "You know, Nils, after seeing our fuel go up like it did on the glacier, it rather worries me to see them stow theirs so close to the emergency flares."

"Where are the flares?"

"Right here." I drew one out from an inside pocket. "If this should find its way into one of those drums, the whole sledge would go up like an oil head explosion."

"I agree," said Nils, taking the flare. "It could happen anytime."

"About twenty seconds after Asia and I drop off?"

"I'd count on it if I were you."

"As much as I hate to waste you on a diversion, there's really no choice. Dolan can't travel on foot and you can't translate Russian. This way you can be sure Dolan completes his part, which is just as important as mine."

There in the darkness we debated the various scenarios possible both before and after the film canister was in my possession. The two things we were waiting for arrived in quick succession. First Asia came up behind us and informed me that the radar beacon was now out of sight over the southeastern horizon. A moment later engines decelerated and our speed fell off.

"Okay, honey, meet me at the rear." When she moved back, I spoke quickly, "This is it, Nils. The flag puller is out. The same goes for you as for Dolan—we should be twenty minutes behind you. Thirty at most. You're not to wait any longer than that. If we don't meet you at the depot within half an hour of the time you arrive, you and Dolan head for Mensa."

He acknowledged it as we shook hands. Then, "Peter, keep an eye on her."

"Just as you always do for me, my friend."

I left him there alone and joined Asia. Taking her hands in mine, I looked into her eyes and watched her try to smile with about the same result as Dolan. What was it with these people? "Your mother's advice is still the best: keep your knees tight together. Land on your feet if you can and cross your arms over your chest so your body can roll. But the big thing is to keep your knees together.''

When her head nodded I pushed us both off.

The ice hadn't softened a bit since we'd left Hell's Flow. If anything, this was even harder. Or perhaps I had merely grown older. I know I felt like it. But there was no time to waste. When the caravan slowed again we would be under the brightest winter blaze Deception Reach had surely ever witnessed in its million years of waiting. I grabbed Asia's hand again, brought her up, and raced with my arm around her into the darkness to the west.

Nils' timing was perfect.

No sooner had the tailgates opened on the last box and arms reached out for the flag puller than the fuel sledge exploded in a spectacular ball of fire that sent a column of billowing orange flame a hundred feet into the air.

It was a magnificent display . . . despite the fact that all of the barrels did not go up simultaneously. That much became clear when subsequent explosions erupted in rapid-fire detonations, each with equally impressive results.

I had hoped some sort of cab-to-cab communication system was in operation—the flag-recovery system argued this belief—but as it turned out, no such device was necessary. That explosion could not have been missed by any of the lookouts in any of the five vehicles. Those in the box facing toward the rear would have sensed it had they been stone-deaf and legally blind, for the heat came to us at fifty yards and the blast literally shook the ice at our feet.

The last tractor halted. The third was next to stop and with it the fourth, and when the lead tractor stopped too, that was that. The door gates immediately opened on all five tractors; we could see personnel racing down both sides of the caravan.

Asia and I turned and ran. A black cloud had begun to build around the blaze exactly as though the night were fighting back against the brightness. It reminded me of the gaseous nebulae amid the blackness of space that snuff out the winter stars. This nebulosity did no less, effectively camouflaging the latter vehicles. As the southeasterly breeze carried it forward, the smoke engulfed one vehicle after another in the caravan, extinguishing headlights and taillights, spotlights and flashlights like so many pinpoints in the night sky. I had been watching for Nils to slip off the back and disappear in the direction we had sent Dolan, but the smoke had formed a perfect screen for his withdrawal.

And for our advance.

We moved forward until we were midway along the caravan and then I stopped to survey the vehicles lined up beyond us yet to be engulfed.

"Where do we start looking?" Asia asked.

"Probably in Fedorev's personal—" Turning to her I saw that she was holding a flashlight close to her body and for one horrifying instant I thought she was going to switch it on. I reached out fast, enclosed its barrel with a firm grip, and only then recognized it as the one I'd borrowed from her and believed to be still in my pocket, the one whose batteries were too far gone to emit the most feeble illumination.

As though aware what I was thinking, Asia smiled and wielded it in mock battle like a club. Until that moment I hadn't realized how fully committed she had become. She wanted to know which tractor was Fedorev's. "It could be any one of the five," she said. "There's no time to search them all."

It was the understatement of the day.

And the days here are six months long.

"When you were with the expedition, coming to Mensa, did Colonel Fedorev ever position his tractor in the middle, with the others fore and aft of him?"

"No. He didn't. Why would he do that?"

"He might not have had a reason then. I think he does now." Even as I spoke the words I knew my conviction was born of hope and not deliberation. Lord knows there had been plenty of time to deliberate the matter. And yet I had a hunch. The electronic equipment and the unusual furnishings in the box of Fedorev's tractor made it unsuitable for either role of dropping off or picking up the shifting flag pullers. There was also the canister to be protected on this return trip. Fedorev might like the idea of having his men positioned around him for simple reasons of security. All that I had considered in the hours I'd lain shivering on the sledge. But my assumption now had another leg, and this one had some real meat on it. No one had alighted from the third vehicle. I'd seen a door open all right and a head had poked momentarily out, but as men hurriedly trooped by on each side of it, the door had closed again without anyone descending. The face had been that of the old radio operator.

I pulled Asia along in a low crouch until we were directly opposite that tractor. Warily I led her to the rear cabin, where the two doors were only slightly ajar.

Then, still kneeling below the door gates, I slipped off my goggles and face mask to peer through the crack, and Asia beside me did the same. Neither one of us got a peek.

With a bang both doors flew open.

Behind each stood a parka-clad trooper and in the hands of each was an automatic weapon pointed directly into our faces. I say "our faces," though both barrels seemed to have an attraction for mine. The guy to my left had a submachine rifle with the action already back; the other held a pistol with a muzzle so large I could have poked my thumb in it.

I didn't move.

The one with the handgun shouted something in Russian I didn't catch, and a moment later I felt something hard grind into my ribs from behind. A fourth man appeared around the corner to my right but on the other side of the tow rope. He was dressed the same as the others and armed the same, but his goggles were unique. They were night glasses. And like an idiot I assumed they were of the starlight type, which magnify infinitesimal available light. What they looked like were infrared glasses, but since those require a source or signal of infrared light, I didn't stop to think: any operator so misguided as to use starlight glasses within a mile of this electric circus would have fried his optic nerves.

More orders came from the pistol packer, whom I now recognized as Lieutenant Whatsizname . . . Shokin, the guy who had spent the night in my room with Major Zhizn, the KGB officer. I didn't catch those orders either, but when the fourth trooper saluted, about-faced very smartly, and disappeared toward the rear of the caravan, I didn't doubt for a second his instructions were to bring Colonel Fedorev with additional troops.

"Meestur Masterson."

I caught that all right.

From behind the two soldiers a third had appeared. It was Major Zhizn. He had been sitting at the back near the radio set and the aged operator waiting for the drift to settle—so to speak—before coming in to enjoy the show. His humorless smile was still frozen in place, but now it was oddly enough his eyes that revealed a kind of eager delight. For the first time since I'd met him, Major Zhizn was happy.

A cold sense of defeat began to fill me. It surged through my body and for the first time that night I realized how tired I truly was. I might have cursed my stupidity. I would, too. Later. But recriminations could wait for defeat; defeat, for death. Just then my mind was pushing aside the fatigue. I was realizing something that should have struck me at once. Without taking a step, Major Zhizn was strutting. He was standing arrogantly between the other two, smoking, with his left arm folded under his right and his right clutching the long hollow filter of his Papirosi like a swagger stick. All of which was incidental.

Zhizn was not armed.

It was only three against my one.

The man who ground his weapon into my back had made a mistake, too. As long as his barrel remained there, I knew precisely where he was and could move accordingly. Of the two before me, Lieutenant Shokin had his hammer forward and I doubted if the first round was fired double-action. I'd take the chance. A second

gained there. Two, if no round were chambered. The
other man had twice glanced toward the rear, over my
head. If only he were to be distracted, however briefly.
He would be the one I'd go for.

In the back of my head was Asia with her bludgeon
of a flashlight. The only one close enough for her to
reach was the man behind me. I didn't doubt for an
instant that she would attempt it. Counting the old
man out it was not even three to one at all but three
to two. Odds I could live with. The sense of defeat
was leaving me. But it had left very little in its
wake. I was empty. Only the cold remained. I was
devoid of any sense or feeling or emotion save for
the cold.

The seconds passed but there was no distraction.

I couldn't wait much longer. In a very short time
the odds would change again, and very much so for
the worse. Every moment worked against me.

It occurred to me that even were Asia in no position
to strike, she could still be our salvation. They would
surely recognize her; that would be all the distraction
I'd need.

I leaned slightly forward, letting the balls of my feet
take my weight. My knees flexed imperceptibly.

Now even the cold had vanished.

Exhaustion was gone.

Any second. Yet no one paid her the slightest mind.

Certainly the light had faded noticeably even in the
last few seconds. As the smoke drifted forward, mask-
ing the headlights of the rearward tractors, our faces
would be harder and harder to discern. Then, too, Asia
was no longer the attractive woman who had been a
part of their expedition. Like me, she was deathly pale.
Lifeless tissue spotted her face, and again like me, she
was a promising candidate for permanent scarring. She
looked like a resurrected victim of Hell's Flow. Like
me.

The surprising thing was that they recognized Peter
Masterson.

The first black vaporous veils wafted past me. It had
reached this far up the caravan. I couldn't afford more

than another few moments, but each moment—at least until Fedorev arrived—was now working for me.

By degrees the smoke gathered until it was all we could manage to see one another. The old man spoke for the first time, indicating, in an ancient tenor accompanied by gestures that even I was able to translate, the two open doors through which the smoke had begun to invade on the very sensitive electronic equipment. Through the same doors the heat had begun to defect—or, in their case, as it was departing without permission, betray the cabin. Major Zhizn glared at him and replied in kind. Then he flicked ashes off his Papirosi and, using it, waved both of us inside.

I took my time helping Asia up in front of me. Then I climbed up and faced the lieutenant. He wasn't looking at me at all but peering instead into the distance through the black clouds.

It was now or never.

I swung in a half-circle, caught the trooper beside me with both forearms, and sent him flying backward onto the ice. As I came around, the pistol was leveled at my midsection and the lieutenant's thumb—fighting his clumsy, thick arctic glove—was working the hammer back.

One second!

I rushed him with both hands out.

Two seconds!

Before I could reach him he made the mistake of taking a step backward in order to equalize the distance between us. He backed right off the tailboard and swung his arms in a futile effort first to regain his balance and subsequently to land on something other than his head.

Zhizn had backed up too. All the way to the radio.

As he fumbled in his parka for his holstered weapon, a 9-millimeter Makarov, my fist caught him just below the right eye with all my weight behind it, and when he dropped, it was with all his weight that he hit the floor of the tractor. In a single movement I whirled and snatched up his pistol, bringing it to bear on the three men below me.

I was too late.

The third trooper could have killed me. He probably
would have, too, but something intervened that frightened him much more than I did with that little popgun.
Nils Hellstrom had appeared out of the black mist like
a mammoth polar bear fully reared, fully riled, with
no more business being in this place than my friend
with his strict instructions. The trooper spun. Nils
plucked him off the ground and, after rendering him
quite senseless, used him as a broom to dust the other
two unfortunates under the tractor.

"They sent a man for reinforcements," I shouted.

He stood after depositing all three in a single heap.
"Resting comfortably under a supply tarp."

I gave him a wink. "Very tidy. As long as you're
here, will you please see that we're not disturbed?"

Asia and I closed the doors and turned to the radio
console.

Darned if that old man wasn't making a dive for
something on the panel. I pushed him aside and
scooped up the prize: a battered, blackened box about
the size of two cigarette cartons. American, not Papirosi. There was only one thing it could be. As I
shoved it in a pocket, the old coot surprised me by
lunging at my arms. He was too old to hit and too
committed to ignore, so I wasted thirty precious seconds wrapping him up and getting him situated in a
corner.

That left just one little errand.

"Tell me how to use this, quick!" I was sitting at
the radio set with its maze of controls all marked in
Cyrillic script.

"I don't know."

I turned full on her. "Why do you think you're
here?"

"Because I don't want to lose you."

Together we faced the machine. It was eight feet
wide and three high off the shelf. There must have
been a hundred knobs and meters, switches and indicator lights.

"Do you see one that says 'on/off' or 'power'?"

She looked around, finally centered on a particular

toggle switch and indicated the upper throw as activated.

A light came on; the radio began to hum.

"Now, where is the frequency adjustment? The tun-
ing knob. It'll say 'hertz' or 'kilohertz.' Something
like that." When several seconds had passed and she
had made no discoveries, I latched on a knob near a
wave-band meter and asked her about it.

"It says cycles."

"That's the same thing. Kilocycles?"

"Uh . . . yes. Cycles in thousands."

After some more translating I held up a hand.
"Okay, I'll figure out the rest." I started to escort
her to the back, but stopped on the one wall that was
white with large-scale survey maps tacked together
in a floor-to-ceiling montage of the expedition's
progress. Detailed in black was an enlargement of
the route I'd seen in Fedorev's map case. Different
colors were used to ink in an apparent triangulation
leading them to the downed U.S. satellite's location,
and still others to plot the magnetic headings that
would take them back to the barrier. I had Asia do
some more translating there but she wasn't much help
and neither was the map, for apparently they had no
designated pickup point. They were obviously going
to descend off the reach and make radio contact with
their aircraft as soon as they ran into clear weather
and fair ice. At the doors, I stopped and told her.
"It's not going to be any easier getting back, Asia,
if we do get back at all. You have your choice of
staying here with them. It's not much of a choice, I
know, but at least you'll be alive."

"In the Soviet Union I am worse than dead. No,
Peter. I am going back with you."

I bent down and kissed her. In that cabin we found
the first warm place the two of us had known together, and our faces, our lips, were so cold and
cracked that any enjoyment we experienced from the
contact was purely transcendental. We made it short.
When I came up I tried to smile and, as I did so, got
my first glimpse of the thing in Robert Dolan that
had put him to it.

"Here," I said, pressing the small automatic into her hand, "you'll need this more than I will."

Then I turned, pushed open the door, and stared.

Half a dozen bodies were strewn haphazardly on the ice in uniform conditions of incapacitation. Nils Hellstrom was calmly stowing them away under the tractor body. Not the slightest sound had we heard. This was the man I had always known to be adamantly opposed to violence of any kind.

"Neighborhood going to hell?"

He looked up.

"Unexpected reinforcements. Ready to go?"

I lowered Asia to him but backed up a step after she was down. "I've still got fifteen minutes left, Nils. Take her to the depot right away. Along with this." I tossed the canister into his hands. "You've got an hour to make it there, right? The important thing now is for that to get back to Mensa. Don't wait any more than the fifteen minutes once you reach Dolan. Understand?"

He didn't like it. But he knew I was right.

This time I made sure he was on his way before closing the doors. I spent another quarter-hour with the machine. At the time I had no idea if it was fifteen minutes wasted or not, for I never was able to raise McMurdo or get any reply on the international emergency frequency. At the end of that time, I headed for the doors brushing against a white steel cabinet bolted to the wall opposite their montage of maps. It was about the size of a small bookshelf. Obviously a first-aid cabinet, though bigger and better stocked than those in the other tractors. A thought struck me. The cover plate was securely padlocked but that didn't bother me, since I knew where they kept the master key.

Outside, the pile of bodies was stirring but otherwise intact. I went forward to the cab, found the transmission assister, and returned to the box. I can now testify that a Russian padlock can withstand no more than half a dozen blows with a ten-pound sledge. Inside I found, as expected, a field medical supply, as hoped, abundantly stocked. Some intemperate searching soon rewarded me with a small vial of tablets that look much the same in any country of origin and whose Russian and English names, I was happy to discover, are pretty near cognates.

I made to leave again—the sledgehammer was still in my hand as a possible weapon—when I happened to sweep a last glance over the radio console.

What the hell, I thought.

It would only take another minute.

Lion by the Tail

What I did next was the sort of stunt one might expect of any greenhorn tourist, an escorted-adventurer fresh off the cruise ship. I got lost.

It was my own damn fault.

Yet at the time I cursed Antarctica in tone and phrase that would have shocked even the most seasoned explorer.

The ice shelf that had glided so smoothly beneath our sledge's runners those last twenty-five miles had somehow—once I was afoot—vanished completely. In its place was an obstacle course. The gently rolling plains had become a rugged range of dunes. A surface sanded runway-flat and smooth by windswept, hard-grained névé had inexplicably here been carved into a myriad obstructions that included ravines and grottoes and jagged barricades of ice. As a matter of fact, every glacial feature that can hinder navigation and whose absence on Deception Reach I had foolishly lamented enjoyed a staggering presence on the terrain between the Soviet caravan and the radar depot.

It didn't happen right away.

I'd backtracked my route away from Fedorev's tractor; once well to the rear of the still-burning fuel sledge, I left the Fuch's Trail and started double-timing to the southeast. In the direction of our last sighting of the radar beacon. Finding the depot was simply a matter of holding that heading until the beacon reappeared. It turned out to be not so simple.

At first I was able to keep a healthy pace.

Health—my immediate health—had called for speed.

All I could muster. But I didn't dare to run. My parka had only begun to dry out and another drenching would have finished me in the long run as surely as a large-caliber Russian bullet with impressive muzzle velocity. Anyway I was too tired and cold. This was a good part of the problem. My knees simply refused to rise. I dragged my feet over the ice, half-jogging, half-Nordic-skiing without benefit of skis.

The first time I went down it was from tripping over a ripple etched not two inches high. The first in an ocean of ripples.

In fact, I had sprawled headlong more times than I could count while the ice was still reasonably accommodating. When the obstacle course began, I was more often prone than plumb.

There had been signs. The most obvious—a warning characteristic to both poles—was the sastrugi, Cheval's *glace ondulée*. These symmetrical wavelike ridges running perpendicular to the direction of the wind are higher and harder on the crests than the ripples; lower, softer in the troughs. It was like walking on railroad ties and required a leapfrog stride to take them in pairs or an awkward shortened step to hit every one. I tried compromising and landing every other time on the crests, but that got me too. The troughs were of maddeningly varying compaction; sometimes my foot wouldn't sink at all and other times it would be embedded up to the knee. Trying to second-guess the snow was impossible.

I didn't know how good I'd had it until the sastrugi undulations began building, separating. Very shortly it was all I could do to leap from crest to crest where misjudging the distance or simply failing to hold the slick rounded surface meant falling into a trough and risking waist-deep burial in snow.

Each wave was higher and wider than the last. Each trough was deeper. Before long they had gathered into the eight-scale swells of a tropical storm. But by then they had lost all claim to symmetry. These swells ran in every direction, doglegged, stopped, abutted one another, and created labyrinthine channels from which it was impossible to see over or navigate through.

Had I Nils Hellstrom's arctic savvy I would have given up the direct route on encountering the sastrugi, as he and Asia had given it up after realizing what that phenomenon forewarned. He had tracked the waves around to the west, picked up the border of the Fuch's Trail and followed it south before turning back to the east around the field of obstacles.

Not Peter Masterson.

After all, Peter Masterson never gives up.

As a result of that unforgivable mistake and the time lost to it, I gave the Soviets their chance to regain the upper hand. Worse, I set the stage for the curse of Hell's Flow to be fulfilled.

By the time I realized this, there was no turning back.

I was staggering mentally and physically from so many brutal landings. My battered sides and legs were throbbing; my sense of direction was so bewildered that finding my way back seemed no less insurmountable a task than pushing on. So I continued. Continued to lose my feet on the climbs, lose time on the detours, lose myself deeper and deeper in the disturbed area.

Slopes barely 15 degrees of grade were so slippery that without an ice ax, they were all but unscalable. It became standard procedure for me to take the hills on hands and knees and glissade down the opposite sides. Though the term *glissade* is inexcusable flattery. I slid down all right, but willy-nilly, and when I got to the bottom, I stopped only by happening upon some obstruction sufficiently unyielding to withstand a high-speed collision with my two hundred pounds. Otherwise, I continued unchecked to the next upward slope.

Fortunately there were many obstacles for me to strike.

One of the little valleys was littered with pillars supporting gale-hewn carvings that could have passed for a nighttime outdoor exhibition of ice sculptures. All of it modern art. All of it decades in the making. The pillars were a series of seracs, irregular pinnacles formed by the imperceptible but methodical movement of the continental ice shelf; atop them the wind had chiseled the compacted neve with its delicate hand, creating here a fragile interpretation of a bush in frazil ice, there a grotesque bulk of twisted growth, and nowhere two of them the same.

Those I didn't slide into I walked into, for that was the rest of my problem, being little better than blind.

This near the south pole as summer approaches, complete darkness prevails only in the midnight period for the sun, while edging toward the horizon, never goes far below it. In spite of the fact that several hours stood between myself and dawn it was possible to see for a very limited distance. The sky was a dark gray, one shade away from black. So too was the ice shelf. From my aspect this meant barely light enough to see but hardly anything that can be seen—ice, after all, is ice. In such limited light my depth perception was practically worthless, and that's not all. Cloudy conditions on the poles often white-blind a traveler in the middle of the summer day; it can happen doubly fast when the same conditions exist at night. The upshot was that I spent much of my journey with hands outstretched.

Occasionally the wind would bring sounds to my ears. Distant whines and poppings. Like high-torque, gasoline engines, I thought, but the wind always carried them away before I could identify the sounds for sure or tell from which direction they had come.

Some time after leaving the exhibition of glacial art I found myself descending into a canyon where progress for a while was dangerously rapid and it became easy to overstep caution. A regular converging of the canyon walls failed to concern me as long as I was headed in the right direction, but when the walls steepened, arced high overhead, and finally met, my world was turned a darker shade of gray, which became, at that point, completely black after all.

Wind had bored a tunnel through the ice. No machinery could have made a neater job of it, for any cross section would have scribed so nearly a perfect circle as makes no difference and the diameter did not vary remarkably from one end to the other.

As soon as I felt the wind in my face, I knew there would be a way out as surely as there had been a way in. I might as well have closed my eyes for all the vision that tunnel afforded me, and yet it was the longest stretch of the evening when I did not fall. My hands were still out and occasionally they confronted sleek walls on my left or right, but for the most part I followed my nose and, though the tunnel twisted side to side like a serpent, was led through without incident.

My welcome to the outside came in a familiar form.

The opening was there—another valley, beyond and below. I stepped to the edge to survey my descent when *bang!* went my feet out from under me. The lip had collapsed. I tried to twist onto my stomach to stop my fall but it was no good. I started rolling, and once that happened I was out of control again. How far I slid I don't know, but I do know that when I came to a rest some time later, I looked up and behind me at the apex of the slope and saw the tunnel opening as no more than a black dot against the gray.

Climbing to the top of the opposite bank gave me a vantage but little cause for confidence. There was no sign of the beacon or my friends. Icy dunes on every side. What of every side I could make out. There was only one small glint of light and that was the one in my brain beginning to dawn on my dilemma.

Without a flashlight I had no sense of time or direction, for I could check neither my watch nor the compass. There might be enough light to see both in a matter of hours but by then it would be too late. One hour was all I had allowed for me to reach the depot. That much time must have already passed. I should have reached it by now. I should have seen the beacon two miles back. So I was in the wrong place—worse, I didn't know where was the right place. But there was no starting over, no turning back. Fedorev's people were surely on my trail. And even if I wanted to, I could neither backtrack my way to the tunnel nor find my route back from there if my life depended on doing so, which, I was at that point convinced, it did.

I swore aloud. Good and loud.

And then I did the one thing no one is permitted here.

Not even a greenhorn tourist.

I panicked.

The next hill was higher yet and I decided that beyond, the beacon would have to be visible. My slide was immediate and painful and I didn't stop until I was at the bottom. Then I was up and scrambling frantically at the higher grade. Three times I fell back to the foot of the slope and had to start over. Each time I did so, it was with an ever-wilder determination.

At the top I found myself panting for breath.

No sign of the depot.

I started running.

How many dunes I crossed is for Antarctica to say. How many times I fell has been permanently erased from my memory by a system of mental defenses genetically in place in the ancestors of man before Antarctica itself calved from the supercontinent of Gondwanaland. Only the last fall is still with me. It wasn't so much the ice as it was my muscles, numb with the multitude of blows and drained of energy. Mentally and physically I was in a state of total depletion. When I started sliding I just lay back and let it come. I must have slipped around and shot headfirst into a hollow in a wall of ice because, when I came to after some little time, that was where I lay. More of a grotto, really. It was a perfect shelter from the wind and a damn decent place to hole up. Assuming one was in no hurry to get anywhere.

My panic was gone.

I sat up and looked out at the rolling clouds overhead and the puffy dunes to every side of me and then just leaned back against the grotto wall and closed my eyes.

There was no question in my mind but that I was lost.

And that was the good news.

Being lost was going to make it damn difficult for the Soviets to find me. I only hoped they were trying, since that would mean they wouldn't get close to the others. If I had made one intelligent move on this entire expedition, it was sending Asia off with Nils. She was better off with him. And so was the canister. Why did I feel as though that were the bad news?

He was the one man who stood a chance of getting back.

Who else could but Nils?

Something heavy and cold settled into my stomach.

Who else would but Nils?

There was a doubt tugging at my guts.

Would he?

Even if that canister were returned to the navy, what would they have for all our trouble? Maybe some infrared photographs of Russian military bases. Perhaps strategic evidence indicating the Russians had violated one or another nuclear treaty. America's security had been breached, our preparedness compromised. I may have been a hopeless cynic but I couldn't help feeling uncomfortable about my role as expendable defender.

It's not that I value my life so highly. I don't. I have no reason to. But Antarctica has a way of putting everything in perspective, and right at that moment I wasn't sure that national security and national preparedness were rather that important.

Our nation was a hut buried ten feet into the barrier.

The Soviet nation is here too, six hundred miles and a hemisphere away similarly buried into the continental ice shelf. We live bomb-shelter existences. But we do not fear bombs. We do not confront one another with ballistic missiles and megaton nuclear weapons. Our mutual enemy here is simply cold. National security for us is sufficient quantities of food for ourselves and fuel for our fires. National preparedness is nothing more than a maintenance of those stores and an alert watch on the fires to see that they are kept under control.

But this was not the reason for my discomfort.

Losing the canister would not mean the end of the world any more than finding it would mean the world's salvation. Still, the idea that we had risked so much on this expedition did not gall. This was no wasted gesture. Our world, ours and the Soviets, should never have been involved with the politics of Cold War waged by people ignorant of what real cold is all about. But the war had come here nevertheless, and now Mensa at least was very much in trouble. This had been our primary responsibility. Recovery of the canister had been a secondary objective. Yet I had trusted Dolan with the one task and now Nils with the other. I had wanted to verify that the transmission system at the radar depot could be used to make one-way contact with the U.S. Navy, but now that was entirely in the hands of Robert Dolan. I was to have brought Asia and the canister to the depot.

But now Nils Hellstrom had them both.

That was the cause for my discomfort.

The redoubtable Nils.

The undoubtable Nils.

He had disobeyed orders to save me—to get Asia and the canister away. Or had he disobeyed orders merely to get the canister? I could hardly believe my suspicions. Not that the suspicions defied belief, for manifestly they did. It was unbelievable that any mind could be capable of such thought. This was the unthinkable. Yet now that the unthinkable had been thought, I knew there was more. The climbing rope that broke—nearly killing me and Carl Johnson in the borehole—had been in Nils' care. It was in his hands when the break occurred. Nils was the only one of us strong enough to break the weld on the borehole gantry, aware—as were we all at Mensa—that Johnson's duties included a visual inspection of the hole itself. When Johnson was smothered in the infirmary he and the killer were alone. But there was only one person at Mensa who knew that Johnson would be alone. That was the man who also knew I would be leaving to go up top and search the tractors. He knew the approximate time that I would go. He knew because I had told him.

Why?

Why would Nils kill Johnson?

What possible motive could he have?

The only thing that occurred to me was the equally incredible fact of Johnson's dosimeter. That badge indicated Johnson had encountered some type of radioactivity. As far as I knew, our portable power plants were the sole sources of radiation at Mensa. We didn't even keep spare fuel rods. But that didn't mean there couldn't be others I didn't know about. Could Johnson have stumbled across something radioactive in the supply wing? Or in the Centaur Project chamber? Processed uranium or even plutonium being smuggled out of the States? Perhaps some nuclear devices. Even, I thought, one or the other being smuggled in. By us. By the Russians. It all seemed too fantastic. And one thing made of it utter nonsense. Nils Hellstrom was the one who had pointed out to me the discoloration of Johnson's badge.

A violent chill overcame me.

My parka was fairly soaked inside. I had the option of sitting where I was and freezing to death within a matter of hours, or getting on the move. The activity would be at once agonizing but it was also the only thing likely to save me.

I wasn't even sure if that's what I wanted.

My hand went to my pocket for the compass, scooped up the contents, and displayed them inches in front of my eyes. Something was wrong. I raised the balaclava and stared again at the single object in my palm. A small vial of pills. I dipped my hand again and came up empty. My compass was gone. Lost in the fight at the tractor or, more probably, on one of my many falls.

Well, that tore it. Popping half a dozen tablets of morphine down my throat would be the quickest and easiest way to go now, although freezing to death—I am told—is really not so unpleasant. Losing the compass should have made up my mind for me, and yet, ironically, it was finding the morphine tablets that did.

Not trusting the vial to my parka again, I stood up and stuffed them deep in my pants pocket before climbing the hill overlooking my hollow to survey.

There was still no sign of light or life. But one thing was clear to me: I could do no good here. Allowing myself to die on Deception Reach would be the only really wasted gesture. I had to make the depot. If Dolan, Nils, and Asia had gone, I would have to make Mensa.

It was a hundred miles.

No one had ever before attempted a long-distance

trek across either Deception Reach or the barrier, alone, on foot, at night, without benefit of direction-finding equipment. Never before had anyone contemplated such a trip with any combination of those handicaps.

The very idea was staggering.

It was impossible.

If I had erred to the east, went west now to find the depot, and missed it again, the next stop would be Vostok II five hundred miles out on Deception Reach. If I had erred to the west and turned east, I might still miss the depot, but I couldn't fail to find the Queen Mauds. Even were I to continue southeast—my best chance of finding the depot, as I didn't really know if I were west, east, or short—and failed to spot the depot, I would hit the mountains eventually. Unfortunately by that time I wouldn't know if I were north or south of the only route to the barrier within walking distance—Hell's Flow. I would have to go back down it. Staggering didn't begin to describe the effect of that little jaunt despite which it would be child's play compared to the one that came next: take a good guess for a heading and start walking the forty miles to Mensa Station. The walk itself would be easy. The odds against success would be astronomical. Instead of approaching the long range of mountains, I would be leaving them behind me, striking out into a black oblivion with only a vague idea of direction and heading. Miss the correct heading by one-half of one degree—a one-in-a-million shot—and I'd pass wide of Mensa by more than a third of a mile. In its current blacked-out condition, I could pass it by a few paces and never know the difference.

All that assumed I knew now which way to start out.

Which of course I did not.

With a sudden deliberation I pulled off my face mask, turned a slow circle on that hilltop, and concentrated on the obscure gray junction of land and sky. I did that three times. Not even using every ounce of my imagination could I permit myself to believe the horizon in any direction was infinitesimally brighter than another. Neither was the wind of any help. Flowing across the undulations it eddied this way and that, up and around, so that the only thing I could feel or perceive was the drift being spun almost vertically aloft like waterspouts or miniature tornadoes.

I watched one whirling up and waited for the tiny ice particles to be carried away. They dispersed without any common motivation. What I actually observed was something else altogether. There was a hole in the clouds. The first I'd seen. And a black patch of sky was moving methodically across the heavens. Its movement alone could tell me little, for variations in the directions of ground winds and winds aloft can approach 180 degrees. Notwithstanding that, my eyes became locked upon it, transfixed as though it held for me the secrets of the universe.

The patch exposed occasional individual stars and a few mysterious clusters—nothing that I could recognize in such an isolated setting. Without the entire constellation, the stars themselves were difficult to . . .

A familiar grouping of four stars became visible.

Diamond-shaped.

A kite. A cross. For me, an arrow.

And then it disappeared behind the moving clouds.

It was the False Cross. I was sure.

But if I were wrong . . .

If it were Crux, the Southern Cross, following it on toward the southeast would take me into the nothingness that is Deception Reach.

No. I was sure.

I did the arithmetic involved with obtaining a heading based on my best estimate of the time and my recollection of the position of that star group. Then, imbued with false courage and false hope, I started walking.

The fact that from that point my progress came more easily and things seemed to go generally well should have been, for me, a sign that something was far from right. That is not to say I did not fall again. I did. Often. And I found myself taking unnecessary detours and spending valuable minutes scaling fantastic specimens of glacial construction that should have been avoided altogether had I known, before topping them, that a detour existed.

By degrees the swells subsided.

My pace picked up.

No less than another forty-five minutes had elapsed, perhaps as much as an hour, before I heard it: the same popping whine that had sounded several times earlier on only to fade before I could identify its source. A Russian snowmobile? Very likely. The Soviets on my trail? No. It came from up ahead. For another ten minutes I followed that sound only, reasonably sure that I approached it rather than moved away. At last I rounded a shelf of ice and ran smack into the depot another hundred yards beyond.

It was ugly. The squat, square metallic body was perched high on four ten-foot legs that raised it above the threat of burial by drifting ice. From out of the top on one side a hexagonal dish was mounted on a brace and pointed skyward. The entire structure was covered with a coat of rime at least an inch thick, which did nothing to dispel its appearance as a prehistoric creature frozen during a not-so-recent ice age. It was beautiful.

But I wasn't seeing that after the first moment.

I acknowledged the rotating beacon. The words *U.S. Navy* painted in red on a side panel were just discernible beneath the rime. Then my eyes fell to the three individuals standing beneath it with the snowmobile, sled, and dogs.

The fools had waited.

For the second time that night I began running.

Nils, as usual, was the first to see me. He and Dolan were standing to one side facing Asia Krokov. She in turn was facing them, holding what appeared to be the automatic pistol I had given her. When Nils' arm shot out, Asia turned, dropped the gun on the ice, and started running toward me. Her ninety pounds struck me at full speed, nearly bowling me over. I faltered for a moment. Then she was in my arms and kissing my bare face and saying something incoherent that I didn't need to hear to understand. I was in no condition to carry her and probably would have gone down if Nils hadn't been there, by then assuming much of my weight and hauling the two of us over to the depot.

"You should've left an hour ago," I shouted at them.

"We tried to," said Dolan. "But your lady friend was most persuasive. Mr. Hellstrom and I found ourselves quite unprepared for feminine charms of her caliber." He displayed the automatic she had dropped.

I turned.

Asia Krokov didn't need a gun to persuade me. What she'd done was unforgivably stupid. Yet I couldn't bring myself to blame her.

"Okay, okay," I said. "How did you make out otherwise?"

Dolan shrugged. "All that can be done has been done."

There was no time to double-check his work. I noted with approval that the sled was all packed; the five huskies, tethered, urged us to be on our way.

"We won't get away fast enough to suit me," said Nils.

Something moved me to glance across the clearing. What I saw in turn caused me to freeze halfway to the snowmobile.

Nils was right.

With one qualification.

Apparently we wouldn't get away at all.

A dozen dark figures had just dashed out from behind a dune. The flashing beacon revealed their intrusion in rapid-fire bursts of red movement of such chilling swiftness and efficiency that they precluded any delusions of resistance.

In spite of the fact they had surprised us completely, their appearance did not come as a complete surprise. On the contrary, I was surprised it had not come earlier. In that same moment I realized our own machine had helped to drown out the sound of their advance, and since they had approached downwind of us— hardly off line from the direction I'd come in—it was no wonder we hadn't heard them. As for seeing them, if anyone should have seen them it was me.

They formed a line right in front of us, close enough

to shake hands. Not a dozen men, after all, but ten. Five in front of Dolan and me, and another five in front of Asia and Nils, who had turned around as I had done and then remained absolutely stationary as I was doing. The ten became a dozen when Colonel Fedorev and Major Zhizn strode up behind them and parted their line like the Red Sea. Nobody stuck out a hand. No reception line this time. No Charles and Lady Di come to tea. Not this time.

Dolan still had the gun, but he wasn't fool enough to point it at anyone. Such was the measure of their confidence that they didn't bother ordering him to lay it down. The two officers ignored him completely. They ignored Asia and Nils, too.

As Zhizn faced me and raised his balaclava, I noted with satisfaction that he sported the first bit of color to his complexion since I'd known him. Of course his face was red in the reddish glare, but below the left eye it was black and swollen. No doubt the balaclava gave him nearly as much discomfort as the antarctic.

Still, it hadn't hurt his attitude.

He was smiling.

Fedorev was not. But just like Zhizn he was looking straight at me. The colonel thrust out his hand palm up and demanded, "The canister, Mr. Masterson, if you please."

I don't mind admitting that Papa Masterson sired one damn fool of a son but, fortunately for me, named him Paul. Peter Masterson did precisely as he was told.

If I had had the canister I would have passed it over without delay. I hadn't, of course, so I asked Nils to hand it to me, and when he had done so, I passed it across to Fedorev. Without further delay. Fedorev gave it only the most cursory inspection to verify its authenticity, stuck it in the pocket of his parka, and glared at me. "What am I to do with you, Masterson?"

"You'll think of something. If you need any help, I'm sure Zhizn there has a few ideas."

Fedorev shook his head. "At our first meeting we were discussing the merits of default as opposed to defeat. This is one contest you should have forfeited. In spite of that, I must admit that you are a most determined man. Never have I known one like you. I am tempted to leave you here just to see how long you manage to survive. Unfortunately I could not remain to watch. Perhaps, though, you can satisfy my curiosity about another matter." He patted his parka pocket. "What can be in this canister that makes it worth the lives of you and your men?"

I could think of nothing to say to that, and that's what I said.

At Fedorev's signal, a snowmobile came into the little clearing. There was a portable radio mounted on the driver's back. Fedorev crossed to the man, grabbed the handset, and talked into it.

Left in command, Zhizn smiled from ear to ear.

It didn't take long for me to figure out what the odds were for us. Even an idiot can count up to zero. But no matter how you added it up, there was only one chance for Asia Krokov and she wouldn't have it staying with me.

Fedorev was quick with his figuring, too; his portable radio couldn't reach much farther than the tractor caravan in this weather. Whether he wanted to communicate with someone at the caravan or have them relay instructions from Moscow, he came back to us disappointed. Communication by radio takes a minimum of two radios. I figured them now for a maximum of one.

Fedorev turned the handset over to his radioman with orders—I guessed—to keep trying. Then he joined us again.

"There's the answer to your question," I told him. "When you can't hope to win and you don't dare to lose, all that's left is to make sure that your opponent dies with you. That's not defeat, Colonel—that's a draw."

His radioman reported on progress with a lot of *"nyets"* and head shaking. Fedorev narrowed his eyes at me.

"We were warned you'd try for it," he said, continuing our conversation as though there'd been no in-

terruption and with no trace of concern in his voice.
"We knew that much even before our expedition was
launched. Your people were frantic about something
the satellite had photographed after we'd blasted it out
of its orbit . . . frantic we might recover the film canister before they could. And one more thing. We knew
your government had a man here in Antarctica. We
didn't know who or where. But Mensa was the only
station close enough to the impact site to be of any
concern to us. You've risked your life getting here, as
well as the lives of these others; so I ask you again,
what is in this canister that could possibly make it
worth taking such chances?"

"Why don't you tell me?"

"I can't. We don't know any more than your people
what these films may show—the satellite's transmitters
had ceased to function. The question remains whether
the infrared camera equipment was malfunctioning,
too."

"Well, you must have a pretty good idea. Whatever
the canister was worth to us, it was worth much more
to you. You've already killed two men. You destroyed
our radio and burned down Mensa Station, condemn-
ing another eight people to freeze to death."

The colonel turned in utter astonishment to Major
Zhizn, whose smug expression was more damning than
any confession.

When Fedorev did drag words from him, neither
Hellstrom, nor Dolan, nor I could get anything of it.
Whatever they had to say, it didn't take long. They
were glaring at each other when I interrupted. What I
had to do couldn't wait any longer.

"Colonel!" Fedorev turned and stared at my sum-
mons. "In case you've failed to notice, we have one
of your people with us." I eased Asia Krokov toward
them. When I raised her goggles and mask, Fedorev
drew back in surprise. So did Asia. She was staring at
me with an expression torn between shock and confusion.

"*Laitenant,*" cried Fedorev.

"She wasn't in on this," I interjected hurriedly.
"All she knew was that we were going to intercept

you and wanted to join you again after her condition was cleared. Asia held my men here at gunpoint until you came in.''

If Colonel Fedorev believed me he gave no indication of it. But Zhizn acted quickly by slipping in, grabbing her by the sleeve, and pulling her into his ranks saying, "Gallantry, Mr. Masterson? We didn't expect that of you. Or perspicacity either. You know perspicacity, Mr. Masterson? Well, at least we were wrong about the gallantry.''

Who was he kidding? I knew we were going to be killed because I knew Zhizn as I knew myself, and I knew that if our positions were reversed I would kill him without hesitation.

"You're saying you don't plan to shoot us?''

He laughed. A laugh to match his smile. "No, Mr. Masterson; I'm saying we do.''

In a single movement Zhizn stepped back out of the line of fire and made a signal to the troopers, who closed in the line, retracting the firing mechanisms of their weapons as they did so.

Fedorev's snarl brought the troopers up short, "Igor Zhiznovich Zhizn!''

The two officers engaged in another exchange that was meaningless to us. Despite Fedorev's authority I judged him to be coming in a distant second. Zhizn's voice never raised; his enigmatic little smile never cracked.

We had seconds to live.

Once the order came we would have no chance at all. Running was out. Not one of us would make it out of the clearing. And where would we run? No. Our only hope was to move before the order came.

I started counting down.

Ten . . .

I could leap at the troopers in front of Dolan and me. Probably take three of them down with me. With luck, get my hands on one of their weapons. Nils, Dolan, and Asia would have to follow my lead.

Nine . . .

The five men in front of Nils were his to deal with. He needed to take them all, and the element of surprise that might be mine for an instant would be lost to him. He'd likely take a few slugs before he reached them. But it would take more than a few to stop him. Of what other human could I expect such an effort?

Eight . . .

Asia must obstruct Fedorev and Zhizn. She would keep the colonel from drawing his pistol if he carried one, and stop Zhizn, whose pistol was still in Dolan's hand, from recovering one of the automatic rifles.

Seven . . .

And Dolan. Those I didn't take down with my flying dive would be for him. And any others that he could handle until either Nils or I secured one of the rifles ourselves. A week ago it would never have occurred to me that I could risk so much on what Robert Dolan might or might not do in a situation like this. Now I had no choice. Somehow, I didn't think he would disappoint us.

Six . . .

Fedorev regarded me severely.

"We are in a most unfortunate position. The events at your station make it impossible for me to take you with us. You understand. And it seems that the major is ill to leave you alive. You three here in the middle of the antarctic."

Five . . .

"Particularly you, Masterson," he added. "If the major and I agree on anything, it is you; something about your character has also impressed him as most indomitable."

I replied, "How perspicacious."

Four . . .

Fedorev barked something while glancing at Nils, Dolan, and me, shook his head sadly the way a judge might before a man who has too often beaten the hangman and for whom he can no longer demonstrate leniency, then he turned and strode off in the direction of their machines.

Three . . .

His final order had been given, a sentence of death.

Two . . .

Zhizn turned to me in a furor. His face red with rage.

One . . .

His mouth came open in a snarl.

Now!

Everything happened at once. My weight shot forward off the ice. The five soldiers centered in the narrow scope of my concentration suddenly right-faced in a body. I jerked back and to the side, stumbling to remain upright, as their weapons were raised again, this time on the huskies still tethered to the snowmobile and sled.

I heard Nils shout.

As I struggled to regain my balance and watched in horror, Nils lunged for the five troopers nearest him at the same time all ten opened fire. The harsh clatter of gunfire shattered any other words or cries. Nils took four of the men down with a single movement, a movement that had taken me by as much surprise as it had them, and had caught me equally flat-footed. The fifth trooper stepped into the fray, pushed his rifle barrel into the sky with both hands, and started the butt down onto Nils' head.

I leapt.

To reach him I had to shove Dolan aside, and that is probably the only thing that saved Dolan's life. Had he tried to use the gun, they would have killed him then and there. The trooper and I went down. Something burned into my back and the dark-gray world went suddenly black as I plummeted dizzily into the most profound of crevasses that had suddenly opened up at my feet.

Somewhere between consciousness and senselessness, far down from the surface of the crevasse but above its depths, I clung to the side. I could see and hear and even move in a torpid, dreamy kind of way. I recollect a rather hazy picture above me of several forms bent over another on the ice, clubbing him repeatedly with their weapons stocks.

My recollection includes an attempt to crawl to him and collapse over his body, but whether or not I made it I do not know. I rather suspect I did, for I did not slip back into that crevasse; I was beaten down by blows that were too real to be a part of any dream.

Death is a force of attraction . . . a kind of gravity. It resists every step we take. With our first movement we challenge the force, after which, for a time at least, inertia is on our side; we yield to the force by slowing; surrender by coming to a stop. Between starting and stopping every man develops his own momentum— that is to say, his own direction, his own speed, and a unique disinclination to modify either. Gravity was pulling me down now. Into that crevasse. Only at the bottom would it cease to attract. I was going faster and faster downward. But Peter Masterson was almost stopped. You might say that the rate at which I was slowing was constantly accelerating and leave it to the engineers to work out an acceptable equation.

By one means or another in that darkness I latched on to the side and started climbing. Blind, I moved toward the pain. The higher I climbed, the more I endured. Whenever the pain became bearable I knew that I was slipping and fought against the pull with even greater force.

As I clambered over the edge this time, my back and shoulders were in agony, but there was light enough to see. I looked. Considering what I saw, it is a wonder I did not release my grip, lean back, and yield to the black, numbing force of the pit.

Dolan was sitting over us with his back to the wind. Somehow—I will never understand the way of it—he had dragged first me and then Nils out of sight of the depot. The smooth gray plains of Deception Reach were on every side of us and nothing more. The Russians had gone. But they had taken everything that could save us along with them. All that I had dreaded before was now true again. We were still a hundred miles from Mensa, still lost, without direction and without supplies. The only difference being I was no longer alone. I had two companions, one crippled and the other beaten into coma. But not Asia Krokov. She was gone too. And there didn't seem to be anything

else on the surface that made hanging on seem worth-
while.

I dragged myself over to a mound on the ice already
shrouded by hoarfrost, and raised an old balaclava
mask.

There was a ghastly bruise across Nils' forehead but
with that exception his wounds did not show. Had we
dared remove parka and inner layers of clothing, his
trunk would no doubt have sported a multitude of colors. Even that would have failed to reveal the true
extent of the damage, for the most serious of his injuries would be internal. Broken ribs. Hemorrhaging.
Damage—perhaps extensive damage—to organs. And
if not a fractured skull then a serious brain concussion.
The only way we could have helped Nils was to keep
him warm and nourished. As it was, we could only
wait for him to die.

I set my jaw, battled to my feet, and stood looking
down at him and Dolan. "I should have spit in Zhizn's
eye," I said to neither of them in particular. "That
was my last chance."

Dolan spoke without looking up. "You would not
have lived to regret it."

"So I didn't. How long will I live to regret that?"

A glow on the near horizon had caught my eye. At
first I took it to be the depot. Yet the beacon was no
longer red or pulsating. It flickered yellow and sent
shimmers of light reflecting off the overcast like miniature auroras australis. Had it been so glaring a beacon earlier, I could never have lost sight of it; I looked
to Dolan for an explanation. He had not moved at all,
sitting frozen with his head down and his eyes avoiding mine. But when I turned again and started limping
toward the light, he jerked up suddenly.

"You can't go back there!"

I came slowly around. "What are you talking
about?"

"After they killed the huskies the Soviets blew up
the radar unit. Set it ablaze. Then threw our sled and
supplies into the fire. The only stuff left is still burning."

I couldn't believe it. If our supplies were not yet

consumed, then we had to salvage whatever we could; even if nothing could be saved, we should be making use of the transient benefits of the flames.

"Christ, why aren't we all back there?"

He shook his head.

"When they blew up the structure they more than likely ruptured the containment shield on the nuclear supply fuel. Strontium 90. It's not even safe for us here a quarter-mile away. When Nils comes to we ought to back away a mile or so if we can get that far."

Nils wasn't coming to. Not if he was down the same crevasse I had fallen in. He had taken a far more terrible beating than I had, and that, coupled with the killing cold, was more than enough to finish him. Radiation poisoning wasn't going to help him at all and it wouldn't do Dolan and me any good either.

This was bad. I can take pain and cope with cold, but radiation just plain scares me. It doesn't hurt. It doesn't warn. It kills. And there's nothing you can do about it. As little as I understood about radioactivity, I knew this much: it is a bombardment of particles too small to be seen. If you place a trillion of the particles side by side, you still can't see them. And they come shooting into your body at something like the speed of light. Some of them blast right through. Others strike harmlessly off cell bodies. When they hit cell nuclei, they destroy. It takes several inches of lead to stop them. Several hundred feet of solid granite. Several miles of air. That is about all I knew. But it was enough.

The two of us each grabbed an arm and dragged Nils until we were exhausted. After a break that was too short in some respects and all too long in another, we dragged him some more. Half a dozen breaks and a full mile later we finally collapsed when Dolan figured we were far enough to avoid any real chance of contamination.

I gave myself only a few moments to regain my strength. After standing, turning a full circle, and taking a mark on our position between the fire and a distant swell, I started back toward the depot.

Dolan shouted for me to come back. I ignored him, and after that, the appeals came more desperately but only at intervals; long before I'd gotten close enough to see the actual tongues of flame above the mounds and had begun circling the clearing at a distance, his cries had ceased altogether.

Eventually I found five hunks of the radar housing that had been blasted outside the clearing. One by one I dragged them to where Nils lay while Dolan sat with his arms folded and his elbows flapping. Two of the twisted metal sheets weren't very large, three or four feet wide at best, but the other three were of good size. When we put them together they made a very adequate shelter. Of course there were some hellacious cracks that made it nothing like windproof, but it was strong enough to support the initial layer of drift that would cover it by morning. After that, it would be solid, windtight, and warm, at least marginally warmer than the outside.

We built the shelter right over Nils' body. When we were done and had joined him inside, I couldn't tell that he had moved an inch.

It was hardly light enough inside to see, but as I huddled beside Nils, checking his pulse and respiration, Dolan must have sensed what I was thinking.

"They really beat him badly," he said. "It was almost as though they were happy of an excuse to beat any one of us and picked on him. Or maybe it was because he was the one carrying the canister."

I nodded, though Dolan couldn't have seen that either, and I knew better the reason. But if Nils hadn't told Dolan about the way he had handled the several Russian soldiers at the caravan, I saw no reason for me to mention it. "I'm surprised," I simply said, "that they didn't kill us all."

He laughed. "Isn't that exactly what they did."

How could I argue with that when I agreed with him? It was certainly true the Russians had left us here to die, and here we were remaining. We were burrowing in, exactly as David Saperstein and his people had done at Mensa. We were waiting, as they had waited, for our momentum to run down.

As much as I wanted to be on the move I couldn't see myself leaving Nils Hellstrom while he lived. Hauling him that one mile had proven it would be folly to take him along without the sled to carry him. Dolan agreed that we should wait to determine Nils' condition, but I really believe he would have accepted any solution that kept him off his leg. No doubt he secretly hoped he would himself be gone before Nils came to or died.

So we holed up.

And so began our four days and nights of hell.

There certainly wasn't room enough in there to do much moving around, had we been so inclined; the shelter's height didn't even permit sitting. We lay on our sides on the ice, conforming our bodies to the odd space Nils' bulk allowed. Curled up in front of him with my right arm and side first stiff then frozen, I was desperate to roll over at regular intervals had that not meant either trading places with Dolan or sticking my feet out the entrance. Dolan himself was not inclined to move at all and, save for shivering and massaging frozen limbs, did not.

As the day progressed we had time enough and more to swap life stories. No real condensation would have been required. No stories were told. I had no interest in Dolan's history and he, as it turned out, already knew mine. Anyway, Dolan had no interest in talking. In the first twelve hours we probably exchanged not a dozen words.

Midday light slipped in like a thief and then fled. Here before we knew it was around; gone before we knew what was missing. After that, the degrees fell by the minute.

Antarctica had dispatched one unwelcome visitor after another. Cold came to stay. The wind was not one, but a dozen strangers, gypsies who had moved their tents and wagons into our back lawn. They banged against our shelter from the southeast for hours and then began swinging around to the northeast. Into the evening drift was blasting through the cracks on our northwest wall and through the entrance. The shrieks were indescribable. A chorus of laments by persistent carolers.

How merciful it would have been had I sunk again into unconsciousness. Neither Dolan nor I was so lucky. We spent a sleepless night suffering the most violent of convulsions. Our only consolation was pain. As long as our extremities stung with cold, we knew they were at least getting some circulation. Whenever the pain disappeared—a warning sign of great danger—we removed our gloves and kneaded our faces, hands, and feet. We took turns blowing on Nils' hands and feet but held off removing any of his snowclothes, for the sudden loss of body heat would have been more debilitating than the slow cooling. And he was definitely cooling off. Much more rapidly than we were. I could tell by his breath—shallow enough to begin with—that his internal temperatures were 10 to 15 degrees below normal.

The same problem in Dolan and me finally forced us to give up warming Nils by blowing. Before the night ended, our breaths were too cool to be of any use. Not only that, but the rapid inhalations required by that practice only served to exacerbate our conditions. We began kneading his limbs along with our own, but even the additional duty didn't keep my hands from growing puffy and stiff between turns. By the morning, even rubbing them had very little effect. Severe chilblain had settled in; we resorted to more and more vigorous massage, which did almost as much damage to the underlying tissue as it did good.

It was simply too damn cold. Sixty degrees below zero at least. Seventy below by late morning and still colder yet by midday. I don't have any hesitation in saying that. We set no record, I know; the Russians had had a team experience a 100 degrees below zero only a few hundred miles to the west, but I daresay they were better supplied.

In spite of all that, I believe I finally slept a bit.

I remember waking in stages. The final stage came when I grasped that the entrance hole had once been dark, and now—though drifts had restricted its diameter by half—suffused light from a noon sun was finding its way in.

Day Two had arrived.

Then I realized that quite some time must have passed since my last kneading of limbs. I tried to get to all fours but nothing happened. Nothing. I became terrified. My arms and shoulders, hips and legs, had become solid blocks of ice. They were literally frozen in place. I spent half an hour coaxing my joints into mobility one excruciating millimeter at a time. When I was finally able to move, my jaws were cramped and tears had formed unbroken icicles down to my chin. I crawled out to witness the event of day.

I could hardly believe what I saw.

The landscape had not changed noticeably, although the dunes may have drifted slightly this way or that. I had changed. A quick inspection showed my hands to be swollen to twice their normal size. The skin was covered in dark-reddish patches; blisters the size of half-dollars ran from the backs of them up my arms. All my fingernails were black. They were also badly suppurating. Yellow pus had collected around my fingertips. It was with no little dismay that I fished out a small signal mirror that I forever kept in an inside pocket, and gazed at the outworldly face it reflected. Dismay turned to alarm. My ears were gone. Probably my nose too and my cheeks and chin would not be far behind. The skin was gray and lifeless. Ugly pustules had literally honeycombed my chin, cheeks, forehead, and neck. Sometime during the night they had begun breaking; now my face was pockmarked with purple patches. At this stage further kneading was hopeless: if I tried massaging them much more, I'd literally rub the skin off my face.

I let the mirror drop. The reflection of overcast lay at my feet. After making one aimless circuit of the shelter, I realized that throwing the mirror away had been a silly gesture, and decided to look for it. But I must have passed right over it without seeing a thing and felt too tired to stop and search.

Freezing to death was throwing my system out of whack. I was listless, though it had been a day since

I had performed any exercise worthy of the name. While I was ravenous for water I had no appetite whatsoever. Yet I'd lost virtually no fluids and required food desperately to maintain internal temperatures. Psychologically I was in no better shape. The situation was more serious by far then than it had been twenty-four hours before, but I was somehow less concerned. Because of my overall fitness I knew the odds favored me surviving at least one more day of these conditions, but when that day was over, I doubted I would care much one way or the other what happened after that.

"Masterson! Come in here!"

I ducked inside.

In the blackness I heard my name called out again. Weak and low. But this time it was not Dolan's voice. Then it was, "He's conscious, Peter."

"Nils! My God, man, how do you feel?"

"Thirsty."

"Scotch or bourbon?"

"Whatever you got . . ."

"It'll have to be neat. We're all out of ice."

Nils tried to laugh, I think, but almost at once he was coughing. When that stopped he said something in a voice so whispered I didn't hear.

He was gone again before I could ask him to repeat it.

Hunched over him as I was, not really seeing him, I knew it was very likely he would never come to again. I was powerless to help him. Inside of me something was raging and I felt again as I had felt at Hell's Flow watching his shelf of ice descend into the abyss. I scrambled outside, stood, and looked around in a fury of desperation. The fire in the distance had long since burned itself out. At least the flames had died. But as I stormed off in that direction I was well aware that the inferno was still very much alive. I was counting on that. The one thing we needed besides food and exercise was heat. All three were to be found a mile to the north at the depot destruction site. Strontium 90 has a half-life of several thousand years and operated the depot power system on the same principle as our plutonium reactor: by boiling fluid and pushing it through a turbine that drives a generator. Whether or not the vessel in which the Strontium 90 was stored remained intact, the hellish stuff would decay and in the process turn out enough BTUs to heat a thousand igloos. It was a measure of my desperation that I actually considered recovering the canister and carting it back.

Fortunately, it was no longer there.

Nothing was there.

The four legs of the depot, standing at rakish angles, were all of the structure that had survived the explosion; they had been embedded too deeply in the ice to be blasted away. They were gone now. The debris of the fire, the carcasses of the dogs, which I had only glimpsed from my earlier circumnavigation, were gone too. Even the minor drifts and mounds within the clearing had been leveled. I was so startled by this mysterious business that I nearly walked right into a lake.

The clearing had melted—everything in it had sunk.

The resulting pool was at least thirty, forty yards across. Wide enough that it had swallowed up the carcasses of the huskies, which, contaminated or otherwise, I had hoped to recover. It was deep too, deeper obviously than the ten-foot legs. The thing that amazed me was that despite its width and depth amid temperatures on the reach approaching 70 degrees below zero, not the thinnest film of ice had formed across its surface. Even the ice edge was mushy and yielded under my feet.

I removed a glove and dipped my hand in the water. It wasn't hot. But it was damn warm.

Baring the other hand, I immersed both to the wrists. The sting was immediate, an indescribable ecstasy.

Eventually, of course, Antarctica would reclaim this affront. The vessel would continue to sink into the two miles of ice shelf until it would be unable to heat the surface sufficiently. How wide would the pool be then? How deep? It didn't matter. The vessel wouldn't stop melting down until it reached the land mass. Perhaps not even then.

Well, I told myself, they had wanted a nuclear

dump under the ice cap. Now it was there. Compared to Chernobyl, it might not have been much of an affront, just as compared to Hanford or Yucca Mountain, it wasn't much of a dump. It was more than enough for me. And it left behind all the water we could possibly want. The problem was I had no vessel to carry it back to the shelter, a debatable misfortune as any amount I could carry would freeze solid before I'd ever get it back. I wasn't even sure it was potable.

After several minutes I decided to dunk my head for a while too—more desperation—and had thrown back my hood and lowered my face to within inches of the water's surface when I spotted it, an oddly shaped little lump also near the edge a few feet to my left.

I knelt to brush aside the layer of drift and so expose a bloodied carcass, its head twisted awkwardly over its back and pinned there seemingly by a bridallike strap of leather snagged in its teeth. It was Thor. He had not been my dog and yet something about this pathetic picture affected me deeply. It was clear what had happened. His body ripped to pieces by bullets, Thor had picked up Nils' scent and dragged himself inch by agonizing inch toward our shelter. He had not gotten out of the clearing before reaching the end of his tether. The last seconds of his life had been spent in a hopeless attempt to bite through the leather leash.

There are damn few men that deserve that kind of loyalty, I told myself. Just maybe Nils was one of them. There are damn few animals that can give it. Peter Masterson had not been one of those. Perhaps I had liked Thor because I had seen in him something I had never found in myself.

The carcass was frozen fast to the ice. I grabbed fur and pulled but failed to budge it. Standing, I lashed out twice with my foot; with the second kick I felt the ice give way beneath me. A small floe slipped out and down into the water and I barely made it back to the edge without going in. I watched the floe capsize, then floe and dog together descend beneath the surface. As hungry as I was, as much as we all needed the meat, there wasn't a darn thing I could do to get it without going for a swim. Which was another way of saying there wasn't a darn thing I could do. Sweating was one thing; actually soaking my clothes by submersion was quite another. Before I had walked the mile back to the shelter in 100 degrees of frost I would become encased in a solid block of frozen material, unable to move, unable to breathe. There are a thousand ways to commit suicide in Antarctica but none more fool-proof than that one.

I returned empty-handed. No heat and no meat.

The exercise was mine alone. And all the way back the only thing I could think about was to keep walking. To miss the shelter in the darkness and not stop to look for it. The two-mile walk had not exhausted me as I had felt it would. I was tired. But less so than when I started out. I was cold and frostbitten. But less so than when I'd emerged an hour before. The swelling of my hands and feet had withdrawn a little.

When the shelter reappeared, I held up at the entrance and tried to talk myself out of crawling back inside. There was no hope for me here. Our time was so drastically limited we needed to spend every minute on the move. I told myself that Bob and Nils were as good as dead no matter what I did. If I were to save my own life, it had to be now.

Apparently my arguments were pretty convincing.

Deception Reach lay before me. I stopped and made a circle. There I was ten paces south of the shelter and I still don't remember taking a single step.

But I'll never forget the ten steps that took me back.

Staying here was giving up.

Going on alone was somehow worse.

I knelt, crawled inside, and burrowed in. And gave up.

On the second night and day several things had changed: we no longer shook. Dolan no longer massaged himself at all. Obviously he had gone completely numb. It was like that for me. I had absolutely no sensation below my thighs. Or past my elbows. I continued the routine, but I no longer felt the need for it. When I finished, my flesh remained insensate to any benefits. The period of pain had passed. Another change was more unexpected: Dolan no longer remained quiet. I would have supposed that as he sank deeper and deeper into hypothermia he would naturally become even more withdrawn. But really it was just the opposite. His outbursts now came frequently . . . often nothing more than a challenge, a profanity, or an irrational observation.

When I came back into the shelter I found him moaning over Nils—"Poor little Dutch boy. Poor little Dutch boy." Dolan knew as well as I did Nils was a Swede. Then he said, "Got your finger stuck in the dike, didn't you?"

Figure that one out.

When he felt me crawling over him he shouted, "What are you going to do when Nils and I are dead?"

I let some few moments pass wondering if he expected me to bury them. "What do you want me to do?"

"Start after them. Get that canister back."

I was too shocked to reply. By the time an appropriate remark came to mind, he wasn't around to hear it . . . yet another change. Cold is an extremely efficient anesthetic. With the pain in our extremities absent for some time we were able to sleep at last. But cold's anesthetizing effect is just as much general as local. We not only could sleep, we did sleep. More than making up for the previous twenty-four hours.

Staying awake became the problem. Or waking up once my mind had begun to slip. Those gypsy winds could bang away without any effect. The shrieking laments might just as well have been sung to an empty house. Even Dolan, scrunched up not two feet away, had to shout to bring me back to the living.

"Something had to be done," Dolan cried. "Time was running out. No one could make a decision; so the decision was made for them."

I had no idea what he was talking about.

"There was a mess," he said. "It had to be cleaned up. You can't blame the garbage man if you don't like the size of his dump."

My brain had become so clogged I felt like a lost ship trying to make way in close pack. I couldn't tell where I was or where I wanted to go until I pushed the floes aside, and always more floes took their place.

"We had to do what we did. And so do you, dammit!"

It didn't sound like his voice.

"Why do you think you're here, Masterson?"

I answered by saying something barely intelligible in a voice that didn't sound like mine. Something about getting a signal out for Mensa.

"I don't mean here. I meant in Antarctica. Why do you think we arranged to bring an outsider like you into the Centaur Project?"

That melted a lot of ice.

"I'm here only because Nils asked for me," I said.

"You've got it backward, Masterson; you're not here because Hellstrom asked for you. Hellstrom is here only because we knew that he would ask for you."

"You're babbling, Dolan."

"Hellstrom was right about you. But so was Zhizn. You're the Unyielding and the Relentless in one, at war with yourself. The only thing capable of defeating you is Peter Masterson. You're extremely perceptive in some ways, but your perception has awful gaps. Mostly about people—and one in particular. Your biggest gap is yourself. You don't even know who you are. Or what you are."

"I know what you are. You're delirious."

"Am I? Look, Peter, everybody knows about you except you. Even the Soviets. Didn't you tell Nils that accident with Johnson in the borehole was no accident at all."

At this point I couldn't have been any more awake. "Nils didn't tell you that!"

"No, he didn't. He told David Saperstein. Before we left Mensa the first time, Saperstein told me. Need to know. As it turned out, no one had to tell me. I suspected it from the beginning.''

''That doesn't surprise me. Yeah, it's true I believe Johnson was murdered. Apparently Nils didn't pass on that I believed you were the one who killed him. Somebody wanted him dead bad enough to try three times. And you were alone with him when he fell in the first place.''

Dolan actually laughed. ''What happened to Johnson in the first place was an accident. Didn't I tell you that? The murderer just used the opportunity to kill the one person who might stand in their way.''

''How did Johnson stand in their way?''

''They were trying to kill you.''

A moment before I would have said his mind was going, and questioned only whether it was with madness or Morpheus he consorted. But this was no private nightmare of Dolan's; it was crazy, yet it was not the ravings of a madman.

''But Johnson was killed,'' I pointed out. ''Or didn't Paulette make her report to Saperstein?''

''Of course, she did. If she says he was killed, then he was. Not because of what he had seen or heard but because of what he might have seen. According to Paulette and Nils, when you left the dispensary the door was open and Johnson was lying so that he stared unseeing out into the hallway. We also figure that some time around then the radio was sabotaged. I believe the saboteur came out of the radio room, looked across the hall, saw Carl Johnson, and couldn't take a chance that Johnson's eyes were all that unseeing. People who plant explosive devices don't draw the line at suffocating comatose victims.

''Then,'' Dolan went on, ''it was back to you. Cutting the rope failed to finish you, so the towlines to the sledges were retied and the Fault-Finder was wrecked. It was your tractor that was supposed to go down a crevasse and you were supposed to be inside—remember you and Nils had decided that only the two of you would operate it. That, setting the fire, cutting the rope . . . the same hand was behind it all. And the same goal. To keep Peter Masterson out of the race.''

I made the mistake of reflecting too long on what Dolan had told me; before I answered him he had slipped away again. I followed him moments later. He had not mentioned the death of Jerry Davis. Had somebody blown him up intentionally in that storeroom, or had he just been in the wrong place at the wrong time? He had said nothing of orbiting spy cameras or black-market plutonium. Nothing of stained dosimeters and borehole Geiger counters. Nor of the one thing that had been bothering me for months, even more in recent days, and uncontrollably so in just the past few hours.

It must have been early morning when he made some noises that convinced me he was waking up. I put it to him point-blank. ''Bob, I want to know who you're working for.''

He mumbled back. I repeated the question and then another time before he replied.

''The same as you.''

I didn't believe it, and I said so. ''What's this business about 'our satellites' and 'we arranged'? 'Need to know' for Christ's sake! You're sure not talking about the Centaur Project. Or any operation at the Mensa I was briefed on. You, Saperstein, Elliston, and Digne. Even Davis and Johnson before they died. You're all involved in something. Mensa's no government operation and you guys aren't military. But you sure aren't like any civilians I've worked with. You call me the outsider, and fine—but what are you in?''

''You fool. Fool.'' Dolan stopped to clear his throat. The interruption seemed to clarify his thoughts as well. ''Mensa is a government operation. It always has been. We all of us are naval officers. Except for Mary Ingram and Nils Hellstrom. The navy had no specialists available with Mary's particular expertise. But she was briefed. She had to be. And her government employment contract gave her clearance. Nils was not. We could have acquired someone with arctic skills—

admittedly not as great as his—but in that case we
would not have had you."

"You don't have me. I may be a fool but I'm not
stupid enough to waste my time working for the military or the government."

"You've never worked for anyone else!"

It hit me like a blow. My mind went from cold to
numb and the power of speech simply left me. If an
ice ax had clobbered me in the skull, neatly cleaving
it in two, the shock could not have been greater.

Dolan didn't wait for me to recover. Almost at once,
he was going on, "When they briefed us on you I
couldn't believe it. It's hard to imagine anyone could
be so dense. But it's true, you really don't know. The
Central Intelligence Agency drafted you out of the
army. Pushed for your court-martial on that insubordination charge, then immediately finagled your re-
cruitment as a security specialist with Arctic Air
Transport. You were no cargo-ship sky marshal. The
security you specialized in throughout Canada and
Greenland was U.S. national security as perceived by
the CIA. When a situation developed in Scandinavia
they contrived your dismissal and had a bogus export
firm operating out of Stockholm offer you a trouble-
shooting position. Again most of the trouble you were
shooting was CIA-related.

"There were other troubles and other jobs. All for
the U.S. government. The firms that hired you were
fronts. Even the society that financed the two polar
expeditions you went on where you ran into Nils
Hellstrom again. Uncommonly uneventful. They
were primarily preparation for this assignment. Then
came the customary dismissal. And Mensa accepted
you and Nils as polar consultants. There was no trick
to convincing you that your attitude was responsible
for your inability to hold a position. Insubordination.
Uncooperative attitude. Loner on the team. Whatever the scene they knew you could be counted on
to play your role to perfection and without benefit of
script. But you were always where they needed you.
Their ace in the hole. The hole card that wasn't to
be used until things were as bad as they could get.

That's what they told us when they assigned you to
the Centaur Project. That you weren't to know. If
anything went wrong, you would do what needed to
be done but you would do better if you didn't know
who hired you. Nils called the tune on you and he's
the only one at Mensa who didn't know your status.
But he was right. You can't be stopped. When they
line you up in front of a firing squad, you'll be mea-
suring distances in your mind and calculating odds.
'If something goes wrong, really wrong,' they told
us, 'put Masterson in charge and do what he tells
you. You won't like it, but do it anyway.' That's
what they said. 'He hates people. He hates himself.
You can't get along with him and you won't like
him. He won't care. Masterson,' they said, 'has no
redeeming qualities. He's perfect for our purposes,
because he also has no feelings and no weaknesses.'
Well, sir, you lived up to your billing precisely in
every respect but one: you started to feel . . . and
you developed a weakness.''

"What are you talking about?" It was the best I
could manage to ask. His description sounded like one
of Major Zhizn to me. My feelings for Zhizn did not
come under the heading of weakness.

"I'm talking about Jerry Davis."

"I had no feeling for Davis."

" That's too bad. Davis died because I had asked
him to keep an eye on someone. I knew you'd never
ask it. So he did it at my request. I'll take the responsibility for getting him killed, since he meant a great
deal to me.''

"That's enough, Bob!"

I jerked half upright, banging my head on the roof.
"Nils!" I could hardly believe it. All of my confusion
and irritation with Dolan was swept aside in a wave
of astonishment, of uncontainable relief. Nils was not
only conscious but by the sound of his voice he'd apparently been so, listening, for some little time. "How
bad are you?" I demanded. "How do you feel?"

"I don't feel; I'm frozen solid. And considering
what I would be feeling if I could feel, it's just as well.
What are you guys doing still here?''

"We were waiting for you."

"Stop waiting. Go. The only way I'd get through that little hole is for you to use that knife of yours as an ice pick and take me out in pieces."

"I'm no better off," I heard Dolan say. "We'd both only slow you down. You've got a job to do and you'd better get going. Don't worry about Nils, I'll stay with him."

"Don't be ridiculous! What do you want me to do, start chasing after the Russian caravan? They picked up all their flags two days ago. Ask Nils how much of a trail will be left after forty-eight hours. I haven't the slightest idea where they're headed. It's a good guess they wanted to arrange a pickup as soon as they made the barrier and found a clear ceiling. But the barrier is a big place."

Dolan sounded alarmed. "My God! Two days. They could have reached the barrier by now and been picked up."

I sensed Nils nodding.

"Maybe," I said. "Maybe they've reached the barrier. I doubt they've been picked up."

"What do you mean?"

"Turnabout. After I broadcast that emergency message, I sabotaged their radio. Destroyed it completely. There's no possibility they'll be able to contact their pickup party."

"You what!"

It was Dolan. Not alarmed, horrified.

Even Nils had risen to an elbow. "Why?" he demanded.

"Why not?"

"Don't you see, Peter, now we do know where they're headed. The odds are they picked up any evidence at their landing site and so there's nothing at that location for them to find or go back to. That means there's only one location on the Ross Ice Shelf, one safe place, that both they and their pickup party know about. The only place that they can both assume the other will go to when they can't make contact by radio."

The glint of dawn was hitting me again. I felt like a damned idiot.

"They'll head to Mensa Station, of course," said Dolan. "Once that happens, they'll have to remove all evidence of their involvement, just like they did at the drop site. Just like they did here. They'll kill everyone at the station.

"Just like they killed us."

11

Virgin Trail

It didn't happen all at once. We lived by inches, by minutes on that march; that's the way we died. My memories of it are only bits and pieces, remnants of a threadbare cloth. So often I found myself walking without knowing why or where. Eventually the reason and the place would come back to me, but the minutes that were lost to oblivion never returned. That was at first. Before Day Three had ended and miles not inches lay behind us, I, at least, was losing time by the hour, oblivious to long stretches of progress and events. Cold, ice, wind, and death had driven it from my mind.

Of Day Four I have no recollection at all.

We had settled upon the slowest possible means for making progress, but I was insistent and neither of the others was of any mind to argue. Both Nils and Dolan were at the point where lying down and allowing the ice to cover them seemed as reasonable as hiking, and as likely to do them any good. Had those arguments been made, they would have been tough to rebut, for we truly had some horrific obstacles to overcome. Aside from the conditions themselves our biggest trouble was direction. We could make a pretty good guess at a heading here, but once the few points of reference around us were out of sight, it would be all but impossible to hold. Even a few degrees off course for the mountains could mean a day or more finding Hell's Flow. Once we descended the glacier and left the mountains for the great barrier, the same few degrees of misdirection would have us among the eternal lost.

I wasn't worried about that. Why should I be? The conditions themselves would almost certainly be our doom long before we reached the mountains.

Maybe Dolan was hinting that he understood all this when he suggested we walk an extended file. "This is the only way to sight a course," he said, and added that as the engineer of the group, he was best suited to hold the line from the rear while we set the pace. I stared at him. Had Robert Dolan hidden motives my brain was too numb to grasp anything beyond the raw suspicion that he had given in all too easily to joining the march in the first place.

I started walking.

Nils followed me out but called for me to hold up before we were very far along. He came up gesturing surreptitiously to the rear, where Dolan had just then started hobbling toward us. It was a pathetic sight to see. Bent almost double, Dolan was taking tortured little half-steps with his left foot and dragging his right behind. After every advance he would pause momentarily, recovering from the last effort and steeling himself for the one to come. Nils asked me—in an exaggerated undertone—if I had taken a look at Dolan's leg.

"No. He wouldn't let me near it."

"You tried?"

"Twice, but only halfheartedly. It was too dark in that igloo to have seen anything anyway. I admit he looks bad."

"Well, I just asked him about it and he insisted he was fine, that a doctor had already checked him over. Did the Soviets have someone examine—"

"Oh, you bet. And prescribed lots of ice and plenty of exercise. That's what we're doing out here. Bob Dolan is babbling. With time-outs for periodic lucidity"—which I had to admit included his analysis of me and the danger to Mensa—"he's been babbling for hours. Despite that, he's right about the line, but I don't want him leading, and if we let him lag, we'll lose him."

I didn't add that I felt much the same way about Nils until I had some reason to believe he wasn't going to fade out again. By the time I'd contrived something, Dolan had reached us and Nils was recommending that we close ranks. He justified it by saying that if we walked together one man's tendency to drift would be compensated by the others. I didn't like it. The idea was okay as far as it went, but it would work just as well with two as with three and I didn't want either of them feeling expendable.

"How about this?" I said. "We'll form a single file, all right, a hundred yards between us. The third man will advance three hundred yards to the front, a hundred beyond the first, line up on the other two, and then wait for the second man to pass him and line up the same way."

It sounded silly, but as I said, there was no argument.

"That will give me a chance to record my reports," said Dolan as he staggered away. I gave him a look, for he had no recorder and no paper; but because he was heading in the right direction, I said nothing more until he was approximately a hundred yards off and then called for him to stop, which he did.

Antarctica is a truly virgin continent. While everything about the antarctic is hostile, it is also true that everything here is pure. A hostile purity that is at the same time a pure hostility. Despite the fact that the snow crystals have lain on the ground for likely hundreds of years, it is absolutely white. Purest white. There is nothing to dirty it. Granules of ice scraped off the surface and melted by one's breath or against the skin are liquid for seconds only, but liquid for the first time in possibly centuries. Anyplace one steps is a place that has never before been trod by human feet— or any other feet, for that matter. In all probability it never will be again. The air is fresh, completely so, and would at these temperatures be rich with oxygen were it not for the fact that we were two miles above sea level. It's the highest continent on earth. Yet the most amazing quality of this virgin land is the utter silence. Nothing is so pure here as the silence.

In calm conditions it is possible to hear a whisper from a block away. Otherwise ordinary conversations can take place from nearly a quarter-mile. Two hundred yards behind I could call to Nils to shift right or left without raising my voice at all. Though Dolan was never closer to me than a hundred yards, except when he was passing me by for the front—or I, him— his voice was never out of earshot.

As I started out for the lead that first time, his words came clearly to me before I'd gotten close to him.

"I'll worry about our heading and you just keep an eye out for their trail. No one can move that many tractors across the ice without leaving some kind of sign. Even if we get ahead of them we'll find trail flags, won't we?"

He knew good and well we were taking the Hell's Flow shortcut rather than follow the Russians the long way around.

When I did close on him I could see he wasn't looking to me for an answer. Or to Nils. Staring off into the sky, Dolan seemed to be consulting a higher authority, and his remarks continued at my back when I passed him.

Ten minutes later when his turn came to pass me, he was still talking. In fact, he never stopped talking. Somehow his mind had created a gulf between itself and reality. His pain was on one side. Antarctica was there too, and so were Nils and I. Across the gulf of words Dolan was safe and sane and warm and comfortable.

Even Nils and I walked dangerously close to the edge. There were my periods of mental drifting during which time I wandered—probably at Nils' direction— or stood listlessly—again on orders—while my consciousness wandered away. Such performance was inexcusable, but I could no longer control my own mind. I was a child at a horror movie, making prolonged and unnecessary trips to the candy counter as an alternative to witnessing the drama. Nils didn't wander mentally or otherwise. When he left us, as he did several times, he just collapsed. The trouble was in his head, the same as it was in mine, but in Nils' case the damage was physical and understandable; while I had nothing but contempt for myself and my behavior, I suffered terribly for Nils. Those first times he was only down for several minutes, but like me, every time he went he was longer coming back.

The only thing that didn't go against us, at least initially, was visibility. We could see fine. Overcast skies never permitted us any sighting of the noon sun or night sky; in fact, we were never to see any hint of horizon. But our dark furs stood out clearly. Free of shade or shadow, the reach allowed us to resolve one another at almost any distance. The subtlest variations in tone from foreground to back were nonexistent. Not so much as a hummock or crater, ridge or valley, disturbed the colorless purity of that world. Actually, it was a universe, a counteruniverse of pure and endless white and we, aliens of another darker dimension, specks of living dust caught between distant galaxies. Our ability to discern distances suffered. Perspective was lost altogether and, inevitably, orientation as well. This was not snowblindness; it was whiteout as I had never experienced it before. Like pilots flying for hours in zero-visibility clouds without any instrumentation, we couldn't tell one side from the other or even up from down. After a while, we just moved, drifting through a white environment with our pathetic ritual of stops and starts.

The lead man would walk until someone, Nils or I, shouted for him to halt. Then he would turn, move left or right, lining up on the back two men, and hold his position until the third and then the second man had passed him in his turn. That continued for endless hours. I didn't keep a count on how many turns we each took walking, or figure out what kind of miles we were making; it's pointless now to attempt it. I know I was walking less than a third of the time. Nils was slow enough, lumbering along at half his normal pace, but Dolan was absolutely leaden, taking as much as half an hour to reach his position with infant steps and agonizing pauses between each. Forty-five minutes out of every hour I spent standing. The walking was bad enough but this was the worst part by far and the times when my condition deteriorated most rapidly. As I stood fighting unconsciousness, my body would shake so violently that it was a struggle to remain erect. As much as an hour might pass before I would move again, and then too often I couldn't. My limbs would be locked and I would have to overbalance myself just to force them to take action, knowing as I did that if I ever went down I might not get up.

At times I almost felt out of body. Absent from it all . . . but still aware, monitoring myself from a distance. One moment I might be staring down at my feet dragging endlessly along, and the next I'd be watching a picture of another Peter Masterson huddled within my parka, hooded head bowed low to the ice, staggering slowly out of sight.

Right after that happened the first time, my brain went out for popcorn, and when it came back, the movie had changed; the cast was the same but the action was altogether different:

I was standing over Dolan while Nils peeled back the leggings of Dolan's furs and untied the drawstring on his finespun cotton inners. That scene would have brought even the most determined malingerer back to responsibility. The dichotomy between skin and cotton was the difference between black and white. Dolan's leg was that dark: not blue—black. Swollen, horribly deformed, the limb was unrecognizable and the stench of rotting flesh unbearable.

Nils looked up at me and in his eyes I saw the same knowledge that I could see in mine from my distance: Dolan had only hours to live. This was gangrene as badly as I'd ever seen or heard of. Were the wound a surface one, I might have scraped some of the dead tissue away with my knife, as excruciating as that would have been for Dolan. But this was entirely internal and the damage was too extensive. Poison had undoubtedly spread throughout his body; even in a modern-hospital setting immediate amputation would probably fail to save him. How he stood the pain without going mad I couldn't fathom; how he stood at all, let alone managed something of a gait, is a question no human is equipped to answer.

As Dolan raised his head off the ice, Nils quickly

began replacing the clothing layers, tying up the boot with abnormal clumsiness.

It occurred to me that something in the picture was wrong.

Nils' hands were bare!

Of all things, he had removed his gloves to work the leather fastenings. I didn't like to see him do that, even for a few seconds. His frozen fingers worked back into the gloves and mittens, then he helped Dolan up.

"I'm carrying you from now on," I heard Nils say.

"No need for that. Help is on the way. Let's just keep on toward those rocks. Got to be some shelter up ahead. Might even find a stand of trees or a brook . . . you never know. Get a good fire going and I'll be right as rain."

Dolan managed to shrug off Nils' arm and stumbled off into the bleached darkness of midafternoon, leaving us only the sad picture of his crippled stride and the running melody of his constant chatter breaking at every step.

I left it to Nils to call Dolan's position because I had no idea which direction to go. Shortly after my turn came to begin walking, I found myself pulling away, panning the three of us from the vantage of distance—an event, I was to learn, that merely heralded imminent departure. I tried fighting but it was no use, for apparently I had neither Nils Hellstrom's strength of body nor Robert Dolan's strength of will.

The sky grew dark and the land darkened precisely to match it and we moved across the gray icescape at our dying pace.

The cold seemed to intensify. Yet this was probably an emotional analysis. When the light goes, cold is the only thing that remains. By this time I was no longer able to rationalize temperatures in terms of degrees, for cold had long since ceased to be a calculable quantity. Like time and space it assumed an infinite character; to our numbed senses, our frozen exteriors, it had become nothing but an immense, immeasurable thing.

The cold simply existed.

Distance had no meaning. I couldn't begin to guess

how much ground we had covered at any point of the march. There were no reference points, no landmarks to mark our progress. Once the remnants of our shelter vanished behind us, it might just as well have been a thousand miles away for our ability to find it. The white vastness seemed as limitless as the universe itself, though it extended only to the limits of our visibility. In the same way, time underwent terrible distortions: while minutes creeped by like hours, too often hours were lost to a moment's lack of concentration. I was present for less than half the night and yet the hours I remember, collected, would consume a lifetime.

We walked.

For hour upon endless hour we walked.

Beyond that, the walking, there is little to record. Only the stops punctuated our progress. There were many stops, some in my memory and others just outside it. At least three of these were when Nils collapsed. One time must have been near midnight, for the antarctic had reached its nadir of spring darkness. We had closed up our distances by half and still had trouble seeing one another with any confidence. I had turned and was lining up my position toward Dolan in the far back when the faint patch of blackness towering between us simply dropped out of sight.

I rushed back, though by this time I was pretty near hobbling myself, found Nils sprawled lifeless over a mound of ice, and lifted his mask. Seeing his face for the first time in days, even in such weak light, startled me so badly I was gripped by horror. He looked like a corpse, deathly white, dark-eyed, and gaunt. In a little while I sensed Dolan's approach and quickly replaced Nils' balaclava before he dropped heavily beside me and traded glances of concern. Again there was nothing to do but wait.

Hellstrom's condition had depressed me terribly. Yet it was not surprising. The demands for nourishment the body makes in these latitudes is difficult to believe. No one, no matter how gluttonous, gains weight in Antarctica. With sufficient calories, our bodies could endure the cold. With additional calories yet, they could survive the march. We had none of us eaten for days and we were traveling through the worst of antarctic weather. It was shocking to see the result on the face of this once prodigious man. The biggest, the strongest among us. But almost as shocking was the knowledge of what the others of us must be like.

Almost an hour passed before he revived. In the meantime I worried that Nils' and my attacks would coincide. As they increased in number and duration, this possibility became all the more certain. In fact, it seemed more than coincidence that it had not already occurred. Nils' attacks were out of his control. I wondered if I could truly say the same for mine.

Once on the move I was determined to maintain a grip.

Again and again I cursed myself under my breath. This man, this creature of flaw and fault, this Peter Masterson, was responsible for everything that had transpired. Yet he alone escapes it with a simple flight of mind. If we all died this night, I told myself, Peter Masterson must be here. I determined that I would be, and prayed I would be the last to perish that I might see my handiwork completed.

I must not escape that.

Our fortunate weather came to an end. With it, visibility. The beginnings of a snowstorm were drawn around us like sheer curtains; we neither felt the snowfall nor perceived it in the gloom of night. The subtle proof of its presence was the absence of anything else. By early morning the subtlety had gone. Massive flakes were a drapery that choked off visibility beyond a matter of yards. Worse, the snow began layering our parkas until we were ourselves as white as the ice. The danger of losing one another in the storm magnified tenfold. We closed up until we were nearly at arm's length, abandoned our procedure for maintaining a heading, and made steady progress for the first time since we had begun. We simply had no conception of which direction we were progressing and none of us would have hazarded a guess as to our heading expecting to be correct within 90 degrees.

Despite my determination, I continued to lose reality. Dolan's voice became a beacon, the last thing I perceived before oblivion swallowed me and the first thing I perceived of reality when I returned. His words were never of any significance, never something to be understood. I had only to understand what and where the words were to be back.

"Six times," I heard him say. "At least six times."

My name was spoken. And something about Strontium 90.

But this voice was Nils'.

It was obvious to me the two men were discussing my wanderings and the many times I had let them down. Only then did it occur to me that I was just reappearing from yet another. It had to be more than six.

"I told him not to go back but he kept going anyway."

"So that's it," Nils said.

My eyes resolved the scene above me. I was lying down and both men were standing over me. Their severe masks could not register loathing, but it had to be there. Then I realized I was wrong. It was worse than loathing. Their voices told me that behind the masks was pity. Their expressions were twins of the ones Nils and I had exchanged watching Dolan begin the expedition or those of Dolan's and mine when Nils had fallen unconscious that first time. Knowing this only increased my self-disgust.

But even with my mind in a rage the comings and goings were out of my control. If anything, this seemed to exacerbate the problem.

Long stretches of the night were lost to me. There were no times by then when I was really alert. Even those hours that should have been mine faded into an endless routine where one step was much like another—one white setting about us, no different from all the rest. After thousands upon thousands of steps and mile after mile of white, any single moment or any one incident was impossible to retrieve. The incidents became transposed in time. And moments afterward I wondered if they ever really happened at all.

But one thing I will never forget. When it came, it was a realization of my worst fears.

Once again I had abandoned my friends. How long I was gone is impossible to say, but when I heard words and began fighting my way back, the process seemed to take forever. The words were fainter, more distant than I had ever heard them. Eventually my mind stirred, though it cannot be said I was alert. I was aware. Consciousness was now merely that: sensation without sensibility, perception without comprehension. I was lying on my back once more. As numb as I was, I could feel the ice beneath me. It had become a part of me; I a part of the ice. A blanket of snow overlay me. Snow trickled through the eye and nose holes of my face mask. There was a faint illumination above me but, this time, no faces. I was alone.

I felt what Nils and Dolan had known nearly two days before. The time had come to quit. The decision required no conscious effort whatsoever. No thought. All I need do was close my eyes.

Painfully, I raised my head and rolled to one side. There, just a short way off was the body of Nils Hellstrom.

I crawled to him on hands and knees.

Outwardly he was cold and still, but I determined that he was alive. Reaching him and making this determination exhausted me. I remained in a heap beside him, half-unconscious, half-sleeping, until he revived on his own some little time later. His movements brought us both around together and together we stood.

I was aware of an odd, quite distant keening that marred the silence. It was like, yet unlike, anything I had heard before. Had I been alert to the significance of this, I would have reacted as Nils was then reacting, swinging his head in circles. It couldn't have been for references or direction; the snowstorm effectively cloaked the absence of reference points and confined us in a small circle of white isolation. The important thing was a sound—a once incessant chatter—we could no longer hear.

Nils turned to me suddenly. "Where's Bob?"

The words struck me a cruel blow. "I . . ."

"He was standing right over you waiting for you to regain consciousness. I felt dizzy and told him I was going to move away just enough to mark our heading. That's all I can remember. I guess I didn't get very far."

"If Dolan was on his own, Nils, he's just walked off."

My words went unanswered.

Nils tottered around, regained his balance barely, and then staggered off like a sot possessed. He cannot have had the remotest notion which direction he was going, for one was precisely the same as another. I held my position, calling continually as a beacon for Nils to return to, and shortly enough he did return, coming in from the opposite direction as he had left.

"Nothing?" I asked.

"Nothing at all. He could be miles away."

"He was in no condition to make miles on his own. The problem is that he could be a few feet away and we'd still never see him. The first time I came to about thirty minutes ago, I swear I heard his voice. It sounded strange. Far off and yet weak. Perhaps I was delirious, but I'm sure it was him."

"Coming from which direction?"

I had no idea. And any guess was beyond me.

"In this storm," Nils added, "his voice wouldn't travel more than just a few feet unless he was upwind."

Wind? For the first time I realized the source of that fearful keening. It was actually quite a blow and we were shouting just to make ourselves heard; I had no recollection of any wind before going down and yet this meant nothing; my recollections were not to be trusted. Until then Dolan's voice had been all that I heard.

Together Nils and I pushed into the storm. Hard-grained crystals blasted our faces, pecking at the balaclavas like hail on a tin roof. The few crystals that breached the eye slots stung horribly. I tried to hold a steady course, should we need to return to our starting point. It was wasted effort. Visibility was so bad we couldn't see more than a few yards on either side of us, and Nils kept tacking back and forth, trying to cover as much ground as he could. The storm frustrated both our objectives. By the time we had gone a dozen paces out we were hopelessly lost and had no prayer of finding our way back.

I bumped into something solid and fell back, almost going down. Before I realized it was Nils, his hands reached out to steady me. "Look, Peter," he said, "suppose Dolan wasn't as delirious as we thought. Maybe when we both collapsed he decided to do what I had done, moving far enough away to hold a heading line. Strayed farther than he intended to. He might have continued talking just hoping that the first one of us that came to would be able to find him."

A flash of hope penetrated my gloom. "If that's true, that he's not completely delirious, then he may still have an idea of our heading."

"And he wouldn't have come this far!"

After a last look around we turned and started back.

With the wind pelting our backs we could at least keep our eyes open, but that didn't mean we could see. Visibility was a circle of white surrounded by parka ruff. Nothing but sheer luck or possibly Dolan himself would ever take credit for our finding him.

At first I thought he was alive.

He was sitting up on his heels with his head slumped forward and his forearms buried in snow at his lap. Through what madness he had contorted his useless leg beneath him was something we would never know, for snow already had drifted above his waist, gathered at his chest as high as his shoulders, and made him merely a frozen bust of a man.

Nils, being Nils, bent down to him, going so far as to discard his own gloves to facilitate raising Dolan's mask.

I didn't need to look, but even for Nils one was enough.

He was set in the ice like concrete. While he appeared limp, our combined strengths were unequal to raising his head or his arms. He had the stiffness of fully developed rigor mortis. But it wasn't. Rigor takes time. Only a 100 degrees of frost can solidify a man as quickly, as completely as this.

Nils could not conceal the desolation he felt. "My God, Peter, why didn't he just lie down?"

I could only shake my head.

When Nils began fumbling back into one of the mittens with fingers that had become almost instantly frostbitten—the wind-chill factor was nearer 200 below zero, and in such conditions exposed flesh will freeze in literally a fraction of a second—I watched dumbfounded, not realizing how small the stubborn thing looked in his giant's hand. Then it hit me. "That's Dolan's mitten," I stammered.

Together we dug into the drift until we completely excavated Dolan's hands resting on his legs. Only the right one was bare. The index finger was straight and stiff; the others locked in a tight fist. He was pointing off into the storm like a sculptured weather vane. Not even my mind could have failed to grasp the significance of that.

Nils had been right about this man. Robert Dolan had known precisely what he was about when he had stepped into the storm to hold our heading. After realizing he had gone too far and would never find his way back unaided, he had kept up his running monologue as long as he had the strength. Sane or not, he knew two things of importance: the direction he believed was our heading, and the fact that none but him could now know it. When he could last no longer, Dolan had braced himself as high as he could in a squatting position so the drift would be longer concealing his body, pulled off his right glove and mitten, and shown us the way. Knowing Dolan as I now did—like everything else, too late by far—I was willing to wager he held on long enough for the hand and arm to become immobilized by cold.

And then he had died.

"What now?" asked Nils.

There was no need to bury him. That job was already well along; before we had made a fraction of a mile, it would be finished, and with an efficiency, a finality that would put any undertaker to shame.

"Now," I said, shrugging and pointing in the direction Dolan had given us, "we start walking."

To say that I have no recollections at all of that fourth day gives the sense of my condition, even though it is not strictly true. There is not one clear memory that I can drag out and say, Yes, this happened that next day after Bob Dolan died. Nevertheless, things happened.

Bob Dolan had died. I knew that.

We started walking again. Events prove that much.

By fits and falls we crossed Deception Reach.

There was no other way.

The sky continued to brighten during the middle part of the morning and darken increasingly late in the midafternoon.

This short daylight was the only way we had for keeping track of the time, and for that reason our days began not at midnight but at noon. By such reckoning we left Dolan late that morning just before the fourth day had begun. I think. I'm not even sure about that. We were both of us dying, Nils and I—more slowly than Dolan, but just as surely.

Procedures were abandoned. We wandered. Sometimes he led the march—usually during my fits—and sometimes it was I who led—generally after his falls. My frequent hazy times no longer interspaced periods of relative clarity. Things had come full circle. The hazy times were now infrequent; moreover, they were surrounded only by darkness.

Losing Bob had affected us in quite different ways. Nils and he had been friends. Something so trite as Dolan's dying gesture was certain to make an impression on the big Swede; I could imagine him resolving that it would not have been made in vain. He struck out with renewed enthusiasm. Though Nils was working on an energy debt even then, his reserves were incredible. I never for a moment believed he would live to see the Queen Maud Mountains, and yet his show of determination was inspiring.

For me Dolan's death only underscored the hopelessness of our attempt. I dragged for miles after that

hating myself for letting him die. Hating myself for
having learned too late how to like him. I hadn't
thought of him as a friend—I never thought of anyone
that way—and I wasn't impressed by dying gestures.
I hated myself for that too.

I was sitting on a ridge of ice.
Alone.
Where I was or which direction I should be moving
were matters with which my mind was unconcerned.
Nils Hellstrom? He was not a part of the picture before
my eyes. And while his absence was disturbing, I felt
no urgency to look about. I had returned to the theater
finding, not an important sequence missed, but that the
movie itself had ended. The actors had gone. The closing scenes had faded to gray. Even the credits had
finished rolling. But the projector, free of film, ran on.
It was time to close my eyes and yet now, oddly
enough, they would not close.
Something compelled me to turn my head.
A hand rested on my shoulder. Several moments
passed before I recognized the hand for what it was,
and more yet before I realized the reason for my confusion. It was bare of glove and mitten. By all appearances it had been so for many hours. Slowly it
sank in that Nils' gloves were still back with Dolan.
The consequences of that oversight were horrifying.
At least I should have been horrified. Oddly enough,
I was unmoved. That Nils' hands would never again
be of any use to him seemed without relevance. Board-
stiff, it lay on my shoulder like a weight, a swollen
misshapen stump with stubs protruding outward that
were no longer fingers. Two were actually broken off
completely, though there was no blood.
It was impossible to understand the comfort that
hand provided me.
I tried to turn in order to face him but found myself
slipping. Too weak to catch myself. The hand came
under me. Another like it slid under my legs and lifted
me childlike into the air.
And then we were moving again. I felt the move-

ment. Each step along the ice. But the steps were not mine.

I was free to close my eyes.

I retched myself into consciousness. Not once, but again and again. After each time I tried to slip back but my stomach reacted so violently that eventually I rolled onto my hands and knees in a spasm of dry heaves. When it was over, I regarded with wonder the utter whiteness of the snow beneath me, marred only by a Rorschach spatter of blood.

Kneeling there on all fours, I scooped up a huge handful of granulated snow, stuffed it under my mask, and tried twice to swallow. No good. Almost immediately it wound up back on the ice—a little reddish but its texture otherwise unaltered. Thirsty as I was, I gave up. The damn stuff was too hard to chew and too cold to melt in my mouth.

I knew even before looking up that we'd entered upon a new day. Day Five? Six or even Seven? No. I'd not survive a week. That thought didn't bother me. I was too concerned about the equally remote chances of surviving today. When I did look up, I was staring directly into the wind.

There was Nils crashed full-length on his chest, his head just inches from mine. He had gone until he collapsed. Given our relative positions, it seemed likely I'd been over his shoulder at the time. Antarctica was proceeding with its routine of operation: if it moves, kill it; if it falls, bury it. Like me, he was covered in drift. I crawled to him and started clearing the pile off his back.

The thing that struck me was the wind. Why was it at his back? It didn't seem likely any front could have come through in just the hours we had lain here, and yet, if Nils had become so disoriented or so senseless that he failed to keep moving into the wind, there was no telling how far we had come in the wrong direction.

I struggled upright. The ice hove and rolled under my feet. Days had passed since I had known cold or pain; I was permanently numb inside and out, but I was not without any feelings at all. Right then I felt

weak, I felt sick, and on top of that I felt seriously
dizzy. Two huge mounds swayed in the distance. Familiar black blisters on a flawlessly white complexion.
Then another sign that my feelings weren't gone altogether: I felt my pulse quicken. I strained to see any
drifting snow beyond a matter of several dozen
yards. Visibility was good enough; it simply wasn't
drifting. Out there the storm had abated completely.
The preternatural calm and quiet of the reach had returned. And yet here, the wind was a full force-four.
Here I sensed the restless roar of an undead beast beneath the ice.

With a wild heart I staggered slowly around.

That became at the same time the most terrifying
and the most rewarding sight that ever confronted my
eyes. I had thought nothing could be more beautiful
than Deception Reach as seen from the top of Hell's
Flow, but this was that too. Deception Reach lay at
my back, and Hell's Flow, a sprawling white ribbon
of ice descending toward the barrier two miles below
and twelve miles beyond, was stretched out before me.
A playground slide reserved exclusively for the children of the gods.

We'd done it.

No. Not we. He. Nils had done it.

I fell to my knees, sobbing, beside him.

Or perhaps I was laughing. At any rate I wasn't
thinking. No sooner had I exposed his head and back
than I grabbed fur and began pulling him out of his
snowbank. The smart thing to do would have been to
hold up there or, if we had to get moving, start heading for one side of the glacier. Not me. The day we'd
left Hell's Flow for the reach my mind had ceased to
function rationally; nothing that had happened since
had caused me to start it up again. Just the opposite.
I wanted to get onto the glacier before the whole thing
turned out to be a hallucination.

I got him turned over, grabbed the front of his parka
with both hands, then tugged and jerked until I'd
dragged him to the head of the glacier. Had we been
going uphill instead of down I don't know what I
would have done. His three hundred pounds—down at

least thirty in just this one week—were still augmented by at least twenty-five pounds of arctic wear and easily that much again of ice and snow. However, once we hit the slope, it was all I could do to hold him back. Before I knew it he had slipped out of my hands; I raced down beside him, got a good grip, and had just started to slow him when the sound came.

I had not heard that sound in five days. Had it been five years or five times five I could not have forgotten.

The ice shuddered violently.

As I whirled back around, I knew what it must be. But that didn't save us.

The glacier ruptured right before my eyes. There was no time to run, no way to dodge. Ice shattered beneath my feet. Suddenly I was sailing into the oblivion of a massive crevasse.

I landed hard on a ledge, rolled against the wall, and looked up dizzily in time to see Nils, twenty feet above me, just then coming over the side along with a small avalanche of ice. Boulder-size chunks exploded all around me. The shrapnel and spray were blinding. I heard a dull crash and leapt out to get him. Something hard struck my arms. When the spray had cleared, I was alone.

There wasn't time to consider options. I vaulted over the edge and started falling again into a gray obscurity. Down and down I plunged. It seemed like minutes; it wasn't. After only a second or two my feet glanced off a slick face and I fell the last few feet upside down. I remember a killing blow to my back and neck, then nothing.

I came to when something jarred me. Nils, I thought. I worked to my feet and felt around with outstretched hands. All I found were two facing sheer walls. I leaned against one—the downhill wall wasn't eight feet away—and peered in vain to my left and right.

The rumblings had stopped. With them, the vibrations. Unbelievably enough, the first sound I heard was water. Running water. Like a brook.

I looked up. The snowstorm had temporarily resumed as drift poured over the uphill edge in volumes that would soon fill the crevasse. It was more blinding than any blizzard. I couldn't even guess at our depth.

Eventually I could make out the base rising slightly to my left and descending on the right. Then I saw him. A small stream of water was running down where the ice sloped away, and there, lying lifeless in a shallow little pool, was Nils Hellstrom. With his feet at one wall and his head at the other, he had damned the stream. I waded over to him.

A hellish shriek stopped me cold as I knelt beside him. I hadn't forgotten this sound either. Countless tons of ice in torment. I stood as though in a trance, my hands pressed against the uphill wall. The rumble had become a distant, high-pitched wail. The quaking had become a steady movement. The crevasse was closing up again! The wail grew louder and louder, nearer and nearer. My head started swimming. It was popcorn time. If anything ever called for immediate intermission, this was it. Why did I stick around?

This time there was no rope. And there was no Nils on the surface to pull me out. Nils was down here with me. He needed saving worse than I did.

What was I waiting for?

I got my arms around Nils' chest and started dragging him down the crevasse. I could never have dragged him up and I had no suspicion that the base would go high enough to take us anywhere near to the top. I could never have dragged him down if the stream hadn't grown so deep and so swift that it carried half of his weight and practically swept us along. All I had to do was keep his head above water. That was all I could do. The walls closed in upon us. I felt the uphill wall—slick with melting water—less than arm's length away. Water was running right off the face and into the waist-high current. It wasn't possible. And yet it was happening.

The screaming of the ice was horrific. It drove right through my brain. I banged from one wall to the other as they closed to barely shoulder-width . . . pushing the river even deeper and faster. I was shouting to Nils in a vain attempt to wake him, but he couldn't have heard it. I couldn't hear myself.

Even the rushing of the water grew intense as we neared the lowest point in the crevasse. Here, another river surged into ours, boiled with desperate confusion, and then swirled into a black rift in the crevasse's downhill side. A second crack running perpendicular to ours.

The ice had closed to within inches, forcing me to turn sideways in order to keep going. At the same time the current had become so powerful that once I turned, I couldn't have stopped on a bet. Even Nils was washed along despite any resistance of the crevasse. The only thing left me was to keep my grip on him so that we would be carried along together.

Where the rivers converged, I slipped feetfirst into the black rift and hung there, the combined torrent pounding against me. Nils was caught in the crevasse. The water pushed as I pulled. Just when the two walls of the crevasse came together, Nils cannoned through. All traces of light disappeared. It was as though the lid of our coffin had slammed shut. We plunged together into utter darkness—a watery darkness. Again two glacial walls. But no floor. We were falling hand in hand, sliding together between the two sheer, slick faces of melting ice. Before I realized what was happening, Nils dropped out of my grasp. I reached out for him but he was just gone. My gloved hand clawed uselessly at the wet wall against my chest. The other wall slid past my back. Water rained down on me from above.

My descent ended in the worst possible way. Sudden impact. A narrow obstruction caught my chest and drove my ribs up into my throat. Had the thick parka not protected me, I have no doubt this would have been the end right then and there. But I wasn't thinking about that. When a two-hundred-pound fist of iron is slammed into your solar plexus you don't think about your good fortune. You think about breathing. After a minute or two, you decide to give your ideas a try. My ideas didn't get very far. I was pinned helplessly. So tightly was I pinned that my chest wouldn't expand even the fraction of an inch for me to take a breath.

Water poured over me in buckets.

Somehow I reached my boot knife and thrust it into the ice above my head. With both hands on the hilt I pulled myself up a single millimeter, took a sip of air, liked it, and pulled again. Four feet higher I breathed with an agonized normality. Wedging both knees under me, I looked up for the first time. The shower continued in an unending deluge. But there was not a drop of light. This fissure didn't penetrate the surface. Assuming I could scale these slick walls the several hundred feet using only my knife—which I didn't for an instant assume that I could—I'd never break through to the top. I had no intention of trying.

Not yet, anyway.

I felt to the sides, but I could not feel Nils' body. I shouted his name, but there was no answer.

He had to be farther below me.

I wormed out of my parka and let it drop.

I turned naturally to see it fall.

The most surprising thing right then should have been that I did, in fact, see it fall. A bloodred light—faint and pulsating, from deep within the fissure—played off the shower of water and walls of ice. My parka disappeared into a gaping wound. That should have been, but wasn't, the most surprising thing. With my light inner layers now completely soaked, it occurred to me for the first time in minutes that I ought to have been half-frozen to death. But I wasn't half-frozen. I wasn't even cold. Surprising didn't really cover what I was going through right then.

In Antarctica, light and water are rare commodities.

Heat, in any quantity, is unimaginable.

Currents of hot air billowed up from below me. The air I breathed was rich with humidity. Heavy with heat. I had survived the night above the crevasse because I had been warm, I had been warmer still once inside.

Now I was hot.

Only one explanation made any sense. Nils and I had suspected that an underground geyser, a kind of geothermic river, had channeled beneath the glacier, accounting for the rushing torrent Nils, Dolan, Asia, and I had only barely survived near the top of Hell's Flow. Of course that was now absurd. Hell's Flow was indeed flowing. It was thawing. And a crust of half-melted mush was being swept down the mountain unchecked. The source of this heat was deep, from the very center of the earth. But that did not explain the throbbing vermilion glow. Neither hot water nor steam would account for that. Boiling magma would. I was then convinced that the real flow here was an active volcano whose eruption was probably hours imminent.

It was a crazy idea. But no more so than the truth.

I traversed over one of the wider areas before starting down. When my feet slipped and the knife failed to hold my weight, I dropped to the bottom of the fissure. Except there was no bottom. The ice simply ended. I tumbled through open space and landed hard on solid rock. The fall broke my back. My legs were broken. When I rolled my broken neck to one side, I saw Nils a few feet away. There was a pool between us but Nils had landed to one side of the water and I to the other, both of us on rock.

It felt like rock. Ice, admittedly, often feels like rock, but there is no such thing as hot ice and therefore the rock-hard surface beneath me, which also felt hot, was rock. We had fallen completely through the glacier!

Seeing him got me to my feet.

My night vision was working overtime.

Though the red glow was barely a candlepower strong—red light does not hamper night vision—there, deep in the belly of the Queen Maud Mountains, I could identify our circumstances.

By all appearances we were inside a grotto, a rock oven of sorts. Granite walls glowing softly like coals surrounded me on all sides except one. That side was open, barred only by a shimmering curtain of red rain. Just beyond the opening was the source of the glow, but I couldn't see it from within the grotto itself. The light seemed to be reflecting off the raindrops.

The heat seemed to emanate from that opening too.

Even there in the grotto with a roof of ice only yards overhead, the temperature was above 100 degrees. Great wisps of vapor wafted from the rock walls, hung overhead like storm clouds, and eventually were carried up toward the glacier by waves of superheated air.

The deluge of water that the glacier sent down was like a tropical shower. It flooded the granite floor, spilled over a stone bank, and disappeared under the shimmering curtain. The sound of its falling, and a lot more water, too, was drowned out by the storm. I sheathed the knife, forded the pool, and verified that Nils' head was out of the water. The light wasn't good enough to do more. Then I moved to the opening. I'd prepared myself for almost anything. A geothermal steamhouse. A massive caldron of boiling lava. Even some devilish creature with horns and goat feet holding court to a chamber of regretfully unrepentant souls. This was, after all, not only the flow of Hell's Flow, it was the hell. In that sense at least I was precisely correct even if what I saw convinced me I'd been wrong about everything else.

The chamber was huge, that much I could tell. The light nearest me was but one of a long row of red blinking lights clinging to the wall at intervals of about a hundred feet. There was an identical row, paralleling this one, on the other side of the chamber. Together they disappeared into the darkness left and right of me, like airport runway lights. This, however, was instrument weather, and visibility didn't permit me to see the end of them in either direction. They were too tiny to illuminate the chamber, however the distance between them and their overall number revealed its vastness. I climbed down the stone waterfall and went up to the nearest red light. It was attached to a rectangular metal box mounted to the granite wall. An electrical panel. The red indicator light blinked on and off from the very center. Above it were some electronic meters and switches. Below was a large knob with a knurled surface and an arrow indicating a clockwise direction of turn. With both hands I rotated the knob 180 degrees.

Lightning flickered.

I looked up.

All hell broke loose.

It came from above: a burst of heavenly light, the first real light I had seen in more than a week.

This was no chamber at all but a natural, if mammoth-sized, granite cavern deep below Hell's Flow. Fifty feet across. Length? It was impossible to say. Visibility was many times what it had been in darkness, but I still couldn't see any ends to the cavern. The natural vaulted rock ceiling, however, was high, at least twice the cavern's breadth. The light came from this ceiling, from a source no more natural than it was supernatural, godly or demonic. A thousand mercury vapor-gas bulbs bolted to the rock had flickered to life. What had seemed to me a blinding brilliance grew brighter with each minute that passed until the cavern became as bright as day. I looked around me in astonishment.

The thunderstorm in here was a veritable cloudburst. Water gushed from every crevice, every hole in the rock no matter how small or how high. Water ran right down the granite walls. It rained off the granite ceiling. My little grotto was only one of dozens, perhaps hundreds of small little caves leading off of this large one, and the waterspill was only one of dozens, perhaps hundreds, that dumped onto the cavern floor. All of these sources were feeding a river of rage that flowed off to my right. This was no mountain stream. It was too deep to wade across and too fast to be swum. Deep and dangerous and damnably warm, I'd no doubt at all.

More astonishing than this were the racks. Between the river and the sides of the chamber. Thirty feet high. Some even higher. They occupied every square foot of space along the rock walls. And these too continued as far as the eye could see on both sides of the river in both directions. The racks themselves were filled with fifty-five-gallon metal drums that stood on wooden pallets. Thousands upon thousands of varicolored drums.

I started walking.

I was doing my best to figure it out. But I was simply too damn dumb. Here, I believed, was salvation. A storage facility of this size—never mind what the hell it's doing here—meant supervision. The lights meant that someone was around or had made arrangements to return before long. It meant that there had to be a way in, as well as a way out. In my dazed condition it never occurred to me these gas lamps might not have been turned on for years or that the entrance might be closed through the winter months, accessible only in summer. How these hellish temperatures fit into that theory never entered my head. The glacier, melting right through the granite ceiling and walls, didn't seem to concern me either.

I stuck to a path between the steeply sloping bank and the racks on my side of the cavern. Very shortly I came across the first of the forklifts on its side half-submerged in the river. I found racks that had toppled, drums that had spilled onto the path or rolled down the bank to the river's edge. Those that had reached the current would be carried far downstream. It was easy to see how this had happened. Water flowing off the walls and under the racks was washing their foundations away.

About every hundred yards I would have to throw another switch to turn on more of the mercury lamps.

After nearly a quarter of a mile I reached a junction of two other canverns. One narrowed slightly and headed up beneath Deception Reach. The other twisted around and went back below the glacier. As natural a pair of geologic features as their contents were unnatural. Similar series of lights overhung each cavern. Along the walls of each were the same racks, though some now held containers of a different sort. To my right, row upon row of oblong canisters, laid on their sides like wine bottles, honeycombed the metal racks. There were literally millions of them, cylindrical sealed tubes, golf-bag-sized, which gleamed of stainless steel. In the other direction the pallets were loaded with single immense casks the size and shape of railroad tank cars.

Down each cavern rushed the same furious river. All three flowed into this junction—a confluence without outlet. The resultant meeting of waters was such a thing that beggars description. Through the chaos of confluent turbulence, wave breaking against wave, swell surging against swell, I was able to see that the picture was not one of utter confusion. There, where the water level should have risen by thousands of gallons each second, it was falling. A whirlpool had formed precisely in the center: a maelstrom, fully twenty yards in diameter, swirling at a dizzying speed. The maelstrom's eye was funnel-shaped, and water, descending the tapered sides, spun faster and faster until at last its centrifugal force seemed to give it the authority to defy gravity. I watched, mesmerized, the clouds of spray be kicked aloft and—vaporized almost immediately in the extreme heat—surge toward the top of the cavern high overhead. It was through those vapors I spotted the entrance. A circular slab of steel nearly half the whirlpool's diameter, mounted on the granite roof like the lid of a missile silo guarding the upper world from the nether.

It was seeing that entrance that shocked me to reason.

I turned hurriedly, moved toward the racks behind me. I had to detour a pile of abandoned pallets before I could get close enough to one of the canisters to see them clearly for the first time.

No need to bother with the fine print.

DANGER! appeared in bold letters.

The symbol below it was foreign to me; I'd been raised with the one that graced public-school basements and the entrances to civic buildings during the uneasy decades of our accommodation with nuclear brinkmanship, black circle on gold with alternating black sections. This looked more like an atom model, a central dot orbited by three other dots at two-hour shifts. But what the hell? Radiation is radiation. And a nuclear dump is still a nuclear dump.

My eyes flew from one to another canister.

The same symbol was stamped on each.

I shivered. In 100 degrees of heat, I shivered.

Now I was seeing the horror of them: drums dented by handling, the sides crawling with corrosion. Here one that had fallen or been washed off a rack was lying near the water with its lid cracked open. There several larger casks with corrugated exteriors that looked like culvert pipe had been crushed when thaw had collapsed a part of the ceiling. Three of them, shells in various states of disrepair, lay waiting their turns to be swallowed up by the current. Rust. Rot. Ruin. All around me, canisters showed the signs of neglect, of inadequate precautions, of heedless hurry.

"Those sons of bitches," I cried aloud.

I started running.

My mind raced ahead. The Geiger counter at the base of our borehole assembly. Mary Ingram's geologic specialties. Paulette Gruber and her odd expertise in radiation treatment. Even the Centaur Project itself, with its continental drilling technique that had to be tested on the ice shelf. Now it all made sense. The United States government must have foreseen many years ago that the nuclear-waste issue would be decades of dilemma with stockpiles of contaminated and toxic material threatening to flood the few inadequate sites authorized for storage. Studies were commissioned. Shoot the damn stuff into outer space, dump it in the ocean, bury it in the deserts of the American West, or hide it under the antarctic icecap. Ten years ago, perhaps twenty or even thirty, they had chosen the easiest, the most politically expedient, the one they thought they could get away with. Because no one was supposed to find out about it. No one was supposed to care.

The flood was dammed and forgotten.

But was it?

The satellite composite I'd seen argued that Washington had kept an eye on its secret. Infrared photographs warned them that something was wrong. A geologic disposal site that should last the ten thousand years of nuclear waste half-life had failed to last even thirty. A hole appeared in the dam. Nasty stuff started leaking out. Enter Mensa. Lookng for uranium ore? Bullshit! We were looking for leaks. Perhaps the project's original purpose had been to drill holes, to locate other sites for geologic disposal, no doubt. Suddenly our job was to plug holes. Or at least to determine how big and how bad the hole was so the proper action could be taken. By the time this water reached the ocean five hundred miles away, it would be too diluted, too dispersed to gauge. Better to set up shop right next to the leak. Where the eye in the sky told them the leak would be.

Then, more bad luck. The satellite was shot down. That one or another one like it, and if one satellite could photograph a heat buildup under Hell's Flow, then so could another. With the satellite transmitters inoperative, probably as a result of the attack, Washington couldn't be sure what the satellite had seen. Neither could they take any chances. Particularly if they had any suspicion that the Russians would try to grab the film canister before the navy could recover it. And why not? The Russians had shot it down; of all the things Dolan had told me, that was the one thing I believed. Fedorev himself had admitted they did. Only one thing had worked in our favor. The satellite had crashed near an American station. Another job for the poor fools of Mensa. One fool in particular.

I reached the ground below our grotto, scrambled up the cliff beside the waterspill, and clawed my way inside.

"Nils," I shouted, "we've got to get the hell outta here!" There he was, precisely where I had left him. In precisely the same position. I drew him farther from the water and then turned him over to remove his balaclava.

I stopped when I had his hood down and his mask off.

In spite of the 100-plus temperatures he was still devoid of color. And he was every bit as stiff as he had been when I'd pulled him out of that snowbank. That much I could rationalize. But not his face. It was no longer Nils Hellstrom's face at all. It had been his, regardless of how hideous it had become, as long as he lived. Now that he was dead, it was his no longer.

I stood over him trembling in disbelief.

He had been dead when he had fallen into the crevasse, dead when I had dragged him off the reach. Dead long before I had even come to. He had died carrying me those last miles to Hell's Flow.

The rocky bank was flying under my feet. At my left the river raced on ahead while to the right the stainless-steel drums with their symbols of horror passed behind me. I paid none of them the slightest mind.

Never had I known this kind of rage.

It sapped me of sight, of reason. Learning about Hell's Flow had been the beginning of my education. Within moments of that time I believed I knew it all. I was wrong. But my education had been brief. Learning about Nils had been the last lesson my mind allowed.

At the confluence of the three rivers I stopped.

The maelstrom was as daunting as though I were seeing it for the first time; I don't believe a mind can carry away the image of such ungovernable fury. Huge columns of vapor still swelled toward the steel door in the vault overhead.

This was the only way in or out for me.

A moment's consideration by any student statistician could have produced some very intimidating odds, assuming, of course, that one is intimidated by the infinite—in this case the infinitely negligible. Even grade-schoolers know that—with odds-making as well as with elementary math—division of zero by any denominator at all consistently yields that result.

Not me. For Peter Masterson school was out.

I scooped up one of the wooden pallets, stepped to the riverbank, inhaled a full measure of hot and heated air, and then, holding the pallet out in front of me, dived directly into the eye of the maelstrom.

12

Scales

The vortex sucked me in so swiftly I had time to register only two facts between that first instant, when the wooden pallet was wrenched out of my hands, and the next, when I found myself being dragged deep below the surface. About the water temperature I had been correct: few hot tubs are hotter. I was wrong about the other: any suggestion that the water in the lower funnel spun in defiance of gravity was purely illusion. It was going down hell bent.

I'd made three complete orbits of the whirlpool in the same number of seconds, each one smaller than the previous, and faster too, when something snatched my feet and yanked me directly into the funnel. Only parachuting into the top of a tornado could compare to it. Before it was over I must have whirled around a hundred times and I don't for a moment believe I could have survived had I not been erect at the time. My arms banged against rock on all sides of me as I spiraled down at high speed through a narrow cleft in the floor of the repository. Down, down I went and around. Then I was through. The whirling stopped. And my descent.

I plunged into a submarine chamber. There the waters churned and pounded; they whipped me about like a soaked rag. Dazed, drained of my senses, I felt as though I had just gone through the spin cycle straight into the rinse.

The first sense to return was panic.

All the air in my lungs was gone, lost in a nightmare

of spume. I had not intentionally exhaled and yet nothing had been saved.

I started thrashing for the surface without any idea how to get there or even which way to go. I was too dizzy. The water was beating so wildly it was certain my sense of balance would be returning last. Of course, it was too dark to see the top. Under any definition of dark. A moonless ocean night is dark; a shuttered basement is dark; that chamber, though, was totally devoid of light. Period. So I was flapping my arms and kicking too—with my boots this was wasted effort—but I had not the slightest confidence I was swimming up.

When something whacked my hand, I jerked back. It had been solid and heavy and moving fast. Cautiously I explored the same blackness again. There was nothing. Whatever it had been was now gone. I began swimming again, more carefully yet. This time my shoulder took the blow, caught by a boulder rushing past with such power it set me doing flips.

I turned and swam back down. My chest was afire but I swam down.

Now I knew an even greater panic.

I was being flushed out with the waste water through the bowels of the Queen Mauds. Aeons of natural drainage had formed this channel, this aqueduct for the subglacial runoff. After so many years it should have eroded to many times its useful size, but the heat from the nuclear waste had brought about a hundredfold increase in the volume of glacier melt. It wasn't even close to big enough. I floated in rushing darkness, head drawn into my chest like a turtle. If I could have pulled in my arms and legs too, I would have done it. These rocky innards that lined the channel wall—ledges, crags, outcroppings—could hit me from any direction, below me, above me, or from either side.

Seconds passed. Fifteen. Perhaps twenty.

The headlong current rolled me here and there.

I grew frantic for air.

My fear of the walls did not lessen, but my frenzy to breathe grew all the more intense. Eventually, it was the only thing that mattered.

Again I started swimming, but this time my balance had recovered to the point that I was fairly sure I headed up. I sculled with one hand and extended the other as high above me as I could reach.

My fingertips, still in water, skidded across a well-worn slab. Projections knocked against my hand and several times I dropped involuntarily. After one of these times I kicked upward feeling for rock, but all that my hands did was thrust out of the water. Without a moment's hesitation I slapped them down, arched my back, and pushed my face above the surface. One desperate inhalation of stale, hot air later, I shot back down.

Another thirty seconds came and went.

I counted every one of them.

Then I did the same thing all over again.

Once again I got away with it. The third time, while launching myself facefirst toward the top, a stone projection caught me right across the jaw. Never have I been struck such a blow. I drifted down only half-conscious until my feet dragged along the bottom of the channel. I came to, dumb with pain but in a worse agony to replace the air that had been slammed from my lungs.

I shoved off toward the top to try again.

The surface was there but the ceiling had withdrawn beyond my reach.

As I inhaled, I knew that other things had changed too. Maybe it was the slapping of the waves. Echoing from higher overhead. Maybe it was the air itself, cooler and fresher. Whatever the reason I seemed instinctively to understand that I was no longer beneath the mountain. And that made sense. I'd been in the water more than a minute. Carried along a lot faster than a man can run.

At the same time I was sure my speed had increased even more. The surface had a wild chop that I felt rather than saw, and it grew wilder with each breath I seized. Waves were breaking all around me. They crashed off the walls with more and more energy; the sounds of these crashes dropped more and more quickly behind me. Yes, the river's speed was increasing, all right.

That made sense too.

I was back. Below the glacier.

The descent off Hell's Flow would be the equivalent of the Colorado River racing down from Pikes Peak. I wouldn't have risked it in a puncture-proof ten-man rubber raft even if Thor Heyerdahl were the other nine men. I didn't even have the wooden pallet. My fur leggings and boots had been almost buoyant for a time; now they'd become waterlogged and heavy as hell. Without a full breath of air I had a constant battle just to stay up. Sixty seconds of treading water had exhausted me. Waves spilled over my head. Swells washed under me and tossed me toward the walls, sometimes stopping just short of contact, too often flattening me against the ice before drawing me back into the flow.

I started shouting whenever I came up for air, just to hear the echo of my voice against the ceiling. Glancing off the walls was bad enough, but the thought of smacking into a low overhang still frightened me so much I continued to shout even after I'd convinced myself the ice was twenty to fifty feet overhead. I kept it up, that is, until I'd swallowed a bucket of hot water and lost my feeble hold on the surface. I ascended under a swell and sank again without ever getting close to the top. Only when a trough exposed my head did I get a gulp of air. Then I was under again.

I came up shouting. But there was no answering echo. The shout that came back amplified a thousand times wasn't mine, it was the glacier. Hell's Flow had its own distinctive cry, and though the only other time I'd heard this particular call had been from the surface, it was a sound a man does not mistake.

The splash of waves and crash of water against ice were lost, drowned by a din of destruction.

The spine of Hell's Flow was splitting in two.

Again.

From below, the sight of the glacier being severed down the middle was even more staggering than it had been from above. A jagged tear of ice two hundred feet thick raced over my head. It shot down the river ahead of me, exposing in its wake a fifty-foot-wide slash of gray sky.

The darkness was thrown aside.

For the first time I could see the true nature of the river, yet I was too staggered by the spectacle above me to notice. The air was filled with ice. Of every size and shape. Billions of tiny particles, frozen shrapnel and huge fragments, rained down from the glacier. When at last I could tear my eyes away and look around me, every horror I had only imagined was revealed as a shocking understatement. That river was the thing of which nightmares are made. A living, heaving, thrashing beast.

Then I spotted it. My pallet.

It was just up ahead across the river.

As I started swimming, the first of the loose debris turned the surface of the water into a battle at sea. No place was free of the shelling. Already running white, the surface became littered with craters from twenty-pounders to ten-kiloton monsters that sent spray halfway up the chasm.

My back was hit several times by smaller pieces.

Then something cracked me on the head. I went under, stunned. When I came up, the wooden pallet was right there. I crawled aboard and paddled into the mainstream.

The river was choked with ice. Bergy bits that rose suddenly from a trough or bobbed on the surface.

Large bergs were calving off the sides. Before I made the middle, a slab big enough to flatten Mensa Station toppled in behind me and surged my wooden life raft and me high into the air. I clung to the slats for dear life, but when we struck the opposite wall, only a miracle and tenpenny nails kept the thing in one piece. We washed back into the central flow as bigger bergs yet careened down on both sides. I was buffeted from one bank to the next by tidal strength waves.

Up ahead was the end of the crevasse. The river disappeared at the foot of the ice into a mouth as black as Satan's soul. In that instant I wanted anything but

to be carried into that maw. In the next, there seemed
no way I would make it.

The north wall near the waterline began to tremble.

As I watched, a cubic acre of ice tore free of the
wall and leaned into the chasm directly in front of me.
There wasn't a hope of avoiding it. It was at least as
wide as the chasm. And it would obliterate everything
in its path.

I was in its path.

A darkness descended over the river.

Over me.

If a fair piece of the sky had hurtled down onto my
head, it would have looked like that berg sliding into
the water. It struck with a deafening crunch, stopped
a matter of feet above the water, and remained there,
pinched between the chasm walls. The current swept
me underneath. I saw fissures race across this rough
roof of ice so close I could have reached up and thrust
my hand in them. No sooner had I passed out from
below it than an explosive shattering of ice came at
my back. The cubic acre shattered into a thousand
pieces that fell in a jumbled mass to the river. A wall
of water picked me up and hurled me, still clinging
mightily to my raft, directly into the black mouth below the chasm's end. My journey was just beginning.

I couldn't know where it would take me. Perhaps
I'd wind up beside Sturdevant in a grotto under Satan's
Gate. Perhaps in a pocket deep within the barrier ice.
More likely I'd be carried down to the frozen sea hundreds of feet below the Ross Ice Shelf, five hundred
miles from the nearest breath of air. It didn't matter
the odds now. There was no turning back. One doesn't
leave the train between stations no matter how dread-
ful the route, the destination, or the fare.

On a one-way ticket you can't look back.

And when you catch the last coach out of hell you
don't bitch about the itinerary.

I don't pretend to understand the thermodynamics
behind that river's course. Down the mountain it traveled between the glacier and the rock. But how the
river, heated though it was, could have penetrated the

ice shelf and channeled so far outward rather than spilling into the ocean are things for others to explain. Even Robert Dolan, whose hot-water boring process used the same principle on a vertical basis, believed that the stream of waste water the satellite had detected extending into the barrier was beneath the ice rather than within it. He had been shocked by the loss of borehole water. It was enough for me that the river did what it did. For fully half an hour I rode the pallet before getting any suspicion that Hell's Flow and the Queen Mauds lay at last behind me. What actually happened after that I reasoned or assumed or occasionally sensed but never saw. I was blind. The crevasse must have closed and sealed again before I was very far away, judging by the totality, the suddenness with which the darkness returned. Yet in the same way I reasoned I had started down Hell's Flow, I knew when the foot of the mountain had been reached. It could have ended in an open hole and waterfall into the subfreezing, subbarrier waters. Instead, the river's rampage eased. What had raged with swift abandon slowed, waves rolled less wildly, and the crashes seemed not so much unrestrained. All this was good news for me, even if I failed to understand it. But one law of thermodynamics was simple enough for even Peter Masterson to grasp, and I sensed that long before the rest: the water was cooling off.

It was still warm. But no longer hot.

The Styx was busy with every size of floe. They choked the surface, often clogging the channel until the warm water melted and dislodged obstructing ice. But always at a price. The cost was in degrees— degrees Fahrenheit, degrees Celsius, degrees Kelvin— but no matter the currency, rate of exchange was all that mattered now: in this case, heat per mile. There were so many miles to go and so many degrees between warm enough to sustain life and cold enough to exhaust it.

This was a race . . . to see which would do me first, the miles or the degrees. Or something else altogether.

My arms were badly torn. My legs and back had taken a brutal battering. My neck ached horribly; ex-

ploring the damage touched off nerves from my forehead to my shoulders and sent bursts of electric torture
down my back. If I were lucky, only the jaw was broken and my spine remained intact. I lay my head
against the wooden slats and closed my eyes. I dared
not sleep. At the same time I needed rest desperately.
My every muscle suffered tonic spasms. My heart
banged audibly. My body was in hysterics, and yet,
compared to my mind, the body itself was positively
catatonic. I counted the seconds through half a minute
forcing myself to a calm. I couldn't concentrate longer.
In my condition half a day wouldn't have been half
long enough.

The night dragged on, the water grew tepid, and the
air between the surface and the high ceiling assumed
a foreboding chill. I was running out of time. The hot-
water dunking had been a quick relief, just what the
doctor might have ordered. But my limbs, my whole
body, had suffered the effects of advanced hypothermia and frostbite over the course of a week. The doctor would have insisted that his patient evacuate the
water before it was allowed to cool.

I started shivering for the first time in hours.

Before long I was shaking with an epileptic frenzy,
my condition worse by far than it had been before I'd
warmed. Convulsions drained the last of my reserves.
Weakness shattered my resistance to the cold.

Under these conditions it is unthinkable a man could
sleep. What I did might be better described another
way.

So I didn't really awake with water in my mouth
and throat so much as I came to. I tried to spit and
managed, but trying to inhale, I only gulped more water in. My arms flailed at the surface. There was no
surface. My fingers found the lower edge of my makeshift raft and frantically I scrambled back aboard.
Alarm was frozen across my face. Not only was it a
terrible way to return, it was the worst way of learning
that too much time had been allowed to pass.

I knew that by the water.

Cool no longer did it justice. This water was cold.

Not freezing perhaps but cold, and the shape I was in, that difference was not likely to count for very much.

My hands shook so badly I couldn't keep a hold on the pallet. I'd try to grip the slats but my fingers had no strength and seemed to spring away of their own accord. Finally I rammed them both between some slats and let them bang around as they saw fit.

The thing that frightened me most was the possibility that I had missed my target. If that were true I wouldn't stop now until I reached the sea. Until the channel dipped the last few feet below the bottom of the barrier. Even if it were up ahead, what condition was it in? Would there be anything to see? Would I see it if there were?

I started kicking. My goal was to reach the northern side, but as much as anything, I needed to keep myself awake. It was a pitiable effort that couldn't have been much less successful in the former if I'd failed in the latter. With useless hands and worthless boots I wasn't making one foot crosscurrent for every hundred I was carried downstream. But at last I collided with something that was not one of the floes and not a part of the flow itself; I put out a hand and felt the bank at arm's reach. I need have no worry about beaching myself unintentionally. Climbing out I should worry about. The ice came straight out of the water, a near vertical slab washed slick and smooth.

As the wall slipped swiftly past my fingers, I glanced automatically upward. A forlorn attempt to judge its height. I saw nothing of the wall. And yet for the first time in hours there was light. A feeble, diffused light passing directly overhead. I turned to watch it disappear. Was my vision dulled by darkness or my thinking dulled by cold? I had a picture in my mind of what I saw, roughly round, about a yard in diameter . . . an opening in the upper wall. But then the dim circle was gone. Too far behind me to be visible. I was left with an obscure memory.

Comprehension struck like a klaxon. The effect was not a cry but a charge that electrified my body. My God! I told myself, that must be it—and I'm being carried right on by.

I kicked against the bank and frantically felt over the wall for a handhold. No, nothing. Pulling out my boot knife, I thrust the blade into the ice—it penetrated less than an inch—gripped the angled haft with both hands, and then just hung there while the current streamed over the full length of my body. My right hand scrambled over the surface for another hold. Still nothing . . . No, wait. A crack hardly that same inch in width ran at a diagonal into the river. I jammed my fingers to the knuckles. It held enough for me to work free the knife and chip out a handhold above the crack.

I'd have traded ten years of my life for an ice ax or an adze. I had only the knife. And nothing like ten hours to trade away. Instead of two or three blows I pecked for minutes at a time to fashion each handhold and step in turn. And the first ones I hollowed out collapsed as soon as I put my weight on it. Twice I fell back into the water. Another time I would have cursed myself bitterly, for I knew better. But I couldn't bring myself to do it. My hands shook so badly it was all I could do to hold on to the knife. Hanging on to the wall bare-handed was almost too much to ask. But shakes or no shakes, ax or no ax, the same rules applied. A steep ice slope is no place to linger. Any ice climb over 60 percent, twenty feet in height or twenty minutes in scaling ought to be detoured. That's good advice for a practiced climber who is rested and in good health. In my case there was no call for self-reproach. I didn't deserve that. Instead, I started doing it right, making all my initial blows horizontal or even slightly upward; once a notch was formed I hacked downward from the upper side. I kept the spacing of handholds regular, far enough to keep their number within reason, close enough to locate blind. Whenever my blade struck with a hollow thud, I abandoned the work and recut farther to the side. I wasn't good enough even in good condition to negotiate fractured ice.

Half an hour later I was fifteen feet above the Styx. I had traversed a good ways upriver but still hadn't got within sight of the spot of light. That wouldn't happen for another hour. It was situated fifty feet from my

landing point at least. Thirty, maybe forty feet above
the waterline. Had it actually opened on the ceiling,
requiring me to negotiate a reverse slope, as an overhang, my position would have been hopeless. Fortunately, it was hollowed into the crotch of ceiling and
wall. I managed to traverse below the light, chipped
out a series of handholds at eye level, and climbed up
by stepping into the lower ones.

I found myself in a burrow.

With my heels braced on one side and my back
against the other, I took a break, the first in more than
two hours.

I was close to mental and physical collapse.

It frightened me the way my heart raced, yet I felt
if my eyes once closed I'd never open them again. My
breath would come in seizures, short and shallow,
when I needed air; when I didn't, I'd be trying to gulp
it down. In between I coughed so violently the taste
of blood never left my mouth.

Part of me knew I could go no farther.

Another part knew this was only the beginning.

Above stretched an impossible climb. Nearly two
hundred feet. Straight up. Some of it I might even
have to worm my way through. The narrowing aperture over my head was obscured by a soft blur of
reflected light. And a heavy fall of ice and snow crystals never once abated. Drift pouring into the borehole. If I hadn't known this was the only opening to
penetrate the barrier ice, I might have doubted it was
the same hole. Nothing looked like it had the last time
I'd been here. Of course, the downhole monitor had
been retracted in pulling Johnson and me to the top.
But even so it seemed roomy. The gash on the side
through which I'd first observed the river channel was
now an open floor. Apparently the lower portion of
the borehole had given way during the last few days.

The significance of this couldn't have been plainer.

There must be no more falls.

From this point on, any slip at all and I wouldn't
stop until I hit the river. The next stop after that would
be the Ross Sea. The end of the line.

I started climbing right away. As much as I needed

the rest, I didn't have a moment to lose. Time was running out. What the repository had done to me I had no way of knowing—my insides felt as though they were swimming in blood, but the meaning of this was a mystery to me. Not so a very clear and terminal case of hypothermia. There is nothing mysterious about freezing to death. About shaking so violently it consumed what little of my energy remained. My exhaustion was fairly near complete. Strength, resolve, even consciousness, were all but gone. The ironic part was that neither radiation poisoning, nor hypothermia, nor exhaustion would be the thing that stopped me from making the climb.

In fact, my greatest fear had nothing to do with my health at all but with my clothes. For the most part they were badly torn. The sleeves of my sweater were ripped to shreds and the skin beneath was in little better shape. My fur leggings were largely intact, though they would never again be of any value as antarctic trappings.

But my fears were much more practical than that.

All my clothes were completely sodden. The outer furs especially were freezing fast. As each minute passed, they, as well as the soaked inner-facing furs and cotton inners, became progressively stiffer. Eventually they would harden like a plaster cast until I was encased in a solid crust of frozen cloth.

So I started up.

While it was comforting to be able to lean against something while climbing and the threat of falling lessened for a time, the shaft was so confining at first that I had to squirm upward and it was impossible to make steps of more than a few inches. I was forced to cut three and four holds to the foot, and with nearly two hundred feet to climb this was insane. After a short time I started cutting them at one-foot intervals, pulling myself up with my arms, my legs hanging straight and stiff against the wall until they found something to jam into. This worked well enough until my arm strength gave out.

Which it did before I was out of the narrowest part of the shaft.

I went back to piddling progress.

My bare hands had lost all feeling after the first hour. By the time the shaft had widened out, my right was frozen fast around the haft of the knife. My arm shook so mightily as I swung at the wall that the blade often struck as much as a foot wild of the target. Several times I stabbed my other hand, though I felt nothing and what little blood exuded congealed almost immediately upon exposure. There was no grip strength left in that hand either. There didn't need to be. My fingers were curled solid into a kind of hook by which I snagged the holds.

By then my clothes were as rigid as armor. I could bend my knees, waist, and ankles barely enough to make the smallest steps. No more. And only my limited movements kept the ice broken in these areas. The material fought me at every turn. Each time I raised a foot the frozen joints had to be broken again. Each time they did, it took just a little more effort and the result was a movement more restricted than the last. I was continually forced to shorten the distance between holes until they were once again only inches apart. Then even these were too great a reach. Somewhere around the halfway mark I found myself hugging the ice in despair. Even with my eyes closed I could not keep the white of it out of my mind. There was nothing else to think about. I wasn't going on. The knife hung at my side, a burden too great to lift. My legs would no longer hold me up. And my brain was arranging a whiteout of its own. Whether the ice gave or I simply let go doesn't seem to matter. I toppled backward, not even conscious enough to brace myself against the opposite wall. But I didn't fall. My head struck ice and my weight was taken up completely within the shell of clothes. That's how stiff they had become. As long as my toes remained in their footholds and my back was supported against the other side, I could relax, even sleep, without fear of falling.

I was too far gone to evaluate the cost of even a moment's rest. Both layers of fur were frozen solid now. Only my activity was keeping the snug cotton inners thawed. They were damnably cold and drew the heat from my body at a much more rapid rate than I produced it. Once I lay still, these too would harden.

All of which didn't mean a thing. I was half asleep before I knew it, completely under before that moment came.

I might just as well have gone to bed in wet concrete.

When I awoke, it had set.

My head was twisted to the side and I looked up to see a small circle of stars at the end of a tunnel. I started at the thought that night had come. Yet light, reflecting off the shower of drift, still filtered down into the shaft.

My body was no longer cold. No longer in pain.

The shaking had ended too.

One can't shake if one can't even move.

Not a single muscle of my lower limbs or torso was free. I started thrashing, so stiff and fixed and frankly confused it didn't occur to me until I almost dislodged my toes from their footholds just how stupid this maneuver was.

The only thing to do was go to work on my clothes. It would have been easier by far if I could have reversed the blade in my hand, but I couldn't let go of the damn thing. If it did break free, I would never again get a good grip on the haft. So I stabbed at the fur on my trunk until my chest and stomach were slashed a dozen times and the torn remnants gave me minimal movement.

After that I started in on my pants legs.

What I ended up with were some raggy-looking cutoffs and two still-mercifully-numb legs that might have been mauled by a polar bear.

I forgot my legs for a moment, and my trunk too, and regarded through the driftfall the last remaining pitch—a sheer face of blue-green glass a hundred feet in height. I shrugged mentally, being too stiff for the other kind, and started climbing.

"All of you. Against that wall."

It was Fedorev's voice without question.

"What do you intend to do with us?" David Saperstein. Weak, but righteously indignant. "Sir, I demand to know your intentions!"

There came a series of barks in Fedorev's Russian. I heard the names Zhizn and Shokin and assumed that he was not alone. Then, "All right, Commander Saperstein, I suppose I owe you that. Call it professional courtesy, one military man to another."

How long the party had been going on I had no idea. Sounds did not begin to penetrate into the shaft until I was within yards of the top. My head was only a matter of feet below the gantry ladder's bottom rung before I was able to distinguish what was being said. I held my position, dully aware that if I could hear them, then they could now hear me. At least my blows. Perhaps my heavy inhalations, too.

"I never wanted anyone hurt, Commander. Despite orders to recover this canister at any cost. What it contains I probably will never know. But I know my orders and my duty: to recover this or, as a last measure, to see to it that no one else ever does. That's all. Nothing was said about destroying any American station or killing American military personnel."

"You're saying you didn't order this station burned?"

"I did not!"

"I don't believe you."

"Neither would I in your place. Unfortunately, whether or not I ordered it, whether or not I was even aware it had been ordered, is beside the point. It was done by people under my command. The responsibility is mine. In the same way I'm responsible for the deaths of two American servicemen here. More directly I'm responsible for the deaths of three others on the high plateau."

There was a muffled cry. A woman's.

"You are surprised?"

"No, sir." Saperstein again. "Lieutenant Krokov's presence told me that."

"Yes, of course. You could assume the rest. So will the world. And the world, like you, Commander, will turn a deaf ear to our denials. Therefore, we prefer it that the charges will never be made."

"I see. What are five more murders?"

I twisted around to face the center of the shaft. There, just a few feet out and only inches above my head, was the foot plate of the gantry ladder. I may or may not be able to make the leap, but there was no way in the world I would have been able to hang on long enough to climb up.

"A sad business. But you are all military people. The prospect of death is not unexpected. You understand that I cannot allow any one of you to live."

"I hope you understand you won't get away with it."

"That, of course, is the problem. What I meant about charges being made. We cannot permit any bodies to be discovered. Have you ever considered how difficult it is to dispose of evidence in this frozen hell? It was all I could do to talk Major Zhizn out of shooting your three men on Deception Reach. He couldn't stand the idea of leaving them alive until I convinced him that prolonged death by exposure was a more tortuous end than a quick bullet. I'll tell you frankly that was not my reasoning. Drifts have buried their bodies by now, but nothing will ever dispose of them. Should they one day be uncovered I don't want them found riddled with Soviet bullets."

When Fedorev paused I could hear Mary Ingram crying.

"Happily," he continued, "you people do have an option. You've dug your own bottomless grave. I noted that more than a week ago, when we came in here that first time . . . when one of your men had fallen down this shaft of yours."

"You're going to throw us down there?"

"If necessary. I would prefer it that you jump."

"You can go to hell!"

Those were the last words I understood. The colonel started moving people around. I heard some shoving and other voices that sounded like those of Shokin and Major Zhizn.

In the confusion I carved my last handhold, reached for the embankment, and pulled myself up until my head just poked over the top. The iron grillwork had been opened in order to permit even the more reluctant members of Mensa an easy time of it. There were only a dozen people in the project chamber. Fedorev hardly needed much firepower to handle this. With the snow drifting over the open ceiling came the sound of his five tractors idling at a discreet distance. The bulk of his forces would be in the tractors huddled against the heaters. If he didn't need them, they were merely witnesses to a thing Fedorev didn't want witnessed.

Asia screamed.

She was standing between Fedorev and Zhizn at the far side of the room near the entrance. Colonel Fedorev wasn't amateur enough to position himself between his hostages and his firepower, and he wasn't insane enough—standing to one side—to stand to the side near the borehole shaft where one would be inclined to fall. Here, where the entire floor sloped sharply into the center, the rushing of ankle-high drift from every quarter under the grillwork and over the edge gave the impression that even the floor itself was so inclined.

Asia's scream stopped as suddenly as it had started. The silence was deafening.

Every head turned as I clawed my way out of the pit, crawled away from the edge, and then fought to my feet with my shredded, bloodied, and frozen garments cracking and tearing in the effort.

The four troopers, Lieutenant Shokin and his three-man firing squad, were nearest. They had wheeled quarter-turns with expressions that, upon seeing me, instantly froze along with their frames into immobility. Never before had they laid eyes on a walking corpse, its face a living death mask, its bare legs and arms the stuff of nightmares, and by the look of them, they never cared to again. Shock didn't begin to describe it; they were aghast.

From the corner of my eye I saw Saperstein and staff against the side wall. Facing the rifles but now looking at me. The three men were haggard and slumped but stiffening at such an otherworldly sight. Paulette was in the worst shape. She showed the frightening effects of a narcotic withdrawal that made her all but oblivious to what was about to happen or to any unexpected players in the game. Beyond her stood Mary Ingram. Mary, regarding me with her scarred beauty agape in astonishment, had clapped her hands over her face.

I started walking.

One step . . . two steps . . . and then three and four. No one moved a muscle, not a word was spoken.

Impossible as it is to believe that no action would be taken against me, that's how it happened. If they'd been so frightened they moved back as I moved forward, I could have at least understood. No. They didn't budge. I closed on the nearest soldier, whose eyes were wide with disbelief and whose mouth was open wide in terror.

I was close enough to reach out and grab his weapon when Mary screamed. Had she not, I believe I could have eased it from his hands. He would not have resisted. Even the other three were so entranced that reaction, any action, was simply beyond their power. But Mary screamed. It was not at all the sort of scream as Asia's. And it had the opposite effect. Whereas Asia's cry had come from the horror of my unrecognizable appearance and had—along with my appearance—petrified the room with fear, Mary had at last recognized me. She was the first who did.

"Oh, God, it's Peter!"

Everyone seemed to come alive.

I snatched the rifle from the first trooper's hands and stepped clumsily back. His two buddies recovered in time to react, but not quite soon enough. I caught one with the stock in the solar plexus and the other with the barrel across his face when he brought his weapon up. Shokin had reached for his pistol. He was out of range of the rifle but not of the bullet. I rammed a frozen stump of a finger through the trigger guard and squeezed. He went down clutching his leg.

When I looked up, I found my rifle barrel pointing straight at Major Zhizn. The gun had been correct. He was reaching for a weapon too but stopped as soon as he realized his would come too late. It was perfect. A chance like this would never come again. All I need do was squeeze. I didn't wonder what Zhizn would do if our positions were reversed. What he would do I

would now do. I was no longer like Zhizn. Now I was
Zhizn. The look in his eye told me that he knew this.
His smile told me that it didn't bother him as much as
it bothered me. Perhaps that was the only difference
that remained between us.

I tried to speak. But damned if my mouth would
open. Blood had congealed across the lifeless gray-
yellow tissue of my face from my nose to my chin.
My jaw was swollen to twice its normal size. When at
last my lips tore apart, I coughed out my demand and
spattered blood into the air with every word.

"Asia, get the canister and come over here with
me."

Fedorev put a hand in front of her but she grabbed
the canister, pulled free of his grip, and started walking. Her face was grim with controlled fear. The closer
she came, the more this fear left her. She grew more
confident with each step. Passing the soldiers sprawled
out on the floor, Asia had even smiled; at the same
time her stride accelerated.

Then things happened fast.

It seems to me that she was running.

Events hit me in a blur of high speed with which
my brain was unable to keep pace.

She raced toward me with her hands outstretched.

Only her face was clear to me. It was no longer
either fearful or smiling. I had recognized both but
now I somehow failed to recognize the girl. Her eyes
were cold. Her lips were drawn back in a rictus of
hate.

David Saperstein called out, "Shoot her, Peter!"

Her palm struck me full on the chest. The automatic
rifle went clattering away. I pitched backward and
crashed heavily, with Asia struggling in my arms. Ice
skimmed beneath us. My hand clawed at the surface
but there was no purchase. Nothing to grab on to except drift. No way to stop. We slid headfirst right toward the embankment. Asia was thrashing with
maniacal fury in an attempt to roll away from me. It
didn't occur to me until too late that she could still
save herself. By then she had torn loose of my grip
and I was left with the canister by default. Together

we slipped right through the grillwork. Side by side we dived over the edge.

Her shriek sliced into the stillness of the pit.

I had an impression of metal just beyond and below me. The base of the gantry ladder spun upward. Now it was over my head. Somehow my right hand snagged the lower rung and I was yanked in a half-circle until I hung at a single arm's length a dozen feet into the hole.

Asia's shriek had faded into nothingness.

I had the canister in one hand, my life in the other, and my desire for both was gone.

"Mr. Masterson!"

A circle had formed above me. Saperstein and Mary on one side. Fedorev and Zhizn on the other believing the situation still within their control.

Fedorev said, "Don't let go, Masterson. We're going to get you up."

A couple of the soldiers had already started onto the gantry; the other, keeping his weapon trained on me, failed to see that Elliston had recovered the rifle I'd dropped and was closing in from the side. Digne was moving in behind the two senior Russian officers with Lieutenant Shokin's pistol.

Fedorev's voice came again. "Pass up the canister first."

"It doesn't belong to you, Colonel."

"Oh, yes it does!" Fedorev's words came rushing out. As though he knew how much time we had left. "You've been told this is a Crest model satellite. Lieutenant Krokov told me you had. 'Crest' is the Russian phonetic for 'Cross.' Cross Four is one of our satellites, not one of yours—a survey satellite whose transmitters had become inoperative. It had no value to us except as a practice target for our satellite-interceptor program. What America wants with it we have no idea. All we knew was that you wanted it badly. And that an attempt would be made by you to steal it. I was content to come and see that no expedition had been launched and be on our way; others in my party had different ideas and Major Zhizn will answer for them. But the film canister is still ours."

I should have known.

Saperstein's instructions to us on the eve of our expedition were still in my mind: "If we can't find it first, we must make sure it will never be found." And now Fedorev. "My orders are to recover it, or to make sure no one else does."

I could feel my hand giving way. "You're wrong," I told him. "It's not yours. It's hers. And so am I."

At that, two men started scrambling down the ladder.

"Please, Peter," Mary sobbed. "For me."

The last words I heard were Saperstein's: "Let it go, Masterson; that's an or—"

I looked up.

A Russian was reaching down a hand.

"That," said Saperstein, "is a suggestion."

For once in my life I decided to do what I'd been told.

I let go my grip.

Epilogue

Antarctic winter officially ends with the sun's first appearance. It seemed somehow fitting that when this event finally happened there would be, not one sun, but three. Nowhere else on earth is the phenomenon of parhelion more striking than here. Instead of the bright spot of light on the solar halo that is common in other latitudes, settling ice crystals in the frigid morning air had created two dog suns of equal dimensions 15 degrees either side of the first.

The upper atmosphere was astonishingly clear and quiet.

From several miles away it was possible to make out the three dots of black weaving about on the westernmost solar surface like transient sunspots that grew bigger with each passing second.

And louder.

The navy Chinooks came pounding over Mensa Station, their thunderous twin rotors driving a storm of drift aloft as they hovered above the ruins, rolled out over a clear patch of ice, and finally touched down. Snow swirled and rolled outside the downwash of air more furiously than any arctic blizzard. The third chopper wavered over the gutted station, clearing out days of drift with a simple wag of the pilot's control stick. Before the rotors had been disengaged or airborne ice could resettle onto the barrier, the after loading ramps were lowered and several dozen arctic-clad U.S. marines came barreling out. Some positioned themselves at the station's perimeter; others formed excavation teams and, moving with a more deliberate pace, descended into the garage.

An inspection of the project chamber was completed without result. Teams immediately broke up and began a wing-by-wing search of the station while the officer-in-charge of the mission supervised their progress from above.

A cry went up.

"They're down here, sir!"

At the officer's signal a line of litters were rushed below by medical personnel. The medics brought their empty litters back out. David Saperstein, walking at the head of his party, hobbled up to the mission OIC, managed a casual stance and a less-than-snappy salute.

"Ideal conditions, Captain! You couldn't have hoped for better if you'd waited a month."

Captain Huggins started. He had expected gratitude, not a rebuke.

"We had little choice, Commander," he said, emphasizing the rank of address.

"You didn't get either of the two Maydays?"

Huggins nodded. "We got three. A cryptic demand for assistance was picked up on the international emergency frequency at about the same time a radar station recorded a Morse SOS from one of our unmanned dishes on Deception Reach. That was five days ago."

"I know it was."

"We also got a very strange message from a Colonel Anatol Fedorev of the Red Army requesting we speed a team to this location as fast as we could. That came early this morning from Moscow."

"He seems to get rather faster service than we do."

Again Captain Huggins drew back. His briefing on the operations and personnel of Mensa had included the station commander, a strict disciplinarian; but what he was hearing didn't jive with his information.

"Who is this Colonel Fedorev?"

"Just a man who learned to settle for a draw."

The captain started to press for information but paused as other survivors filed by.

Jules Digne and Tom Elliston—deathly pale and gaunt, and ambulatory only under the most liberal interpretation of the word—stumbled past, shrugging any offers of assistance by the medical corps.

"Those men should be on stretchers, Commander."

"I don't think so, Captain. We've been staying active. Can't afford to lie down out here. Anyway, our polar adviser would never have stood for it. As a matter of fact, we were organizing a foot party to McMurdo when we heard your choppers coming in."

"Four hundred miles! You can't be serious!"

"Don't bank on it, Captain."

Huggins was more than slightly put off. He'd been told this was a tight crew, but their sense of independence seemed to him to border insubordination.

The last litter was carried out by two marines. A medic walked to one side but it was obvious even from a distance that he was not the physician in charge. That function was being carried on rather arrogantly by Paulette Gruber. The rescue party had found her gruff, insulting, and overbearing—in short, her usual bedside manner. Paulette was her old self—morphine has that effect on addicts, even Russian morphine, and stolen Russian morphine at that.

Captain Huggins halted the litter. A young woman who walked with the patient's hand in hers stopped too. He was stung by the immediate impression of great beauty marred by wounds, and yet the woman's dazzling eyes and absorbing smile made the scars seem somehow trifling concerns. He followed Mary Ingram's gaze to the figure on the litter.

"Jesus!" He winced and turned away, finding the picture of his unusually forlorn medic a welcome haven for his eyes.

"Severe hypothermia, Captain. I've never seen worse. Frostbite, gangrene, hemorrhaging, fractured jaw, contusions and lacerations too numerous to count, concussion, and worst by far, according to the doctor here, massive radiation poisoning."

"Will he . . . ?"

The medic pursed his lips and sadly wagged his head.

"Die, dammit," snapped Paulette. "The word, dear, is 'die.' And your medic here may be a little shy on gumption, but he's right about one thing. The answer is no. Peter Masterson won't die. Not soon anyway. Oh, he's in bad shape and he's going to be in a hospital for a long time, but you know something?'' She had stepped close to the captain and pushed an insolent finger into his chest. "The damn navy's going to pay for it.''

Paulette waved the litter on, and the two marines, never shy on gumption, marched ahead at her command.

The captain shook his head in disbelief. "It's not my place to say, Commander, but I do believe your physician—''

"I believe her too,'' said Saperstein quickly. Then he started walking.

"Commander!''

Saperstein stopped, turned slowly around.

"I'm trying to make allowances for what you and your personnel have endured. But all the same I think your report on this matter is going to make for some interesting reading.''

"That draw I was telling you about—it was really kind of a deal, don't you see? I'll honor it. Which means I may not make a report.''

"You may have to,'' said Huggins.

Saperstein shook his head wearily, started off, and then turned back to the captain, almost—but not quite—smiling.

"In that case,'' he said, "I won't.'' Commander Saperstein hobbled off behind his people.

About the author

Stephen Forbes was born in Topeka, Kansas, and educated at Tulsa University and the Defense Information School. He has worked as a newspaper and magazine editor, a private investigator, a martial arts instructor, and as a parachute jumpmaster. He is currently an independent contractor in Montana, where he lives with his family.

Ø

SPELLBINDING THRILLERS

☐ **THE KEY TO REBECCA by Ken Follett.** A #1 nationwide bestseller! Alex Wolff, "The Sphinx," must send ruthless, Nazi agent Rommel, the secrets that would unlock the doors to Cairo and ultimate Nazi triumph in the war. "Brilliant adventure by the most romantic of all top thriller writers!" —*Time* (155106—$4.95)

☐ **PAPER MONEY by Ken Follett.** A fast-moving, super suspenseful caper by the master spellbinder. Felix Laski is a powerful corporate raider who built an empire and shook the stock market. Ambitious moves led him to an affair with a bored wife and to masterminding for a professional criminal. (159047—$4.50)

☐ **EYE OF THE NEEDLE by Ken Follett.** His code name was *The Needle*. He was a tall, handsome German aristocrat of extraordinary intelligence— England's most dangerous enemy. H knew the secret that could win the war for Hitler ... and Lucy Rose was the only one who could stop him. ... (155246—$4.95)*

☐ **LIE DOWN WITH LIONS by Ken Follett.** Two men on opposite sides of the cold war—and the beautiful Englishwoman torn between them—caught in romantic adventures from Paris to Afghanistan! "Rivals his Eye of the Needle for sheer suspense."—*Washington Post* (146425—$4.95)

*Prices slightly higher in Canada

Buy them at your local

bookstore or use coupon

on next page for ordering.

There's an epidemic with 27 million victims. And no visible symptoms.

It's an epidemic of people who can't read.

Believe it or not, 27 million Americans are functionally illiterate, about one adult in five.

The solution to this problem is you... when you join the fight against illiteracy. So call the Coalition for Literacy at toll-free **1-800-228-8813** and volunteer.

Volunteer Against Illiteracy. The only degree you need is a degree of caring.